**UNDER TWIN SUNS
ON THE PLANET MAALSTROM**

**FLORES OF THE
TURLICUM
FIGHTS MAALSTROM's
ENIGMATIC FORCES**

**IN THE TRADITION OF
EDGAR RICE BURROUGHS
AND ROBERT E. HOWARD**

The shadows deepened and Flores' eyes adjusted and he suddenly wondered why he had thought the man was old. The person who stood before him was not old at all, but young. An irsrem dagger glinted with starlight–Flores was glad he had not plunged blindly forward under his first impulse. Behind the first man appeared four more shadows, moving quickly, glass blades flashing.

The first stepped toward Flores.

"So that is it." The Ven noble nodded. No mystery remained. "Good, then. What better time to die than the present?"

More Heroic Fantasy
from DARK LOTUS BOOKS
in the tradition of
Robert E. Howard
&
Edgar Rice Burroughs

THE MAALSTROM SERIES:

BOOK 1
MAALSTROM

by
Glenn Lazar Roberts

In the midst of war with the tyrant Nesos, Flores of the Turlicum is trapped in the Temple of Vensa where he falls under the spell of the priestess Amina, the most beautiful gila of the Three Valleys. First half of the The Selk King.

"If you enjoyed Game of Thrones or Joseph Campbell, you'll love Maalstrom." —John Picha

"An ever-surprising plot down to the last page, the last paragraph, the last sentence."
—Sirius Reviews

"A beautifully written fantasy saga."
—Writer's Digest

From Dark Lotus Books
JUST PLAIN WEIRD:
Life at the touch of a button…or death!

FRENZY

by
Glenn Lazar Roberts

The hurricane party went well–until someone locked the doors. Now the partygoers' only escape from the Research Center's basement is through a labyrinth of rapidly flooding tunnels with drug gangs, psychics, a stock fraud, and one-minute piranhas created by experimental 'genechips.' Weird sci-fi run amok.

"A terrifically fun read! Glenn Lazar Roberts squeezes a lot of horror, mystery and plain old fun into his new novel... My suggestion? Grab a copy as fast as you can and read this face-paced novel."
—Jerry D. Mohrlang, author of Sarawak.

"A plot worthy of the movies. Frenzy by Glenn Lazar Roberts is a perfect example of building tension... Just when you think you have it all figured out, the plot twists again and sends you giddily in a different direction."
—Michael Fox, author of Theater Boy.

More of the JUST PLAIN WEIRD
from Dark Lotus Books:
A tale of the fantastic and macabre...

THE GLOW
by
Glenn Lazar Roberts

Sam Trencher has a problem. To keep from exploding into flames, he must keep the exact same coins in each pocket. Six years ago he left his home town and his girl. Now he's coming back to find her–but can't tell what's real and what's not...and his temperature is rising.

"Non-stop chills from Glenn Lazar Roberts, master of the macabre."
                                        —*Sirius Reviews*

THE ADVENTURES OF THE RADIATED LESBIAN NUN
by
Glenn Lazar Roberts

Pop the Thunderbird wine and break open the nopalitos. Because Maggie, the Radiated Lesbian Nun and Queen of the champion roller derby team The Warriors, is igniting fires and breaking hearts from Santa Monica to across the galaxy! Political correctness may never recover from these *no-holds-barred* mercilessly satirical novels by Glenn Lazar Roberts.

"Nuts!" —*Sirius Reviews*

The Selk King

by

Glenn Lazar Roberts

Dark Lotus Books
Home of the
Just Plain Weird

DEDICATION
To Mervyn Peake, who floated
perpetually on a sea of script
&
Joseph Campbell, who taught us that
there are no–and can never be–
humans without myth

THE SELK KING first published by Dark Lotus Books, 2001. Second printing 2016. Copyright 1999 by Glenn L Roberts. All rights reserved. This book may not be reproduced in whole or in part, by any means, without written permission of the publisher, except by reviewers who may quote brief passages in reviews.

ISBN 978-0-9675809-1-3

This work is speculative fiction and intended for entertainment only. All characters and events are fictional and any resemblance to real persons or incidents or institutions is entirely coincidental.

Cover Design and story art by Glenn Lazar Roberts.

CONTENTS

I flee to the Lord of Dawn,
from the Evil He created,
from the night when it falls,
from gilas who twist what should be straight,
from the One that Envies all.

I flee to the Lord of Man,
the King of Man, his God,
from the One who sneaks through portals,
who whispers evil in the hearts of men,
and the ways of selks and mortals.

—The Holy Quran
Surahs 'Falaq' and 'al-Nas'

THE SELK KING

CHAPTER 1

RENDEZVOUS

Flores almost failed to recognize him. The object of his vigil emerged from the river atop a reven and scrambled up the muddy bank streaming water, only withdrawing the spur from the beast's neck when on level ground. The swimmer dismounted. Beast and man shook off the excess water, raising a cloud of steam in the cool morning air of early spring. The swimmer's head had recently been shaved and his hair begun to grow out again, his bare chest glistened, and a glass sword dangled at his side. His complexion was dark–darker than Flores remembered–and his face and body were entirely hairless, lending his features, dominated as they were by a strong and bluntly angled chin, a flat appearance. The swimmer scanned the treeline along the riverbank, glanced back to the Island of the Lurenmurg, then began to lead his reven with reins in one hand and scabbarded sword in the other. He moved systematically, beginning with the point of the riverbend directly opposite the isle, and probed carefully with his scabbard each pile of leaves.

The Lord of the Turlicum spurred his mount from the protecting trees and approached. The dark man ceased probing and turned. A few paces distant the Turlicum halted, leather reins sliding the length of his reven's curling neck. The dark man stared without expression, his face revealing so little of his thoughts that he might have worn a mask.

Flores dismounted.

"You always knew, did you not, Flores."

The noble shrugged. "You could have employed greater subtlety, Macius. Your story was transparent from the first–not to say preposterous. However, I must admit, had I been in your place, I would have been more direct."

Macius said nothing but peered at a bulky sack tied to the saddle. A ripple played along the reven's neck, followed by a sinuous twist of its massive tail.

Flores nodded. "They are indeed useful."

"How many?" asked Macius.

"Seven. All in good order."

"And what is your price?"

Flores frowned.

"Remember, Flores–I am only a poor adventurer. I have no estates to put money in my pocket like Simet nobles."

"I am surprised, Macius. Do you think I desire only money, then? Am I of such limited imagination?"

Flores drew his sword, and Macius' wooden mask suddenly paled, but the noble turned toward the island in the channel. He waved the glass rapier letting the irsrem prisms that comprised his weapon glint. Soon Macius noted a ship approaching upon the water, oars dipping.

"It was not you, but Yezd, created these, was it not Macius? Yezd–the true master of your castle–and he who sought to keep you penned within it."

Macius said nothing.

"No matter," added Flores, "but I must ask of you a question." The Turlicum Lord peered carefully at the shorter, stockier man. "The Island of the Sun God, Macius–does it in truth exist? And have you been there?"

For a long moment Macius stood in silence, motionless. Finally, he nodded, a strange look in his eyes.

Flores lapsed into thought and watched the ship slowly expand. When it had come quite close, he untied the sack and removed one device. He handed the contraption of tube, cup, and excised reven gill to Macius, who received it with widening eyes.

"I am going there, Macius, to the Island of the Sun God, and I need a navigator–a murshid–one who can guide me without fail. The remaining gills I will need to get my men ashore and avoid the winged malkops who guard the Isle." He looked at Macius. "Will you direct my ship? When my task is accomplished, all of the devices will be yours."

With a bland expression the dark man inspected the gill, turning it over in his hands. The brush and dirt had been removed; it seemed as new as the day it was made. Flores noted the thick muscles of Macius' arms tense with sudden renewed energy.

"Why, Flores? It is the city of the selks, the workers of the sky, their lair from which they roam the world. Vensor the Sun God has forbidden mortals to set foot there. That is why his servants guard it so well." He raised his chin. "What could be of interest to you in such a place?"

The noble's lower lip projected further than usual. His dark eyes flashed. "In violation of all the laws of Vensor, the malkops have stolen Amina while the life was still within her. She once saved my life. I have sworn to repay the debt."

Macius' eyebrows arched in surprise. "But, Flores, you know that she is a gila, one of the forbidden sex?"

Something in Macius' tone took Flores aback. Instead of the contempt and hostility he had expected for consorting with a tool of Atasan and using its forbidden speech, he thought he detected irony in Macius' voice, or an unconcern that bordered on impiety.

"Is she?"

Macius nodded. "There is no doubt. A gila, Flores–a woman. Do you not fear the reaction of others? The hand of every man will be against you." Macius glanced toward the galley. "The law of Vensor forbids consorting with her kind–men fear their powers, even as they long to possess them."

"My men are trustworthy, Macius, and these are my best. Moreover I wish no consort, but only to repay my debt."

"You are determined to find her?"

Flores sighed. "I would go to Heaven itself."

"But to Hell, Flores?"

He nodded. "There too, if I must."

Macius glanced at the gill and at the galley with its men at the oars and square sail rising on the mast. He chuckled softly, then raised his face to the sky and laughed aloud. He planted his strong legs in the sod of the riverbank and hopped with his arms outthrust, then paused, his face still frozen in its characteristic immobility. Flores watched in puzzlement.

"So you would defy God and Man and cast fortune to the winds for the sake of a woman–a gila–who may lie dead even as we speak. Such a gesture is worthy of Vensor Himself. And worthy of the aid of a simple thief such as myself." Macius glowed with admiration.

Flores glanced overhead where streaks of cumulus passed swiftly through the stratosphere, immune to the suns' rays warming his flesh. Unconsciously, he scanned the open expanse for suspended tell-tale dots. Finding nothing, he returned his gaze to his companion.

"What may we expect to find there, Macius?"

The navigator and thief opened his mouth, then hesitated.

Flores nodded. "I understand...piety stops your tongue. No matter, we have swords in plenty." He stared at the mud clotting his sandals, then again looked up. "Do you think she can be saved?"

The dark man shrugged. "If she awoke in flight, her bearers could have been startled, and lost their hold..."

Flores shook his head. "I cannot bear it. If she lives I must know. You will pilot my ship, then?"

Macius solemnly nodded. "Yes, Flores. I will take you to the Isle of Vensor, the home of the malkops, to find your priestess. But–" He turned a guarded glance upon the Turlicum Lord, "may I request of you an indulgence for my time, some compensation besides the gills, which, after all, are mere curiosities, and not silver or gold?"

Flores nodded. "Name it–if it is reasonable."

"A slight thing, really. Allow me to remove from the Island and keep for myself anything of value that we may encounter–in the event that we find anything besides bones of the dead, that is–so that the trip shall be worth my time."

"Remove the lawful property of Vensor, Macius? I am no thief. I want only to settle my debt, though it be to the enemy of Vensor."

"Trifles only, Flores. Mementos–" Macius affected a carefree gesture.

The Turlicum thought again, then shook his head.

"I go not to anger Vensor, or to place my burdens upon Him. We carry swords only to protect ourselves from the anger of his minions." Flores squinted at the suns. He nodded to himself. "I will pay you for your services out of my own pocket."

Macius' fingers curled upon empty palms.

"If it concerns you so, I pledge that I will match in value whatever trifles you may find upon the Isle that take your fancy. I will pay you myself when we return."

Macius stared hard at Flores. The Turlicum Lord thought he perceived an undertow of humor, again expressed in Macius' own inscrutable manner.

"The thought displeases me," continued Flores. "It is my will that none who accompany me are to disturb what does not concern us, and as my employee you will be subject to my orders. I forbid it. Let us not speak again of removing Vensor's property."

The navigator said nothing but stared past him at the vessel, now drifting close to shore.

Flores Sumvensor of the Turlicum, noble, Assemblyman, and newly elected king of the ancient city of Ven, waved again to the galley. Answering waves signaled recognition. Two oarsmen leaped into the water and clambered with vigor onto the bank; Flores handed one the reins of his reven and Macius passed his reins to the other.

"Your mount will be in Ven when we return, my friend. And now we leave."

As if he found the fact of little interest, Macius turned his palms up, and together they waded into the wide river and swam to the boat. A knotted rope was lowered over the side, and with the aid of the projecting oars they clambered aboard. The word 'Grest,' sniffer of the wind, was emblazoned on its side in spidery Vensor script. The men on board, attired in faded unwashed tunics, were of the tribe of Turlicum, the clansmen of Flores, and included Isav, Flores' chieftain and veteran of the Battle of the Plateau, and Revd, a leader of militia. Once the wind had died, forty of his clan pulled oars while eight others handled the ropes. Isav and Revd cast sidelong glances at Macius as he gained the deck. Neither was pleased at the prospect of sailing with a rogue and professional thief at the rudder.

Macius counted the oarsmen. "Too many, Sir Flores. We'll need more room for supplies."

"But the oars–"

"We won't follow a coastline, but the open sea. The mainsail will carry us well enough." A hint of a smile again played over Macius' face as he planted his feet upon the gangway.

"And the malkops–"

"You must understand, Flores. We cannot gain what you wish by force. Swords will be needed, but deceit will be our main weapon–deceit and surprise and the divine favor of our benefactor divine Gethos. A ship packed with warriors will only alert the Isle's guardians and bring their anger upon us."

Without waiting for the Turlicum to direct him, Macius settled near the rudder in the place reserved for the pilot. Flores nodded and motioned twenty men to swim to shore, ignoring his officers' protests. Macius counted, shook his head, and Flores signaled another ten to go. The remaining twenty hauled the ropes. The sail raced to the top of the mast. With a loud snap the canvas billowed outward and the ship lurched forward, beginning the long journey to the southern sea.

Flores negotiated the gangway and rejoined Macius. "How far is the Island of Vensor?"

"Far, Flores. First we must put in at Vaw."

Flores nodded. His own vessels had traded at that port on occasion, though none of his clansmen now on board the Grest. He himself knew little of it. "Your home city, is it not?"

"It has been long since I was there. There are safer ports, but Vaw straddles our route and we will need provisions. I once knew of merchants who could supply a ship such as ours. We shall see if they still can when we arrive. But I think that while in Vaw we should be cautious–remember that I am still wanted by Prince–I mean 'King'–Kot. I was once widely known, but with some care there is no reason to expect anyone to recognize me in the short time that we shall be in port. Afterwards, we shall spend much time on the open ocean. The way is not hard; it requires only patience and courage."

"Or ignorance and folly," called Isav as he approached, not bothering to conceal his distaste for Macius. The chieftain drew Flores out of earshot and Macius returned his gaze to the river and pulled the rudder in silence.

The days rolled by. The season turned and the cool rains of early spring changed to warm monsoons. Brown marshlands with forests of bare tree-trunks covered the horizon like a graveyard of ships, registering little change with the new season. Occasionally they passed skiffs and yawls making the long journey to Asan or Sipan, and finally the ship reached the mouth of the Tlaam, the tributary that fed those two cities, once subject to the city of Neset, as it also fed Neset itself in the dry distant highlands. The galley continued toward the sea, relying mostly on the oars with the change in wind direction.

Flores was a man of fifty-six as measured in the short sixteen-hour Maalstrom days; a man in his prime. Slender, aristocratic, muscles sculpted as if planned and developed to suit; his clipped black beard shaved to rid himself of parasites acquired in the western forest–perhaps the same reason Macius had shaved his head. The lines around his eyes, formerly lined with humor, were now cross-printed with pain. Standing at the wale before the bright barbell of the overlapping suns, palatine flapping in the moist breeze, the noble clenched and unclenched his crippled right hand. He smiled. The mausoleum with its rough-hewn statue crumbled further each day. And Amina beckoned.

The crew worked much and spoke little. Though they welcomed the end of the long war with the Nesets, the final defeat of the conqueror Nesos and the instatement of Flores as king by the assembly had only relieved the city's physical exhaustion, not dispelled its spiritual malaise. Like a heavy weight, depression lay upon each crewmember of the Grest, excluding only the foreigner Macius. No Assemblyman fully comprehended the import of the death of the Queen of Ven. However, every subject, every citizen of the ancient capital had felt the subtle change that found reflection in each event. The final catastrophe had befallen the city–the Sun-god had withdrawn His favor from His offspring. The priestesses of the Temple had blocked the passage through which Flores had led his warriors into the citadel, and the dark stronghold had returned to its former mysterious and forbidden ways. And with the exception of a final ritual, no child had been granted the city since the death of Vensa. After granting Flores the throne, which they did almost as an afterthought for saving Ven's Temple from the Neset-sa, the Assemblymen abandoned plans to pursue the war to Neset–or any other plans necessary for the survival of Ven–and spent their days in fervent prayer, hoping for a renewal of the ancient covenant of the calling for sons by Vensor.

They waited in vain. The assembly was a tomb; Ven a graveyard. All knew the city of glass would die–Vensa had said as much with her final breath. Vens drifted from the city to die or scavenge in the wilds, and Flores too had felt the gloom and sought solace in his memories of the priestess Amina with eyes the color of night and skin like purple clouds. Then it was that Flores conceived his plan: he would follow Amina to Heaven and learn whether she still lived. If she lived, and wished to leave, he would bring her back, in accordance with the law of Vensor. He would live with her and protect her. If she no longer lived, he would return to Ven alone and accept the common fate of the city. At the end of either path lay peace. Flores smiled. He could feel the weight lifting.

With an assistant to help, Macius threw his weight against the rudder's wide spar to negotiate a curve in the river. Gulls circling overhead announced the presence of fishermen. Skiffs appeared, floating in the marsh. Men leaned over the side, their bronzed backs shining, ropes connected to a gaggle of geese that paddled close by. Each rope encircled the neck of a bird, its owner drawing his bird in and extracting the catch as it plucked fish out of the depths of the river. A few coins procured fish for the Vens' evening meal.

The days passed rapidly. The marshes broadened, the trees shrank and vanished, the vegetation melted into a deep, rich green. The swamp broke up, alternating brackish lagoons with patches of soil. Then salt-spray blew upon them and the land peeled away and the vast open sea stretched beyond their sight. Heeding the advice of Macius, Flores struck a course south by south-east across the bay of Ud toward the isle of Vaw and its capital.

CHAPTER 2

VAW

The port of Vaw opened before the Grest on a bright cloud-driven day. Breakwaters outthrust on either side completed the natural formation of the harbor, and skiffs and galleys appeared in a complicated traffic converging on the entrance and spreading along the upswept coast. Vaw was smaller than Ven, much smaller, having been founded only in the last century after the powerful and ancient city of Morl had died leaving the northern sea empty of men. Most Vaw-sa recalled in legends, however, the greatness of its predecessor and some still remembered the few decrepit survivors found among the ruins of Morl when the first children of Vaw quarried there to build their own town. Now the dynasty of Kot reigned proudly with gem-encrusted glass and ocean reven, policing or pirating the waters, depending on whether one had paid or omitted the requisite taxes to their coffers.

"Behold Vaw–" Macius spread a hand to encompass the expanding city and its harbor, "–first city of thieves. Be wary of your purse, Flores. If a stratagem occurs to them, they will not hesitate to take what they may from you and your men. It is best not to mix with them or attract attention to our ship while in port. And do not reveal that you are royalty. The Vaw-sa recognize no city. They would take you and hold you for ransom."

As a vessel neared the Grest, sped by glistening rows of harnessed reven-na, Flores raised the customer's purple trading pennon. In response to their drivers' tugs, the Vaw reven slowed and the vessel neared the Grest. A youthful chargé, tumid with self-importance, displayed a bright yellow cloak of Kot authority and called to them from the bow. Macius elbowed Flores and indicated that their barrels be opened.

"Cargo?" The inquiry penetrated the salty wind as from a great distance.

Macius spoke to Flores with his face averted. "Hold up your grain and salt vok. He doesn't want to come aboard if he can avoid it."

Several Vens raised handsful for the Vaws to see, pointlessly thought Flores, since he could be smuggling contraband in other barrels or a score of places on the Grest that would be invisible from the deck of the other vessel. The wind blew much away and in annoyance Flores motioned for the cargo to be repacked.

"New to Vaw?" echoed the official's voice.

Macius clutched Flores' arm and cupped his hand. "Yes!"

"Docking fee! South dock!" The official pointed to their starboard side. "Three mir!" The tollsman raised an arm indicating immediate payment.

Flores looked to Macius inquiringly. The pilot nodded and indicated with his eyes that Flores should throw a bag of coins onto the other ship. As the coins landed, Flores wondered who would have been responsible if the toss had erred. He suspected it would not have been the tollsman.

Minutes later the Grest slid into position beside the south dock. A youth tardily retrieved and secured the rope. The quay, twenty feet across and five hundred feet from end to shore, was of wooden clapboards and something of a rickety affair, but solid enough, and represented a substantial investment for Vaw. The center strip of the dock was uncluttered and gave access to the wharves of the city's waterfront district. The quay's periphery was alive with workmen and sailors mending nets and ropes or unloading vessels.

Anxious to feel something steady beneath their feet again, even clapboards, the Vens closed with the dock. Flores dropped to the boards. He tipped the youth who had secured the Grest's rope and the boy returned a sullen glance, apparently for the size of the coin. Shouting a banal vulgarism with the easy spontaneity of long habit, he promptly deserted them and moved up the quay where other vessels drew near.

Macius leaped onto the dock and puffed out his chest with a deep draught of Vaw air. He drew his cloak in closer and leaned toward his employer, while glancing furtively about him in that part-joyful, part-mocking, part-earnest manner that Flores found so disconcerting and so unreadable.

"I shall return soon. Be on guard, Sir Flores. Do not assume that matters are as they appear among Vaw-sa for they excel only in thievery and deceit. Not the King himself is safe from their swindles, which often embarrass his court and leave their victims without a mir to their name." He stepped back and pronounced melodramatically, "Some men are beasts and some beasts men. How little can the eyes of mortals see!"

While Macius strode toward the city, Flores frowned. He watched the shrinking back of the pilot until it vanished in the crowd circulating on the wharf. After several minutes the Turlicum stretched his arms and passed his gaze over the harbor. His concern for readjusting to solid land proved exaggerated as his poise rapidly reasserted itself. Smiling and taking in the clean air, Flores had begun to turn when suddenly he cringed in reaction to a shout that someone at his elbow had delivered directly into his ear.

"Fee!"

Flores turned and found himself facing another yellow-cloaked official. Worked silver shone from a leather cap on his head and his skirt was new and dignified. An assistant stood by his side with rapier helve ostentatiously displayed.

"For what is this fee?" inquired Flores with politeness as he rubbed the offended organ. "Docking?"

The man passed a supercilious glance over the Ven. "No." He swelled with dignity. "The quay toll. Three mir." The man held out an empty palm.

Flores looked to Isav. The captain shrugged. Flores loosed a pouch, counted the coins and placed them carefully in the outstretched hand of the Vaw. The tollsman turned and marched further up the dock, away from the city.

The remaining Vens had stepped off the Grest and stretched with groans of relief. Flores forbade them to leave the dock–he wanted no trouble to delay their journey. Awash in light the port spread before them like a land of fables; Flores took it in and scanned the heights that surrounded the harbor on three sides. Vaw itself lay on a hill and from the quay one could see atop the acropolis the dark temple and knife-like spire where the Vaw priests tended their mysterious duties. Flores glanced back to the quay where his surprised gaze settled on another bit of yellow. Flanked by an attendant, the newest viceroy of the King of Vaw descended on the Grest like a predator.

When he arrived the agent stopped and held out his palm, his clean yellow cloak flapping smartly. "Fee!"

Flores peered at the bureaucrat with skepticism.

"Sir, if this is the docking fee or the quay toll," asked Flores, "we have already paid."

An incredulous and condescending smile seized the Vaw's lips. "What is this? You would tell an official of King Kot his business? Well, sir, you may have paid the dock or the quay tax. But I am here on the command of the King to collect the wharf tax! Three mir! Or you can unlash your boat and find another port!"

Flores opened his mouth to speak, but Isav caught his arm and whispered, "Remember what Macius said–they will use any pretext. And we want no trouble." Flores nodded. He counted out three mir–again–and handed the sum over to whom he now regarded to be little more than yellow-cloaked bandits.

The agent smiled at his attendants, absorbing their humor, then returned his attention to Flores. He snapped his fingers and his attendant pulled his rapier half free of its scabbard. "Plus one–" the agent's voice dripped malice, "–or I shall call the gendarmes!" Subduing his pride, Flores reluctantly delivered it. Without another word, the Vaw-sa turned and marched away. When the agent had gone some distance, far beyond apprehension by the Vens, Isav nudged Flores and pointed. The Turlicum put a hand to his forehead to shield his gaze and saw the 'agent' remove his cloak, carefully fold it, and place it inside his shirt. The agent then removed his cap and placed it beside the cloak. He and his assistant mingled with a group of stevedores unloading a boat and were soon lost among their number.

Isav shrugged. Flores sat upon one of the barrels his men had unloaded, his eyes wandering over the visages of the silent dock workers. Contempt and amusement showed in the faces of the workers. He began to suspect that he had been swindled by known impostors and that no Vaw would deign to enlighten them, having concluded that the newcomers were too slow to discern developments on their own. Flores sighed. Perhaps they were right.

Some minutes later the Vens' attention was drawn by a disturbance on the quay. Flores noticed a Vaw worker pause from loading the galley lashed next to theirs and shove a passerby apparently without cause. The victim lost his footing and fell. However, with the admiration of the Vens, and to all appearances undeserving of such treatment, the victim regained his feet and returned the insult to his attacker so that the culprit fell upon his backside. Without delay the first man leaped to his feet and for several minutes they shoved each other, both remaining expressionless and silent during the entire encounter. At any moment, Flores expected them to escalate to blows. None of the stevedores or fishermen intervened or even seemed to notice the duel. Perceiving a dagger within the belt of one, Flores shook his head–how brave was the man's opponent to resist an armed attacker with bare flesh, how tragic that the conflict must soon be resolved by resort to that cruel weapon. But then, to the bewilderment of the Vens, the pair suddenly embraced–the two now seemed to be the closest of friends.

Flores shook his head but had no time to contemplate the strange custom. The rapid approach of yet another representative of the King, his yellow cloak uplifted like the wings of an angry hornet, again distracted him. The official with the usual armed attendant marched to the Grest and halted. Flores met him, this time determined not to be hoodwinked. Laborers up and down the dock halted their work to stare. Approaching the Grest, the King's agent halted and peered about for a responsible party. His gaze alighted on Flores.

"How long have you been at this dock?" demanded the official, who might have been a twin of the previous agent.

Flores noted with interest that although the agent's badges were fresh and bright, his hands were callused and his skin roughened by exposure to the weather. They were the hands of a workman.

"A few minutes only, sir," he answered with a brief polite bow.

The Vaw passed a careful glance over Flores and his vessel, noting various unobvious details.

"No matter. We are now here. Your fee is three mir. Let's hurry it up now, we've much else to do. The ships are coming in by the dozen today." The man extended and spread a conspicuously empty hand. A glance from Isav reminded him of the necessity of anonymity for their vessel.

Flores displayed his most congenial diplomatic smile. He forced a laugh. "Kind, sir. The fee is already paid. The King's man collected the docking fee while we were yet on the water. Your colleague collected the quay fee only moments ago. Then his companion obtained the wharf tax after him, before proceeding up the pier. If you are diligent and hurry, doubtless you can overtake him and retrieve your share. But we have already paid."

The Vaw looked at Flores as if he had lapsed into insanity. "Already paid? Impossible!" Several dock workers sniggered and elbowed each other. "There is no 'quay fee'! And what is a 'wharf tax'? What an imbecilic idea! Some oafs have impersonated agents of the King. Only I have the authority to levy pier taxes." In his anger he dropped his cloak. His assistant, open-mouthed with vicarious outrage, retrieved it and brushed off algae.

The official suddenly calmed and looked hard into the eyes of Flores. "Listen!" he pointed. "Do you think you can outwit Fish, a third-degree initiate of Kot? Is that your game?"

Flores drew himself to his full height, relieved to speak honestly. "Sir, I stand before you and say in all truthfulness that we have already paid toll to three persons with yellow cloaks, each of whom had an armed attendant by his side." Flores swung his arm. "Any of these dock workers can attest to that." As one the workers averted their eyes and returned to their respective interests, as oblivious as they had been earlier to the shoving match.

Surprisingly, Fish suddenly dropped his gaze to the deck and nodded. He sighed with resignation. "Indeed I understand. We have had trouble with people impersonating the King's agents for some time. We've tried stamps and receipts, but they are soon forged. We put out rewards, and keep a constant watch, but if people will not report these criminals, what are we to do?" He shrugged his shoulders. "Obviously we cannot cease collecting taxes." Fish shook his head in deprecation of the pathetic state of affairs in Vaw. "But fortunately for Vaw–and unfortunately for you," he pointed again, "the pier tax must still be paid. Nothing changes that. I can't help you if you are slow in the attic and paid your required fees to some wandering vagabonds off the street!" Fish signaled to his assistant who casually revealed his rapier's sword handle and the tollsman thrust out his palm a second time.

Reluctantly, Flores counted out three more coins.

"By the way..." The man peered at the ship's inscription and jingled his coins. He inquired in a gentle tone, "What is the name of your vessel?"

"Grest."

"By the way, Grest. If you want to stay out of trouble in Vaw, just remember." His finger thumped Flores' chest. "My name is Fish and I'm the only agent of the King on the south dock–everyone knows me. They call me Fish because of my wide mouth." Flores wondered what was wide about it, but Fish placed his fingers in his cheeks and pulled and Flores accepted the caricature as not too implausible. "This cloak and my temper prove it. If any riffraff has the balls to appear before you demanding money, yellow cloak or no, you have my permission to give it to him right in the nose." He shook his fist uncomfortably close to Flores' face. "Then call me. I'll haul him off by his thumbs and he'll never look like anyone again–even himself. Now, good day, Grest. And watch yourself."

The man turned and marched toward the city, vanishing in the crowd that mingled on the wharf, and retaining his cloak to the last, as Flores and Isav noted with care. Satisfied that they had finally contacted the correct party, and relieved that there would be no more interruptions from the King's officials or their facsimiles, Flores directed his men to unload the other empty barrels from the boat. There were only a half dozen, but his men managed to drop and break one of them on the dock anyway and Flores bit his lip in irritation, not from the loss of a barrel but for the added attention that was drawn to their ship, noting the continuing stares from workers, haughty stares that now bordered on impudence.

Several minutes passed and Flores began to wish for the quick return of Macius, despite the knowledge that his navigator had in fact been gone but a short while, when Isav suddenly groaned. Flores followed his gaze and was stunned to see yet another yellow-draped figure picking its way with exaggerated care along the dock.

The latest agent of the King–if that is what he was–was short, stocky, and strong. Flores noted smugly as the official and his retinue of three armed assistants neared that his cloak was faded, his leather cap torn and without decoration, and his boots soiled–this 'agent' was different from all the others who had come before.

Flores glanced at his twenty clansmen and nudged Isav.

"What did Fish say?"

"With his permission!"

The two turned their backs–this obvious impostor had best keep walking. Dockside laborers above and below the Grest halted their work and watched the approach of the 'official' with close attention.

A few moments later a finger tapped Flores upon his shoulder.

Flores ignored it.

The finger tapped again.

Again Flores ignored it.

He heard someone draw breath sharply in irritation.

Flores clenched his fist and exchanged a knowing glance with Isav. If he heard once more the word

"Fee!" someone shouted in his ear.

Twirling, Flores and Isav simultaneously swung. For one moment the squat yellow-cloaked figure leaned like an ancient monolith, its extraordinarily wide mouth zagging like a fault line under the imprint of eight knuckles. Slowly the official's eyes lowered from their empyrean reflection and with difficulty refocused. Then the cloaked man fell backwards upon the wharf to a loud report of clapboards.

For several moments no one moved. Then howls of glee arose from the stevedores, who doubled over, devastated with happiness.

"Fish!" the attendants gasped and knelt beside the stricken man. With casual curiosity, and immediate knowledge of what punishment was likely to follow their assault on an agent of the King, Flores noted the peculiar physiographic feature which their victim possessed. The man's mouth, Flores thought, was the widest he had ever seen. As the agent's legendary temper swelled, the lips came to life and writhed across the man's face like angry snakes.

For a moment the surge abated as Fish froze in strangled apoplexy, then the official gasped and the laborers regained their composure and returned to their ropes and barrels. The volcano welled again and the King's agent, apparently unharmed, struggled to his feet bellowing with the voice of a male reven newly cognizant of the theft of his harem.

"I'll kill 'em!" roared Fish. "I'll starve 'em I'll drown 'em I'll strangle 'em! I'll lock them in the deepest cell in Vaw! I'll tie this one to a baited ros, and the other to its mate! Then I'll hang 'em, and poison 'em too..." These threats were followed by an ever more imaginative crescendo of proclamations concerning the fate of the Grest's crew, and of Flores and Isav in particular, as Fish stamped and leaped about the deck in unison with the leaping into his brain of each new terrible configuration of mortal revenge. Another minute passed and one of Fish's attendants who had been eyeing the Grest grasped the official's arm. Fish turned on the gaunt man and smote his assistant savagely. The purple bruise that emerged soon outshined his own.

"You said there would be no more trouble on the dock if we hang a few!" Fish screamed. He grabbed his companion, revealing an unexpected strength by lifting and rattling him. Though his assistant was taller he was no match for Fish's compact sinews. "Idiot! Don't you call this trouble? They almost killed me! Tomorrow bring more men on the rounds. More men, I tell you! And more weapons! I want no repeat of this! No repeat! Do you hear?"

Observing Fish's solid frame Flores could well understand his apparent full recovery–he was to all appearances unscathed, his ego suffering more than his jaw. Fish's companion did not resist his rough treatment but succeeded in finally securing the attention of his boss. Pulling him out of earshot, he whispered in Fish's ear for several minutes. Slowly the lips calmed. Then they began to arch and jerk in response to changes in Fish's mood. A frown formed momentarily then melted into a cynical smile.

Flores looked at Isav. Both Isav and Revd were white with suspense and eyed the city for signs of approaching warriors.

"Well?" inquired Flores in a calm voice. "Perhaps we should appeal to his natural reason as a universal trait of Vensor-sa." Isav displayed subtle signals to the crew who moved casually but quickly to position themselves between Flores and the Vaw-sa and to secure their retreat to the boat. Flores watched but felt no confidence in the Grest's ability to outrun the Vaws' swift patrol craft.

Fish returned, still fuming but under control. His eyes bulged.

"Fee! For docking!" For emphasis Fish slammed a blunt fist upon the Vens' other barrel-top and shattered the staves like matchwood. His three attendants were outnumbered by the Vens, but, with their home port at their backs, arrogantly confident of their superiority. They half-bared their swords. Reluctantly, Flores counted out three more coins into the attendant's waiting hands. Fish calmed and brushed himself. He glared at the Grest, at the Vens, but especially at Flores. Then, inexplicably, since the Vens now expected the entire weight of officialdom to fall upon them, without further action, Fish and his attendants turned, and, with a few malicious lingering glances toward the Grest and occasional cuffs of dock workers slow to vacate their path, retired in the direction of the city.

Confused, but relieved, Flores ordered his men to board and prepare for a quick departure, awaiting only the return of their pilot. Fish had vanished, the dock workers had returned in good spirits to their mundane activities, and the Grest was ready to sail, when a breathless Macius reappeared, his face still obscured by his hood, his gaze passing swiftly from face to face like an errant butterfly.

"There has been trouble," Flores said.

Macius looked at him and cocked an ear.

"We struck the King's Overseer of the dock when he came to collect his fee."

Macius said nothing but shifted his weight as an athlete might when securing a more certain pose prior to a competition.

Isav stepped closer.

"My apologies, Flores," said Macius. "I had forgotten the full extent of the hazards that newcomers face."

Isav broke in with ill-concealed distaste for Macius. "Why didn't you tell us of these deceptions before we docked? You may have condemned us to a Vaw prison." He turned to Flores. "I told you he could not be trusted. He meant for this to happen."

The Vaw gazed the length of the pier, saying nothing.

Flores waved a hand. "If so, then why did he return?"

"I fear that your captain may be correct," continued Macius. "It was not my intention to hinder us, but it seems that by bringing you to Vaw I have needlessly placed us all in danger."

The Turlicum shook his head. "No. We cannot eat oars or drink sea water. You were right. We must take on supplies." He glanced toward the city. "But we should depart at once. If only we had some way of out-running the harnessed reven of their patrol boats."

"Perhaps that will not be necessary," said Macius. "The Overseer's authority is limited to this dock. Your men can push off, then drop anchor. This man Fish may want the Grest, but the King never seizes ships. Bad business for a port. Fish would not openly violate the king's direct command. But we should not delay–no one in Vaw can be trusted after dark." Macius passed his glance over the harbor. "I was not able to find whom I wished in the city, but there are others in Vaw as resourceful. With no delays–and for hard mir–we can still get what we need. Send a man with me into the city with fifty mir, Flores, and we can be gone by dusk."

The Ven shook his head. "I will not risk my men in a strange city with such a burden. Throats are cut for far less than fifty mir. I will accompany you myself."

CHAPTER 3

THE ORACLE

"The city must defend itself! It must take heart and organize!"

Ust-Terenol-Calomar leaned forward, jeweled hands on vest, thumbs out-thrusting the silver shirring to emphasize his words. A handful of nobles of the city of Ven gazed with disinterest from the back benches of the Assemblyhall. The oval chamber with its concentric rows of expensive marble seats was bathed in light penetrating the translucent irsrem dome that roofed the immense structure, but the light could not dispel the darkness and depression that oppressed the heart of each—except the heart of Ust. Where the others slouched or moved listlessly about, most Simet-sa indeed preferring to spend the last days of the city ensconced in their clan domiciles or engaged in private religious pursuits, only Ust was energetic and enthused with solving the problems of governing the city and its empire.

"Why do you lean upon your hand, Nilsit, leader of a renowned and ancient clan? Why do you lie upon your back, Toosel, when at any moment foreign warriors may enter the city and pillage your estate, our Temple, our city?" Earnestly he swung his sharp bearded chin from side to side, inspecting each face for a positive response.

The nobles glanced at Ust then returned to their gloomy preoccupations. Several stood and walked out. One entered the chamber, seeming to have arrived entirely by chance so desultory did he appear, walking aimlessly about for some length of time before settling on a bench some distance from the small group that sat near Ust. Across the hall a Simet aristocrat let out a cry of despair and addressed the dome: "Vensor! What were our sins? How can we redeem ourselves?" Without waiting for a reply, he buried his face in his hands and quietly sobbed.

"The city deserves to die," said Toosel without rising.

"No! The city will live!" expostulated Ust, staring down upon him.

Toosel looked at Ust and shrugged. "You may live with your fantasies. What is it to me? We," he looked about him at the cavernous theater, almost empty of life, and continued, "the responsible Simet-sa, the leaders of the city, would rather live with our feet on Maalstrom." He shook his head. "No, Ust, you are wrong. We have failed Vensor. His Temple was violated. Defiled. His spirit no longer resides within the city. All know what that portends."

A noble by his side sat up straight and shook a finger at the Calomar. "Since the sacking of the Temple by the Neset-sa, our city has not had a single child delivered by Vensor's guardians. No children for six months. The clans cannot renew their numbers. Men have no sons. The city has no guidance from Vensor, we cannot consult the oracle, the Temple will not accept our gifts, we cannot worship the deities or glimpse the idol of the Sun-god."

Toosel rose and removed his blue and silver assemblyman's vest and tossed the expensive garment on the floor at the feet of his comrades. "There. There lies the future of Ven! There lies the assembly! There lie we, in the eyes of God–abandoned, forsaken, guilty, despised by our Creator."

"No!" interrupted Ust. "The children will be delivered. The Temple will again open. Vensor has not deserted us, he merely rests in order to renew his strength. We must have faith and rely upon his goodwill. I tell you we will again worship the deities, we will again see Vensor, we will again consult the oracle." Ust's sallow face searched the visages of his colleagues poignantly, seeking some indication of life, of will, of energy. He glanced up to where a large throne of irsrem sat upon a dais amid the benches, empty.

"I ask you once more. Appoint me dictator of the city. Give me the authority to defend the city from marauders. I swear I will organize Ven and deal with its enemies. I will do as Numsenmur would have done in this crisis. I will whip the indolent, scourge the recalcitrant–and Vensor will listen and open wide the gates of his loving bounty. I promise you this. I can save Ven! Give me the power as you once gave it to Serclasler and the Turlicum!" Ust paused, bearded chin quivering, mouth open, his hands clutching empty air.

Sighs answered.

"Aaah!" Ust flung the lot of them away with a toss of his hand. Turning, he stormed out of the chamber.

Crossing the grounds, Ust entered the Way of Murfenmas and stared in horror at the ruins of the central bazaar. Fires had broken out among the stands, columns of smoke trailing into the sky. No one moved to extinguish them. If the flames spread to the city they would engulf the tenements and become irresistible. More dejected and stunned with each moment, Ust walked toward the Holy Temple of Ven. The city was collapsing, dissolving before his eyes. Bodies lay upon the ground where their murderers had left them, some with the instruments of death still protruding. Gangs of youths and children beat pedestrians with sticks and pelted them with stones. Ust dodged one, felt for his rapier, and hurried on.

Near the Temple he halted. Acolytes of the House of Prostitution, holy eunuchs with shaven heads, were advancing toward the platform of the eremites along the elevated walkway that joined the House to the Eunuch Guild. He followed their black forms until they arrived at the landing, a high tower of wooden clapboards from which the acolytes by habit observed the suns during public celebrations. Several of the eunuchs were blind. These were the holiest of the sacerdotes, the most dedicated observers of Vensor, whose devotion was such that they had burned out their eyes from long sessions of staring into His shining orbs. Collecting at the base of the tower, the blind one by one climbed the ladder and formed a circle upon the landing.

Ust's skin crawled as he contemplated what purpose the slaves of Soorkrul, the Eunuch Lord of Ven, may have in these last of times, when the world itself was collapsing into ruin. As Ust watched, one opened a leather pouch and began to smear its sticky contents upon the shaven head of each, including his own. A crowd gathered. A spark flashed—more sparks, and a small torch flared. Casually, the priest with the torch touched it to the head of each eunuch, the man's head bursting into flame as he did so. Finally, he touched his own. For several minutes the crowd stared, too horror-struck to move, while the eunuchs stood, linked hands and began slowly to dance, their heads sputtering in the afternoon suns. Then, as by previous arrangement, they began to sing their traditional chant to the Sun-god. No sooner did they begin singing than their voices were transformed into shrieks. Lurching and beating upon their heads with their hands, the eunuchs turned and stumbled, or dove over the side of the platform to ply the ground at the feet of the crowd, which panicked and fled. Ust covered his face with his hands and wondered how he could ever have thought that Ven would survive, that the Temple would reopen, that he, no more than a man, could renew a civilization and lead it to new heights of grandeur and prosperity.

The last acolyte lay crushed and smoldering and the plaza before the

Temple sprawled empty and desolate before the saddened gaze of Ust, when a sullen gong sounded from deep within the mysterious and secluded Temple. Washing across the city, its waves of sound searched out every soul, every ear, every person whether noble or commoner, summoning them to the Temple for a renewal of the ancient covenant between Vensor and His Children, a renewal of his eldritch promise to those whom He elected from among all the life of the Universe–to summon the Chosen once again to another calling for the sons of Vensor.

Ust stared at the massive Temple gate. Appearing above the lintel, black-swathed figures moved. He listened closely for sounds and heard soft mewling. With a shout the Calomar lifted one hand, lowered it, then drew his sword, and swung it in great circles above his head.

"Vensor!" he called in unison with the suddenly energized Vens surrounding him. "Vensor has forgiven us! He has renewed his energy!" A throng of Vens crowded into the plaza. Ust began to chant, "Vensor! Vensor!" and others joined in, shouting and gesticulating. Within minutes a multitude covered the square, pouring into the plaza from the far corners of the city with flutes and gongs and drums, crying with joy at the salvation of Ven, of the world.

Ust noticed Sendas and Simlet among the arrivals. Motioning for them to follow, he approached Toosel, who appeared clutching the magistrate's rattan cane of office, and disheveled vest.

"Hand the cane to me," Ust demanded, "I shall preside over the ceremony."

Toosel made no move to deliver it. "You have not been elected to the post of magistrate. I shall give it only to the magistrate."

"There is no magistrate," exclaimed Ust. "I can fulfill the duty until one is elected."

"You shall not. We must elect someone and then hand him the cane."

"Then let us elect one!"

"Don't be absurd. There is no time." Toosel turned away.

Ust turned to Sendas. "You vote for me! I vote for me! He votes for me." Pointing to another Simet, "And you vote for you! I win! Now hand me the cane." Ust reached out his hand.

"Stand back or I will strike you."

Ust grabbed Toosel and they began to wrestle. A crowd of Simet-sa gathered, commoners backing off, once again afraid, with the return of authority, to offend Simet nobles, even by accident. Seizing Ust, the nobles dragged him off Toosel and pushed him down. They lifted Toosel and brushed the dirt off him.

Nilsit shook a fist at Ust. "We have no time to elect anyone, you pretentious braggart. Desist from your ridiculous fantasies and leave brother Toosel alone. He already possesses the magistrate's cane, so he might as well act as magistrate for the coming ceremony."

Ust stamped one foot, tried to kick Toosel, but missed and nearly fell. Laughter rose from his colleagues. Ust regained his balance.

"You fools! Don't you understand that the time for your foul and feeble elections has passed? Never again shall we sit and calmly elect a leader to do the assembly's dirty work and take the blame when our plans collapse." His voice dripped with venom. "The Serclasler's executions ended all that. The Republic is dead and the Turlicum is gone. The only question is who will next sit on the throne of Ven. I demand that you elect me king as we stand here, or I shall organize my clan and seize power as did the Serclasler!"

The nobles, who had finally begun to listen to their colleague, tittered. "Ha! Listen to him squeak; he rants of dictators and kings! Ust, the coward. Ust, the fool! He longs to be King of Ven!" The speaker elbowed a companion, and they broke into laughter. They folded their arms and stared upon the Calomar with amused contempt.

"And how will you seize power, dear Ust," said Nilsit. "Your former protector, Numsenmur, is dead, and his son is loyal to the Assembly. Your clan cannot challenge the great clans alone. Perhaps you think it your destiny that Vensor give you the mantle."

Ust glared at them. "If you must know, that is exactly so." The others cocked their ears and Ust raised his voice. "Yes, it is my destiny. Vensor Himself wills that I be King of Ven. And it will indeed happen."

The Simet-sa, their numbers now swelled to dozens, roared with laughter. They gasped with hilarity at the idea of a heavenly mandate for the least respected member of the assembly.

"I demand that the question be put to the oracle! If necessary I will voice it myself." Ust pointed again to the nobles. "I said that the Temple would re-open. You would not listen to me, but behold—the gates open! I told you that we had not lost the goodwill of Vensor. While you lay upon your backs in self-pity, I kept faith in Ven! Now I tell you that if you consult the oracle, you will find that I am favored in the sight of God, and that it is His intention to place me over you as your King!"

The Simet-sa ceased laughing, something in Ust's tone suggesting that his utterances might be based on more than fancy.

Toosel shrugged his shoulders. "If you are so adamant that you would disrupt city business and submit this insane and ambitious desire of yours to the oracle, so be it. You will only succeed in humiliating yourself further. But since that appears to be your purpose, and you will not be dissuaded, then I agree to put your request to the Temple." He looked about him and the others nodded agreement.

The second gong sounded from the spire within the Temple. The huge gates began to lift. The Simet-sa, suddenly in control and organized, commanded soldiers to hold back the rabble, and approached the courtyard of the calling for sons. Most of the stone altars were bare, but crying and kicking upon the altars in the courtyard lay four male infants. Without waiting for the ceremony, the nobles rushed forward. One of the infants lay upon the altar of the Lurenmurg. How ironic the twists of fate–after years of patient waiting, the dead Sruk finally had a son.

The infants were soon claimed and removed and the nobles proceeded to the steamy chamber of the idols where they placed the hurriedly assembled offerings, all the city could amass with such brief notice: rorerush and ses, flesh of lyart and hen, wine, fruit, rich cloths, oil, and the finest that the city possessed in worked gold and silver. These were placed before the idols of the Clan of Vensor: stony Nantifus; Talen, claws reaching for prey; Tumsenet, roots and trunk finely carved; Nvediteg, lightning bolts aimed at the unwary; and Gethos, fish scales glinting blue in the mist. And behind, joined to the Temple proper and looming over the chamber, the golden sphere of Vensor, tiny hands on knees, minuscule head surmounted by an efferent aureole, its eyes emitting smoke, its groin a steady flume of steam.

Toosel, Nilsit, and–not to be put off–Ust mounted the long narrow stairway that arched perilously from the floor before the idol to a platform just below the flaming eyes of the golden idol of Vensor. Toosel rang the small gong resting on the platform, then leaned upon the railing. He opened the scroll that lay below the gong and read:

"Our Lord Vensor, Father of the Universe, Just and Merciful Giver of Life, Protector of the Sacred Spring, Bringer of Victory, Imposer of Order, God of Justice, Master of the Malkops, we beseech thee today to give your attention to your unworthy children, in the following:"

Toosel glanced at Ust, who stood staring upward into the murky eyes of God, the flames throwing shadows upon his face, the heat and moisture causing sweat to bead and trickle down his neck.

"One of our number, a fellow named Ust-Teredol-Calomar, claims that he is favored in your eyes and that you wish to make him King of Ven. Is this true?"

A minute elapsed.

At last, emanating from the mouth of the idol came a thin but commanding voice. "The Creator commands: food."

Silence followed.

No man ever suffered as did the least respected member of the assembly in that moment. Nilsit and Toosel turned and smiled upon a tiny fragment of a man, a pygmy in a Brobdingnagian universe, his reputation shrunk to such proportions that he seemed veritably to implode and become invisible.

Then Vensor cleared His throat. "And, oh yes, the one named Ust-Terenol is indeed favored. You will appoint him King–unless he wishes otherwise."

CHAPTER 4

PLOTS WITHIN PLOTS

The dwindling suns glinted upon the variegated profusion spanning the harbor of Vaw, warming the torsos of two vok-clad figures wending through the mob toward an abrupt facade of shops and narrow alleyways. Macius lowered his cowl over his head, and after the incident on the pier Flores also wished not to be recognized and avoided staring directly at any Vaw-sa. He hoped their stay would be short. As the pair disappeared into the twisted tunnels of the city, a youth of sullen expression and tousled hair turned and hurried along the seawalk, melting into a tide of masculine faces. Moments later the youth re-emerged at the entrance to a squat and faded yellow edifice. An ill-washed sentinel awoke. With a sign of recognition he motioned the youth to enter. The boy passed through a darkened hallway. He halted before a soiled and scarred wooden door. Uncurling his fingers from about a small coin, he withdrew his hand from his pocket and knocked.

"Enter!"

Clumsily the boy opened the door. He shut it behind him.

"Well?" demanded the voice. "What do you here? I told you to watch those rogues. I want to know what they are doing every moment."

The full lips of Fish lay across his thick-set jaw like tentacles draped upon a melon. He leaned forward in a worn wicker chair. The joints groaned beneath his weight. Momentarily transfixed by the peculiar physiognomy of the king's Overseer, the youth stared. The lips began to frown, and he dropped his gaze.

"They've left–I mean two of the men you told me to watch–including one of the two who struck you."

Fish rubbed his lips where the fists of the two men had connected.

"They entered the city a few moments ago–"

"Fool!" Fish rose and struck the table. "Follow them! Do not lose them!

Report back to me as soon as you learn their destination!" The lips stretched in an absurd caricature of a smile, splitting the bullet head obscenely, and a gold coin appeared between the agent's hammer fingers. The youth made no move to accept it.

"There is more?" Squinting, Fish sat again and leaned forward.

The youth nodded. He glanced at a gaunt assistant to the King's Overseer standing a few paces away, and stepped behind the desk. The boy whispered in Fish's ear. The agent's eyes and mouth slowly relaxed, then tightened as the boy spoke.

"You're certain it was he?"

A nod assured him of the information.

With a ping the coin spun into the youth's waiting hand. The door slammed shut. The king's agent turned to his companion.

The taller man resumed speaking. "As I was saying, our men can be gathered within the hour. And when darkness comes we can rush the boat. We have not registered them, they will not be missed. Shall I tell the men to prepare? Your revenge will be sweet." A gloomy smile almost brightened the visage of the gaunt man, his own jaw still revealing the effects of Fish's abuse.

The third-initiate of Kot frowned. His fingertips slid along his face, and ran over dull stubble. "Yes. Tell them to prepare. But we shall not take their ship—not yet, anyway. There is another matter I wish to attend to first."

⇛⇖

Macius and Flores followed the twisting alleyway, climbing steadily higher toward the black temple mounted on the acropolis. The houses tumbled helter-skelter, at times meeting overhead to plunge their path in shadow. The pair watched the descent of the suns with apprehension, gauging the time that remained till night should envelop them. Before rising again, the avenue leveled and, presently, on a plateau beyond sight of the harbor, Macius found the complex he sought.

Casually eyeing the passersby in front of the shop, he entered. Steam seeped from a dark aperture at the rear, emitted by invisible irsrem smelters, and curled about implements and weapons suspended from the walls for the perusal of buyers. A sharp scent of corta hung in the air. A customer finished his business in the shadowy interior, paid the clerk, and passed into the cleaner air of the open street.

Macius approached the clerk and pulled back his cowl. Though Flores observed the man closely, no glint of recognition showed in the clerk's eyes. Suddenly, without expression or apparent cause, the shopkeeper drove a fist into Macius' shoulder. Macius returned the blow and for a minute the pair traded punches and shoves as Flores stared, shocked into inaction. If not for fear of arrest, and Macius' warning against any contact with Vaw officials, Flores would have summoned the police. Finally the clerk and Macius ceased pummeling each other, and, without a sound, embraced like old comrades. Macius lay a heavy hand on the clerk's shoulder and together they entered an adjoining room. The door swung shut.

The minutes passed and Macius and the shopkeeper had not reappeared. Flores glanced about the interior of the smoky shop. He looked for some place to sit. There was none. Observing the Vaw-sa on the street, he noted that many seemed almost identical to Macius. Most were also hairless, almond-eyed, dark, and frequently muscular. But Flores shook his head–there were so many exceptions, like the King's agent Fish, that he could not be sure who might be traders like him and who were natives of the city.

"A worm-sword. It was to be ready today."

Flores turned. He beheld a yellow-capped official with the shopkeeper's youthful assistant, an alert guard by the official's side. The youth nodded and exited to retrieve the order. Flores averted his gaze and affected an interest in the rows of glass tools and devices hanging about the walls. In the shop of Macius' friend, the eye of officialdom was even less welcome than on the wharf.

"You!"

Flores feigned interest in a glass blade suspended before him.

"No use looking away, it is you whom I am addressing." The official approached, his attendant following, hand on helve. The man stopped before Flores. He took one corner of Flores' fur cape between two fingers and twilled it. "Not of Vaw make. Where did you get this?"

The man eyed Flores' features. "Not of Vaw birth." He gazed quizzically at Flores, who noted the same hairless, olive-hued skin evident in Macius and most of the other persons he had seen thus far in Vaw. "Ah. A foreigner. And this of foreign make." He rubbed the cloth again, then snorted. "No matter. It is inferior."

The shopkeeper's assistant returned, bearing a wickedly cast irsrem rapier, the blade of which snaked left and right before terminating in a double-pronged tip.

The official lifted it, felt the weighted handle and cut the air. "Fine work. Your master is justly admired."

The youth again nodded deeply. "It is his specialty and pride, sir. He makes them only for trusted friends and intimates."

The official grunted in satisfaction. Handing the weapon to his assistant, he handed a bag of coins to the youth, turned, and left.

A moment later Macius and the master of the shop emerged from the backroom. Macius pulled his friend roughly toward Flores. "Flores, may I present Stalkin, a friend from the old days when together we haunted the back alleys of Vaw and made every merchant along the dock wary of the night."

Flores nodded to the shopkeeper and smiled. The man laid a glance upon him that seemed to Flores akin to both amusement and conceit–to Flores's relief this dark and muscular Vaw did not repeat his elaborate introduction with him. Stalkin's face was hairless, but broader than that of Macius, he stood taller, and his arms were more muscular, and scarred in places–from accidents with hot glass, Flores assumed. Flores noted that Stalkin's legs, left bare by the same workers' skirt worn in Ven, were massive, due, Flores again assumed, to long hours spent working with essence and heavy ore of corta.

Stalkin motioned them to accompany him and they re-entered the adjoining room, shutting the thin wooden door behind them. He drew chairs about a wooden table.

"Then it is agreed," said Macius. "Enough dried lyart and ses-bread and fresh water for twenty men for two months. In all, twenty barrels." Macius looked at Flores and pointed to a pocket. The Turlicum produced a heavy and compact roll of coins and Macius handed them to Stalkin. The shopkeeper snapped his finger. The youth entered with such little delay that he must have been listening at the door. Stalkin flung the coins.

"If what Surge says–"

"Surge?" queried Flores.

Stalkin looked at Macius. The pilot turned to the Ven. "Macius is my public name. Surge is my initiation name."

Flores stared without comprehension.

Stalkin continued in a deep resonant voice. "If what Surge says concerning the Overseer is true, I cannot bring the supplies to your ship on the south dock. It will be too dangerous. But I have a warehouse close to the western pier. Precisely at midnight bring your ship to the western pier and dock in the first empty stall by the seawall. The barrels you need will be there and ready. My men will load them for you."

Nodding, Macius and Flores rose and departed.

Once outside, the pair followed the avenue back toward the wharf. With the approaching darkness, the crowd of Vaw-sa was thinning and Flores and Macius felt less need to conceal themselves. Flores felt even more unsure of his companion.

"Surge? Or Macius?"

"Among Vaw-sa I am Surge. Among Vens, Macius."

"Which–"

"Macius, Flores. Or Surge if you wish..."

Flores nodded. "If Fish discovers our plans, Macius, we shall be hard put to escape. How is this Stalkin fellow? How much do you trust him?"

Macius walked quickly, leading the way at each fork and turn of the street with confidence. "Fear not for Stalkin. In our youth we stripped many a wealthy merchant together." Pride rang in Macius' voice. "We shall leave the south dock immediately. Fish will not expect that. If he intends anything, he will collect his thugs–all that he can coerce or bribe into plundering the Grest–and expect to take us at night. But we," Macius raised a hand and gestured with the finesse of a maestro, "we shall be at the western pier, loading the Grest with the help of Stalkin, after which we shall vanish in the night. Before Fish discovers our deception and dispatches patrol boats, we'll be upon the open ocean, beyond his reach."

The street twisted before them and spun off galleries and branches, some obvious cul-de-sacs, others opening onto avenues. A few led perceptibly down toward the harbor, while others seemed to double back and lead up the hillside. Blank walls and roofs blocked their view so that although they could smell the salt air of the sea they could not glimpse the open water or the wharf where the Grest was tied. Macius followed the path unerringly, however, taking each turn with a knowing eye. He strode quickly and, as Flores slowed on occasion to glance at the new sights about him, a distance of several meters soon intervened.

"Watch your path, dog!"

Flores turned his glance from the facade of a roadside inn and beheld an old man blocking him, leaning upon a stick.

"I said, watch your path!" The ancient figure stared upward with defiance into the face of Flores, the man's lower lip entirely covering his upper, his one good eye contacting each of Flores' eyes in turn. "Dog!"

Flores smiled. "Forgiveness, sir. It was my fault."

"Of course it was." He shook his hand, still clutching the staff, in Flores' face. "Who said it wasn't?" His one eye blinked. "Go ahead, try something. Lay a hand on me. I'll show you what I'm made of."

Flores stepped back and walked on, giving the old man a wide berth.

"Dog, I said!" The cry came drifting after him.

Flores halted. Before him the road, now empty of traffic, forked, to reveal a right-hand path that seemed to lead downward in the direction of the docks, and a left-hand path that apparently led upward toward the heart of the city. Macius was nowhere in view. Flores frowned. The suns had set and darkness was only moments away. Already gloom obscured much of the street and plunged the alleys in impenetrable shadow.

"The wharf must lie this way," he muttered. He turned to the right and hurried on. He paused. The path ended in a blank wall. Except for a single tightly shuttered window beyond his reach, the cul-de-sac was featureless. No outlet existed except the road that Flores had followed.

"The road ends. It must have been the other route."

Even as he spoke to himself, the last sunrays illumined the roof of the apartment before him, and winked out. Above, outlined by the roofs of the surrounding apartments, the first stars of the night appeared. About him all was quiet; no movement or breath disturbed the heavy humid air. Flores turned, took a step, and halted–a figure stood before him. Instinctively, he grasped the handle of his sword. Beyond the figure that blocked his path lay the empty street, now immersed in shadow. The figure expanded. The tight place in his stomach relaxed and Flores forced a smile. It was the harmless old man, whom Flores had accidentally brushed a few moments earlier.

"Pardon my haste, sir. I had thought my companion entered with me. I wish to find him." Flores stepped forward.

The old man took a step and blocked him again.

"Sir, if you were offended by my action, I apologize. My act was entirely accidental. I assure you I shall take care not to disturb you again."

The old man did not move but remained bent and blocking his path. For an instant the thought occurred to Flores that perhaps this was actually Macius, who, after assuming a disguise for some obscure purpose, had slipped behind him. Then the shadows deepened and Flores' eyes adjusted and he suddenly wondered why he had thought the man was old. The person who stood before him was not old at all, but young. And an irsrem dagger in his hand glinted with starlight–Flores was glad he had not plunged blindly forward under his first impulse. Behind the first man appeared four more shadows, moving quickly, glass blades flashing.

The first stepped toward Flores.

"So that is it." The Ven noble nodded. No mystery remained. "Good, then. What better time to die than the present?"

The Vaw lunged with his dagger. As Flores expected, the first lunge was a feint and the Ven, who had not reacted to the first thrust, twisted to avoid the second, then with his right hand slipped his blade deep into the man's left lung. For an instant the Ven warrior glimpsed an intimacy as much emotional as physical with the mind that drained before his gaze. The ruffian's brown eyes rolled spasmodically in his glabrous face as his life gushed into his clothing.

The second attacker lunged–Flores yanked his blade free to counter him. His victim attempted to scream but spewed a shower of blood on his companion before collapsing.

His companions gasped. They stared in shock at their fallen comrade. Flores reflected on a basic principle of combat: the mutilated will throw an enemy's camp into turmoil.

"Revenge!" The cry reverberated off the walls of the cul-de-sac and, were they in Ven, would have aroused the neighborhood. More of their gang must be near, thought Flores. He peered past them, half expecting to see King Kot emerge from the shadows at the head of an army.

Flores wasted no time but employed his next tactic. He rushed upon the foremost, and, since the other had compensated for a right-handed fighter, switched his dagger from right to left, and met the rapier skill-fully with his own blade. How often had this simple deception ended an encounter almost before it had begun! He closed and rolled. Sparks popped where glass met glass. Blades stabbed the ground about them, but he continued rolling until he felt a pair of legs bow and collapse upon them both. As Flores rose to meet the next onslaught, his opponent raised himself and stared in shock at a dark ring that spread across his torso. The night took on a red glow as Flores felt Atasan awake and take breath. The well-drilled automaton within him detached his conscious mind and began to direct each move. His blade spun to lap gently at the jugular in another victim's neck. Another pressed forward, tossing aside his baldric for greater motion. Flores backed him over his fallen comrade. He stumbled and was transfixed before he fell.

Despite the shouts of his attackers, no other ruffians had appeared to join them, and the last one paused. Apparently he realized the superiority of the swordplay of their intended victim. But he could not flee–Flores now stood between him and the exit. His eyes inspected the walls of his prison as had the eyes of Flores moments before, sweeping the high para-pets for a way out. Then, steeling himself to his fate, he whipped aside his nightcape to reveal a wickedly fused irsrem blade with twin prongs snaking in one hand. Rushing forward, he engaged the Ven in a complex net of parries and thrusts. Evading his jabs with some difficulty, Flores slipped on the gravel and nearly fell. He dug in his heel and met the man head on, parrying each thrust as rapidly as delivered, his glass blade spilling a constellation of sparks on the ground and drenching the air with ozone. Pebbles rasped from the alley and the Vaw paused to grin, apparently still expecting assistance–in surprise he looked down to where Flores's dagger had penetrated his midriff. Flores tore it free, and the hideous thing that had moments before been a man staggered backwards, spilling organs on the ground.

"Flores! Thank Vensor! You live!"

Flores paused, his dagger weaving, awaiting the next red kiss.

"Macius?"

The Vaw rushed forward from the shadows, and halted. The thief whistled. "Five! And with only your dagger!" Two of the bodies took shallow breaths. Surprisingly, Flores' first victim still lived and crawled toward the avenue as they watched, silent as ever. Flores ignored him, wiped his blade on a corner projection, and belted it.

"Miraculous. You are unhurt?"

Flores nodded.

"I became lost," added Macius. "I doubled back. Then someone clubbed me and I fell. When I awoke I heard shouts and came running."

The Turlicum peered carefully at his companion, who knew the alleys of Vaw better than any man alive and whose criminal exploits and deceptions were famous across the seas.

"Look," the Vaw leaned and pointed to a welt upon the back of his head. "I cannot understand it. I was not even robbed. Why would someone club me and leave me, but not take my purse?"

Flores stood for another moment, listening to the grisly sounds by their feet. "Let's go."

Macius turned and together they exited the alley. They followed the left-hand fork. Within minutes they were upon the Grest, Macius informing the others of the ambush and of their plans for the rendezvous. Soon the Grest pushed away from the south dock and, with lights extinguished, the crew huddled in the cool night air counting the hours to midnight.

Macius watched the sky and shivered. A dense cover of clouds drifted in from the east, and, like the hull of a capsized ship, the dome of the Maalstrom night sank into the sea. Gethos, then Tumsenet, vanished. Nvediteg, Talen, and fiery Atasan followed. The Vaw would have far preferred to bask in the eye of the deity of fortune than to hide in this endless pitch night. He glanced at the carved totem mounted fore of the ship; at least his scaly image remained to remind Macius of the real Gethos above. Macius motioned and Flores silently touched the others on their arms. Twenty oars thrust out and sank into the water, pulling the Grest toward the western pier.

As they neared the pier nothing at first was visible. No light shone–as should be the case, Flores reassured himself. Passing a line of moored cargo vessels, they drifted close to where Macius believed the first stall should be, then a brief whistle carried to them from closer in to shore.

"He waves to us," said Isav, squinting in the dark.

"I see, yes." Flores tapped Macius and pointed.

Several minutes passed and the Grest drifted quietly into the first stall by the seawall and touched the pier. Waiting hands caught their flung rope and looped it about a cleat. On the right the seawall ran parallel to the ship, permitting a clear view of the shore's esplanade and a row of adjoining flat brick warehouses. A half-dozen barrels lined the dock fore of the ship–fewer than agreed upon, Flores noted. Several Vaw-sa tended them. Flores frowned. There were more than necessary; at least a score moved in the darkness. But the presence of Stalkin, cloaked and peering about with exaggerated furtiveness, reassured Flores.

"Quickly," Stalkin hissed as Flores and Macius boarded the pier. "There has been activity on the south dock–I do not know what happened, but I wish to finish as soon as I may." Stalkin looked at Flores. "Anyway, we were in luck. There is no sentry on the western pier tonight." Stalkin shrugged. "Who knows what happened to him?" He drew his finger across his neck and grinned.

"The barrels–" began Flores. "–this is not even half of what I purchased."

Stalkin nodded. "The rest are in the warehouse. I could not get enough help to bring them–help I could trust, that is." Eyeing the many Vaw-sa workers that Stalkin had recruited for the task, he wondered just how many Vaw-sa it took to load twenty barrels. The shopkeeper glanced across the esplanade. "There. The first building belongs to me. Send your men there, mine will remain here and load these."

Flores looked to Isav. His captain shook his head.

"No," said Flores. "Send half of your men with half of mine. And you stay here until they are loaded." A subtle but effective touching of the handle of his glass rapier evoked a moment of silence.

Stalkin paused. "An excellent suggestion." The smithy turned to Macius. "And you, Surge, must accompany the Vens and show them which barrels to bring. The ones that bear my mark are the correct ones."

Ten Vens joined Macius and half the Vaw-sa and moved up the pier in the direction of the dark squat warehouse. At the threshold of the seawall they paused, then moved quickly and noiselessly across the open esplanade. Moments later Flores glimpsed a wide gate in the side of the warehouse swing open. Blackness engulfed them.

Upon the dock Flores selected two hogsheads at random and removed their covers: dried lyart and fresh water, as requested. He smiled and nodded to Isav and Revd. "Take hold," whispered Isav. Stalkin turned and grasped one side of a barrel and together he and Isav swung it into the waiting hands of Turlicum warriors within the Grest, who placed the barrel beside the gangway in an open space that lacked oarbenches. A minute passed and two more barrels were loaded. Soon none remained on the dock.

Flores casually eyed the Vaw-sa but saw nothing to indicate that beneath their jerkins hidden weapons lurked, although even had such been the case, an illicit affair such as theirs, he admitted, deserved such precautions. Flores glanced at Isav. The ever-suspicious officer peered carefully at Stalkin. Flores followed his glance and noticed that the shopkeeper seemed unduly nervous and kept his eyes on the warehouse. None had emerged from the building. Re-mounting the pier, Flores joined Isav, Revd and Stalkin and they exchanged glances, the same thought passing among them.

Stalkin turned. "A moment's delay, that is all. They must find the correct barrels and carry them to the entrance."

Flores jumped. A high shriek rose from the building. For one long moment it hung in the air, then abruptly ceased. Seconds passed–figure burst from the warehouse gate and began a mad dash across the esplanade. No one on the dock moved, all eyes riveted on the approaching figure, which moments later was revealed to be Macius. Behind him the warehouse expelled a mob of ruffians who turned toward the dock in pursuit, brandishing clubs and daggers. Flores frowned, momentarily uncertain as to whether Macius was fleeing the mob or leading them. Then Macius was upon them.

"Away! Push off!" he gasped. "Fish has found us!"

Flores grabbed Macius' arm. "My men! Where are they?"

The thief shook his head. "Dead! All dead! But I managed to take revenge for one. You must have heard him when I struck." The thief held up his dagger as proof, the blade stained red.

"And you believe him?" Isav grasped Flores by the shoulder. "Thanks to this cutthroat, only ten of us remain out of fifty who set out from Ven!

How will we manage the oars?"

His voice was drowned by a moan from Stalkin. "Fish! It is Fish! He will spare no one! He will not let me live after assisting you, but will kill me and all my men! If we stay in Vaw we are doomed!" He glanced at the mob approaching the pier, eerily silent but for the clatter of their weapons. He covered his eyes and groaned.

Flores and Isav exchanged glances, again communicating the same thought.

"Get on board!" Flores shouted. "Take an oar! Hurry, if we push off now we may lose their patrol craft in the night."

His eyes lighting with sudden inspiration, Stalkin yelled to his men to jump onto the Grest. They quickly obeyed. Macius, Isav, Revd and Flores followed. Two oars contacted the dock and strong sinews pushed the Grest clear. When the first of the armed mob arrived and halted at the pier's edge, the new crew were settled into place and the ship already half-turned toward the sea. Silently their shadowy forms lined the dock, a hundred strong, clubs and daggers etching blacker shadows in the night, their anonymous figures breathing in deep drafts, waiting calmly like some impersonal force of nature to swallow the small boat. Once more the oars dipped and the ship moved away from the dock, away from Vaw, away from the brooding black temple on its acropolis that calmly watched the small drama unfold without interest or expression.

The ship turned and got underway. Passing through the artificial reefs of the harbor entrance, it had shrunk to a dot and was headed for the open sea under a billowing sail and twenty thrusting oars, when a short stocky man elbowed his way to the front of the mob. With careful deference, the ruffians parted to admit him. Perched on the edge of the clapboards, unmindful of the slick dark algae beneath his hard booted feet, the full lips of Fish snaked across his lantern-jaw in a smug and satisfied smile. He nodded to himself as if some careful plan had just commenced operating, meshing like the gears and pinions of a precise apparatus. He turned and again vanished among his cronies.

❧ ଊ ଓ ❧

CHAPTER 5

THE ASSIGNATION

The occupant of the massive throne turned a furrowed brow upon the assembled Simet-sa of Ven. Ust squirmed. Unable to find a comfortable pose in the solid-glass seat, he shifted his weight, then paused, fearful that his attempts to relieve its hardness might be construed as unkingly to his subjects. Silently he gazed upon the multitude of eyes upturned in expectation of a pronouncement from their king, a pronouncement that would solve the problem at hand.

"Repeat the last statement."

A quiet groan escaped the lips of the nobility. Some rolled their eyes; others turned to refresh themselves with drinks; others whispered in the ears of consorts and colleagues, while directing amused expressions toward the throne. Standing in the proscenium, an elderly noble in red vest moved his hand and an assistant raised a scroll and read a second time what was written.

"Plaintiff has charged plaintee with violating a partnership agreement, in which the lessor, that is the plaintiff, provided land and money for a business, and lessee, that is the plaintee, agreed to deliver one-half of the profits from the business to lessor. Plaintiff has charged plaintee with diverting all of the profits to salary and showing a net loss so that plaintiff has been defrauded of his rightful compensation."

Upon the dais recently constructed to support the massive throne, Ust smoothed his sky-blue cape, noting casually the astrological symbols in-sewn in the style of the late king of Neset.

"The answer is simple, Judge Osis." He held up the royal sceptre with his left hand. "Let the plaintiff be compensated—"

The red-vested official bowed, his pale eyes peering from an enormous growth of eyebrows whitened with age. "A thousand apologies, my king, but it does not end there."

Ust frowned and lowered the sceptre. "Proceed."

"Lessee has countersued, and, as plaintiff, has charged lessor, that is the plaintee, with leasing to a rival business in an adjoining lot thus ruining the profit potential of the partnership."

Ust's brows flattened across his temple. "Then the first party is the guilty one!"

"Indeed, that is so," continued the official, "or it would be so except for the fact that lessee has also subleased to third party, that is the rival business, and lessor has now sued third party in a separate suit. The plaintiff in the first case charges that the lessee in the second case has colluded with plaintee in the third case to divert profits in their business to salary as well."

As if to summon aid, Ust glanced to his right, where a balding aristocrat with bulging midriff stood alongside the throne. Dos continued to stare quietly ahead.

"So," ventured Ust, returning his attention to the proscenium, "the plaintiff in the first case has charged the lessee in the second case with plotting with the plaintiff in the third case."

"No, my king," corrected the judge, his brows almost hiding his eyes. "The plaintiff in the first case charged the lessee in the second case with plotting with the plaintee in the third case."

"Did I say different? The lessee in the first case has charged the lessor in the third case with plotting against him."

"But no, sire! The lessee in the first case *is* the lessor in the third case!"

"You said the lessor in the second case was the lessee in the first case."

"Indeed so, but the plaintiff in the first case is the plaintiff in the third case, and the lessor in the third case is the lessee in the second case."

Ust shifted again in his seat. "Then the plaintiff in the first case is the wronged party and should be compensated!"

"Not entirely, O Ruler of the Vensors. For, as the lessee in the third case has pointed out in a fourth lawsuit, the plaintiff in the first case had no claim to the land that he leased to the plaintee in the third case, who is now the subject of a fifth suit from its true owner."

"Then the third party has been wronged and should be compensated by the lessor in the third case–"

"Yes, or rather, perhaps not. Or more precisely, simply no. You see, sire, they came to the plaintiff in the first case of their own accord, claiming to own the land themselves, and sought to collude with the lessor in the first case in order to drive the lessor in the third case out of business."

"Then it is conspiracy to defraud the plaintee in the second case!"

"Not in the least, O Brother of Moons! The plaintee in the second case was the perpetrator of the fraud!"

"Then the victim must be the plaintiff in the third case!"

The judge shook his head and Ust glanced to his left. Seated beside the throne, surrounded by drinks and cushions, Sendas of the Molersal loudly imbibed a beverage. He had not been listening to the debate and he paused, cup on lip, to meet Ust's gaze. Ust exhaled in annoyance and returned his attention to the judge.

"Or rather," said Ust, "the victim is the lessor in the second case–that is what I meant to say."

The judge still shook his head and Ust sat higher in his throne. "The victim is the lessor in the first case?"

The judge raised his enormous eyebrows, while the nobility exchanged subtle smirks.

Ust gripped the throne-arms tightly. "The victim is indeed the plaintiff in the first case–I heard you say it!"

"I did not, sire."

"Indeed you did–I heard you myself!"

"Let us explain our dilemma once more, O Wisest of Men–"

"Enough! What I wish to know is why you bring such to your king! My time is precious, as is the time of the assembly."

The beard parted and the aged judge replied, "The plaintiffs have appealed to the throne as the final arbiter. It is their right under Vensor law...now that His Majesty has taken this right away from the Public Commission."

Ust narrowed his eyes and tapped the throne-arm with an index finger. How would the fashioner of his throne, whose expanse he had such difficulty filling, have dealt with this? Numsenmur of the Serclaslers had possessed no advantage that he did not also possess–excepting perhaps more numerous and more ruthless followers. Ust's gaze rested upon an impassive youth seated among neutrals in the audience. Why had Lirsus, son of Numsenmur, withdrawn his clan from the ranks of his father's allies? If I could inspire the same confidence as the Serclasler once did and regain the loyalty of his Heir...

Ust held up the royal sceptre. "Let the headsman execute the plaintee in the first case."

The Simet-sa of the assembly gasped. Ust smiled. Now he felt like Numsenmur. A tug at his elbow distracted him.

"That would not be wise, Sire," said Dos, leaning and whispering in his ear.

"No?" sneered Ust.

"No, my King. The plaintee in the first case is an important personage in the Selemnev clan."

"The Selemnev?" Ust too whispered, cupping his voice to conceal the exchange. "But they supported that traitorous Turlicum, and even now are haughty and defy my will."

Dos' owl-eyes grew large. "Precisely, Sire. Which is why you cannot harm their interests. Were they to take up arms against you, it would be difficult to contain them; their clan is strong and ill-disposed to us. It would be best not to anger their leader, Latkin–and certainly not while he sits in the assembly."

Ust frowned. Across the chamber Latkin stood, fingers toying with the helve of his rapier. Ust thought a moment, then addressed the assembly. "I rescind my order."

He raised the sceptre again. "Let the headsman execute the plaintee in the second case!"

Again sharp breaths rippled through the assembly, and Ust's advisor pulled his sleeve.

Ust yanked it free. "What now?"

"That also would not be wise, Sire."

"And why not?"

"The plaintiff in the second case is a member of the Leredol clan, my King."

"And?"

"The Leredol are neutral. If you anger them, they might join with the Selemnev."

The Calomar gazed across the assembly and saw Fursel of the Leredol rise and move casually to the side of Latkin. Ust flung his hand. "Is there no one then I can execute? Execute the plaintee in the third case!"

"But, Sire," exclaimed Dos, "I am the plaintee in the third case!"

Ust slammed the throne-arm. "Then rescind both orders and a pox on you all!" He fumed, the bemused expressions of the Assembly–and the triumphant faces of his enemies–seeming to smile down upon him, despite the fact that their benches were situated well below the level of the throne.

Ust narrowed his eyes and leaned forward. "I order the right of final appeal restored to the Public Commission so that no more of my time will be wasted on trivial matters. I charge it to investigate matters fully. And," Ust glanced at Dos, "since my advisor seems to lack objectivity in this affair, I appoint Sendas of the Molersal as the Commission's head!" Sendas ceased his noisy consumption and stared at Ust in surprise. Ust looked again upon Dos. "I trust the noble Sendas to root out corruption wherever it may lead!"

Ust turned to the attendees. "And, since you, Judge Osis, cannot seem to distinguish between important issues and trivial ones, you will relinquish your judge's seat and henceforth clean stables for the butchers guild...so that you may learn to recognize what is truly trivial."

Dos bent to whisper, but Ust cut him off. "This audience is over!"

Judge Osis stood open-mouthed. "But, sire, I am old–"

"That is all!"

His pale eyes moistening, the judge lowered his head and, joined by his assistant, backed away from the throne, and out of the chamber.

Opposite Ust, seated close together amid the sloping benches, several Simet-sa looked carefully at one another, then, as by mutual agreement, one of their number rose slowly to his feet. Mosum of the Kalikum placed his hands on his obese hips. He breathed deeply as if preparing to utter words that might evoke hard consequences for their locuter. "Sir Ust–"

"I am your king, now, man. Address me so."

Mosum raised his chin. "Sir Ust. King of Ven. As an honest noble of Ven–"

"Enough, subject Mosum. Sit! If you cannot address the throne properly, then you will address no one."

Several Simet-sa grumbled.

"I must remind you, King Ust–"

Ust leaped to his feet. "Sit, I said, you foul bag of lard!" The Calomar stared, his small pop-eyes shot with red. "Unless you wish the anger of the holy oracle upon your head!"

Mosum grew quiet but remained standing. "According to the rules of the assembly, I have the right to speak."

"Unless I revoke that right, and I revoke it now–"

Several nobles rose to their feet beside Mosum, hands on helves, while their bodyguards moved closer. Ust's own guards glanced nervously at Dos. His advisor's hand fell once more upon his arm.

"Sire, I advise you to permit Sir Mosum to speak."

"Then have him address me in a proper manner!"

"Whatever the manner, Sire, as a Simet he has the right."

"Numsenmur–"

"–is dead, Sire!" Dos urged. "We must console our enemies, my King.

At least until we are more certain of our strength."

Ust gazed into his advisor's round eyes and gradually calmed. Finally, he nodded, and returned his attention to the assembly.

"Sir Mosum, you may speak your mind–but," he leaned forward, "remember that I tolerate no disrespect."

Mosum let his hands fall by his side and resumed. "King Ust. You must know that no criticism is implied in my words, but as an honest noble of Ven and son of divine Vensor, when an evil is done–or perhaps I should say, when a rightness has been neglected–it is my duty, as it is the duty of all Vensor-sa, to stand and speak my mind."

Ust leaned back to stare.

"As every assemblyman has the right to speak in this chamber, every nobleman has the right to continue in his offices and privileges, unless this body of virtuous men votes to repeal those privileges. Flores–"

A harsh laugh rang from the throne. "Flores? That slow-footed cripple, that fatuous coward, that traitor who conspires with the enemies of Ven...?"

"The Turlicum remains head of the Public Commission. The throne cannot appoint the Molersal, or anyone, in his place without the approval of the assembly."

The Assembly murmured their agreement.

The frown on the face of Ust deepened.

Mosum continued. "The holy oracle spoke, and as devoted servants of our God, the Divine Twin, and loyal to the fount of our spawning, we hastened to obey, and elected Your Majesty to the throne of Ven, and we have no regrets in this. Indeed how could we, since the chief joy in our lives is the fulfillment of Vensor's will? However, it must be said, King Ust, that not only is our city unused to living beneath a monarch, but that when the oracle proclaimed you king, we already had one–Flores of the Turlicum–whom we awarded Numsenmur's throne in gratitude for having saved Vensor's holy Temple upon the defeat and expulsion of the barbarous Neset-sa."

"Flores again?" sneered Ust. "It seems you let this man dominate your every thought." Ust snorted. "I tell you the Turlicum cannot be trusted. When the city was desolate and vulnerable, he took a single ship and vanished. Indeed he seems to make a habit of leaving the city in the lurch. The Turlicum is dead, Kalikum; he will never return. Take hold of your senses, and tell his clan to disband. They will not see their lord again in their lifetimes, and the clans could make use of recruits from a famous warrior tribe–inferior though they may be."

"Still, before the throne can appoint a new head of the Commission, the assembly must first remove its present head–"

Ust sat up in his throne. "Then let us do so. I would rid myself of this parasite and be done with him once for all." Ust swept his cape to one side, exposing his jeweled sceptre. "It is proposed: that the Simet noble and chief of the Turlicum–" He paused in mid-sneer to glare once more at his advisor, who had again placed his hand upon his arm.

"Now what would you have me do," Ust hissed, "or rather refrain from doing, since that seems to be your chief preoccupation?"

"Sire, it would be a mistake to take such a vote."

"And why, pray tell?" he demanded.

"In the eyes of the assembly, you would be comparing the popularity of the throne to the popularity of one who did not actually rule and hence rendered no decisions. My King, to rule is to alienate. In not sitting upon the throne, the Turlicum made no enemies, provoked no opposition. Such a vote would bring the throne no benefit, only demonstrate any weakness for all to see."

"Weakness? Before a dead man? You forget: I have allies. They will not fail the throne. A dead man cannot beat a live one, no matter how popular."

Dos lowered his eyes. "If His Majesty is certain that the throne will not overreach itself and create a martyr where there was none..."

Ust gazed calmly at Dos. "You worry too much, old man. You need a rest. I intend to take this vote today and dispose of the matter permanently. You yourself will put the resolution to the Assembly."

Dos straightened and stared into space and Ust returned his attention to the chamber. The king snapped his finger and Dos spoke, his voice booming. "It is proposed: that the Simet noble and chief of the Turlicum– who has been missing for a month leaving no word of his whereabouts and can now be presumed dead–be removed from his position as head of the Public Commission, and that Sendas of the Molersal be appointed to replace him."

The assembly fumbled beneath their seats for their voting blocks, each choosing a black wooden block to affirm the resolution or a white block to deny it. A loud clattering of boards reverberated through the chamber as the blocks tumbled in a pile upon the floor.

Ust stared, unable to speak, his own black block still in his hand. The marbled floor before him was almost hidden beneath a windrow of white wooden boards that gleamed and shined like snow, and, unclouded by a single spot of black, betrayed the same purity. Ust turned to stare at

Sendas. The Molersal stifled a yawn, his black board propping a phalanx of drinks.

A maze of chambers opened before the King, who smiled despite his disappointment with the assembly. Although the new royal home was still incomplete, its rooms and corridors were strewn with luxurious furnishings. Before another month, Ust's reconstruction of the Hall of Vim would be finished and, he thought with delight, he would hold court in the first real palace in Ven. Confiscation of the wealth of Sruk of the Lurenmurg had enabled him to undertake the project. Should his plans progress, confiscation of the wealth of other clans would enable him to complete it. Passing warriors of Molersal and Hutsutsem, he thought of Sendas and Dos and frowned. How tragic that his glorious rule should depend on the likes of them! After looting the Lurenmurg, he had granted the former warriors of Sruk to Dos to reconstitute his own long-neglected clan. Given the warriors' loyalty to the itinerant diplomat, he had little choice.

He came to a massive double door guarded by Tumlefler and Spandicum–soldiers of Revtal and Simlet–and his own few but reliable Calomar, and was reassured. No warriors of Dos or Sendas were stationed by his private rooms. He could not–dared not–forget that the two nobles had once tried to assassinate a reigning king of Ven... The bumblers; he trusted them not at all. How could he when Sendas was distinguished only by incapacity, and Dos had once tried to save himself by turning on his colleagues? Dos' explanations had been profuse and long-winded–after Ust's election to the throne by the muse of the sacred spring! Ust sighed. He was a ros chained to rum-na. Well, he thought, let them bask in my shadow for now. I have a weapon that will soon free me of tremulous advisors and traitorous Simet-sa forever! He had invoked it once and become King of Ven. And, Gethos and Vensor willing, he would invoke it again and crush his enemies more thoroughly than even the dead Tyrant of the East could have imagined. Exultant, he entered his quarters and caught sight of several languid youths in the dark garments of the Eunuch Guild reclining in a back room. Again he smiled. Directing the sentinels before the outer door to bolt and guard it well, Ust the King of Ven, Brother of Moons, elect of the Divine Twin, and genius of the progeny of Zeyd, entered the rooms of his harem and released the portiere.

Night fell.

Dressed in dark clothing devoid of distinguishing features, a silent figure left the Hall of Vim and approached the iron grating that shut the Hall and the assembly off from the city's central plaza. He lifted his cowl and signaled to the sentinels at the gate. By prearrangement the gate opened, and the figure, after loosening a glass rapier in its scabbard and nervously touching the handle of a poniard, slipped into the darkness.

A half-hour passed and Ust emerged from the warren slums of Ven. A thousand feet distant loomed the forbidding ramparts of the Temple, that massive edifice which, until its violation by the Neset-sa, had never known the tread of a hostile warrior, and which, after the invasion, had returned within hours to its former isolation. He gazed at the high merlons that dominated the skyline, dense clouds drifting slowly over the battlements. All was quiet. Ust breathed deeply, rubbed the sweat from his palm on his doublet, and stepped into the plaza.

Moments later he arrived at the base of the Temple. He glanced back. In the umbra of the night the slums presented no more than a dull mass, no glimmer of light disturbing the slumber of the city. No one followed. Satisfied, he turned and tapped quietly upon a section of wall, a section invisible in the daylight as well as the night, but with an unsuspected potential for those with the knowledge to make it work. For a time he stood silently, waiting, watching.

Finally, a slight noise emanated, as though through thick slate, something between a scratch and a tap. Immediately Ust responded, and again waited, his eyes shifting as if conscious of being observed. A sliding sound escaped as a heavy bolt was withdrawn. Ust waited a full minute more. Then, stepping to the wall, he pushed with both hands and a portion of the stone swung away. Placing both legs within the aperture, he slid within and the section swung back where it locked with an audible click, and Ust knew that even if the panel were detected from the exterior, no amount of force would suffice to pry it free.

He was enveloped in blackness. Stretching his hand above him, he felt, as he had expected, an uncomfortably low ceiling that prevented him from standing erect. On either side his fingers encountered surfaces completing the outline of a roughly-hewn corridor, a passage lined with undressed ashlar. He moved slowly, paralleling the outer rampart, until his eyes caught a glimpse of a single lonely flame, no more than a candle, spilling white smoke into the darkness. He hurried forward, then paused. He was in an intersection of tunnels, each like the one he had exited. Mentally he reviewed his instructions. Depositing his weapons with care upon the stony floor, he took up the candle, and entered another tunnel. Minutes passed and the tunnel ended. With a gentle push, he opened a second trap and stepped into a large, dully lit chamber.

The chamber displayed a high, coffered ceiling and the Calomar stretched, relieved to stand his full height. Exhaling with vigor, he peered. He saw round beds covered by linens of quality and beauty. He saw corners filled with finely carved chests, the interiors of which, he knew, were equally tasteful. He saw tapestries on the walls, brocaded, as he recalled from his previous visits, in typical Temple style, focusing upon idealized representations of an unclothed gila flush with youth and allurement, awaiting the embrace of a handsome man with wings. The man hovered above in anticipation of that blasphemous act of which Ust had heard whispered all his life, but had only recently come partly to understand: the mingling of the sexes, the attraction of a man for the female order–the crime of feminality. He made the sign of Vensor, and thought of his soul, but could not prevent his eye from lingering over the full satiny image of the woman. His gaze wandered further. A similar arras lay beneath his feet, serving as a rug, and upon tables and shelves were a profusion of glass images, delicately wrought and expensive, most recognizable as animals common to Maalstrom, but some not, which fact Ust found puzzling.

Across the room a second door, equipped with gilded handles and iron brackets, was visible. The room was empty and he crossed to an exquisitely manufactured wide, low table of rorewood and placed the candle within a lamp placed for that purpose upon it. Caressing the rorewood with his eyes, he admired its durability more than its appearance. It might have existed for five hundred years–or longer. There was hardly any limit to its lifespan, and its strength approached that of iron. What he could get for such an item in the market! How he wished his own chambers matched the wealth of his visitant.

A rasp sounded. The gilded handles turned and the door opened. A figure entered and shut it, pausing to slide a stout bar of rorewood behind the brackets. Entering the circle of light, the newcomer halted, and Ust beheld a small person clothed in sweeping folds of black, all skin invisible but that of face and hands. The body was thin, the garment despite its thick volume unable to flesh it out in any satisfactory fashion. The feet were covered with loose-fitting shoes with baggy tops and soft vamp, and dust from the tunnels clung like webs to the hem of the dark heavy garment. The hands were thin, emaciated. Spots marred their surface. The face was wrinkled like yesterday's sun-dried fruit, long since overripe and shriveled. His eyes passed over the sere skin of the newcomer and noted the strange delicacy of the features, which even the obvious age and voluminous folds of clothing could not entirely obscure. As he looked into the dun-colored eyes, the lips pursed in an unmistakable expression of disapproval and Ust found himself longing to withdraw, to shrink, to plunge back into the tunnel and vanish in its depths. With an effort he wrestled the impulse down, even if he could not quite strangle it, and raised his bearded chin. Rubbing the sweat from his palms, he flashed a thin smile.

"You are late," said the woman. Her voice was as sharp and thin as the fingers.

Ust's smile died. "I came when I could. I was detained by my business in the court."

"What care I for your petty affairs? Sit upon the bed, and hurry. My patience wears thin." The old woman stepped forward and lit more candles, till the room glowed with light.

Ust approached the nearest bed and began to remove his boots. "My affairs may be petty to you, gila, but to me there is nothing more important than my court."

The old woman turned to face him, her stare drilling him. "Do not speak to me thus! You will address me as Wijah, and you will watch your tongue. I will not allow holy Sisters to be slandered in the confines of the Temple–certainly not by a mere man! Save your insults for the gilas of the city. This is the Temple of Vensa. Here women give the orders, and men obey! And I have a name. It is Wijah. You will use it."

Ust nodded and removed his doublet. "As you wish...Wijah. I apologize. But you must understand. This is difficult for me. And dangerous–you cannot know how dangerous. If my subjects were to discover that I venture out of the palace alone on occasion, or worse, discover what we do here–"

"Ha! Do you think it any less dangerous for me? If the Queen were to find out it would mean the Ritual of Penitence!" She halted and clapped a hand to her mouth as if she had revealed a secret. She pointed her finger. "But do not think that that knowledge will avail you ought! The Queen cares not a whit for you. Should we be discovered, you would executed without delay."

Wijah stabbed her finger toward the broad expanse of mattress. "Now. Remove your clothing. And lie upon my bedding. I do not wish to take much time. My soul is in danger each moment you are in this room."

Ust stood and removed his tunic.

"Quickly! I have no time."

He hurried and soon lay supine in the shifting flames of the lamps while Wijah disrobed. He raised himself upon one elbow. "Wijah. I must ask of you something. You must help me once more. Speak through the oracle as you did before and command that the assembly obey me; give me the power to execute those who resist. They will listen to you. They obey the oracle."

Wijah laughed. "Indeed so, you wretched scum of a man! And if you do not satisfy me, they will listen when I tell them to cast you bound into the sea, or have you thrown to ros-na!" She cackled as she unwrapped the vast garment of shadow. "You will do as I wish or pay the consequences!" Within another moment the old woman stood naked before him, and ran her hands along her emaciated flesh. She smiled and closed her eyes, contemplating the pleasure to be hers, her hands lifting her low shriveled breasts. "Now rise up, man, and satisfy me. I wish to lie beneath you."

Wijah lay upon the bed and accepted the embrace of Ust, who shut his eyes as he did so. As he began to do his duty, he spoke. "Wijah, about the oracle..."

"Quiet, man! I must concentrate. Our efforts thus far have been inadequate—I am still not pregnant, and grow impatient."

"Pregnant?" he said, his tongue stumbling over the unfamiliar word.

"Do not concern yourself. As a child of the city you would not know of it."

A few moments later he relaxed and Ust stood and reached for his clothes.

"What? So soon? And with so little result?" She snorted. As Ust reached for his doublet, her features resumed their sour expression. "No! Do not clothe. We must try again. Come, man, and mount me!"

Ust hesitated. "I cannot. It is over..."

She sat up, her mouth open. "What? How is that possible?" She pointed her accusing finger. "Each time you do thus! Oh, how will I give birth to new generations with you for a husband? I will be lucky to mother a single scrawny egg! We must try again."

"Woman, I grow tired."

"You will obey me—unless you wish to anger the oracle!"

He breathed deeply, and nodded.

She lay upon the bed and Ust soon mounted her.

The bed began to rock. "Wijah," he began again, his brows twisted with worry, "about the oracle. Your first oracle was not sufficient. The Simet-sa mock me, and perceive that Vensor does not fully back my status. It seemed to them that the oracle elected me in uncertain fashion."

"I was busy, man. I had more important things to think about. The Queen was hungry, as usual."

"This should be corrected. I need a second oracle, to confirm my position, to give me power to harm my enemies."

"Cease your prattle, man, and concentrate!"

Ust sweated and wheezed. "Here. You must labor."

They rolled and Wijah sat on top of him. She began to thrust, then stopped. "You oaf! My effort is wasted! You have died!"

She sat on the edge of the bed and put her face in her hands while Ust sat up. "After several attempts I still remain barren." Wijah spoke bitterly, as if voicing a thought that remained always in her mind. "I cannot understand it–unless it is because you are such a poor specimen."

Ust stared at her blankly. His eyes wandered to his nude body, which was strong and full of life.

The old woman stood and raised her fists in the air. "Oh why did I meet you when the Temple was open? Why could I not have encountered a more virile child of Vensor? A thousand years of glory could have been mine! But fate drew me to you–of the hundreds of specimens roaming the Temple–to you! I am ready to put on yellow, but, despite my best efforts, I remain barren." Bitterness fell from her words like dust. "To think that, after violating every oath and principle of my life, my immortality should hang on your small and feeble member. But...I dare not risk another."

"I am sorry...perhaps next time–"

"Yes. Regather your strength. I expect vigor when next we meet. Next time you will not fail me."

Ust swallowed and slipped his tunic over his head. "You will speak, then, through the oracle? And help me in the city? It is of the greatest importance."

"Forget your throne!" snapped Wijah. "The oracle has other business to attend to." The priestess took up one end of the clumsy black garment and swathed herself. "The Queen is young, and at the height of her powers. She wants a man to dally with."

"I don't understand. What 'Queen'?"

Wijah paused and stared, as if debating whether to reply. She shrugged and resumed her wrapping. "The Queen of the Temple. A new Vensa, whom fate has smiled upon and selected from within these walls–over those who some believe were more deserving. We live to serve her pleasures. She is young and slim and healthy. A woman of incomparable beauty, indeed the most beautiful gila on Maalstrom. The man who could resist her temptations has not lived. And her one desire now is a man."

"You say your Queen...is a gila?" Ust contemplated the image upon the tapestry, its smooth flesh firm with youth and moisture. His gaze wandered to the sere form of Wijah and he shuddered.

Wijah noticed. Her shrill voice rose. "But don't you occupy yourself with thoughts of her! I know of your lustful desires, and your deceit! Oh, how well we priestesses know the nature of your kind–better than you know yourselves. But, pathetic as you are, I have claimed you for mine!" Wijah held a weakly clenched fist before Ust's disheveled beard, driving him back though he was at least twice her weight and considerably taller. "And you will remain so! If I ever hear that you have touched another gila besides me, I swear by the spirit of Vensa that I will have your hands cut from your arms! And if I find that you have looked upon another gila unclothed, after looking upon your eternal mate–which is Wijah–I will have the very eyes gouged from your head!"

She seized both his hands and placed them over his heart. "Now swear that you will be loyal to Wijah forever. And do not forget: one word from me, and you will forfeit your throne and your life! One breath, one hint from the oracle, and the slaves of the city–your 'subjects' as you say– will rush to tear you to pieces!"

The King of Ven trembled, his heart pounding beneath his palms. He dropped to one knee. "Do not speak thus! You must know, Wijah, that there is none other on Maalstrom who would not do all that he can to ensure your happiness! None other loves you as do I!" He grabbed one shriveled hand and kissed it and looked into her eyes. "I swear by my undying love that I will never touch another."

The old woman smiled, then descended to her knees and placed his hands upon her shrunken breast. "Now repeat your oath."

Ust repeated what he had said, then both rose to their feet.

The sour frown returned. "Now listen well. I do not wish to repeat myself. I cannot bother with your needs during the next session. The Queen has business that requires my time. The next oracle will call for a special session of holy worship–the Divine Communion. No such session has been held in the Temple for centuries. It has been long since the other Vensa was interested–long since she was capable. But the new queen is eager and impatient. You are to select a single man from among the men of the city. The one chosen will be admitted to the grotto beneath the room of the idols and there enjoy loveplay in the arms of the Queen, with doe-eyed gilas to serve him and enhance his pleasure. After which he will be released back into the city unharmed. Then the Queen will be ready to fulfill her destiny...such is the reward for he who is chosen."

"But, my love, by what means are we to choose him?"

"What does that matter? By whatever means you desire. Neither the Queen nor I care, so long as he is not ill or deranged."

Ust's lips parted in contemplation of the mentioned loveplay.

"And anyone may participate?"

"Of course. Anyone–except you! You are mine, and you have sworn, and if you break your vow I will use the oracle to search you out wherever you may be, and destroy you utterly!" The fist shook a second time. Ust extended his arms in terror.

"Wijah, my love! I have sworn. It is only you I desire. Do not fear. I will return again to make love to you, though I place my life in danger each time I do so."

The old woman calmed. "That is well. For in truth you place your life in greater danger if you do not. Now take this candle, and leave the way you came; once you depart, the trap will lock of itself, as always. Now I must depart as well. Each moment I remain with you endangers not only my flesh, but my soul."

Ust stepped into the tunnel and the trapdoor closed behind. The Calomar penetrated some distance, holding the candle before him like a beacon. Once he was certain that he was far beyond the point where he could be heard from the chamber of Wijah, he turned his head and glanced back in the old woman's direction. A sneer crossed his lips. " 'Undying love'...I'd sooner love a lyart." He wiped his hands on his tunic as if to clean them, then faced forward once more. "So she would use the oracle against me, would she?" He snorted, his brows drawing tightly together. "We shall see. For the present better slavery to one, than slavery to many. But once I gain her cooperation, and win her trust–then, when the city obeys me in everything," he paused to glance nervously behind him again, "I will no longer leave my poniard in the tunnel. That was a bad slip letting me know that she is in the same danger as I. That means she has confided in no one. And once she is gone, none within these walls will be aware that I was ever here. Or that I am not truly favored by Vensor."

He shambled further and came to the intersection.

"Now, which tunnel was it?" Ust turned and glimpsed a cloud of white dust rise from a bed of crushed bones within the entrance to one of the other shafts. A gust of air whirled and he was plunged into darkness. He swayed, dizzy from the sudden absence of light.

"So. The exit lies this way." He stepped forward and collided with a wall. Felt his forehead. "Surely, then, it lies to the left." Stepping again, he found himself between exits. He paused, felt a chill along his spine–he had lost the way. With a slow moan the ghostly wind blew again and he shivered, his nostrils filling with ancient desiccated vapors suggestive of tombs crumbling through millennia. Sweat coated his skin. Whichever way the exit lies, he thought, I cannot stay here. Even were my cries to attract assistance I would be executed for violating the Temple. Extending his fingers once more, he detected a groove in the side of the tunnel, marking it as the correct passage. Ah! He placed the lamp on the floor and began to move, following the rough wall of the tunnel with his hand.

After a while the tunnel elled to the left, but still offered no light to guide him. Again he halted–he was in the wrong tunnel after all, and had now lost the intersection as well. Panic seized him. His soul shouted for him to run–but which way? He inched gradually forward. Finally, just when he felt he could not endure another moment of the blackness, a pale glimmer appeared. Another ell angled opposite to the first. He followed cautiously and arrived at last in a chamber of peculiar shape and construction, the atmosphere viscid with moist heat. The upper reaches were obscured in a perpetual fog, whose overflow spilled through a grill of inadequate size into what appeared to be a larger and poorly lit chamber whose ceiling swam with steam. On his left, the moisture billowed without respite from a steep passage gouged from live stone that spiraled downward towards damper, but better lit regions. Hot air gushed, leaving his tunic clinging to his skin. In annoyance he removed the garment and wrung it.

Glancing up, he froze.

At first he could not believe his eyes, and, convinced that the heat must have addled his brain, tapped the side of his head. This produced no change and he shut them tight. But when he reopened them, the vision was still there. Standing within the mouth of the passage, its suffuse light and vapor enveloping the vision, was a living manifestation of the tapestry on Wijah's wall. A gila gazed upon him with a serene and confident smile, the water forming rills and rivulets upon her bare curving torso. The tapestry took one step, and another, then stood directly before his awe-struck face. Soft hands touched his chest. They stroked, rubbing the water into his skin, no more than a caress, tracing the flow of pectorals to biceps and forearms. Ust dropped the wet tunic on the stony floor and the vision stepped closer and stared into his unblinking eyes. A gentle finger shut his gaping mouth. Palms found his cheeks; framed his mouth; kissed it. Sliding back and away, its hands entwined with his, the vision moved toward the passage with Ust in tow. It glanced back once to smile sweetly upon him, and descended the stairwell, while Ust, his brain recalling something someone had once said about a steam-laden grotto and a gila of unrivaled beauty, silently followed.

∾ ₧ ₨ ∾

CHAPTER 6

BLUE SEAS

The Grest sped through the black boundless night propelled by oars and canvas, the crew putting all their muscle into the effort, fear of the King's Overseer and his cohort of ruffians impelling them. Peering into the darkness for signs of patrol craft, and listening for strange oars and splashing reven-na, the crew sought to place as much distance as possible between themselves and Vaw before dawn. Flores directed the vessel toward the west so that when the suns did appear, the vessels of their pursuers would be outlined and not their own, enabling them to remain in darkness for a few more precious moments. However, when the suns did finally come and their spreading light ignited a wide clean sky, no other vessels appeared. Flores shook his head. Although relieved, he still frowned. Was their success due to his stratagem, or to other less certain circumstances? Signaling the rowers to rest, he glanced at his navigator, and pondered.

Plying a wide arc over the course of the next few days, the Grest turned gradually south and then east and finally, on their fourth day out from Vaw, re-entered the main sea route following the trade winds toward the southeast. No other stops would be necessary for the remainder of the voyage, save the unpopulated nameless rocky isle that lay in sight of their final destination, where they would finally touch shore. While traveling the main route, other vessels often hove in sight, sails straining or oars dipping, heading south by southeast toward the mysterious cities of the most distant Vensor-sa, or returning from those exotic ports. A few vessels accompanied them on this leg of the journey, keeping pace at a distance, but showing no interest nor giving hint of any association with Vaw.

The days rolled by, then one evening the constellation of Atasan appeared on the southern horizon, and their pilot turned into the wind and directed the ship toward the southwest, taking care to keep the prime star of the vortexed cluster directly above the prow and its carven image of the god of fortune. Their companion vessels peeled off, continuing south by east. The Grest's crew could see the surprised expressions on the other crewmen's faces as the Grest plunged into the twilight depths of the swelling western ocean, as if pursuing the setting suns themselves in their mad quest. They could see the pious gesticulations of the other crews as they gazed heavenward and prayed for the unlucky strangers, who must be at the mercy of a deranged pilot or fanatical captain.

Flores spent the time fore of the vessel, one hand resting on the scaly totem of Gethos and the other upon the wale. The windspray sharred his skin and with each sea-swell of the boat twisted his dark hair. He found the rogue Macius—or was it Surge?—ever more absorbing, and ever more inscrutable. Sitting by the rudder, he appeared relaxed and confident. Each night with the advent of twilight he would study the sky, searching out the first stars, and trace constellations, beginning with Nantifus—a difficult task due to the great number of stars visible on Maalstrom. Since he had studied the heavens as part of his Simet education, Flores could trace a few, but putting forth to sea was a different feat altogether. Macius knew more than Flores, including the stars of the southern sky, and had no need of charts. He was indeed a pilot, a murshid, Flores noted. Again he found himself pondering the man. What other hidden traits, or secret inclinations, did the dark man possess?

The Turlicum let his gaze slide over the rag-tag crew of Vaw-sa and regretted having permitted Macius his dagger. The thief's popularity among his compatriots, who also bore arms, made it now too risky to retrieve the weapon. It was no less risky to disarm the other Vaws. Still, there seemed no need, as the newcomers worked hard. This too puzzled Flores. For men who had only recently become fugitives from their city, they seemed unduly cheerful and optimistic. Not even the revelation by Flores that their ship's goal was the fabled and inviolable Island of the Sun-god dampened their enthusiasm. If anything they were encouraged, glancing often at their pilot and taking inspiration from his presence. The most famous son of Vaw, renowned for his exploits, had returned in safety from the Isle once before, had he not? All of the Vaw-sa were thieves and seamen, and if the most enterprising thief and seaman of the far-spread ocean assured them of their welfare, they should be well satisfied, so they murmured. At the very least they stood the best chance they might of surviving the journey, after which they could return to their homes, and hope that Fish will have forgotten or forgiven their offense.

Still, Flores wondered why they should be so enthusiastic. From their occasional singing one might think they expected some more tangible reward than mere survival for another month.

The captain let his gaze rest on Stalkin. Here was another matter. The man's broad flat face, habitually creased with a conceited curl of one lip, moved restlessly about, and refused to converse. At times, after learning of their destination, Stalkin would perch at the stern for long periods beside Macius, though Isav asserted that few words were ever exchanged. Flores found his dislike for the smithy growing by degrees. Although relieved that the shopkeeper represented no threat to his command, he was still disappointed. Stalkin might have been better company on the long voyage.

Flores glanced at Isav. The captain, once an official of the irsrem guild, took his turn at an oar. Flores nodded. Isav would prefer the activity to inspecting the watery waste that surrounded them. His nature not allowing him to relax, the captain, together with Flores' second militia chief, Revd, warily observed their navigator and the Vaw-sa. Perhaps, Flores noted, Isav's nose for betrayal would preserve him in the southern seas as it had the year before in Ven.

Most disconcerting, however, was the fact that his own kinsmen were becoming listless. They pulled the oars with less vigor than did the Vaws, nervously scanned the skies, and often murmured together while glancing resentfully at Flores. The passage of two weeks on the open sea, in the cramped condition of the small vessel, with only a single tent erected in the center to break the increasing glare of the suns, worsened their mood even more. They knew nothing of Macius, or the southern sea, were not experienced sailors and had no interest in Flores' obsession, and their resolve was little bolstered by the tales of the previous exploits of 'Surge' as related to them by the Vaws, although, as the days passed, perhaps they too found the experience and fame of Macius to carry more weight than the tenuous and bizarre purpose of their own leader, who fastened himself to the forward totem, as if, envying Macius his luck, he had decided to forsake his own talismans for those of his more famous pilot. Would clan ties, so strong in Ven, prove more fragile elsewhere? The pain lines around Flores' eyes deepened. Each mile with no land in sight, each day adrift in the vast viridescent waste, with their frail ship exposed like a wound to the cerulean expanse, brought a visible strengthening of his men's fears–and of his own.

The Vens were especially disturbed by the appearance of the constellation Atasan. Invisible from their home, the Vens had never before glimpsed the strange cluster with so portentous an appellation, and the import of their voyage began to weigh ever more heavily and–their anxiety concerning what manner of reception might await them at the end of their journey, their goal being so much less legitimate than it had been in their last port–to work upon them. With the change in direction, the need for their sinews to work the oars became greater, while their interest lessened, and their energy could not be made up by the increased effort of the Vaw-sa, who finally also began to slacken as the ship penetrated ever deeper into the unknown and forbidden waters. They may well have ceased rowing altogether, if not for their fear of stagnating in doldrums, and their awareness of the vulnerability of the ship to sudden squalls, and the continuing consumption of their dwindling supplies. Flores began to believe that the presence of Macius alone persuaded the others, both Vens and Vaws, to continue on their course, and although still distrustful of Macius' motives, the Turlicum finally was as glad as the rest of the crew that the famous murshid and no other steered the craft.

As it was, the crew came to regard the azure and vermilion sky as somehow menacing, as if their lives depended on secrecy, darkness, and evasion. As the ship penetrated more deeply into the unknown, even the officers became seized by this obsession and began constantly to watch the skies. The white clouds above folded and merged and blew, at times roiling till they seemed to brush the mast, at other times dissipating till the sky shone clear as crystal, and, although Vensor still ignored their vessel, the crew came to feel that this was only because He had not yet detected them or that He merely awaited an opportune moment to demonstrate His power and His will, as if waiting patiently for them to complete their transgression and place themselves utterly beyond redemption before He showed His displeasure, and inflicted His vengeance and judgment upon them, in His good time and way.

The days grew steadily warmer and longer and became gradually intolerable in their heat. The crew began to view the suns with revulsion, their fear and guilt interweaving with exhaustion under the merciless glare of the blinding rays. Like the Eyes of God the suns waxed greater, the angry yellow orbs scouring the waters, searing all within their sight, as Vensor waited patiently, drawing His plans, gathering His strength for the inevitable retribution against those who would dare to set foot in Heaven, dare to violate the word and law of God.

Then it was, when they lay exhausted and depressed under the unrelenting glare, having long since abandoned progress to their sail, rowing only in short relays, and feebly at best, and, despite the emptiness of the vast shimmering blueness that spread on all sides, refraining from needless banter, as if ears as well as eyes might detect them, then it was that one of the Ven crewmen pointed skyward. The others followed his line of sight and grew silent. Far above, flapping lazily on broad outstretched wings, soared a malkop, one of the denizens, the guardians, of Vensor's holy isle. At such a distance hardly more was discernible than wings and torso, but, as its course crossed theirs, or rather paralleled and overtook them, its features grew more distinct, and the crewmen finally ceased rowing altogether.

None dared speak.

As the creature drifted overhead, undeterred from its single-minded task, indeed apparently unaware of their presence, the crewmen viewed the creature in detail. It possessed those features they knew well from the skies above their native cities, but here—in the midst of the southern ocean, a month from land but in close vicinity to the malkop's divine habitation—its features seemed alien and menacing. The face of the selk, as the Vaws termed the creature, was pretty and pale and for all appearances quite human, having a slender quality that was somehow deeply provocative and attracted even as it repelled. Voiceless, like all malkops, the creature yet radiated unmistakable moods in the turn of its mouth and lips, smiling or frowning as might a man, and to all appearances from similar cause. Its hair was fair and blond, straight and flowing down about its slim and delicate neck, the swift currents of air sometimes blowing the sun-bleached strands above and back, and sometimes allowing them to droop down about its neck and across its bosom. The shoulders were similarly delicate, although deformed by the massive outgrowth of wing muscles bulging just below. The wings themselves were smooth and glabrous, no trace of feathers or down being visible, sustaining themselves rather with taut skin stretched across bone and cartilage.

Its midriff was as flat as that of an athletic man, but smoother and hairless and with a delicately pinched waist, not exaggeratedly narrow, but well-formed, as if sculpted from rare and precious stone, again presenting a strangely pleasing quality. Most disturbing of all to the crewmen, however, were the pair of symmetrical fleshy globes or ovoids suspended from its chest, each crowned by an organ of great emotional and philosophical import to all Vensor-sa, the universal symbol of Atasan, the sign of animal reproduction and femininity, the sign of the forbidden sex—the teat.

Vensor-sa could not explain why the creatures of Vensor, those assigned by Heaven to defend it, indeed themselves being the inhabitants of Heaven, should bear the mark of the enemy of Mankind, the opposer of the will of Vensor, but some mysteries are not to be fathomed. Whether the creature possessed the other unmistakable sign of Atasan, the organ of feminine reproduction itself, ubiquitous in the animal kingdom of the divine Talen, but totally lacking among Vensor-sa, as the citizens of the cities of glass pridefully and repeatedly avowed, the crew could not discern, since the hips of the malkop were draped with the usual plain sewn dirty brown garment worn by all selks. No Ven in fact had ever glimpsed what lay beneath that common garment of the malkops. And to speculate on such a matter was too close to heresy in the eyes of most for any to voice such perverse desire.

The creature's legs were strong, slim, and lithe. Bare of clothing, they hung below the suspended animal like the limbs of hornets, while the arms, far stronger than their slim appearance might suggest, clasped the usual burden of a malkop engaged upon its dour and eternal task. The corpse of a recently deceased child of Vensor–a man–hung limply in its grasp, the funeral garments still clinging to its torso, although now tattered from exposure to the elements during the long trip to Vensor's abode. The crew made the sign of God upon their chests and gazed silently until the selk had passed from sight, merging with the vermilion streaked sunset that hung like a tapestry above the erect prow of the vessel.

Night brought no comfort to the crew, but only more of the endless stifling heat, and fear of what the rest of the journey might bring. The next days passed without incident. Once more the skies were the playground of clouds, misting, billowing, whipping across the heavens in pursuit of each other, expanding to fill the horizons, or, without warning, evaporating to leave the bright sky clear and vulnerable. One morning daylight arrived to reveal a blanket of grey obscuring the heavens and drifting so low that the mast of the vessel seemed to ply the clouds as the hull clove the waters, their existence as it were bounded by the most narrowly conceived of Aristotelian spheres compressing the space occupied by the frail vessel and its crew to a wide narrow plane, pressing upon them simultaneously from above and below. The crew felt relief not only for the temporary shelter from the hammering rays of the suns, but also for the increased sense of safety from detection. They hoped the cover would continue till they arrived at their destination. Macius shook his head. As long as the cover lasted he could not locate the small island that was their goal. They should prefer a clean sky, he explained, adding that there was no need to fear the malkops. So long as the Grest remained on the eastern side of the rocky isle, the guardians would ignore the vessel and leave the crew in peace.

For several days the mist endured, as if a great storm vented its fury in some distant part of the ocean, providing the crew welcome relief and boosting their spirits. Then it broke and dissipated to reveal a clear sky that had cooled considerably. The men, however, far from enjoying the change in temperature, felt the return of all their fears—for far above them, compassing the welkin from horizon to horizon, moved a belt of black dots, or clots, like strings of beads connected by invisible thread, gaps and patches supervening in places, but no part of the sky entirely clear of their mysterious and menacing forms. Moving in several directions along interconnecting arcs, one branch stretched back the way the Grest had come, toward the northeast and bending slightly toward the east, while a second branch extended northwards, in the direction, Flores assumed, of the valleys of the three rivers, the Hedronmas, Suma, and Tlaam, where Ven and all of the cities he knew stood, the entire region of Ven's dominance reduced in his mind's eye to a small facet of a vast organization that encompassed the world, indeed more than the world, of a plan that included both Heaven and Hell in its stupendous and grand design. From their vantage point the crew could see clearly the two great arms merge to form a third that continued south-westward, unrelenting toward their goal.

The crew turned their eyes to the murshid.

Surge glanced above them at the selks suspended in the distance, then brushed some lint from his faded brown tunic. "It is time to turn south. We shall be ashore by evening."

The crew burst with energy. The yardarm was turned and the mainsail refastened, and twenty oars splashed into the water, the Grest launching itself in the new direction, cool wind and visions of solid ground at their journey's end reinvigorating them.

They soon lost view of the selks and encountered a sky that was at once clear, cool, and empty of Vensor's guardians. For a day their prow rode the waves, then abruptly, miraculously it seemed after the long weeks of watery desolation, land hove into view. The heart of every crewman never knew such joy as when their vessel neared the small rocky cliff that jutted from the midst of the elemental deep, poised so perilously that Flores feared that should he shut his eyes but for a moment, he might re-open them to find that the waves had swept the island under and re-asserted their jealous supremacy.

Nearing the rocky refuge, he found that the crags were more firmly fixed in their bed than he had supposed, a hard and imposing jag rising straight from the angry waves, the waters never ceasing their assault on this challenge, each heave of the sea sending a dense column of watery brine crashing against the rock, with a river of foam running perpetually back whence it came, the boom and tumult of the wash reverberating without surcease. A hundred feet above the Grest the stony walls loomed, giving no harbor to the vessel, and the steep sides of the cliffs admitted no holds to climbers should the vessel drop anchor for the purpose. To halt would have been suicide in any event, for the gigantic heaves of the sea against the rocky outgrowth, and the fierce currents that played around its base, would have smashed in moments any ship whose pilot might be so foolish as to attempt it.

Macius steered the ship eastward, and, finding that the island was shaped in a crescent, followed the extrados of the curve along its eastern shore until he had arrived at a position southeast of the isle, and near the end of its southern arc. Here, they rounded a blockish promontory, and a sandy beach opened before them, providing sufficient space for a dozen Grests, and leading the crew's gaze up into a lush interior such as they had not guessed existed from the austerity of the outer cliffs. Palms, and trees laden with bright fruit, waved in the humid air. Having glimpsed such after their long ordeal, the men could well believe the isle lay but a short distance from Heaven. The ship approached the beach, and slid to a halt on the soft sea bottom. Shouting, the crew spilled ashore. Ropes were produced, and the crew scrambled quickly onto the beach, pulling the vessel after. Within minutes they had dragged the ship securely onto the hot sand.

The interior was of a higher altitude than the beach, and, together with the circumscribing cliffs, hid from their view the horizon in all directions save east so long as they stood upon the shore. Climbing steeply from the shore they found themselves on a plateau that sloped upwards until it met the cliff walls that compassed the isle on its remaining three sides. On the southern half of the isle, the plateau being comparatively low in these parts, it had to rise sharply to meet the flanking heights, so that any who stood amidst the palms found themselves well sheltered from the elements and as comfortable as one might hope on a deserted rocky crag in unknown waters. On the northern half of the isle, however, the plateau was higher. Here the vegetation was sparse and the crew found themselves more exposed since the plateau had to rise but a short distance to meet the precipitous shoreline. As one moved north the skies became increasingly visible until, near the northern tip of the isle, one attained the summit and found the horizons outspread below, all things being visible to one ensconced in this lofty aerie excepting only the beach at the southern end, which was obscured by the verdant groves.

Flores and Isav, with Macius behind, mounted the summit, and halted. Far to the south a belt of black specks, such as they had glimpsed in the morning, was suspended in the sky in a vast arc. Although at a lower altitude than the selks they had previously seen, these were also more distant, visible in no greater detail. On the other hand, the belt was now more dense, appearing more like a distant storm than living creatures.

Of more interest to Flores than this highway of selks, however, was its terminus upon the west. Here a smear of white presented itself, almost featureless, stretching away to the south until it receded into the blue of the endless sky and sea. Shining through the white, on those occasions when the clouds parted, or when the suns set behind them, glittered all the colors of the rainbow, like a beacon, sharp though still distant. The white was cloud and mist, the other, some less certain material. It was apparent that the Holy Isle of Vensor was incomparably larger than the fragment beneath their feet.

Also visible was a shorter stretch of beach on the western side of their crag, not far below where they stood. By means of a precipitous approach a path led from this sandy strip to the summit. This western beach could well accommodate several ships, noted Flores, should one desire a more direct approach, though he recalled the warnings of Macius concerning activity on this side of the island.

The men returned to the oasis and laid out a rudimentary camp. For the remainder of the day no one discussed the land that, after their long and perilous voyage, had finally come within sight. The crew slept and ate and rested and wandered about, savoring their long-delayed freedom, none of their chiefs wishing to spoil the mood by the exercise of their authority. However, their joy, it seemed to Flores, was not at all like that of the condemned granted a temporary reprieve. Far from relieved that they would not have to scale the Isle, they now seemed disappointed. The mystery had deepened. Flores could not imagine why the crew, especially the Vaw-sa, should be upset to encounter obstacles in completing a quest that was not only impractical but impious—should not they rather be relieved that the expedition's difficulties had become insurmountable, and they could now return home without having violated the law of Vensor? Their dejection and murmuring were so patent that the quest seemed more theirs than the Turlicum's.

Leaving the men, Flores explored the island on all sides, and returned alone to the summit. For the remainder of the day he sat and viewed the distant land and the locust-like swarm clouding the horizon to the south. The crash of sea on rock carried to his ears ceaselessly. But he did not see or hear. Superimposed on the obscure distant smudge wedged between sky and sea, was a delicate hand removing a veil from a face of hypnotic beauty with olive skin and jet-black hair. Something in Flores' soul ached at the thought that Amina, having been so recently freed from her long imprisonment in the Temple of Ven, had suffered abduction yet again, and now lay in a prison of even greater remove and isolation.

Dusk approached, and he returned to the camp, a sputtering fire of driftwood guiding his approach. Nearing the flame he heard voices raised in argument. He halted in the darkness.

Faces appeared in the fire's light. All the crew were visible, save Macius.

"Gold, I tell you. Gold! All the mir you could hope to lay your weary eyes upon. And other treasures. It lies but that short distance to the Isle!" Stalkin held up his palms, imaginary coins slipping through his fingers.

Isav faced Stalkin, a ring of Vens and Vaw-sa crouched around the two. "This is insurrection!" yelled Isav. "We are here not to rob the holy Isle. Our Lord is a pious man and has forbidden us to remove the property of Vensor."

The flat broad-chinned face of Stalkin stared newt-like in the corona of the flames, eyes widening till the white shone from entirely round his pupils. A sarcastic smile turned the corners of his mouth. He seemed to have entirely recovered his poise.

"I remind you again, dear Isav. He is not 'our' lord, but yours. And what does that matter, here, in the vastness of this watery desert? On the sea all men are equal. If the ship goes down, your employer will die as surely as we commoners, his privileges would not have the weight of a single grain of sand."

"You ingrate–speaking of the Turlicum's death? And to his own clansmen! And after he saved your neck from those cutthroats in Vaw!"

Olive and pink alternated on the face of Stalkin as the sarcastic smile extended across the width of his features. "You may believe that if you like." The Vaw gazed slyly about him at the others. "As for me, I am for putting it to a vote."

"A subversive idea!" interjected Isav.

Revd backed him. "The authority of the Turlicum does not depend on anyone's goodwill, and certainly not that of Vaw-sa."

"And what care we for your customs? We have our own ways." The Vaw leader turned to his followers. "Who wants to decide this matter by vote?" he shouted.

All of the Vaw-sa quickly raised their arms.

Revd rose and stood beside Isav.

"And how many Ven-sa?" added Stalkin with confidence, as if he already knew the answer to his question.

Hesitantly, four arms rose. Then, having seen their own number, two more, with more assurance. Only four remained to support the Ven captains.

"Now that we have settled how we will run things, let us put our question to the vote as well," said Stalkin. He addressed the others again. "Who wishes to waste our time with the dead–and a *gila* as I hear–when our provisions are short, and measureless reward lies now within our reach?"

Cries of encouragement rose from the crewmen, drowning the protests of Isav and Revd.

Stalkin shouted. "Our leader Surge has spoken well of what he saw upon the Isle! Gold! Jewels! Mir! Enough to carpet this rock we sit upon! Surge brought us here in safety. We may accept what he says as truth. Let us take the ship tomorrow–before dawn, to avoid the malkops–and load it with the treasures of the Isle. Then, after the eyes of Vensor have sunk beneath the waves, we shall return here to distribute it under the cover of darkness."

The others, both Vens and Vaws, exploded with enthusiasm.

"This is folly," interrupted Revd. "If you try to pillage the Isle, you will anger the guardians. Has it not occurred to you that if it were possible to remove anything, someone would have done so before now? I guarantee you will perish before you touch land. Or, even if you do make it to shore, you will only provoke Vensor's vengeance before you again depart."

"And what of abducting Vensor's subjects?" replied Stalkin, a look of amazement on his face. "This will not provoke His anger? The Turlicum wishes to bring down upon our heads the wrath of the entire Island–and for what? A gila! And what is our payment for that? Poverty and death! We would risk our lives just as surely if we follow your employer than if we look to our own interests. Can you not see? He is mad! No sane man would undertake such a quest. When will his journey end? How far must he search? He must scour all of Heaven to find what he seeks, but we–we have only to reach the shore to accomplish our purpose." He passed a gleaming eye over the quiet crew, and whispered. "Surge has said that the jewels lie scattered almost upon the beach itself!"

"It is not for you to judge our Lord, sir, and I warn you not to speak of him again in such a manner–or you will find yourself challenged." Isav laid his hand upon his sword's pommel and pulled the blade partly from its scabbard.

Unlike the Ven-sa, those of Vaw had no swords, and Stalkin grew quiet.

"Think of what you are saying," said Revd, addressing the Vens who had sided with Stalkin. "Look from the summit; you will see the guardians poised at this moment to prevent us from approaching. They remain aloft night and day. You would indeed be destroyed–Macius said that as well. Have you forgotten his warning so soon? He reached shore only by waiting until a storm occurred which sent the selks scurrying to Heaven for safety. You cannot reach the island by boat at other times, even by night, and were we to sit here until a storm arrived, we would not have time to load the ship and return before the wind died and the malkops resumed their flight. Even if successful you would drown beneath the waves. At any rate, we would starve long before such a storm arrives."

"Then," Stalkin gently asked, "pray tell us: how do you plan to get ashore? You must have some plan in mind, or you would not have come so far–nor Surge."

Isav and Revd exchanged quiet glances.

Flores stepped into the circle of light. The others lapsed into silence. Picking up some driftwood, the Turlicum tossed it into the flames. For a time no sound was heard but the snapping of dry limbs.

"You are right, Stalkin. I do have a plan. And tomorrow, you shall not only see it, but you shall participate. And if you desire, you yourself shall be the first to step onto the Island of Vensor." He threw another stick onto the fire. "We cannot take the ship, so we cannot remove many valuables. And no more than seven of us may go. But, if what you say concerning the island is true, and something of value does indeed lie there, and if it be important to you that you avail yourself of such, I shall allow you to return with a few souvenirs of our visit...mementos. In fact, you have my permission to return with all that you can carry."

The crew leaped to their feet.

"Flores! Flores! Long live Turlicum! Long live Ven!" The Vens laughed and patted each other on their backs, their faith in their leader restored. Stalkin, however, continued to frown.

Flores continued. "You may accompany Surge and I and choose for yourself what to take, or to testify to the others when we return that we found nothing of value. And my two captains will go. And Toom and Meld also." Flores indicated two of the Vens who had sided with him during the argument.

Stalkin's brows furrowed. "That leaves two Vaw-sa. Are Surge and I to carry the treasure alone, then? Those of us who wish their reward number sixteen—can two carry enough to satisfy sixteen?"

The crew murmured.

Flores prodded the fire, while the tension again rose. "Then Toom and Meld may stay."

"And one captain."

For a long moment the camp was silent. Stalkin stood opposite Flores, fists on hips, waiting for another capitulation. The opposing sides moved subtlely to opposite sides of the fire, the swords of Flores' faction outweighed by those of the Ven turncoats and the daggers of the ten Vaws.

Finally, he spoke. "And one captain—Isav."

The tension vanished. The Vaws nodded to each other, grumbling assent, and the Vens again shouted their joy. Stalkin was not entirely pleased, but he grunted and turned away. Within minutes the crew dispersed, some lying down to sleep, others wandering off to savor the night or tend to private matters before bedding down.

Flores stirred the fire a few minutes more, then stood.

Isav approached and the pair moved next to a trunk.

"Flores," Isav said softly, "why have you allowed the Vaw-sa to go and none of our own but Revd? Will you not be in danger with only Revd's sword for support?"

The Simet noble gazed into the night, the surf booming ceaselessly beyond the palms. He breathed deep the moist wind and exhaled.

"Better to have them with me, Isav, where I can see their eyes and faces, than here where they can plot behind my back. On Vensor's Isle they will be too busy to plot. And should our activities arouse the selks despite our precautions, who would you rather bear the first onrush of Vensor's guardians—your kin, or those we distrust? I do not believe it is so simple a matter to rob Vensor in his lair, else Macius would today be rich. As for Macius, I saw not his face among the Vaws. I would know the true motives of our pilot, and do not wish to leave him alone in the vicinity of our ship... Only he knows what lies ahead."

"Macius!" Isav spat. "Do not trust him, I tell you. He is their ringleader. It was he put Stalkin to this. He who ordered you murdered in the streets of Vaw. Lost his way, indeed! He is an accomplice of Fish, and on the dock left us to confront Fish alone. And only he escaped the Overseer's ambush. Accidents do not happen in threes!" Isav sighed. "It is perhaps best that you have concealed your suspicions. Still I would not turn my back in his presence. You, however–you would swim to Heaven itself in the company of his gang!" Isav shook his head.

Flores opened his mouth to answer. "Patience. Here is what you are to do while I am gone..." The two stepped beyond the camp and their conversation was swallowed in the gloom. As the Turlicum chiefs vanished, another face took form in the renewed light of the fire. Surge appeared from where he had been standing in the darkness behind a palm-trunk and watched the spot where they had vanished in the shadows. A bright gleam was in his eye.

CHAPTER 7

WHITE BONES

Before dawn they assembled. Flores returned to the vessel and entered. He pulled aside a shroud that had remained undisturbed for the duration of the voyage, extracted a large sack, and rejoined the crew. Summoning the others to follow, Flores climbed to the island's northern crest, where, flush in the cool salt breeze that blew perpetually in from the sea, he surveyed the blackness of the pre-dawn sky. They had lit no torch and, after muffling irsrem and metal to prevent inadvertent noise, they descended to the beach without incident.

In the shelter of the escarpment, five Vaw-sa and Flores and Revd stripped off their clothing and donned close-fitting loincloths, thrusting within their belts daggers and pouches of dried lyart sufficient to last several days and nights. Flores then lay his sack upon the sand and opened it. Within were the seven water-breathing devices of Yezd. Taking them up in turn, Flores stretched the excised reven gill, rubber and twine over the face of each crewman and when each was in place, the seven slipped quietly into the surf. In a short time they had mastered the technique of breathing underwater, and returned briefly to shore where a last meal of lyart flesh was washed down with barreled water. Finally they entered the sea and dropped from sight.

The hours underwater passed with agonizing slowness. Each man was a passable swimmer, or better, but the unfamiliarity of the gills and the knowledge that they dared not surface for any reason made the journey difficult. With the arrival of dawn, the swimmers made better progress, but no swimmer can exert himself for an entire day, and they soon found themselves pausing frequently for rest and reorientation, at which times Macius would gesture and hurry them on. Even when each felt that his exhaustion must overwhelm him, still Macius drew them forward. As the sea bottom rose to meet the surface, the light again grew faint, then feeble, and the shadows returned, and in shallow water that moved with each passing wave, the seven halted. Night was complete. At last Macius signaled, and after a short rest they scurried through the surf.

They saw a narrow strand of beach that met a wall of grey. The wall's flat surface ran obliquely up into blackness. Flores became uneasy as he realized that what he had heretofore believed was part of the bedrock of the island, was in actuality an artifact. Set within the grey wall was a circle of black, perhaps twenty feet in height. Into this circle Macius plunged. Clambering up a sharp slope of loose particles and fragments, Flores followed. He could not see his companions, though he could hear their breaths alongside, and before long the slope leveled permitting the seven to draw together and whisper under the echo of waves.

A noise, as of someone abrading an object, rasped, and a flame burst into view. The flat visage of Macius was huddled. Removing their gills, the men gathered round, while the Vaw set fire to a small pile of tinder. From a pouch, Macius withdrew a piece of tallow and applied it to a length of driftwood. He lit it. The branch glowed with light casting a weak but broad net of rays.

Flores caught his breath. They stood within a low wide cavern that meandered into darkness in all directions save back down the slope where, small and distant, Flores could barely discern the outline of the aperture. The ceiling hung low. Its gibbous swells billowed fifteen feet above their heads, though in places dipped towards the floor, which itself undulated although providing sufficient space to walk about.

And glittered. Iridescent drops, embedded in hard translucent glass, sparkled in their eyes with all the colors of the rainbow. Could this be other than the coarsest, most earth-bound portion of Heaven, its very refuse, as it were? Flores moved one foot and a jet of white dust rose and remained suspended, immune to the breezes that swirled about the entrance. Indeed the ground seemed to consist entirely of dust, its pale greyness forming hillocks where the roof receded, valleys where it obtruded, as if earth and heaven strove to meet, but were unable anywhere to succeed. Flores shuddered. Claustrophobia crept upon him. Given the absence of pillars to uphold the vast roof, it seemed on the verge of collapse, the crystalline element, in its desire to remain untainted by the dust, defying the laws of nature.

Macius waved the torch and moved toward the interior of the Island. Linking hands, Flores and Revd kept several paces apart from the Vaws, though not so far as to lose sight of them. The cavern proved to be uniform in its composition. The same soft floor and delicate roof opening before them with regularity. They might have moved in circles, or have put a hull to its white waves, were it not for the clear sense of purpose exhibited by Macius, and the presence of occasional interruptions in the dunes. Negotiating the powdery slopes, Flores noted a darker structure emerge from the depths. A walkway of bricks about three feet in width would at times appear from beneath the grey drifts and sweep a straight line until arriving at an angle, whereupon the crumbling and pitted brick-work would arrow away again only to burrow in another windrow of grey. Since the bricks extruded only seldom from beneath the folds of dust, and never offered a straight path long enough to be of use, Flores for the most part ignored them, and trudged after Macius. The Turlicum glanced at one Vaw and noticed him wrinkle his nose. Flores did like-wise, and noted that as they progressed a subtle offensiveness of the air grew, increasing steadily the more deeply they penetrated the chamber.

The hours passed. At length, when Flores felt he could go no further, having been already exhausted beyond endurance by the swim, he no-ticed the torch's reflection at a point some distance before them as upon a mirror, and Flores became aware that they approached the terminus to the cavern. A ribbon of shiny darkness emerged. The seven arrived at a wall of dense rock, whose smooth surface of tachylite gleamed.

"Here," said Macius, "is where we shall bed. Sleep long. We must wait until the remainder of the night and an entire day have passed before we venture forth again." He sat and produced damp strips of lyart flesh and nibbled.

Flores drew close to Macius and sat. "Where will we go from here? Is there some way to approach...the more inhabited regions?"

The Vaw slid a sensuous finger across the skin of the wall. "Soon, Flo-res, soon." He eyed the ceiling, which met the wall with a seamless web. "We are not within Heaven yet, but within its bowels. Here we are safe—the malkops do not enter due to the cavern's lowness and the lack of light. Their wings are large. The space is small. They do not like such places, but prefer the suns."

"And where do we find our reward?" interjected Stalkin, his eyes rov-ing on his flat face like marbles on a table.

"Above. There are other chambers—"

"Used by the malkops?" inquired Flores.

"The next chamber—not. Stalkin will encounter what he desires first, Flores. The chambers you wish lie beyond." His finger drew a circular pattern on the igneous rock at his back, relishing the illusion of wetness. "Tomorrow you shall see. It is easier to show than to explain."

The party of seven lay upon the powdery ground and relaxed, as much as they were able contemplating the vast weight suspended perpetually above. Within moments, however, their exhaustion overtook them and they collapsed into profound sleep.

When Flores next awoke the others were moving about. Revd stirred and briefly sampled his ration, leaving the remainder for the future, as did the Vaw-sa. Macius had gone.

Soon the thief reappeared, however, and motioned for the others to rise. "Make no noise. Come. The suns have set. We have an entire night to explore."

Flores nodded. Relighting their torch, the seven advanced with the wall upon their left, and after a short time paused, startled, for the impregnable glass of the ceiling, whose strength and durability kept their claustrophobia at bay, had collapsed and blocked their path. They stepped closer and discovered that the massive spur was a ramp—a slope of glass that, emerging from the grey tide like nacre from dross, gave access to higher levels through a tunnel that penetrated the ceiling at a steep angle.

"Vensor be praised," said Revd in relief. "This material is not only beautiful, but steadfast."

"Let us hope that its strength rests on more than Vensor's will," added Flores.

Macius looked at them in surprise. "There is nothing to fear. Do you not recognize, Flores, that which made your city strong—the glass-smith's treasure?"

Flores gaped. "Irsrem!"

"Yes. And made not by human hands."

The next level, thought Flores, must be similarly filled for the irsrem ramp was partially obscured by currents of dust that lay upon it in rills and streams, collecting in wide pools about its base. And more. Flores' hair raised upon his neck as he observed bones intermixed with the dust, to all appearances human.

Torch in one hand and gill in the other, Macius set foot upon the ramp. He climbed silently, displaying none of the reaction of his comrades. As they moved up the ramp, the odor grew. Now menacing, the stench hovered, invisible but potent.

The ramp gave onto another cave. This cave was similar to the first, and cast equally in darkness. The dim light of Macius' torch, seemingly inextinguishable—and Flores found himself wondering whether the thief had left the stick and tinder during his previous visit with the expectation of returning with such a party as this, and also wondered how the murshid could think that seven could profit more than one–burned on with only slightly diminished capacity, the light revealing a roof no different from the first, its gibbous irsrem marching away until vanishing in the surrounding night. On occasion isolated glints and glimmers flashed from remote distances as if sly conspirators signaled with mirrors while awaiting an opportunity to strike. Flores found himself listening for the sound of drums. None came. From their first step the Island of the Sun-God had been bathed in silence–a silence of the dead. Only their muffled breathing and the soft slick of their bared feet on glass disrupted the region's eternal peace.

Before resuming their climb up the curving ramp, the band examined the second cave. The ceiling in the chamber was of the same height as the first, but interrupted by a natural formation that was missing from the chamber below. This second chamber contained stalagmites or stumps, five-foot wide growths that pushed from amid the debris to terminate in a lacerated peak at a height just above their heads. The stumps occurred every hundred feet or so, their white moon-crater trunks rising like corpse-fingers, precisely spaced as far as the torch revealed.

Over each pillar was inscribed in the ceiling a circle of approximately the same width, the irsrem within the circle being of different composition, and coffered, as if some glass-smith with inexhaustible supplies had plugged a gap that had once existed over each stump. And each trunk rested–or rather slowly crumbled, since their surface gave before Flores' touch as easily as water, sending a stream of dust to join the expanding piles about their bases–within a net of obtusely angled walkways similar to those which Flores had glimpsed in the cave below. Here the paths were identical, but were visible to a greater extent and not as pitted and marked as formerly. Set at intervals equidistant from each trunk, the paths of brown brickwork formed a terrazzo of huge hexagons that angled away in the darkness, each hex circumscribing one trunk, though many of the walkways seemed to have crumbled away, leaving no trace even where the dust was shallow. Were it not for the greater vista afforded by the torch, and the glittering reflections of the glass in the ceiling, no pattern in fact would be discernible, the destruction being great. Here, also, the gradually accumulating piles of dust from the disintegrating forest seemed destined to obscure what remained. Flores gazed upon the ghostly trunks. What purpose could they have served? Had the formation indeed any purpose, or had it replicated of its own accord, upon some occult motive of nature?

The observers, however, gave little more than a glance to the trunks and brickwork for, as they penetrated the dark arcade, their attention was distracted by a sensation of treading on something brittle, each step resulting in a loud report as their weight caused the floor to collapse a short distance, as might a carpet of empty eggshells. Macius lowered the torch and the others recoiled.

The floor was bones. Not covered, as one might expect, with reassuring patches of more natural substance appearing between, but composed entirely, exclusively of bones. From stump to stump grey skulls, yellow ulnae, white ribs, and stained femurs underlay their feet in a single vast reservoir, all trace of flesh or clothing having long vanished, the bones themselves now crumbling of their own weight, having no longer the integrity even to harm the bared feet of the intruders. And again, as far as the observers could tell, most were of human origin, no representative of Talen's animal kingdom being obvious among them, though it was difficult to tell in the crush, and Flores thought he noticed several long, thin examples that could not belong to any child of Vensor.

"Take care with that flame, I beg of you," said Kip. "This cave will explode if your sparks drift into the pit and ignite it."

"No," corrected Surge. "The trunks exude a substance that renders the bones useless for fire. I learned that on my previous visit. Only the occasional body deposited beyond their reach—for example those upon this ramp—are capable of burning."

Flores shook his head. "How far does this cavern extend?" His voice drifted quietly, muffled by the peculiar carpet. "As far as the shore, like that below?"

The thief stared straight ahead. "To the shore—and beyond. I believe each cavern encircles the Island in its entirety, Flores. And the Island of Vensor is larger than all others. Before, I tried to walk its length. But I managed to view only a small part." He glanced back down the ramp. "There are many apertures such as the one we entered. But there is only one ramp. There is a central core to the structure which I have not been able to penetrate—the ramps seem to coil about it. The wall," he tapped the tachylite, "houses the core, while the ramp leads to the populated regions of the Island. Perhaps the core can be penetrated from those regions, Flores. If you are successful, then we may learn."

Macius glanced up the ramp where it vanished in another tunnel. With apprehension Flores followed his glance, but saw nothing but shadows.

"Come," said Macius, "we have little time; the dawn will be upon us sooner than you suppose, and once the suns rise on the surface, their light will seep in and our activities may be seen. When that occurs we will have to retreat here or below where the selks do not go and wait for the night before setting forth again. Although their sight is excellent by night as well as day, the selks do not frequent the caves at night for fear of injuring their wings. Even so, I cannot emphasize enough the importance of remaining quiet and hidden–the selks must not suspect that their realm has been invaded." He thrust his head forward and hunched his shoulders. "We must become rats, gentlemen. For in the eyes of God's minions, that is what we are–violators of their nether fields, trespassers in places where we do not belong." He turned his wooden face upon them. "Rats, sirs. Rats!"

Moving in a peculiar way that left the impression that he had already taken on his new identity, Macius left his stick of deadwood upon the ramp, the brand now giving forth no more than a feeble glow. His shoulders hunched and his fingers curled like claws. "We shall have no need of a torch after this. The stick shall remain here for our use when we return. First we shall view the upper cave...and Stalkin may gather what he wishes."

The glass-smith smiled, his eager tongue traveling the length of his mouth.

Leaving the second cave, which, mercifully, in Flores' view, they did not have to cross, the seven resumed their climb and entered the darkened tunnel. Immediately the odor that had followed them since their appearance on the Island increased immensely. As they rose through the gradually curving tube, great waves of stench assaulted them, each stronger than the last, until several removed their loincloths and placed them across their mouths, or replaced their gills over their nostrils to filter out the odor. To no avail. Nearing the egress of what seemed again a climb of great height and duration, they bent forward as in a gale, the gases of a thousand tombs inundating them, their mephitic outpouring pounding their senses like hammers.

Finally the tunnel ended and they stepped forward to view the latest invention of a contradictory god. The third cavern differed from the others. First, in that the span from floor to roof was greater than before. Of similar composition as the other caves, the ceiling loomed some forty feet above the floor so that the claustrophobic fear which previously had colored the mood of the seven vanished. Next, the party had emerged far above the ground, the tunnel debouching only ten feet from the roof so that, standing upon the ramp which here ran nearly horizontal, they were able to view the entire cave from on high, nothing impeding the panorama before them, which, the cavern being alive with incandescence, lay open to their inspection.

The ceiling shone and glittered far beyond that of the lower levels, reflecting a glow that emanated from a forest of pillars, stretching as far as they could see, and disappearing only where distance made the high roof seem to merge finally with the ground. And, also unlike below, the pillars in this cave remained firmly in contact with the roof, the stumps having grown directly into the irsrem, or rather had not yet deteriorated from this, their living state. The boles, still white and soft, now ran with light throughout their length, narrowing gradually from floor to ceiling, where they embedded themselves in a spectacle of color.

Despite their luminescence, however, the boles presented to the men no more pleasing an aspect than formerly, there being something fulsome, viscid, and unnatural about their bloated trunks which were disuniform in their circumference as a sense of proportion demanded, their being something deficient in the dull light they exuded, with certain mottled patches emitting more brightness than others. Still, what the source lacked, the ceiling returned many-fold, as might the child of a miser grown wealthy, and eager to spread his good fortune over all.

In the suffuse glow, Flores glimpsed more brickwork, less pocked and crumbling than before. Here the walkways were revealed to be not mere paths, but architecture, consisting of walls of cemented bricks that rose some distance above the ground, each hexagon spanning fifty feet or so to imprison a glowing trunk, the interior of each hex clearly visible from the perch upon the ramp. Both boles and hexes were far-flung, being part of a single mysterious structure that spun its web into the distance and was interrupted only by twisting avenues or, more precisely, a maze, accessible from the ramp by means of a steep series of steps descending to the floor, and which seemed to wend its tangled way into the interior without purpose or logic.

Indeed, in contemplating the floor, the little band reacted as one, gasping with horror and surprise. One Vaw retched. Another re-entered the culvert and covered his eyes, while Revd and Flores inhaled sharply through their loincloths, and said nothing, but coughed. The remainder, Stalkin included, put their hands to their mouths and moved next to Macius, who alone did not react but stood calmly, his eyes moving rapidly across the scene as if viewing a thing familiar.

To his shock, Flores felt he comprehended what he viewed, at least in part, and not only for the ghastly logic of the vista before him, but for the familiarity of the scene. In his mind he traveled to another cavern a world away that had a similar roof and similar brickwork–the pits beneath the palace of Numsenmur. There, in the midst of death he had encountered life. Now, gazing upon the undulating plain interrupted by its hexagonic cells with their boles immured like potted plants, his eyes perceived a more final death, and the hope that he had nurtured of finding the source of that life–of his life–the gila Amina of the Temple of Vensor–sank into a deep despair.

For within the cave stretched a new kind of floor, a material unguessed but in the mind of the manic, the offensiveness of its nature matched only by its unlimited vastness and depth, and Flores realized that the caverns which they had thus far traversed were in fact of equal depth to that which he now viewed, and identical in purpose, being only older and abandoned for the smallness of their ulage. Flores' eyes widened. Momently he perceived as an explosion in his brain the full immensity of Maalstrom, the cold symmetry of time and sex and death. In the honeycomb before him was the universe–disorder within order within disorder nested in infinite succession, each level more subtle and puzzling than the last, the puzzle indeed composing the universe itself, which followed its own concord, its own logic set from the beginning of time, and was forever veiled until Fortune, for reasons of Her own, pulled the fabric aside for a single brief moment of clarity...

They had discovered the source of the stench. Following no apparent order or design, the corpses of centuries of effort by malkops, those tireless workers of the sky, lay strewn in their multitude before the intruders, sinking under their cumulated weight as they decayed, in their growing density more obedient to the authority of nature than any had been alive. Despite their funeral garments and ritual gear and warrior weapons and careful toilet administered by loved ones, who had performed their final rites with affection and punctuality in the fervid belief that their kin would henceforth dwell in the Eye of Vensor, the selks, whose malignant presence Flores soundly cursed as a conspiracy and a plague, had cast them like refuse into these dark pits to rot, forever exiled from the welkin.

Within him something broke, and Flores knew that no longer would he view God's creation with deference, or even indifference, but, given the opportunity, would slip his blade into the very heart of the Divine. For there must be life–even in death. In his head was confusion no longer. As Vensa had ruled in Ven, masking her tyranny with oracles to evade the anger of her subjects, so Atasan ruled in Heaven, deceiving Vensor-sa with mythic tales of a happy land where the souls of the dead spoke with Vensor, deceiving even Vensa in her watery bed, who was as much a captive as Flores. There was no Vensor–or the Divine Twin existed but was blind–and the suns saw no more than a priest in whose burned-out orbs they shone, cold to life even while hot. Atasan–the beloved son of Vensor, the mad creator of Maalstrom whose one goal was the destruction of Humankind, was the only god it had, the only god it could ever have, enslaving not only the queens, and through them the insect-men of their cities, but ruling even in Heaven and in Hell. Indeed, there was no difference between them–one was but another name for the other, and Heavenhell together governed Maalstrom, as the head governs the body, and the heart the soul. Flores' soul squirmed. All that he knew was wrong.

Slowly, and agape, the seven descended the steep flight of steps. Here a dissolving foot lodged in a laborer's face, there the head of a silver-clad noble was buried in detritus. To one side a youth lay as dropped, on broken arms. Between were eunuchs and warriors, old men and infants, and others, humiliated, shamed, silent. None spoke with Vensor, none basked in the suns, none lived in the Eye of God. All were imprisoned in darkness, chained eternal to Atasan, their souls in torment. Like low cries of the dead, quiet creaking came to Flores' ears, as the interior of the pit slowly settled in a metamorphic crush. Flores felt his mind unhinge. What unholy variety of rock took form in its depths? Why did the selks desire to build their homes of flesh-brick? Was it more durable than skulls when petrified? An obscene squelch erupted from a hidden pool of liquid as the unnatural tectonics followed its putrid course, shattered walls testifying to the age of the process. Flores' eyes teared from the stench. The maze contained no streets. In fact there was no maze–rather through the centuries the shifting tides had felled the walls in random patterns, leaving avenues and alleys, openings and angles, plazas and cul-de-sacs. Rising eight feet or so above the top-most layer of carcasses, the brickwork that remained meandered blindly, no less sinister for its inadvertence.

Following Macius' arm, the Vaw-sa sighted an object. As they neared they became heedless, ignoring those whose dignity they violated, and rushed to take it in their hands. Stalkin, the strongest, and the fleetest, arrived first and yanked a golden necklace done in herringbone free of its owner's neck. It glittered in the light of the trunks. The Vaw grinned. Removing a crumpled sack from his pouch, he dropped the necklace within. He then exchanged the sack for a delicate silken bag and proceeded to ransack the pockets of the corpse. The others halted, eyes on Stalkin.

Surge watched Flores and Revd. The thought crossed the Turlicum's mind that the pilot had been unusually subdued since their advent on the Island. None of his former energy seemed present. Instead a cautious wariness hovered about him, and Flores felt somehow certain that this change was due to something other than the malkops, from whose meddling they were apparently safe.

"Flores," said Macius. "I wish to avail myself now of your promise to me, which you made upon the shore of the Hedronmas. I have fulfilled my oath and done for you as I pledged."

"I agree, Surge. You have my permission—as do the others." They glanced at Stalkin and the three Vaws, who had already turned their attention to the treasures before them, began to gather them amid expressions of joy. "But remember: the purpose of this expedition is to rescue Amina. You may take what you can carry, as may the others, but you are not to leave without me. After you have gathered what you wish, you and the others are to wait in the cavern below, with Revd, while I reconnoiter above. When I return—or after the passage of one full day—you may depart, but not till then. And I shall wish to consult with you before I climb the ramp."

The thief of Vaw passed his inscrutable gaze again across Flores, but said nothing. None of his habitual humor was present. Casually he sat. He took up a stray pair of boots and upended them to clear them of bones. He placed the boots on his feet. The other Vaws followed his example. Then, without another word, Surge turned and leaped into the flesh-pit with the agility of a gazelle. Soon he had moved far away, beyond the others, his quick eyes scrutinizing every corpse with cold efficiency. Flores watched, wondering, since he seemed to pass over many fine examples of wealth. Did he perhaps search for some specific object in all this vast cemetery? Flores shrugged, and turned to Revd.

"We need boots as well," he began. He gazed down upon the desolation. "And in all this charnel there must be weapons."

"Weapons?" Revd repeated.

"Yes. Our daggers are reassuring, but I do not wish to face the selks without a sword, or, even better, a pike."

A squeal of pleasure arose from the pit. One of the Vaws, perched on a spine of broken brick like an eater of carrion, displayed a breastplate of gold. He tied it about his own breast and returned to the hunt. More exclamations followed.

"When I have found a suitable sword, I will wish to explore the upper passage. I am afraid I must then leave you alone with them—I cannot ask you to risk your life along with mine in the upper chambers."

"But, Sire, you will have need of my help–"

"You will remain here. I order it."

Revd nodded.

"But do not turn your back on these thieves while I am not present to help you."

"Do not worry. I can handle this rabble."

"I have no doubt of that. But take care. And do not lose your gill. After I return–assuming I still live–we will return together to the Grest in the company of Macius. But if necessary, for instance if they become unruly, or if I fail to return by sundown, leave without me and rejoin Isav. He has his own instructions and is doubtless fulfilling them even now. I have my gill as you have yours. We need no guide to find our way back."

Revd nodded, and gripped his gill more tightly.

"And now I must find a sword, a light rapier of glass. It will protect us against our companions as well as the malkops. If only we had some means of felling them from the sky, before they strike."

"Perhaps this will do..." Revd pointed to a twisted length of wood.

"A bow!"

Revd grinned. "And arrows. Its owner must have been a renowned hunter in life."

"Good. Somewhere in all this cave there must be rapiers as well."

Flores gave a last adjustment to his boots, and, with an expression of disgust, forced himself to leave the irsrem of the steps and descend to the macabre landscape of the cavern.

"I will catch up to you in a moment," said Revd. "The gut requires re-stringing."

The chieftain nodded and ventured across the pits. Soon he lost sight of Revd. Rapiers were rarer than he had supposed. He advanced along a central avenue, the murals encasing their rows of shattered trunks, their weird glow casting shadows over the forms beneath his feet. At first Flores could not shake a feeling of infinite desecration, every step a violation of something sacred, a crime committed. He found his eyes wandering about him as if the shadows hid vengeful malkops waiting only an unguarded moment to spring. But the ceiling held no shadows, but coruscated with light like frozen flame. And soon he found that he no longer thought of what lay beneath his feet, and he moved forward without fear.

He advanced with difficulty. It was necessary to keep one hand clasped always to his mouth to filter the air through his loincloth. Once he lost his balance, plunging his other hand wrist-deep in muck. With a shudder, and a haste akin to panic, he rose and cleaned his hand on patches of crumbling leather. He calmed himself and proceeded. He passed swiftly along alleys, peered into pits, climbed up ridges, then backtracked and set upon new courses, viewed new lines of sight. He found and tested several short rapiers, but rejected them, and ignored the armor as well, as too bulky to wear.

He learned that he was correct in his belief that not only Vensor-sa were brought to the Isle. What he suspected were malkops also lay in varying stages of putrescence, but were always dismembered in fragments, making it difficult to be certain.

And Macius had been right about other matters as well. At Flores' feet were strewn a profusion of baubles, gems, and medals. Even the less rare objects would be worth a fortune in Ven if he could get them to the ship. Flores shuddered at the thought. Let the others strip the dead–to the least of the jewels was attached obscenity, as repellent to Flores as the Isle's guardians. Besides, he had other business. Doubtless the Vaw-sa, whom Flores could no longer see nor hear, were still filling their sacks and pockets, and lashing plates of gold over limbs, but the Turlicum could not free his mind of the image that floated just below his consciousness–the image of Amina spurred him on.

He paused. Inside a cul-de-sac whose walls framed a crumbled entrance lay the remains of a large Vensor warrior with glass armor. His web-shrouded skull lay against the trunk and beside the shield his disarticulated hand still clutched a rapier-pike six feet in length with one end molded into a firm handle. Placing his gill upon an irsrem shield by the entrance, Flores entered the cell. He weighed the haft. A strong blade, suitable for his purposes. He turned to rejoin Revd...

✎ 𝕰𝕺𝕮𝕾 ✍

Stalkin glanced once at Flores and Revd as they stood upon the stairway talking with Macius. The glass-smith overtook the other Vaw-sa.

"Wait." Stalkin jerked his head toward the stairs. The others glanced stealthily back and pretended to remain occupied with their stripping of bodies.

A moment later Macius sprang from the stairs and strode rapidly over the undulating corpses to vanish amid the brickwork, and Flores then eased into the pits. The walls swallowed him, and Revd was alone.

"Draw closer, my pretty ones, and listen." The three ruffians, their smooth hairless faces spoiled by the licks of knife-blades, moved closer, still pretending to inspect the dead. Stalkin resumed his monologue. "Our master, praise him and his cleverness, has brought us thus far. It was he put these jewels in our pockets. He gave us these suits of gold instead of glass, he whose plot tricked these idiot Ven-sa into inviting us aboard their ship and leading us to their goal–this world of treasure now before us. Has he been successful, my pets? Has he fulfilled his word, even as he promised?"

"Indeed, Stalkin, he has!" The Vaws grinned wolfishly through the cloths that they kept about their nostrils. Their ears absorbed every flinty sound their chieftain made.

Stalkin hacked with horrid effect, and continued. "Now I tell you the moment has finally come when we are to complete the last part of his plan." He paused to look back. Only Revd could be seen, just beyond hearing. The Ven captain glanced once in their direction, then returned his attention to his longbow.

"Once the deed is done all will be finished. The treasure will be ours– not merely what we can carry upon our bodies, but all that we can pile into their ship! And more–why limit ourselves to this fragile and puny boat? Our master has promised more ships. And men! All that we must do is rid ourselves of these Vens!" He clutched an imaginary dagger and pretended to rip open a heart. "First these two, then those upon the isle. Then we shall have our way clear, with all of their sea devices in our possession to bring the wealth of a thousand years to our chests. Riches beyond dream! Our master was right–'stay with them till the end,' he said, before even we tread upon the boat, 'and you shall discover not only their goal but their method. Only then should you strike,' he said. And now, by the eye of Vensor, we shall!"

He unsheathed his dagger, and turned a subtle glance back toward the stair. "Leave this one to me. You follow Flores. And take care. Make no noise but use that which lies within the heart of every Vaw–stealth and deceit. Now...make your city proud!"

Nodding again, the three Vaws covered their nostrils and started off to- ward the bend of brickwork where Flores had last been seen. Stalkin turned toward Revd. He smirked his olive lips and flexed his massive biceps. A rush of pleasure took him as he contemplated the deed. It would be no harder than brazing irsrem. And more invigorating. He stole closer, and sank into the muck to knee-level. Forced to grip the straps and pull them out with a loud squip, he clambered to a locale of freshly dead, their bloated torsos still retaining firmness, their skins flaying be- neath his boots. Desiring some distraction to allay any suspicion that

Revd might entertain, he paused to gather several rings from bony fingers and place them within his sack. Then he clambered to the stairs. Revd remained engrossed with restringing the bow.

"Revd, dear sir. Might I speak with you a moment?"

The Ven glanced up, displeased. Or bored.

"A good tool that. It will feather their tails without a doubt, should we need it." Stalkin paused, quiet. "I wanted to speak with you alone, dear Revd. Might I broach the subject?" A salacious glint shone in the Vaw's eyes. He ran one hand over a muscular arm, his face orgulous with narcissism.

"Save your passion for the eunuchs of your city. Or broach with one of the deceased malkops–they will prove more cooperative." He sniffed and coughed, bringing his loincloth back to his mouth.

Stalkin had drawn quite close. He now mounted the last step and stood beside Revd. "Is there no chance, then, of my affection being returned?" The Vaw breathed deep as if in the throes of passion.

"None."

"May I express my disappointment, then?"

Revd turned to face him. "I have given you no sign. You have no call to–" Revd heaved as one of Stalkin's sturdy hands clapped heavily across his mouth, stifling his cry with the loincloth. His eyes exploded as the other, wrapped about a dagger, ripped into his abdomen and traveled up and through his ribs. The rainbow on his face turned crimson. Still holding shut his mouth, Stalkin snapped out a length of twine he had secreted and wound it about Revd's neck, strangling permanently his death cry. The body fell into the pit. Stalkin dropped beside it and quickly covered it with corpses.

Meanwhile, the three Vaws advanced up the avenue which Flores had entered. The cordwood flesh was here more uniform in appearance than elsewhere, perhaps victims of the same disaster in some far country. The corpses were firm and only ridges of bricks broke the monotony of the corridor, like a snake with red ribs. The six-walled cells alternately opened before them, and closed to preserve their secrets. Within, the white trunks drank the soft pusculence with their tentacles, squeezing forth their facsimile of life.

Unable to locate their prey, the Vaw-sa at first maintained their pretense of hunting for jewels and gold. But at each broken pile of bricks they paused to listen and wink. At length the three ceased moving and their eyes mutually embraced. A reven gill–Flores' breathing device–rested upon a plate of irsrem at the foot of a crumpled wall.

He was within.

Three blades slid free.

A slithering sounded and one Vaw glanced down–gasped. A white head floated in the cave light, its beaded eyes black against a skull shorn of skin, the close-set orbs searching for prey. Mounting the ridge at the entrance, the head rose on lizard forelegs, bucking as for a mate. Its red-rimmed eyes focused on the naked Vaw, its upward-curved tusk snapped with enough force to split stone.

"A jungle ros!"

Unable to check his thrust, the second Vaw struck. Then turned and fled.

They rushed back to Stalkin who glanced, with Revd's bow uplifted.

"Is the deed done?" Stalkin frowned.

"Flee! It is almost upon us!"

The swarthy glass-smith narrowed his eyes and lowered the bow, still skeptical. "Did you find the Ven chieftain? Did you kill him?"

"Flee if you value your life! It is hungry and almost upon us!"

"But–"

The nearest Vaw paused, his chest working with exertion. "I tell you the beast took the Turlicum. We must depart at once! Look–we have our gold. Our sacks are full; our limbs are plated with the stuff."

"True..." Stalkin glanced nervously across the pit, looking for movement. "But what of Lesk?"

The two looked around. Their companion was not in sight. "He must be as dead as the Turlicum. Would he have delayed if he still lived? We must flee at once!"

"I should confirm this–the master will be displeased if Flores still lives."

The other Vaw clutched at his waist. "Look! Here is proof–his gill. Would Flores have abandoned the device if he still lived? They are done for, I tell you. We must depart this devil's hole before our bodies join them!"

Stalkin slowly nodded, then gave in. "Alright. But first fill the sacks. And lash the plates well. I do not wish to return empty-handed. Our comrades might then prove as dangerous as any ros." He descended to the pit again and soon returned with several lengths of rope, which he used to tie the treasure-sack of each man about his neck. Quickly the three stuffed what was in reach into the bags, and fastened their plates more firmly about their limbs. They turned to mount the long staircase.

Stalkin halted. "Surge!" he swore. "What has happened to our murshid?"

A small sound crept behind him. He turned and jumped, despite the burden of his heavy sack an arrow leaping into place within the bow. The thief stood quietly, staring up at them from the pit.

"Surge! You come upon us like a moth, without a sound."

"You mount the stairs?" Macius inspected their preparations, his eyes already shifting to his flanks. "Flores has entered the upper zones?"

"The Turlicum has entered a new zone altogether. As has his comrade." Stalkin pointed to the pits where a bloody leg protruded from beneath a pile of corpses. Surge registered no reaction. "And," continued Stalkin, "we are leaving these caves while we still have our lives and our loot." Stalkin and the others hurried up the stairs. Surge hesitated, then followed.

"–we can return with a larger party–"

"–you say the Turlicum is dead?"

"–his body lies below–"

"–where are the Ven's devices?"

"–and Lesk, Vensor take him–"

"And from what are they dead?"

"–Lesk has his; I do not–"

"–of a demon, a demon of the Isle–"

"–you are certain?"

"–I asked you to watch the gills–"

"–and Lesk also? You saw their bodies?"

"–I watch only my feet when I am running–"

"–I saw the demon–that is enough for me–"

"–you must keep quiet in these caves, you will attract the selks."

"–selk or ros, I long for the open sky and wish not to remain another night in these regions–"

"–head of a demon you say?"

"–I hold his gill in my hand!"

"–what kind of demon?"

"–its roar thundered in my ears–"

"–a ros–but not a ros–"

"–I saw the trunk of the tree glowing through its body–"

"–yet it roared to rouse the dead–"

"–I heard nothing–"

"–nor I–"

"–yet it fair deafened me–"

"–and me–"

"–I waited not to feel its jaw upon my neck–"

"–we will return to the isle at once–"

"–without Flores?"

"Of course without Flores. Did I not say he was taken by the creature? No worry, you are the murshid, not he."

"–we have gained what we sought–"

"–quiet while we climb, do not disturb the guardians–"

The four Vaws reached the ramp at the head of the stairway. Briefly they paused to glance across the pits, the inspection revealing nothing in the gloomy landscape. They turned and halted.

"Look!"

One of the two Vaws who had returned from stalking Flores yelled through his loincloth and pointed across the cave to the midst of the pits. A small figure advanced, a commotion or movement hovering about it so that it appeared no more than a blur. Whatever it was, it was not a ros.

"Into the tunnel, quickly," hissed Stalkin.

They entered the ramp leading to the lower caves. Swiftly they descended through the culvert, their lungs working the thick air. Emerging on the ramp at the second level, Stalkin felt for the torch which they had left. He found it and handed it to Surge.

"Here is the brand. Light it quickly, I do not wish to delay any more than necessary."

The thief produced a flint and iron. He selected a bone from among the many about the cave and quickly crushed it into powder. With the flint, he struck sparks into the pile.

The others glanced apprehensively back up the tunnel.

Soon the brand flared anew and Surge held it up to guide their approach to the other tunnel-mouth. While Surge lit the torch, the others, except for Stalkin, sat and rested. They lurched to their feet, stumbling under the weight of their golden armor and sacks of treasure.

"Wait...*listen!*" Stalkin, who had hung back and stood within the mouth of the upper tunnel, motioned for silence and directed his ear to the upper ramp. A dim but definite rustling carried from within the tube, its echo traveling from what seemed a great distance, but growing louder. The Vaws exchanged terrified glances. Flinging his sack across one shoulder, Stalkin notched an arrow to his bow. They plunged into the tunnel leading to the first level.

Another seemingly interminable length of time elapsed, with the Vaws wheezing in the noxious atmosphere, and clambering down the steeply graded tube. Several times one paused to rest or catch his breath, but

Stalkin, who brought up the rear, jerked and hurried him on. With the passage of what seemed another inordinate stretch of time, they finally emerged from the ramp on the first level. Spilling from the entrance, they set out across the dunes of bone-dust. An hour passed. Then another. Finally, Macius halted. The others shouted. He had extinguished the torch in a windrow of dust.

"What is the reason for that? We have not yet found the passage out of this foul region!"

"We will not need it. Look!"

The Vaws gazed across the cavern.

"Dawn comes."

Indeed the darkness was not as complete as before. Light seeped in from some distant source.

"We erred in our estimation. Or delayed too long," said Kip.

"Or marched too slowly!" said Stalkin. "On, on quickly! Or we will be caught between whatever follows us and the workers of the sky. We must exit and gain the water at once."

Their senses no longer assaulted by the stench of the third level, and too impelled by their haste to pause to reclothe, they cast their loincloths in the dust and hurried toward the exit, the light growing swiftly about them. Although Surge was the least burdened, having no more than a sheath and dagger and his water-breathing device, he soon fell behind until some distance separated him from the others.

Kip slowed his pace.

"Hurry your legs. The thing will catch us—I do not wish to end as did the Turlicum."

"How, Fel?" Kip wheezed. "These plates are heavy. I cannot run with all this gold."

"Run you must!"

"I must discard some—" Kip reached a hand into his sack and dropped a bracelet upon the ground. Stalkin stopped short and his dagger sprang from its sheath. It hovered over Kip like a cobra.

"Retrieve it—or die."

With a trembling hand, Kip picked up the bracelet and placed it again within the sack. The glass-smith lowered the blade and pushed his face close to the other's. "If you throw aside so much as one item, Kip, I shall gut you as I did the Ven. Do not cast aside what we struggled so hard to obtain."

The Vaw nodded. Swinging the sack behind him, he shuffled forward.

"And you, Fel? Has your sack become too burdensome to carry?"

The other Vaw blinked.

"Indeed no, Stalkin. I am strong–I will not lose the gold."

"No, you will not. Or you will lose your life as well. Remember my warning."

Stalkin glanced at Surge. The murshid stood silently behind the others, swaying as if before a wind. A slight noise emanated from the cavern at their backs. They turned. Nothing could be seen in the gloom and Surge looked back at Stalkin. The smithy grinned with fear.

"The aperture lies ahead. Quickly!"

Kip and Fel hurried forward, and arrived at the crest of the slope that led down to the aperture. Scrambling down the slope, they halted at its base. They placed their palms on their foreheads to shield their eyes. Within the aperture were the suns, curving just above the horizon, their bright rays stabbing into the cavern. A narrow beach of sand fell gently away to the sea.

Stalkin paused again. His eyes scoped the portion of sky visible from the aperture. "Surge, is it safe? Can we make it across the beach?"

The thief shrugged. "I do not know. I have not ventured forth upon the Island during daylight. It may be safe. It may not." Peering cautiously outside the aperture, he gazed upward. The sky was empty and serene and deliciously cool with a moist breeze.

Stalkin breathed the air with vigor. "Surely nothing can happen on such a morning–not in Vensor's world, at least. It is a dawn to surpass all dawns."

They glanced once more at each other and set their jaws. Stalkin placed an arrow within his bow and loosened the several others he had within the mouth of the sack. Each settled his gill over his nostrils. They adjusted the twine; discarded their boots. Four blades glinted. There could be no mistakes.

"Now–"

Kip and Fel rushed into the open, Stalkin close behind. The beach was perhaps fifty feet in width. They covered half the distance and no more than a few moments remained before they would gain the security of the waves. Sand kicked up as they sprang forward. They panted encouragement–they would make it.

Kip stumbled. For a moment he puzzled as to how he could remain erect while his foot suspended strangely above the sand. He glanced up. On either side a malkop gripped him, leather wings beating. Fel and Stalkin stared in round-mouthed surprise. Kip's eyes locked with those that held him. He grimaced. The pretty visages he had glimpsed so often before were dark with rage. They made no sound, but one of the selks unclasped a hand and bared dagger-like claws. Kip moaned.

As if in a trance, the others watched. Behind and above Kip loomed the artifact whose presence they had only sensed the previous night. Now, the wall awash in light, Fel's jaw slowly opened as he contemplated its full expanse, and Stalkin fell to his knees. They gazed upon a flat shining surface, the slope of a pyramid that swept its massive height as far as the eye could see until it vanished in mists of white, its upper levels clothed in cloud. Reflecting the suns, the surface glowed and coruscated with all the colors of the rainbow. Like its interior, its outer face was composed entirely of irsrem, from its invisible crest suspended dizzily above, to the base that was enmeshed in the same ignoble sand beneath their feet. Its sheer size staggered them, and Stalkin found himself wondering how anyone could have thought–insect progeny as they were–that they could intrude at will and penetrate its mysteries. The ramp alone must require weeks to walk, its circumference years. How vast the structure; how deep the pits; how ancient the practice that had filled the lower two levels! Indeed, how much more time would be required before the city outlived its usefulness and became nothing more than an immense tomb for the dead.

For city it was. At intervals across the sky-crawling surface occasional vents were punched, in the shape of fan-windows. At a distance up the glittering slope, directly above the aperture that opened upon the first cavern, loomed one of these vents, close enough that the Vaws could see that its lower tangent was thronged with winged malkops, standing on the lip in their hundreds. In angry silence they observed the lonely figures far below upon the sand, as might humans view vermin which had trespassed. Other selks hovered about the entrance. In the distance they saw a stormcloud–more selks advancing airborne.

"How...?"

Fel glanced at his feet. His eyes followed the tracks which the seven had left in the sand when they had first emerged from the water, two nights before. In the night they had seen nothing–before or behind. He shuddered. The selks must have seen their tracks at first light and been waiting for them to re-emerge. Vensor–or Atasan–was ready to take His revenge.

The selks flew higher with Kip. Several more closed about the unlucky Vaw, who was momentarily obscured. He reappeared and the Vaws could see that each selk had seized a limb. He disintegrated. Flapping higher with their grisly trophies, the selks entered still another vent further up the slope to the third level. The one in need of cadavers.

The two Vaws trembled.

A wave of selks spilled from the aperture, diving swiftly.

"Quick!" cried Stalkin through his gill. "Into the water!"

The Vaws ran. Not time enough–they could not make the deeper stretches. The smithy turned and raised his bow with the arrow still notched. He loosed it into the body of the nearest selk. It found its mark. With a silent scream the creature tumbled to the sand, flopped, and lay still. He fixed a second arrow, and was startled as a dark body sped past; Surge dove efficiently into the sea. The second arrow went wide. Aiming another, Stalkin brought down a second selk, then threw the bow away. Turning, he too vanished amid the waves. A swarm of selks glided after.

Fel pulled gold ingots from his sack and flung them at the creatures. Surprisingly, this caused them to hesitate, and Fel, in turn, took the opportunity to cast aside his burden. He dove into the same wave that had consumed Stalkin and the weight of his remaining sack of gold took him under.

The selks peered angrily about. Like hornets they swarmed along the coast. But the beach was empty but for the two murdered selks and a tangle of baubles, and at length the creatures calmed and returned to the vents. The sea tumbled upon the shore. It gave no hint of where the intruders had gone; offered no comment on the spasm of violence it had witnessed. Steady and eternal, it caressed the sand, already dulling the gold's bright gleam.

CHAPTER 8

IN THE PALM-GROVE

Stalkin paused to inspect the water about him. Despite his efforts, his motion could not be described as swimming, for the burden of his golden plates prevented him from maintaining the requisite bouyancy, with the result that his efforts fell somewhere between a crawl and a staggering upon the bottom. He also kept his sack, the mouth of which was tied with a length of twine and looped about his neck, which further prevented him from making swift progress. He gazed about. The surface of the water was several feet over his head, and he squinted through the brine to locate Macius–of the fate of Fel he was less certain.

At first no other shadow was visible in the dark waters, at least no shadow that might indicate a child of Vensor, but as he shrugged and prepared to resume the long journey to the smaller isle, a splotch suddenly took shape. Fel had survived! Stalkin snorted, sending bubbles spurting through the fluid. As his companion neared, he tapped one of the plates, his other fist upon his dagger. Lose them–and die. Fel understood and nodded. Of Surge no sign was visible. With a slow wave of his hand, Stalkin led the way into the deep.

The day passed sluggish as sap, the murky discs of the suns drifting across the sky without concern for the men plodding in the sea. Their pace seemed intolerably slow. At times Stalkin glanced back at Fel with disapproval. The sailor of Vaw, though less burdened than the muscular smithy, fell steadily behind; his breath came with increasing difficulty.

Hours passed. The suns attained zenith and again began to sink. The thick sinews of the smithy pumped steadily against the sod, the algae rising about him in a wake that quietly broadened to encompass the other man. Fel followed as best he could. He often staggered, or paused. He halted to sit. Stalkin turned, looked, and again snorted. The weakling! He had failed him at every turn–if only he, Stalkin, could carry more weight, he would have no need of the wretch... From a score of feet ahead he contemplated the sailor. A shadow emerged from the deeper darkness. Like a specter it floated just within view, too distant for detail. Stalkin's brows flattened, his eyes, red with brine, unable to make it out. In a flash of white, it vanished–it was not Macius. Stalkin chilled. Fel had not seen. Slowly Stalkin pivoted and began to move away while Fel forced himself once more to his feet.

Gradually the day expired, like a dumb beast whose life slowly drained, the darkness of the nether world gathering eagerly to consume it. The suns had gone and Stalkin knew that they would again be immersed in blackness before they could gain the shore. They would have to walk hours in darkness. Stalkin's muscles creaked, rebuking him. But obeyed. Stalkin was blessed with strength. Blessed? No, he corrected himself. Praise Vensor, the world is as it is, and none other is possible–this world is blessed for the fact that I am in it. My body has not failed me yet–and will not so long as I face any child of Vensor... His legs lurched, the dense strands knotted with energy. He glanced back. Behind Fel the white blur was joined by a second. Stalkin grew nervous and educed more effort from his sinews.

The lie of the sea bottom changed and Stalkin found himself moving upward. The suns having set, he could see no more than a few yards ahead, the murky water lit dimly with starlight. The shore ran just ahead. He paused. Perhaps it was better that he return with Fel. Should the others find his own baubles inadequate, he could point to his companion and let their anger fall on him. A companion had proved useful when the selks had gone after Kip. Poor Kip...the *fool*. He should have been stronger! The gods favor the strong; the overweening; the willful. The weak return to compost. Stalkin smirked–they deserved no better. He turned to display another contemptuous smile in Fel's direction, and his eyes widened. What audacity! He had gone. What would the others say? Whom could he mock in his hour of triumph?

Turning, Stalkin retraced his steps and his colleague soon returned to view. Fel sat beside a cabbage-like growth that floated flaccid tendrils in the drink, one arm outstretched as if to relieve the cramp of a bicep. Stalkin moon-walked closer to jerk him to his feet. They had survived the most spectacular feat in centuries–and here he sat!

Stalkin slowed. Dozens of white tendrils clung to Fel's legs. The hand with the blade was tightly bound and his free arm stretched not in relief, but, he now realized, in succor. Unable to scream and locked in the plant's embrace, Fel could do nought else but hope for Stalkin's return.

His eyes shone round with fear. To save him Stalkin had only to take his hand and pull.

Stalkin smiled. For such moments did he live. He freed his dagger. Fel relaxed. Pulling loose a strap that secured a golden plate upon the sailor's unencumbered arm, he cut it, and put the plate in his sack. Fel stared, confused. Stalkin cut loose another and placed it also within his bag. Fel began to struggle. The white strands clasped tighter, moving about his waist. A third, then a fourth plate came free and joined the others and Stalkin paused to flash a last silent smirk at the doomed man. Snapping off Fel's gill, he stuffed it in as well. Then, pivoting slowly around, he accelerated his glittering bulk through the waters and headed for the beach. The white blurs reappeared. Behind, Stalkin heard a muffled scream, barely audible, shudder through the liquid.

Waves crashed.

After the silence of the deep, the sudden noise was deafening. Stalkin lurched forward, alternating thick limbs in the surf. He had returned to where he had begun, the narrow stretch of beach on the western side of the small rocky crag. Alone in the night, the heavy sack resting beside him on the sand, he gazed... Where was his welcome?

He cupped his hands. "Hellooo!"

The empty cliffs and caves threw his deep voice back. Vacant.

Divesting himself of his gewgaws and golden armor and gill, he stuffed all in the sack and placed the sack in the cave, then climbed the path to the crest. Without the burden of the metal, the climb was facile and he soon drew himself up to full height upon the peak, breathing in the clean air. He was tired, but his athletic sinews still not exhausted. He glanced about the small plateau. The night was bright, the stars twinkling like leaves on an aspen. The moons shone in their many colors, casting green and red tints on the wind-whipped rocks. The endless crash of water on stone carried from beyond the rim. No fire flickered in the direction of the grove; no living sound emanated.

He was alone.

Could the selks have struck while he was in the water and carried off the crew? Had Macius died as well? Had the murshid not survived the journey back? That would be a stroke of bad luck, he reflected, and a brief pang of regret passed through him as he realized that he might have killed his last companion. But his predicament was still not insuperable. For the last phase of the plan he needed the assistance of no one–not even the murshid. He inhaled and prepared to gather wood.

Crackling penetrated the darkness.

Stalkin peered, hope rising, for in the end even he did not wish to be alone.

"Ho there! It is I, Stalkin! I have returned from the Island of Vensor! Will you not welcome me?"

A sudden whirring sounded and his legs folded, pain shooting through them. He fell. Snaps sounded again as of feet on twigs. The rainbow blade of a rapier glittered at his throat.

"Say no word." The voice turned to others: "Take his arms and bind them. Take him to the camp."

The crew of the Grest appeared from the darkness. They produced a length of rope and in silence bound Stalkin's wrists behind his back. With Isav and six Vens watching, bared swords in their hands, the Vaws, with the assistance of the remaining Vens, untied the bola that had struck him and raised him to his feet. Stalkin noticed that two of the Vens who had before sided with the Vaws, Telemer and Fronek, had rejoined their former comrades. His eyes grew large as Macius approached from one side. The pilot's wrists were tied as well. Only the Vens possessed weapons. The Vaws had lost both daggers and swords.

"Can you walk?" asked Isav.

Stalkin nodded, though in truth he was not certain. His legs hurt badly. He blinked, his eyes still smarting from the water.

"You will walk to the camp. Tomorrow you will answer my questions— you and Macius. Think carefully before you answer. If I do not get a satisfactory accounting of what happened to Flores and Revd, you will not live to see the sunset."

Stalkin opened his mouth to speak.

The blade leaped to his neck. "Say nothing now, or I will kill you and learn what I wish from Macius."

The smithy shut his mouth, and turned and limped away.

Silence lay heavy upon the troop as they descended. The rapiers of the Vens, ephors guarding helots, flashed warily in the moonlight. Isav turned his foot to avoid a slither of lizards green like malachite. They turned red in the fiery beam of Atasan, their backs burnishing with rage. The second chief in the Turlicum clan followed, eyeing the bound giant before him with cold purpose. The warm tropical air felt unfamiliar against his light northern skin. Devilish scenes sprang into his mind in the humid night, scenes that did not bear repeating. He had loved Flores. Since the youthful Heir had chosen him from among the aides of the orphanage, already scarred from lashwork, he had listened and watched, always with Flores' welfare in mind. His chief had not returned—his revenge would be as ferocious as his love. His eye glinted with regret. Again he had been proven right in his seeming unreasoning suspicions. He had said that Flores was too trusting, and, as the year before in Ven, so now in the southern seas, his feel for treachery was justified. Again he wished he had been wrong, that Macius–for it was surely he who masterminded the plot–had not intended from the beginning to betray.

The palm-grove swallowed them. Two Vaws restocked the fire with brush from the oasis and a Ven struck sparks into the tinder. Soon a fire burned, hardly more than another star in the bright vastness of the night. At a gesture from Isav, the Vens who possessed swords directed Macius and Stalkin to lie by the fire and two Vens sat beside them as sentinels, while the rest of the crew lay upon the earth beneath the palms. For the remainder of the night they slept, exhaustion extracting its toll of time.

Morning came. Isav rose and stretched. He approached his two prisoners and observed them. They lay upon their sides, their backs turned away, the two guards squatting close by, still awake if not as watchful as the prior evening. The chief sniffed the cool air; his ears drank in the calls of the gulls. He could not ask for finer weather. Too bad the day would be ruined by the unpleasant task ahead. He glanced to the shore, where the hull of the Grest could be seen alone upon the beach like a dragon from the deep. The tide was out.

With his boot, Isav nudged Macius and Stalkin. They were awake.

"So you have not husbanded your strength. That is unfortunate. You will have need of it today." The hard glint in Isav's eyes was still there. "I suppose, though, that anticipation of your trial disturbed your sleep to some degree. It did mine, though that will mean little to you."

The two Vaw prisoners gazed silently at Isav, saying nothing. Stalkin squirmed, less used to privation than was Macius.

The other members of the island's new rulers gathered about the three. Besides Telemer and Fronek–the two Vens who had guarded them–there were Toom and Meld, and Gwolior and Zeydad. They glared at the four Ven turncoats who had sided with the Vaws, and who had not been allowed to possess arms. The Vaw-sa sulked, returning their stares with equal force. Besides Macius and Stalkin, the Vaw-sa numbered five.

Isav kneeled, balancing himself on one heel. "I did not wish to make this difficult, Macius, so I will give you an opportunity to tell me of your free will what you did upon the Island and in what way you disposed of Flores and Revd. I promise that your end will be swift and painless if you cooperate in this. I wish only to know what happened. I admit that the Turlicum brought some of this upon himself by bringing such as you to this distant spot. It is obvious that from the beginning of the voyage you have had this result in mind and have maneuvered Flores and the Grest so as to bring us to this. You are the mastermind and Stalkin is your agent, is he not? Come, tell me. I will eventually get it out of you no matter what. It is you who concocted this plan to kill Flores, in order to be free to loot the Island of Vensor without restriction. Now, speak! I do not wish to employ more drastic measures. And do not think that your status as pilot will save you. We needed you to find our goal–we need no guide to return but only to sail north and east. Enough of your eternal reserve. We will now find out what your heart really desires and what you have done to get it."

All the crew stood or sat before the murshid, some watching intently, the rest pretending not to listen.

"I did not kill Flores," said Macius.

Isav stared. "But...he is dead."

"I do not know."

Stalkin was watching Macius with a strange look in his eyes as if the pilot spoke in some new and incomprehensible language.

"I did not kill him. I did not see him killed. I did not see his body. In fact, dear Isav, there is nothing more to say. I have done nothing but what I promised before we sailed–no more and no less."

Isav dropped his eyes, a look of doom about him. He withdrew a dagger from his belt. "We shall see."

He turned suddenly to Stalkin and grasped one of the large man's forearms and unfolded it, laying the venation bare. Isav snapped his eyes up–the smithy's bonds were gone.

Stalkin erupted to his feet. He gripped Isav by the shoulders, lifted the Ven, and with a roar threw him across the clearing. The two Vens who had stood sentinel pulled rapiers from a wrapping of canvas and tossed them to the Vaw-sa and those Vens without arms. Stalkin snatched one. He spun it, producing a merry whistling.

"Now, 'dear Isav,' " cried Stalkin, "we shall see who tickles who on this day! And who shall live to collect the reward that I hid in the caves below. And who the selks will carry off to rot in the gardens of Hell!"

The two Vens who had freed him crossed blades with Toom and Meld.

"Fine work, Telemer," continued Stalkin, "Good play, Fronek. As I told you in the dark before you cut our bonds, I brought enough treasure for all. Each shall have a share. You will live out your lives in plenty, with slaves and harems at your call–and gilas! Whatever you desire! Now strike. For Gethos and Nantifus, for fortune and gold, drive these Vens away; drive them off the isle and into the sea!"

Retrieving the weapons, the Vaws shouted with glee and with the aid of the four Ven traitors, reinforced by Telemer and Fronek, fell upon the remaining Vens with fury.

"Back!" called Isav as several mutineers clustered about Gwolior.

The Ven fell, his skin exploding beneath the scythe-like swords, as stripped of its integument as the palms. His screams rang above the eager ejaculations of his attackers.

"Revenge!" shouted the remainder. They rushed to avenge him and passed their rapiers through the bodies of Fronek and a Vaw. But the others rushed in. They hammered them back. The clot of warriors were pushed to the edge of the clearing, and then into the grove, the greater weight of the mutineers outflanking them, forcing them back.

"Pursue them!" called Stalkin to the others from the undergrowth. "The reward is gold! And silver! And mir! We have but to kill them and all will be ours! Onward my own, my lovelies!"

The mutineers pressed forward and the resisting Vens turned and fled. Emerging from the grove, they regrouped on the upward slope. They backed away as their attackers massed, and followed.

Isav paused to catch his breath. "Telemer! Haf! How can you fight your city-mates? Your own clansmen? Have you no shame?"

They laughed and spat. "There is no longer any clan. You should have joined with us, Isav, instead of living in the past! The Turlicum is dead–and his Heir–Ven harbors only spirits anymore. We have no city! But before we die we shall be rich; and pity any who stands between us and our gold!"

The mutineers fanned out, seeking to use their greater number to surround them. Isav gestured and his men fell back, retreating up the slope.

"You cannot escape us, Isav," said Stalkin. "Give up. I will let you live."

Isav made no answer but steadily climbed, the four surviving warriors walking backwards in the form of a diamond. The mutineers did not follow. The Vens then reversed and climbed the slope until they stood upon the small plateau of the island. Here a section of igneous rock had fragmented to form a small glen and Isav directed the others to take refuge in the lee of these fragments. The approaches from the grove were visible and, so long as daylight remained, it would be impossible for the mutineers to come upon them unawares.

Zeydad settled behind a rock and watched. "They are returning to the palms."

Isav looked. The mutineers had indeed turned and were heading for the shelter of the grove. Isav could see Stalkin gesticulate.

"Our smithy from Vaw still cheers them on."

"Indeed," said Isav, "but you may be sure that he takes his orders from Macius."

"Oh?" inquired Zeydad. "I do not recall seeing him strike a blow."

The Turlicum chief knitted his brows. "You are right. I do not recall seeing him after the fighting began."

The others agreed.

"He is not among them."

"Yet they do his bidding!"

"The coward!"

Isav leaned back and watched seagulls spiral.

Night fell. The bright-specked dome slipped into the waves, returning the fiery moons to their orbits, and the four lit no fire that might tempt their enemies to sneak upon them in the darkness. The breeze that blew in from the sea remained warm and humid, enervating their energies, a delicious relaxation rendering thoughts of war and conflict superfluous. Still, two remained awake when the others slept so that the approaches were always under watch.

When day again broke, the four were surprised to see the mutineers emerge en masse from the drop that led to the western beach, with gold and trinkets in their hands. Under Stalkin's direction, they had managed to evade their watch and under the cover of the night had silently obtained the treasure which Stalkin had so deftly employed to ensure his survival. Isav, inclined to believe the smithy was deceiving the others and had in fact brought no treasure, was the most surprised. He had expected a final assault before dawn.

Still bereft of Macius, the mutineers collected on the lip of the rim then marched back to the grove in a body, wary of interference from the Vensa in the rocks. Again they disappeared within the trees.

Zeydad smacked his lips and withdrew a piece of reven flesh from a pouch. The others gazed at him until he produced several more and, with veiled reluctance, shared them.

"Damn!" swore Toom. "We cannot remain here. There is no fresh water or food upon the island except for what is on the Grest."

"We can troll for fish–"

"–only if we can do so without interruption." Toom placed his chin in his hands. A weak plume of smoke filtered from among the trees. "See!

They eat well. They will soon have strength while we are unable to move. How long can we last here in these rocks?"

"Yes," added Meld. "Another night and I will be so weak that I will not be able to fight."

Isav shrugged. "We cannot let them know. As far as they are concerned, we have sufficient food for a month. We must make them think that. At least until we have devised a strategy for defeating them. Come, I wish to hear your ideas." They edged closer and began to speak in low tones. An hour later they grew quiet, no clear plan having taken form. Without food or water and greatly outnumbered they could see no escape from their predicament but a sudden attack by night on the mutineers. Stalkin would probably have arranged an ambush, however, expecting just such a move. They thought, and waited.

The day drifted by without incident. In the late morning they consumed the last of the reven and began to feel their thirst. Circling the sky, the smoke from the grove slowly thickened. They licked their lips. Whatever the mutineers ate, it was well-cooked. With each new spill of ash their mouths watered, their imaginations inflating the object of the fire to the status of a banquet. Overhead, the suns crossed and plummeted. While they watched, the clouds that obscured the reaches of Heaven momentarily broke, sending rays of red and gold stabbing skyward. Then the white veil returned and the Island lapsed into its former state of mystery.

Late afternoon came and the Vaws emerged from the trees and placed their dead in the open, where, as if by sorcery, several malkops appeared and flew off with the corpses, heading for the Island. Isav chilled–he had not really believed that the workers of the sky were watching them. But why not? What was different about this crag that they should let their charges lie and rot, while nowhere else? All men lived at the eternal mercy of Heaven, it seemed, wherever they might be.

He sighed. The duskline approached, skidding across the sea, another short Maalstrom day of sixteen hours drawing to a close. About the dark rocks of the wind-swept plateau the shadows spread like pools whose dams had burst, clothing all in ink. Suddenly Isav noticed Stalkin standing close before them and cursed himself for having allowed his attention to wander and enable the Vaw to advance without challenge. Behind him, the smoke from the grove had ceased, the fire now extinguished.

The mesomorphic Vaw smiled a smile of subtlety and triumph.

"Isav!" His deep voice boomed across them like surf.

The four Ven-sa did not reply but gazed to either side, alert to attacks from their flanks.

"Isav!" came the voice a second time. "Toom! Meld! Zeydad!" Stalkin stood alone, though several of his Vaw companions could be seen just within the cover of the palms. "Come out! I must speak with you! I wish to parley!"

Isav stood. His suspicious mind reviewed the various permutations for treachery and murder entailed in following the other's request. The Vaw was alone and unarmed. The others were within the far grove, which contained no wood appropriate for constructing bows. They could not throw rocks from that distance. If they started from the trees, Isav and his men could regain the cover of their shelter before they arrived. On the other hand, they could themselves fall upon Stalkin and cut him down. The Vaw before them grinned, his marble eyes rolling across the olive-colored plain of his face like an upturned crab. Isav pursed his lips and swore–there had to be a trick. He attempted to click his tongue but failed. It was beginning to swell. They needed water, and quick.

He stood, saying nothing. Stepping from the shelter of the blockish fragments, he approached the Vaw. When he came within ten feet, Stalkin began to move back.

"That is close enough; I do not wish to be within arms-length of your blade should you dislike my terms and decide to run me through." Stalkin grinned again. He was in good spirits.

Isav passed his glance slowly over the body of the Vaw, attempting to search out hidden daggers. Behind him, the three other Vens rose and walked to within several feet of Isav. Their leader raised his chin.

"What terms? And with regards to what manner of settlement except that of your immediate surrender?"

Stalkin folded his arms and laughed good-naturedly. "Kind Isav, don't be so unsociable with your old friend. I bear you no ill will despite what you said to me yesterday, and all those terrible threats you made. I wish only the most cordial and relaxed relations between us. There is no reason for us to fight; you saw for yourself that we took the treasure. Instead of bringing up the gold, we could have struck you in the night. We could have killed you all–you know this. But we didn't! We wish no trouble, but merely to go about our business, which dear Flores–Vensor honor him–allowed us, and I hasten to add that as Macius did not kill your Flores, neither did I, nor any of my men, but that he and Revd were taken by the malkops because they were careless, and two of my men as well who fell victim to them while attempting a rescue. But we still have two gills! And we have brought back what is only the first batch of the gold. There is plenty for all. Indeed, more than we can handle! And still more where it came from for those who exercise care! Why don't we work together and pool our energies for the purpose of looting the Island for the benefit of all? Ask your own comrades–surely they agree with me."

The others said nothing but their eyes wandered briefly to Isav. Hunger and thirst made Stalkin's words persuasive.

"The truth is, dear Isav, we need you. After your most unkind stroke killed Fronek–my friend–whom I had personally promised vast stores of treasure last night, and for which he cut my bonds and secured the weapons from the Grest–and I would have fulfilled my promise by swimming to the treasure rooms of Vensor's Island myself if necessary– and after your men killed Split as well, an old comrade of mine from my youth in Vaw–Vensor knows I have reason to order the rest of my comrades to kill you here and now. But I will not for we each need the other, and we can benefit by working together. We are going about our business, as your Turlicum allowed–Vensor honor him–and we are dividing up the gold, and preparing to depart." He tilted his head and gazed slyly at the Turlicum chief, "You would not wish to remain behind on this desolate rock with nothing but slimy fish to eat, would you? And rainwater? I think not. So join us. We number ten, eleven including Macius–though we have not seen him of late..." He peered between them at the rocks as if the murshid might be among them, "And eleven is not enough to man the oars with success. If you join us we will number fifteen, that would ease the work at the oars greatly. Your citymates long to see you; they wish no conflict within their own city, their own tribe. So join us! Your Flores is dead. You have no gills of your own. You have done all that honor requires in memory of the Turlicum. What more can be done? Turn a new leaf. We have food and drink for all, and no desire for vengeance. Only your cooperation in getting the booty off this speck of dirt and back to civilized zones, where I promise to let you and your men go your ways without interference of any kind. Come, now what do you say to my offer? Is it not kind? Is it not generous?"

Isav found himself nodding as Stalkin spoke. He tried to speak and found that his tongue had swollen further as he stood–he had not thought that the effects of deprivation would come so quickly. He thought: yes– I am no longer young. The effects will not be delayed or shallow as on the younger men, but swift and harsh. Just within the cornice of the grove, the other Vaws stood nonchalantly about, the declining suns shining on their faces. He shrugged. There was nothing else to do.

He swallowed hard and his voice croaked. "We shall return, and I promise that my men will not molest you–but only provided that you share the stores and the gold immediately and without deception, but in good faith. And we shall sleep by ourselves and keep all our arms. And my men, at least these three, shall remain under my command, not yours nor that of any Vaw. And we shall eat in common from the same bowls–after the food has been well-mixed–just so no…'misunderstandings' or 'unfortunate accidents' occur."

The Vaw nodded and flexed his massive chest. His skin had deepened in the suns to a rich shade of dusk, a paler streak visible at the line of his loincloth. "A wise choice, my lovely. We shall be comrades again–and friends."

He turned and waved to his companions in the grove. Although Isav had expected them to emerge upon the concluding of their treaty, they did not, but withdrew deeper into the wood. Isav hesitated, but the decision had been made and after a moment he and the three Vens moved in a body toward the trees led by Stalkin, who was in truth unarmed just as he had said. The Vaw walked with his back to Isav and within easy reach of the militia captain's weapon–one thrust and the mutineers would lose their strongest and most voluble member. Perhaps what he said was true.

The gathering dusk rendered the interior of the grove impervious to their gaze. Though the palms were bereft of branches along their trunks, fronds and brush interceded between them, leaving open only a few paths to the center of the oasis free of entangling greenery, the brush obscuring not only the remainder of the grove but most of the isle beyond it, including the wide stretch of beach along its southern shore. Arriving at the center of the oasis, the four Vens saw that the fire had not gone out but had burned low, the remains of its brighter life circumscribing it in the form of a bed of soft grey ash. Several men stood around the fire as well and as Isav stared he grew more uneasy. Unclear at first as to the reason, he gazed casually about, and, as he often did when distrustful of his company, began to count those present and their weapons. Then he realized: he saw no Vens but his own. The five Ven-sa who had sided with Stalkin in the dispute over the gold were missing.

Isav turned to the Vaw.

"The gold," offered Stalkin. "I can see it is on your mind! Fear not, it lies just beyond the grove beneath the hang of the palms spread upon a patch of canvas from the boat. We could not leave it on yonder side where a sally from you and your men could steal it, could we?"

Passing through the oasis, they came to the trinkets. Even as Stalkin had said, the gold was outspread upon the canvas, the metal bright and sparkling in the suns. Gathered in a semicircle about the trinkets and plates were the five Vens whose absence had alarmed Isav, sitting in cloaks and tunics upon a magenta and crimson canvas, their backs to the grove as if guarding the treasure. Isav breathed more easily.

"You see, dear Isav? Your men are doing double duty: watching the coast for enemies at the same time that they prevent the malkops from swooping down and making off with our gold. How generous they are with their time!"

The Vaw laughed over the forms of the Vens, his arms akimbo with arrogance, his laugh too loud, his face too expressive. At the base of Isav's spine, the distrust became a chill and began to crawl upwards by inches. His eyes settled upon the five forms before him and widened. That which he had thought was a canvas from the Grest was in reality a wide pool of blood, the hot sand imbued with the substance. Stepping forward, and meeting no resistance from the Vaws, who eyed him with the casual assurance of predators eyeing rum-na, Isav perceived that each of his erstwhile comrades bore gashes across the throat as if five blades had struck at once, their clothing drenched a shade darker than the crimson sand. From the shelter of the rocks they had heard nothing–there had been no time for them to scream.

Isav trembled. He still held his sword, as did the other three Vens, and he gazed at the Vaws. Why commit such a deed? Stalkin had done nought but even the odds between them–then Isav's gaze was drawn to the beach and he wondered why he had failed to notice the change–not one, but four galleys lay upon it. He stepped forward. Paused. A body of men ran towards the grove, kicking up white puffs of sand. Blades flashed in their hands.

Stalkin smiled with sensuous triumph. "Give in to me now, my lovelies, and perhaps my Master will let you live. But I warn you not to anger him–he is tired from his voyage and has lost the last of his patience. Watch your tongue and do not become greedy as did these and perhaps you will yet survive your journey."

With that Stalkin backed away. Isav was still puzzled and made ready to dive into the trees, when Macius appeared beside Stalkin.

"You bloody dog!" erupted Isav. "You and your slaves have murdered us all! Of twenty brave and hardy men, only we four remain. A pathetic remnant! And for what? Trinkets!" He raised his sword. "I swear before Vensor that however long it takes I will have my revenge on you for this deed–and for all the evil deeds you have performed in your bloody trek across the seas. Look well upon this scene, Macius! For eventually it will be your undoing!"

Macius stood calmly and said nothing, the inscrutable as intrinsic to him as his roving eyes, which clacked and moved like those of a wooden puppet. No muscle upon his face reacted to the Ven's tirade, but he looked to the grove, where, with a crackling of twigs, another body of men emerged from the palms, numbering as many as those who approached across the sand. Bearing an assortment of iron and irsrem swords, with glass plates of armor and gnarled clubs they advanced into the fading rays of the suns until they came between Isav and the gold. Their ranks parted and a squat bulk came into view, sliding like a monolith in the sand.

Stalkin lowered his head with deference. The smithy's voice grew quiet and respectful. "Master, your plan worked without a flaw. All the Vens but these are dead. And the Turlicum's treasure, only a small part of which you see before you now, is ours."

Moving his bulk with unseemly ease, the newcomer halted his gait beside the five slaughtered Ven-sa. One massive hand, equipped with digits more like tongs than fingers, took hold of the head of one of the dead Vens and twisted. With a horrid crack the bone snapped. The corpse fell on its side. The bullet head rose to view its remaining prey through glassy blue-green orbs, thick lips rippling with a welling up of humor, and a voluminous mouth wider than any Isav had seen parted to emit a low mocking laugh, plangent in the huge barreled chest. Inspector of the wharves of the fecund city of Vaw, third-degree initiate of the cult of the living Kot, slave of the Golden Cyclops and the eternal whirling sceptre, Fish raised high his hands and two score of ruffians closed about the Vens. To his right the sinking suns, now merged into a single glory as they blazed and flamed about the crystalline rim of Heaven, shot forth a rainbow tongue and lit his ichtheous features as it might a savage totem, snouts and fangs implicit in every turn and glance. Isav let fall his arm. His sword slipped dumbly from his grasp.

CHAPTER 9

DIVINE COMMUNION

Ust of the Calomar, King of Ven, inhaled the warm air of early summer. The spire at the center of the Temple, stabbing skyward like a warrior's pike, grew silent and the echoes of its recent reverberation traveled among the insulae of the city to wash over the richly adorned figure of its king. For a moment, silence reigned. Then, while stragglers emerged from the city to join the citizenry gathered before the Temple, the irsrem gate that walled off the citadel from Ven squealed. It began to open. Ust gazed from atop a reven; the creature was attired in as fine and regal a manner as he. The King had gone to great effort to increase the dignity attaching to the royal office. All, both the skeptical and the reverent, must know who ruled in Ven.

Beside him stood Sendas and Dos. They were flanked by Revtal and Simlet. His supporters and advisors were on foot. None of the customary palanquins were present, nor other reven-na—only the king now rode. Behind him Tumlefler and Spandicum warriors listened and watched the crowd, and a core of Calomar, down-curved fangs of ros-na framing the face of each—another innovation that had had the desired effect upon the gullible masses, who were suitably impressed at the ability of any who could slaughter the fearsome beasts.

As the portcullis cranked aloft, Ust scrutinized the subjects—*his* subjects. The royal eye paused briefly on a section of Temple that contained a hidden entrance. Then hastily moved on. None must learn The Secret. A line of soldiers held the crowd back from the smaller gathering of nobles. Once the gate was raised, the latter would get first pick of the charges within, as dictated by long centuries of custom. For a moment Ust desired to lead them, but his eye came to the magistrate who held the rattan cane, Toosel of the Tooselwat, sporting the list of aristocratic houses. He directed his glance elsewhere. Some things not even a king could change. Ust puckered his thin white lips. In time...

His reven grew restless and leaped, executing a shallow curvet. It hissed with impatience and the tongue darted out, conveying the movement down its long neck and streamlined body to terminate with a ripple in its tail. Ust stroked the smooth grey neck. It rumbled with pleasure through the muzzle. The creature, more at home in water than on land, craved moisture. He leaned and spat on one gill and the beast gurgled, then grew quiet.

Across the plaza near the Avenue of Zeyd overlooking the Temple, rose the platform of the eremites, a high landing accessed by stairs from a long peninsula leading to the Eunuch Guild, on which the martyrs attained union with the divine while staring into the suns. As had Soorkrul, the Lord of the Guild, from his own special seat upon the landing–until the siege of Nesos. Ust watched several dark-clothed eunuchs climb the stair to the platform and begin their grisly rite without their master. Ust nodded with satisfaction. The reclusive monk had not been seen for months. He could proceed as planned.

The portcullis ceased moving and Toosel signaled for the ceremony to begin. Inside the Temple, laid bare by the gate, was the courtyard of the infants, each child crying upon an ancient and eroded altar. One by one the magistrate recited the names of the aristocratic houses, and one by one the nobility entered to claim their tribal heirs, followed by the common folk, unclaimed infants being packed off for servitude within the orphanage. Divesting themselves of their arms, the crowd proceeded to the room of idols where the usual assortment of gifts and foods were deposited. Ust, accompanied by Toosel and Nilsit–and also by Simlet who kept one hand in his jerkin which led others to suspect that he had not quite divested himself of all his weapons–mounted the fragile arch to the mouth of the statue of Vensor.

Came the voice: "Vensor wishes divine communion with a mortal of the city. You will bring him to the postern and return for him in seven days... And the Creator commands: more food!" Descending, the nobles remanded to the Assembly to discuss the best method of fulfilling Heaven's instructions.

"Tradition is clear," began Toosel in the soft glow of the Assembly Hall. "At the behest of the Eunuch Guild, which governs our acts in matters such as these, upon the date the fourteenth of Murfenmas in the thirtieth century–being the most recent occasion that Vensor's Temple requested Communion with a mortal–it was established that such one is to be chosen by lot from among the nobles of the city, and that this noble is then to be delivered by his peers to the postern. After the passing of the stated period of time and his release from Vensor's house, he is to be bound and gagged without having spoken and escorted by military garrison to the limits of the city's territory where he will be released and permanently exiled lest he reveal the holy secrets and contaminate our town, thus risking the withdrawal of Vensor's grace from His children." Toosel hooked his fingers in his jeweled Assemblyman's vest. "Since this is clearly the proper course for us to follow in the present instance, I hereby motion—"

"One moment, Sir Toosel," interrupted Ust. Toosel ceased speaking and the king leaned back in his hard glass throne and crossed one leg over the other, his hands on the hyaloid arms. "I wish to ask of you something before we conclude this matter, which seems to me indeed to be shot with haste."

The Assembly looked to their lord. A few smirked expecting a repetition of his previous demarche.

"Kind sirs. My dear subjects," the royal lips curled with relish at the feel of the latter phrase, "I would like to submit to you a question—an interrogation—concerning the fitness of this method which you say has been hallowed by tradition." His tongue pushed out one cheek toward his advisor Dos, who momently believed he was being summoned by some obscure code, but halted when a reproving glare was flashed.

Toosel played games with his brows. "My king, I do not understand. Tradition dictates that the matter is settled, determined."

"It is not settled nor is it determined, Toosel," sneered the ruler of the three valleys, "and it shall not be until your king, who has been placed upon this throne and over you by God Himself, declares it so." Ust paused and stared into space with a smile as if contemplating some exquisite pleasure not shared by the others. "It seems to me, dear Toosel, that the method by which we select this lucky—I mean this unfortunate—soul who shall be forced to spend a week in the arms of the deity is not something that Vensor has ever concerned himself with. As I recall, the method that we are to use was not discussed by the oracle. Am I not correct in this?" He turned an open countenance upon the nobles.

"True, O King," ventured Toosel. "It was not specified, but was left to us to determine. And to the Eunuch Guild, which speaks for the Assembly in such matters."

"Which is just my point, Tooselwat." Ust raised his chin and peered down upon the noble. "The Guild does not speak for the Assembly. The Guild does not speak for me."

The nobles exchanged glances. What could Ust be getting at? What provocation would they next have to endure from the boor upon the throne?

"In fact," continued Ust, "insofar as I can tell, the Guild does not speak at all at the moment, and has not for some time. As our former king has vanished, so has the soul of our religion. And as I have been appointed as a steward to the throne–at least until we may establish the facts of what happened to the Turlicum–so it is only logical that until we establish what has befallen Guildmaster Soorkrul, I should assume the...um, stewardship of the Guild as well." Gasps rose from the ranks of the nobility. "At least as far as deciding matters such as the method of choosing the candidate for Communion with the Divine."

The Assembly calmed and Toosel looked to Mosum and Nilsit for an explanation. None was forthcoming. They did not know how to regard the Lord of the Guild in the first place, a mysterious entity whose face and features were as unknown to the rest of Ven as the topography of the poles. All that any had ever seen of him was his black-clothed figure as it stood upon the landing of the platform of the eremites, gazing with unrestrained joy into the searing orbs of God. He seemed as remote and terrifying as Vensor Himself. His domination of questions of ritual and worship, established by long tradition, was virtual complete, though the Guild itself, despite, or perhaps because of, its monopoly of essence of irsrem, was forbidden to meddle in politics. The Guildmaster's monopoly on the training and provision of eunuch-consorts to the rest of the city, however, left open one avenue that more than a few nobles believed had not been ignored.

"Given that we have heard nothing from the Guild for these many months since the desecration of the city by the Neset-sa, and given that we now have an urgent matter placed before us by God to consider, and since this Assembly has made no formal ruling on the authority of the Guild to officiate in this matter, I hereby move that the Assembly take it upon itself to implement the Temple's instructions, without reference to the Guild."

Still unaware in which direction this would lead, a number of Assemblymen nodded agreement. There was no denying the importance of the matter. The Temple could not be put off.

Toosel looked to his colleagues, including Dos, to ascertain their feelings. They shrugged. "Agreed, my king. The Assembly assents to this."

Ust smiled. Finally he no longer followed, but led. Soon he would command.

Toosel continued. "And by what method shall we choose the unfortunate noble whom the city shall afterwards exile?" Toosel did not wait for a reply. "We may choose among ourselves by lot, as before. Or we may conduct a tournament should we wish to select the bravest; or we may release a captive from the mines should we desire the most base. If by lot, a mean commoner may be chosen. This would be unworthy of our city. If by tournament the city would lose its best warrior. If–"

"By my command he shall not be challenged or exiled," said Ust, "and we need not debate the method." Foreheads wrinkled throughout the Assembly. "I myself shall do the deed. And I shall return to the throne when it is done." Every eye in the Hall turned his way, shock transforming their expressions. "And I make this sacrifice out of my deep love for Ven and my selfless devotion to Vensor and His children. And we shall then hear the oracle and shall obey its commands in all that it says concerning the throne and Ven and each person in this chamber, who all should beware lest the eyes of God rest upon him even now."

For once the Assembly was too stunned to reply. With quiet satisfaction and a growing sense of triumph, Ust leaned into his seat and contemplated the confusion he had wrought. No one rose to speak–even Dos stared immobile at his master whom he began to suspect was unpredictable to a point approaching danger for both the throne and for himself. Ust twitched a finger. Toosel, for once cowed, responded and motioned for the next order of business, then sat and placed his chin in his hand. Could the least-respected member of the Assembly in fact enjoy the very ear of God?

The next order of business involved a delegation from the newly reoccupied cities of the Suma, the cities that had defected to Neset in the midst of the recent war. Ven soldiers now sat in their assembly halls or guarded their palaces while they sent hostages and tribute to the Capital. Elders and youths from Toor and Salaman came in, escorted by Ven warriors.

"Increase their taxes!" called Ust in response to the first delegation.

"Redraw their boundaries giving more to Ven," Ust judged in response to the second.

"More hostages. And more youths for my harem," he demanded peremptorily of the third. He then grew bored and permitted Dos to represent him in the seemingly endless stream of petitioners and pleadings while he toyed with the tippets of his sleeves.

At length the delegations ceased and a minor functionary of one of the more obscure municipal departments rose to discuss some minor matters:

first, an extension of the system of aqueducts beyond the city walls to insulae previously ignored; second, a complaint from the scribal guild that a newcomer was practicing without the guild's approval and so what if he was clever and wrote better than the licensed scribes and had paid his dues it could not be allowed because he was a foreigner and the guild chief had not approved him.

The monotonous droning dragged on through much of the afternoon, and its end was still not in sight, when Ust became aware of a figure standing within the exit between the benches in a place where he could have sworn an Assembly guard had stood. The figure was not attired like a guard but was clothed in a clumsy dark cassock which hid all skin but face and hands. The head was shaved. The hands pale.

The figure moved. Slowly it walked into view of the entire chamber ignoring the Simet who currently spoke, prattling on even after the rest of the nobles had diverted their attention to the intruder. Ust tensed. No eunuchs were allowed within the Assembly except as consorts of Simet-sa, and then only in the company of their betters, with the proviso that they conduct themselves with the humility proper to their station. By chance, today no consorts were present. This eunuch stood tall, and walked with a spring of arrogance. His features were orgulous and haughty. It was plain that he expected the attention of the chamber–and relished it.

"Eunuch! How did you get in? My guards have orders not to permit stragglers to cross these premises." Ust's voice was not as firm as he had wished. Something about the Eunuch Guild and its ways always eluded him, suggesting a potency he could not explain, but feared. Their practices of mutilation were as intimidating to him as they were mysterious. And for that very reason.

The eunuch, of average build and a face assembled from plates with sharp angles halted and stared calmly ahead.

"Have you no sense, man? This body is in session. Get out!" Ust signaled to the gate guards.

The dark messenger bowed briefly, a cold look about him. "My master sends his word–Soorkrul of the Holy Order."

Ust raised his hand, reversing the previous signal, and the Assembly guardsmen paused.

The eunuch continued. "My master sends his word–Soorkrul of the Eunuch Guild, teacher to the enlightened, Maalstrom's guardian of souls. I...am his mouthpiece." The ambassador raised his chin and folded his hands within the sleeves of his cassock. Then he waited as if his statement required an answer, from the throne or from others within the chamber. No one spoke and the minutes passed until Ust began to shift in his chair from discomfort.

"Well," the king finally sneered, "did he tell you to inform us of his word, or have you now said all that you wish to? If so, then you have the king's permission to leave and I would that you do so and cease interrupting the important business of this–"

The voice spat: "Soorkrul has heard. He hears much–he hears all. He has heard of the blasphemy spoken by the Simet Ust of the Calomar from the pale throne of Ven. He has heard of the willful independence of the Simet Ust, of his plan to participate in Divine Communion with Vensor– and has forbidden it. It is sacrilege! My master sends his word: the mortal soul once entwined with godhead is contaminated, polluted; it becomes a source of blasphemy and evil! Soorkrul of the Guild, who even now contemplates the divine from his abode, safeguarding the souls of all that live, even those within this room who are forever ungrateful, has decreed that the banishment be changed to death. Any who loves the deity shall be burned! His body shall be destroyed and scattered in the Hedronmas lest his foul sins endanger the grace under which we live. Any–including Ust of the Calomar." The eunuch's sneer matched the king's.

The eunuch said no more but turned and walked from the chamber to vanish in the corridor leading to the exit.

The king stared as if struck. His lips moved but no sound escaped. Finally a growl erupted. "Arrest him!" Ust leaped to his feet. "Bring him back!" He shook his fists. "I will know who put this impostor to this if I have to torture him for a week!" One red-rimmed eye fell on Toosel. "If this is a plot of you and your cronies, I swear I shall not rest until I have your heads on poles!" His stare was returned with equal hatred and barely disguised defiance, and the many soldiers and warriors who loitered about the hall began to move quietly toward their lords, responding to the subtle signals they showed. Those loyal to the throne directed alarmed looks to Dos. The counsel to the king did nothing, but blinked at the gesticulating form upon the throne.

Ust returned his gaze to the corridor. The guards reappeared alone. They shrugged their shoulders.

Ust slammed the throne arms. "Tumlefler! Spandicum! I wish to see you in my private quarters. At once!" One hand summoned Revtal and Simlet, the other Dos, and Ust stepped from the dais and mounted the stairs to the floor of the Assembly Hall where the other nobles–subjects of the throne in the minds of none–waited warily for their 'king' to gather his men and depart.

Ust stood. Behind the throne, across the entrance to a small anteroom which Ust had recently constructed for quiet breaks between the arduous duties of governance, a curtain moved. As Ust descended the stairs, the portiere was yanked suddenly but quietly aside. A man in red appeared. Swiftly he traversed the steps behind the king. Above Ust, he halted. A dagger flashed.

"Aah!"

Ust twisted. By chance his foot slipped and he fell upon his side so that the descending blade ripped through cloth.

Warriors in ros-na fangs snapped out rapiers. The assassin turned and sought to flee back up the steps to the anteroom, but their pikes caught him and lifted, his blood spraying like rain. He shrieked. They dropped him on the steps.

Dos and Simlet helped Ust to his feet. He trembled. Incredibly, he was unscathed. They stared upon the dying man. The assassin had bushy eyebrows, white with age. He gurgled. "You...would destroy me...without a hearing...without honor..." With a groan, Judge Osis died.

Ust's skin contracted. Eyes shifting, he twirled. Ust clapped for his soldiers, and hurried from the Assembly Hall. He must gain the safety of his palace before the rest of the conspiracy unfolded.

ॐ ೮ ೮ ॐ

CHAPTER 10

THE PILLAR

Flores turned to rejoin Revd–paused. Beside the warrior whose rapier he had taken, lay a selk that had recently died. Its fragile, pale body with wings folded beneath as if in pain lay open to Flores' inspection–a thing rare in itself–excepting only the foxed brown loincloth it wore. Flores nodded. Modest even in death. About its neck clung the remnants of a sack, the tatters soiling a stay that encircled, and a plexus of bruises and lacerations attested to vigorous but futile efforts to dislodge it. Violence had been done elsewhere as well. The left leg ended in a stump, just above the ankle. Its mouth was bloody. Flores recoiled. The selk had severed its own limb. His brow raised. What unkind fate had brought the creature to such an end? The dismembered foot lay beside it, and Flores shuddered. Even the foot had been brought. Such purpose! Such devotion to task! Pity stirred within, and a flicker of admiration, then his gaze wandered to the dark ranks of dead and he again wished to stamp the animal with his boot.

A flicker caught his eye. From the selk's hand, light flashed and Flores bent closer to look, recalling that Vensor's malkops wear no jewelry. He pulled its arm into the glow of the trunk, saw a small circle of glass, and grunted. Such insolence. A malkop should not possess what Vensor-sa have made.

Flores tore it free.

He raised the trinket above him. In the twilight of the pits it shone with a hundred colors, and the noble placed it upon one hand, surprised at how easily it slid across the bones to rest upon his wrist. A perfect fit. He smiled, glanced down, and his anger re-emerged, coalescing, as it had so often in the past, in the image of death he had harbored since a child, a ros taking shape in his mind, its fangs and claws seeking flesh. He stepped from the cul-de-sac.

A knife flashed.

He fell. Looking up, he beheld the comrades of Stalkin, the three Vaw-sa, smirking down upon him. Flores swore—once more he had let his guard down. He glanced at the wound; by chance the blade had passed between his arm and his side inflicting no more than a scratch and he struggled to regain his footing though he knew he could not move fast enough to intercept the blades that must follow. He took a breath...the Veil was parting...

The daggers remained suspended. He grew impatient. Why did they stand as if frozen? Why did they delay? Life was not so precious that he would struggle in his final moment, they must finish the deed; they must grant him an end with honor. He stared; their faces were yellow with fright. Another moment and they had missed their chance—Flores now stood upon the ridge, rapier in hand. Their treachery angered him more than he had supposed it would, and a thirst for revenge seized hold.

To his surprise, two of the Vaw-sa let out a sudden cry. Flinging aside their daggers, they turned and fled. The third seemed riveted. Then he too tore himself loose and clambered away. Flores rubbed his chin and glanced behind him. The cul-de-sac was empty. True, he was a Simet warrior, and yes the blood-lust of Atasan was upon him, but even thieves were brave enough when the odds were on their side. Why had they hesitated? What did they fear so? He looked for his gill and glowered—they had taken it. If he did not recover the device, he could never leave the Island, but would remain in these death-pits forever. Leaving the pit, he advanced toward the steps. It was one thing to seek his life; it was quite another to steal his property. For that, they must pay.

Emerging in the avenue, he looked up and sighted the Vaw-sa collecting upon the stairway to the ramp. They gazed in his direction, gesticulating and jabbering. Stalkin led the way; Macius followed. Contemplating the perfidy of the latter—his murshid—his rage turned to sullen hatred. The thief had indeed meant to murder him, had probably planned to from the start. Flores strode forward. He was outnumbered, but would leave good account of himself. The Vaw-sa turned and climbed the steps. Again they refused combat. Why? Even with his sword, they must surely prevail! He half-climbed and half-walked, making for the steps, halted. A leg red with gore extruded from corpses beside the steps. It was Revd. The ros sprang again to life, and Flores mounted the steps determined to overtake the murderers.

At the entrance to the tunnel he paused, fearing another ambush, but this proved unfounded and Flores plunged into the tunnel. A faint glimmer appeared–Macius' torch. Flores let this guide him and forged ahead. But the Vaw-sa continued to increase the distance between them. They had the advantage of light, while he had not only to feel clumsily for his path, but to guard against sudden ambush. Try as he might, he could not close the gap.

The torch winked out and Flores found himself immersed in blackness. He felt his way forward, more by intuition than by his senses, until finally the ceiling opened up and he realized he was at the second level of caves. He pressed on. A subtle glow grew. The first level opened and his eyes were met by a light that softly permeated the cave. In relief he rushed forward.

Far ahead they reappeared–Revd's killers. They glanced back. Upon seeing him, they talked excitedly, then turned and vanished again. Flores hurried, his lust for vengeance mixed with fear of abandonment on the Isle. The light brightened and his heart leapt; he could now see tracks in the dust. At last he arrived at the crest of the slope that led out to the beach beneath open sky. Sea breezes whirled within and he breathed deep, realizing that clean air, like clean water, has a distinctive smell and taste.

A shriek tore. Sliding to the bottom of the hillside, Flores halted and peered. From the lee of the cavern he saw a stretch of open shore and the small interval of sand that separated the cave from the sea. The suns had just moved from behind the horizon and shone bright and yellow on his face. The beach was empty. He inched forward. A dense flock of malkops was rising in the wind, heading for higher altitudes, while several more hovered over the sand and blocked the aperture.

Retreating back into the cave, Flores passed a grimy hand over his unshorn head and chin and sat. Of the seven only he remained–and he had lost his gill. Like Amina, he too was now marooned on what he had once regarded as the Island of Vensor, but which, as it turned out, was more akin to the abode of Atasan. Macius' luck, it seemed, had finally failed. For himself–and Flores as well.

For a time the Turlicum sat within the lee of the cave and thought, expecting the malkops to swoop suddenly upon him and put him out of his misery. He almost wished they would. Nothing had brought success. He was indeed lost, as lost and as dead as the corpses on the upper level, though his body still took breath. That, however, was mere illusion. His body still moved, but his soul lived now in the realm of the dead–none ever returned from the regions beyond the Veil. Innocent phrases ran through his mind. Love conquers all; hope springs eternal; faith moves mountains. He smirked. Platitudes all! Rather: whom the gods would slay, they first make mad. Now there was a judgment rooted in fact!

He sighed and weighed his rapier. He felt a twinge of energy and his dejection lessened. In truth all was not yet ended–he did still breathe, and he possessed a good sword, and he still possessed several strips of lyart. He was not yet mad. That state may lie in view, but it remained at bay–for now. And his goal lay before him. Somewhere within this edifice was Amina, and Heaven had many sanctuaries from which one might explore the remaining reaches. Macius' admonition to think like a rat returned, and Flores found it apt and reassuring. They were indeed vermin, and like vermin he must take care not to be caught in the open, at least while the suns shone. The fact that the suggestion came from his enemy was of no consequence–he could learn from enemies as well as friends.

Flores stood. His cut had already closed. Consuming several of the lyart strips, his spirits lifted. He might be alone, but on the other hand the others, with their obsession with gold and wealth which required him to constantly watch them and plot to avoid assassination or ambush, had been in truth only a hindrance. Their deaths had freed him. And his queen waited. Unconcerned with what would happen after he found her, or how he might depart the Island without his gill, or how he might rescue Amina, he set out for the ramp as the first step not only in rescuing his consort, but in satisfying his first and more primal need–slaking his thirst.

Eventually the familiar wall of tachylite reemerged. Flores averted his gaze. The surface reflected as well as a mirror but he declined to look. He knew his appearance had become hideous, even more so by the wound. Once he found water he would wash it–along with the rest of his body.

The ramp appeared. He ascended, and sometime later emerged on the second level. He found that here too a faint light seeped in from the distant vents, relieving the darkness just enough to enable him to distinguish the outlines of bones in the cavern's fulsome pits. He found Macius' torch, and placed it with care beside the entrance to the next tunnel, though he did not see how he might light it without Macius' iron and flint. Recalling the stench, he again removed his breechclout and shielded his nostrils. Then entered the tunnel.

A half-hour passed and he halted at the exit. Nothing had changed. His lips rippled. He recalled the gill that had belonged to Revd. The Vaw-sa might have neglected to take it; if so he could secure it for when he was ready to leave... The Turlicum descended the stairs to look again at his chieftain. He pulled aside the bodies that Stalkin had heaped upon his friend, and set his jaw. Both culprit and victim were dead. But no gill. For a time he scoured the area, but gave up. His thirst had grown steadily and again he reflected: in all this land there must be water. Malkops must drink as well as Vensor-sa. He placed his foot on the first step—and heard a flapping of air.

Flores turned. Twenty feet from him a malkop hovered. Engrossed with selecting a spot in which to place a corpse within its grasp, the great wings beat the air with vigor. This was ill luck. Should he flee, the creature would surely see him and alert the others; should he remain, it may discover him, with the same result. He might be lucky and kill it, but to what purpose, here in the pits? He sought the levels above, the regions of light—that was where the object of his passion would be. He must not be found so soon! He inched back, deeper into the umbra.

The air swirled and a second malkop appeared beside the first. Within moments a third had joined and the three flapped closer to where he stood. Flores halted, half in shadow. What chance had he now? He could not kill them all. But should even one escape, it would return with hundreds.

The first malkop turned its head and gazed in Flores' direction. His heart stopped. Its humanoid eyes gazed down upon him, the pupils focusing with purpose and intelligence. It glided closer. The Turlicum gripped his rapier tighter—if it should come in range... To his surprise the creature paused some ten feet from him, and opened its mouth. The lips began to purse and ripple as if speaking in some strange tongue but Flores could hear no noise. Flores made no reply and finally the malkop turned away. With a slapping sound, the creatures released their burdens into a nearby hexagon, and flapped beyond his sight.

The Turlicum let his breath go. The encounter had been close. He sat. Despite the shadows in the pit, the creature must have seen him. Perhaps the coruscating light had provided sufficient camouflage. Perhaps it had made its gestures from habit, or instinct. Or perhaps its eyes were like those of the rum-na of the northern plains and could see nought but movement. Flores had made no sound, nor had he moved. He shook his head—corpses remain still always, but the creatures sight them from the furthest reaches of the sky, even at night. So what had motivated the creature? Why had it not attacked him as Macius had said it must?

Flores relieved his tension by tapping the glass with his fingers and gazed upward at the ramp, and the entrance which flanked it, the entrance that rose to the mysterious upper levels. Perhaps the creatures simply left to retrieve reinforcements before returning to finish him off, and had not wished to alarm him. He frowned and gripped his rapier. Why put off the inevitable? If he must die–and he suspected that he would never leave the Land of Vensor alive–then let it be in battle, attempting to win his goal.

He rose. The minions of Heavenhell would not catch him hiding among the dead like a frightened eunuch. With a jaunty spring he cut the air with his sword, and climbed the stairs that led to the ramp. At the summit he turned. The cave remained empty. Still unsure as to precisely what had happened, he entered the tunnel and climbed.

A longer stretch of time passed than that which had intervened between the several previous levels, and the tunnel had not yet ended. His thirst grew. Soon, he felt, he must satisfy it, or begin to lose his mind. At last, however, the character of the tunnel changed and he supposed he must be nearing its terminus, but he could not be certain for the translucence of the irsrem allowed light to seep gradually upon him until it filled the entire tube with its glow. This, combined with a steadily growing drumming, left him uneasy as he advanced, the sound falling dully on his ears.

The tunnel ceased.

Beneath the lip of the overhang he paused, stunned yet again by the strange caprice of God. Since emerging from the sea, he had believed that he moved beneath a city and that its chambers had loomed overhead, halls and cells and corridors ramified within. But what his eyes now glimpsed was nothing of the sort: instead he stood beneath a lowering sky, watching rain tumble from clouds, their sheets enveloping an array of tall trees. Between the trunks swept streams. A network of torrents rushed away toward some invisible distant sink.

Having grown accustomed to the dark chambers below, the scene took him suddenly aback. Where he had expected desert, he found greenery and grass, an oasis such as one might find in paradise should mortals, and not gods, govern it. Except this garden was more than a mere oasis, being outspread without limit, and lush beyond words. Flores was ready to believe that he had indeed found the abode of Vensor, and placed in abeyance (though he could not quite forget the death-pits) his former desire to murder its Creator.

After a time the rain slowed and he was able to view the land in more detail. How could he have come to the surface of the city? How high must he have climbed to now witness open sky? He had walked far, he knew, but had not suspected that he had mounted to the top of the Island's cloud-riven structure. While he ruminated, the trees multiplied before him in their endless columns, row upon row of white pale trunks marching away in their serried ranks.

The rain died. The streams began to ebb and Flores found that the water had not disturbed the grass that lay between, but had been diverted into a series of spillways or aqueducts, thus preserving the grounds and orchard from the worst of its energy. Flores stepped forward. The trees were not thick, but were spaced about one every sixty feet, each displaying a thick fascicle of branches at its top. The branches, however, were not like those of other trees, but appeared more like tendrils, clean of sessile growths and leaves, and pendulous with fruit. Flores eyed the fruit, and was reminded of his hunger. He glanced at the ground. None of the fruit had fallen–or if had, had been washed away by the rain. At least, however, he could slake his thirst. Crossing a patch of unkempt grass, he entered one of the culverts, and paused. It was empty; all of the rain had been efficiently diverted. He peered about. Could he truly be in a land brimming with food and water, yet continue to starve and thirst?

Behind was the entrance to the tunnel. It stood stark and unsupported amid the trees, partially obscured by the stilted boles. The central shaft had gone. Flores thought of his guide with annoyance. Why had Macius not spoken to him of this? He must have known the region existed. But Flores already knew the answer to his question–he would not have believed Macius. Who would? There was something unreal and artificial about all that he saw. He turned to take in the view. The trees stretched into the distance, grey, tubular, and wet, the low-slung clouds prepared to spill their dark burden again. They reminded him of the ghostly trunks he had seen on the levels below; the resemblance was marked. In sudden recognition, his brows rose–these were they.

The trees upon which he gazed were not merely similar to those below, or of the same species, but were the very same, the trunks having penetrated the entire thickness of glass to emerge here, in the open air, where they could absorb the moisture and atmosphere. He glanced at the trunks and noted that they met the ground without ripple or bulge, plunging straight into the earth like needles, the grass about them no more than a mat of soil and vegetation laid upon the glass to give it the appearance of an orchard. He again nodded. Another piece of the puzzle had fallen into place. What more would Heaven offer? An answer suggested itself and Flores glanced skyward. The broad umbrella of the trees' fascicles obscured his view and he leaped within the aqueduct and set off at a trot.

At its terminus, he halted. Before him, by the edge of the orchard washed a lake dotted with sedge where fish leaped. A row of glass spill-ways lined its shore, the water's remnants inpouring, causing the agile surface to ripple. The clouds were breaking. Within moments they dissipated, and a rainbow glinted, a rainbow that joined horizon to horizon and filled the sky. *Irsrem*. Like rafters in a dome, a vast wall of glass ran from the seashore behind the orchard to an invisible point above, returning to ground level at some reach beyond the far horizon.

A construct.

Or a terrarium. Housing what the minions of Vensor thought valuable–or necessary–the death-pit trees, whose roots sucked life from death. And something else imposed itself on his vision. Flores lowered his gaze and beheld many thousands of meters removed and thousands more in height, a black tower of tachylite, huge, smooth and gleaming in the filtered light of the glass. It rose like the axis of the world, dominating the sky, its surface clean of defect, its dimensions set by gods. A flawless cylinder, it narrowed abruptly at periodic intervals like a ziggurat, every surface either horizontal or vertical, the attenuate upper end joining the lofty glass ceiling in a riot of mist and color. Clouds lingered about the edifice. Other than the intermittent interruptions in its diameter, platforms apparently from which one could view the plain, no features were visible.

To both right and left the orchard led away, but ceased in the direction of the pylon. In the region between orchard and tower stretched not only the lake, but a tongue of land, a wide isthmus–strewn with meadows resplendent with flowers. No footpath was visible. Indeed he would have been surprised had his eyes found a path. He was, after all, in a realm of winged creatures. And, as he realized with a start, Macius had not been wrong after all. The black tower was the shaft that his guide had described, the continuation of the black wall below, which had been but the first stage of many, and only the first and thickest pediment, made necessary by the fact that its component material was mere stone and not the tears of gods. Flores smiled. The ramp, therefore, must continue as well, as Macius had said.

Flores stepped off the spillway and waded into the lake. Its surface was still broken by the flood. He drank his fill, relishing the rush of renewed energy and health. If it was poisoned he could do no better–he must slake his thirst. Though less pure than he would have preferred, the water was not poisoned, and Flores soon felt ready to proceed. He climbed back onto the culvert.

The spillway had widened and deepened as he neared the lake, and, with a little more effort, he climbed out of the large duct, crossed the peninsula of grass, and lowered himself to the floor of the adjoining flume. He must next satisfy his hunger. Perhaps the water had not washed away all the fruit, but permitted some to remain within a duct. He decided to search each culvert and proceeded to climb into the adjoining one. This search required some time and while he climbed he kept one eye on the sky lest the clouds regather and again submerge the channels while he stood within. But the clouds did not gather. And the rain did not fall. And neither did the suns shine through the massive glass above, but their filtered light glowed softly, casting a warm and humid yellow on his face.

At length he emerged from the trees upon the grassy tongue of land. He had found no fallen fruit. The rain had been more efficient in cleansing the orchard than he had supposed. He turned to the water. He would have to catch fish instead. But how? He had no tools, no net, nor hook, nor pole, nor bait–only the single rapier by his side. And his hunger had grown stronger. He approached what appeared to be a small pond, and became suddenly gelid.

Wings.

Flores slowly turned. Above, hovering near the tops of the trees, fluttered a band of malkops. They had not seen him but seemed engrossed with the fruit that grew upon the limbs. Red bulbs with yellow striations hung in their ripeness and the creatures smacked their lips in anticipation. One reached its hand towards a globe. Flores noted the lack of means to store any gathered fruit and wondered how the creature would transport it. Others joined the first, and then the entire group, numbering perhaps fifty creatures in all, settled among the branches. A fierce commotion ensued. Moments later they rose, each clutching one or two branches in its hands, and leaving the tree shorn. Several nibbled their trophies.

So, thought Flores, the malkops ate not only the fruit, but even the stems they grew upon. Their harvest was as efficient as the rain–nothing was wasted. He began to suspect that the fruit was never allowed to litter the ground, but was consumed the moment it ripened. He frowned. Might they deal with their enemies as efficiently? He continued to peer as the selks rose in an updraft, no trace of disagreement or conflict among them, as if each was but a cell in a vaster organization. Was it instinct, or intelligence? Flores shrugged. What did it matter, since the result was the same?

As the malkops gained height, the Turlicum made no move, a picture in his mind of him being torn apart as the tree had been. He waited for them to vanish and hoped he would be missed on the plain below, and indeed it appeared as if they would not see him as they glided in wide circles, preparing to depart. Suddenly one separated from the band and plunged. Without warning it fell toward Flores.

He caught his breath. In his mind he had reviewed how he would respond when faced with the consequence of his deed, of his intrusion into the sacred realm of Heavenhell. He had no doubt that Vensor would eventually extract His vengeance, and that this vengeance would be mortal. Now it had come; here, on this open plain, at the hands of a band of malkops. He could neither hide nor flee. The orchard was too far; the lake too vast. No–he would have to fight. He gripped his rapier more tightly and again prepared to spear the creature the moment it came within range. The selks would find an armed Simet warrior more difficult to dismember than a plant.

To his surprise, however, the selk did not attack, nor did it hover agitatedly above him, as had the previous one, but landed upright no more than ten feet away. The creature stepped forward and smiled. Flores inspected its pale form, rarely visible to Vensor-sa except at a distance. Its voluptuous hips curved. Its lips puckered as if desiring to kiss. Disloyal to his will, Flores' feet moved closer. With a supreme effort he halted. He swallowed, absorbed, despite his knowledge of the danger of the encounter, by the creature's notorious beauty: the flowing blond hair, the strong and well-formed legs, the trim narrow waist, and inevitably, though his soul still fought valiantly to resist further corruption by the agents of Atasan, by the nipple-crowned breasts that thrust primly forward. Its pale skin glistened with water that had fallen from the fruit-laden branches in its grasp. Droplets clung to one cheek.

For the nonce Flores forgot where he was, forgot who he was, so whelmed was he by the situation. Never in all the long chronicles of Maalstrom had a mortal encountered a denizen of Heaven so closely as he did now. It occurred to him that perhaps such meetings had occurred many times before but with the unlucky protagonist not having survived to tell of it. He knew he would not.

His ruminations were interrupted as the creature twisted its lips. Like the malkop he had seen on the level below, this one too began to form and shape its mouth in imitation of speech, while smiling and staring. There was no mistaking whom he meant; they were alone in the field; it saw him, and no other. One branch was lifted and paused in air, as if the creature offered a meal. His brows rose. He said nothing, and the creature cocked its head. As if something were the matter, it peered at his arms, and pointed. Again it jabbered in eerie silence. Finally, it glanced at its companions, who still circled above. Flores had not accepted the branch. Turning, it cast it at Flores' feet, and sprang skyward. With a rush of air, it rejoined its mates and the band resumed its flight, vanishing at length in the vicinity of the black pillar and its surrounding mist.

Flores inwardly crumpled. Again he had been convinced that his last moment had come, and again the creatures had allowed him to live. Why? Could Macius have been wrong about the selks, while right about the geography of Heaven? Could the selks in truth be well-disposed to violators of their privacy, and hospitable to strangers such as he? Then why had Macius insisted on remaining hidden? Did they turn violent only in the event of burglary? Why indeed did the creatures live on the Island? And what use did they have for treasure when they let it rot and sink among corpses of the dead? Moreover, if they did resent the intrusion of thieves, how might they respond to the seizure of Amina, their captive?

He shrugged. There seemed no possible explanation. However, at least they had not molested him, and seemed not to care whether he proceeded. They had even provided him with food. Flores raised the branch and tasted it. It was sweet and not at all unappetizing. Before he realized it, he found that he had consumed the entire branch. His fatigue evaporated and he felt renewed. Again he turned to the lake to quench his thirst. He bent over the now calm water of the pond–he leaped.

He spun, sword cutting air. Then paused. Where was the creature he had just glimpsed about to attack him from behind? He blinked in confusion. He was alone. Perplexed, he returned to the water, and peered. There, on the calm surface floated the head of a malkop–the very creature, if he was not mistaken, that had confronted him but a few moments before. He stared in shock. In the mirrored water of the lake, the brown eyes of the selk peered deep into his own, its brows furrowed similarly in thought. No other face was present. Flores stepped back and inspected limbs, rapier, torso–all appeared as it should. He then lay flat upon the shore and exposed his upper body, taking care not to disturb the surface. He saw only a winged worker of the sky in every detail. His eyes beheld, clearly visible, the breasts with teats, the monstrous wings with leather pinions, and, edging further over the water, the strong firm legs, and dirty brown loincloth. His mouth opened–*its* mouth opened. He blinked–*it* blinked. He smiled–*it* smiled. He rose, stepped back, and took a breath. What manner of mischief was this? What arcane magic or sorcery afflicted the pond? He moved to another lagoon. The malkop followed.

He tried a third; no difference.

He sat and thought. Had he indeed died in the pits only to be reborn in the shape of a malkop? What power could render him such? He raised one hand to view himself again, and his eyes settled on his wrist.

An idea flashed.

He returned to the edge of the lake. While gazing into the water, he slowly removed the bracelet. In an instant the malkop vanished and he gazed upon an unkempt adventurer, whose eyes leered from an unwashed and bearded face. Yesss. He looked now upon his true self. Replacing the bracelet, he saw the malkop return, the change too swift for words. He breathed deep. All became clear: the fleeing Vaw-sa; the malkop in the pit; the selk he had just encountered. Each had believed he was one of the winged creatures–or perhaps something else. It was the bracelet deluded them! The words of Macius rushed back: 'Rats–think like rats!' and Flores laughed. Not rats, but selks! He glanced down and found that the image had warped. Slowly it melted and began to refocus, then a new image snapped into place. A rat. Flores caught his breath. His mind went blank and he thought of himself, and the image disappeared to be replaced once again by his own. He recalled the encounter with the selk. In an instant its image came back into focus.

For a time he remained thus, bent over the edge of the pool. The shadows lengthened. The duskline swept the dome, plunging first the tower then the vast lake into dusk. As darkness swiftly gathered at the end of this most eventful day, more malkops appeared from behind the orchard, where Flores surmised a wide vent pierced the glass, and their bodies hurtled pillarward, climbing swiftly. Flores kept the bracelet on till they had gone, and sought shelter beneath the trees.

Night came.

Upon the meadow Flores lay, contemplating the vast dome overhead. The temperature had dropped several degrees, but no more so than to make him more comfortable. Truly, he was in Heaven. And in Hell. And truly, as Macius had said, the life of a child of Vensor was not over till the gods had had their jest. What fate had brought him to this land of gods and devils? What fate remained? Was his destiny written in the stars before ever he was born? Or was it possible for one to overturn one's fate, to challenge the gods in their stronghold, make them justify their deeds, their cruel manipulation of men? He wondered. Can a mortal in the end best the gods? Something deep within said yes, to keep faith, that his lover, the enigma of Atasan, priestess of the brooding Temple of Ven, lay somewhere before him, gazing perhaps at that moment upon the same stars as he, with similar thoughts of her lost paramour. With luck, and daring, and a trickster's device, he would find his queen before he breathed his last. Vensor himself could not stop him.

He sighed. The Maalstrom sky was flush with white stars. But, here, beneath the dome of God, their orbs winked in a hundred colors and the rushing moons were muted. Their shadows moved as behind thick veils, as if Heaven wished to hide the secrets of its rule. A moist breeze moved his hair. On the horizon a column of shadow was silhouetted. What would he find in the morning? To what strange terminus did the black tower lead, suspended as it was among the clouds? Did the obscurity of Heaven perhaps hide some weakness that would open itself to the bold? Tomorrow. His mind afire with fancy, he closed his eyes and slept.

Flores awoke to a hissing and for a moment he believed he was again within the adit that led to the selks' terrarium, rain beating upon it. He rose to his feet. The cool air of early morning revealed a sky clear of clouds. He stood upon a peninsula of grass between palm-trunks, while below, the lake rippled with fish. From its edge the meadow ran along the isthmus into the distance in the direction of the black tower and a bright smudge on the horizon signaled the location of the suns, still veiled by the irsrem dome. He could see no cause for the hissing, which ebbed and flowed. At length he shrugged and turned his attention to more important matters.

He was hungry. The trees remained inaccessible, their fruit unattainable. He recalled the fish and waded into the shallows, and, despite his lack of tools, and to his own surprise, soon caught one on the blade of his rapier. Though raw, he consumed it with relish—he did not wish to draw attention to himself by lighting a fire and thus displaying a talent no malkop possessed. A draught of water followed. Splashing more upon his face, he paused to practice the bracelet's magic again using the surface of the pond as a mirror. Several moments sufficed to fix the image he desired; that of the malkop which had given him the branch.

He stood. Taking up the sword, he cut the air; then placed it in his belt. The bracelet would be his main weapon. As Macius had said: deceit and surprise and the divine favor of Gethos. With amusement he thought of the thief's obsession with the god of luck. Flores preferred to rely on more tangible tools—his sword and the quickness of his arm. Still, the bauble would be useful. It had saved his life more than once already.

Finally he was prepared. With a glance overhead in the direction of the domewall, which determined that no malkop was aloft, he set boldly forth. He felt vigorous...confident even, and thought of Macius' boasting of his exploits when they had first met. He would not be bested so easily. He too was capable of bearding Vensor in his lair! Almost at once, however, a sprinkle of dots shot forth, much too low to evade, and Flores retreated to the grove, fearing a repetition of the previous day's encounter. But the dots did not pause, but passed over, and climbed at great speed. Again they vanished in the direction of the tower. A sudden thought caused Flores to frown. Macius had apparently not come this far. What if he was wrong and the ramp ended at this level, giving no access to the upper levels of the tower except by wing? What use, after all, did selks have for ramps? If the black surface proved impossible to climb, how could he reach the upper reaches? And if he could not go forward, how long would he last in this land with nothing but an oasis for shelter? He chewed his lower lip. There was but one way to find out. When the malkops had gone and the sky again cleared, Flores set out.

Although the meadows on the isthmus were thick with yellow-flowered altheas, Flores made good time. A gentle breeze fluttered the slender green leaves and the flowers sagged their bell-lobes at waist level so that his thighs were soon smeared with pollen. For hours he strode forward, ever toward the black pillar that gradually grew before him. No hills or variation appeared to hinder his progress, and the flowers themselves were almost uniform in their height and distribution. At length he could no longer see the lake, and his mind began to imagine that he had entered a similar inland sea, this one yellow, as the cool breeze rippled its surface in waves. Once he again heard the hissing which had earlier attracted his attention. Again it receded and vanished, while the rippling of the meadow continued, hence was not made by the wind.

Mid-afternoon came, and the black pillar began to take on more definite shape. It remained a ziggurat, but its size had increased beyond all imagining, and not merely due to the lack of any neighboring structure. Indeed Flores realized that he had seen no other structures of any kind since entering the terrarium. The upper reaches were invisible. Not only were they swathed in cloud, but from distance the pinnacle seemed to merge with the sky, enveloped as it was by the irsrem dome.

Flores paused to smack at his leg. Before the blow landed, he halted. A leroo. A hornet of the most ancient variety, old before the first Zeyd took Maalstrom from the giants of the Urlis, moved along one thigh, the green stiff-winged creature swinging its hungry insect eyes over the clinging yellow dust. A rush of adrenaline washed over Flores. He suppressed it and grew still. A single sting from the animal brought much pain; the stings of many, death. Flores slipped into the meditative mood he employed when he probed their spherical nests. On those occasions he would place his hands on either side and the emotion-charged glass would induce them to trance, with the result that he had only once been stung. But now he was in the open, with no glass to manipulate, and no assistance should the creature attack.

A proboscis flicked. Flores tensed, then slowly relaxed. It lapped again. Flores smiled—the most sensual pleasure flowed through him. The proboscis licked a third time and Flores desired more. How long had he observed leroo-sa, how long had he probed their nest which sat within his study, taking precautions against their aggression, without guessing that they possessed such a talent! He raised his brows; best not to reveal his discovery to others—the cult might catch on among the more jaded Simet-sa with incalculable results for Ven. None other need know his secret...a second insect landed and Flores looked beyond it at the flowers. The hissing returned and turned into a buzzing. A torrent of insects approached.

This would not do. Despite the pleasure of their grooming, Flores realized they were applying a soporific substance. Who knew if the effect would last? A drug administered by a thousand such probosces might prove as fatal as their stings. At the same time, however, he was aware of the danger should he thwart their desire and they release their anger en masse. The buzzing swelled. Somehow, he thought with growing desperation, he must ignore the effect and push on. Flores glanced beyond the meadow to the tower. Most of the distance had been crossed and the rim of the base loomed no more than five hundred meters ahead. Between him and the black wall the flowers gradually thinned until at the foot of its cliff-like face they died altogether leaving only thin grass on the ground. He staggered. His limbs were growing numb. He must make the open patch or succumb to the desire to lie amid the flowers and sleep. From such sleep he knew he would never wake.

The desire grew stronger with each step. His legs, thick with life, dragged one before the other in torment. His mind pleaded for rest—yet paradoxically at the same time for more attention from his tormentors. One part of his mind began to plead with the rest to slow or pause just for a moment to catch his breath and why push forward anyway since he was doomed no matter what and this meadow was as good a place to die as any. Flores pinched himself, careful not to harm any leroo-sa, and staggered on. He stumbled and an angry buzzing sounded. He caught his balance, and pushed forward.

How much time finally passed Flores did not know, but the flowers finally ended, and at last he lurched into the grass-lawned clearing at the
base of the darkened tower. Through the haze he noticed that the insects
had gone, though whether this was due to the fact that they preferred the
flowers to his skin, or the fact that they had removed the last of the
pollen, he could not tell. At the foot of the cliff he fell to his knees. He
collapsed in the grass and slept.

His sleep was long and dreamless and he awoke suddenly, refreshed,
but with a feeling that eyes were upon him. Jerking himself up, he
looked. The sky was still clear, and Flores breathed in relief, though he
was careful to keep the image of the malkop fixed firmly in his mind
lest he be observed without his knowledge. The suns had dived low while
he slept, and now, obscured by the eternal glass, were perched low on
the horizon, though dimmer than he thought they should be, in comparison to the brightness of the morning. No shadow was cast by the cliff.
The darkness instead gathered slowly, as if unseen fires emitted smoke
in secret.

He stood. The numbness had vanished. His fear, it seemed, had exaggerated the danger, and Flores resolved not to weaken so easily in the
future. Still, he had to admit, the experience had been both menacing
and euphoric, and he realized that he had lost sight of the difference, the
pleasure overlaying the pain so that the two seemed to merge, one en-
twining with the other. Much as had occurred in a similar episode, he
reflected. A core of joy from his encounter with Amina shone always
through pain, and he shut his eyes to embrace it. Nothing would halt his
pursuit. The pleasure-pain of his relationship with Amina would again
be his.

He sighed.

Turning, he glanced at the cliff-face—and halted as if struck. A phalanx
of eyes stared. To the limit of his vision, figures twined and twisted,
sculpture writhing on its surface in a visual cacophony of glass. The face
of the tower was a dark forest, with no spaces visible among the works,
which feature led the eye ever deeper into its tangles until the wall itself
seemed to vanish, as if the rock had sprouted black ivy, its loops and
stitches reproducing itself in a jungle of translucent life. In wonder he
stretched out a hand. The glass was slick, and unexpectedly warm. His
eye could not make out what he felt, but, moving back from the tower,
Flores realized that he gazed upon representations of living creatures,
carved—or polished—with infinite care and ability from the living volcanic
stone.

The most of what fell within his purview were versions of the land's denizens, malkops of the Sun-God. But the array did not stop with them. There were also figures of other life-forms of Maalstrom, including rumna, reven-na, and ros-na, birds and insects, and other species he could not identify, but carved on arbitrary scales, as if the mind that had conceived the stupendous project–stupendous for, as he realized while gazing overhead, the entire tower was covered, indeed seemed entirely composed, of the rambling ebony carvings–had been afflicted with a sense of disproportion that bordered on madness, blowing the insignificant absurdly huge, or shrinking the sizable to nothing. Yet, as he progressed, and encountered the beginning of a wide flat ramp of smooth tachylite and mounted the ramp upward, he began to realize that what he saw was not random, yet neither was it planned, but rather was a continuous celebration–or dirge, he thought–of life, without plot or structure, experience alone guiding the seeker. Each event in the life of a malkop was captured in the glistening glass. A peculiar medium, he thought, since the selks were pale and white. What master had directed the effort? What motive had led to this medium, which recast the race in such darkness? What meaning, if any, lay beneath it? Flores shook his head as he climbed–he had not guessed that the fumbling creatures, whom he had believed driven by mere instinct, were capable of such deft artistry. Or were they? He shrugged. Perhaps the answer lay ahead.

As he climbed the ramp's slow spiral, the figures took on more substance, or his eyes learned to distinguish them better. A frequent character was a vast bloated thing with arms so small that it could not feed itself, relying instead on nursemaids to assist. This was always in the act of expelling seeds or lozenges. Flores frowned at the feminine reproduction, which marked it as Atasan's own, though his memory of Vensa, the Queen of Ven, left him uneasy and bereft of explanation. Another frequent actor was a stiff-winged insect that flew ever-present above. It too was blown hugely out of proportion so that it often dominated the panels. This, too, he had glimpsed in Vensa's Temple. Most of the representations, however, were of Vensor's winged malkops, flying hither and yon through the sky, returning with corpses for the pits, or carrying large lozenges and sundry items through the air, or walking through halls and chambers of artificial geometric construction.

At times these were engaged in other, less familiar, activities, which Flores found both more disturbing and less comprehensible. In some panels the winged creatures converged to tear open a lozenge. In others they taught smaller versions of themselves to fly. In still others–Flores hesitated and wondered at the wisdom of his boldness–individual selks were pulled savagely apart by their comrades, and the fragments taken to the pits. More panels depicted selks devouring trees. And others showed them lifting their breechclouts amid strange scenery and coupling with things whose trunks were rooted in the ground. The blasphemy and outrage of Vensor's own engaging in the act of Atasan, and the shock at his discovery that the signs of Atasan were not limited to their breasts, caused Flores to turn his gaze aside. Additional panels of the destruction of selks at the hands of mysterious predators left Flores ill from the detail of the work: the open spewing mouths, the silent screams of horror. At least they were mortal, he reflected. The denizens of Heavenhell could die.

Flores fingered his sword-handle, and strode on. Not all of the panels were recognizable. Those that portrayed a sphere above a pit remained a mystery. As did others that portrayed selks and insects slipping inside darkened windows to commit vile acts on sleeping Vensor-sa. What people were these, he wondered, who lived amid great wealth, strangely clothed, and with gila-sa? Only once did he encounter script–it was the universal script of Vensor-sa, but–though its presence here, in the zone of Vensor, was in itself thought-provoking–it was only a single quote from the poetic cycle of the Zeyd, one of the most enigmatic quotes of an enigmatic epic: *fi baitihi ra'allah, tahlimu kthulhuu mautaa.* Perhaps the answer to that lay ahead as well. Birth–life–sex–death. The panels marched without end, portraying millennia of sensual, unspiritual existence. Orgy followed feeding followed lynching like night on day, until he grew jaded with the materialism and the sacrilege.

As Flores climbed he paid less attention to the sculptures, which showed no sign of diminishing, or of altering their tale. Their execution remained exquisite. Indeed the perfection of the work varied not a whit, no defect or mar to be found. Having seen but a fraction of the whole, Flores nevertheless felt confident that the entire tower was no different, but remained as perfect and as flawless as what he had viewed. The time of its creation was inestimable: an hour earlier–or an epoch.

Flores climbed. And, despite the strange–even macabre–air of the darkened panels, with their depravity, lust and violence, Flores' spirits rose. He began to feel that his abandonment on the Island was fortuitous, for through all of the panels he saw no evidence of Vensor-sa in the land of the malkops, and nothing that guaranteed his destruction, and the shadow that moved on the dark ramp before him bore wings, so his confidence steadily rose, and his ill will for the malkops lessened, even extending to the Vaw-sa who had marooned him. So long as he did not attempt to fly, he might move among the selks at will, and was glad he had encountered the tower to warn him of what he might find. He paused by a sculpture of a spiraling ramp. A malkop with a broken wing walked upon it. He breathed in relief. If they constructed ramps for their injured, they should not consign him to the pits when he arrived.

But where did the creatures dwell? No opening led inside the tower, and Flores soon dismissed this possibility since the selks seemed to frequent only its pinnacle. And he knew what lay in the pits. That left only up, the direction in which the injured malkop in the panel traveled.

Flores came to a landing, which gave upon the first level of the ziggurat. An avenue led to the next vertical section, and another curving ramp. In the deepening dusk, Flores rested his eyes on the forest of tangled sculpture. An arctic landscape flanked the avenue, but black as night, and even more realistic than those sculptures rooted in the side of the tower.

Flores turned to view the meadow. The dome's compass had grown, and Flores for a moment forgot that he stood within a construct, the glass interfering little with the downpouring rays, which stirred clouds of steam from the trees and the lake. The lake curved round mile upon mile so at length it formed a moat between the circumscribing bands of meadow and orchard, pierced by many isthmuses. Beyond, the orchard extended in a vast belt. Among the trees shone iridescence. He nodded. The aqueducts, for drainage. More were visible in the distance. The ramp had taken him to the north and west so that the tower now blocked the east but allowed him to view toward the south. On his right the domewall continued, but seemed to meet no counterpart, and Flores wondered what upheld the roof over the more distant regions. He squinted and glimpsed a plateau toward the west and scattered sunlit hills that faded into the horizon. The hairs raised on his neck as he realized that the entire span he had traversed was but a small part of Vensor's own.

Then the selks came. Appearing in the dusk like a locust-swarm, a humming grew as they approached. Flores took care to mask himself, now needing no mirror to aid him, and, though several glanced in his direction, they flew by unconcerned. Near the tower they ascended, wind signaling their passage. Amid the drifting cloud, Flores thought he saw portals; the selks entered and vanished. More appeared in the opposite direction, spilling forth like bats.

Affected, he supposed, by the lingering effects of the hornets' soporific drug, Flores found he could go no further and lay down amid a drone of whirring and clicking. He closed his eyes and slept.

❧ ❦ ❧

CHAPTER 11

HEAVENHELL

Flores awoke with the suns and first mistook the clicking he heard for birds. Then he remembered, and composed his selk-guise before moving beyond the eaves of the sculpture and standing upright in the avenue. The selks flew without ebb. A belt of the creatures now stretched unbroken from the portals to the far horizon. Flocks hovered over the orchard to the east. The suns had not had time to raise any moisture, and the dome was still free of clouds. He was famished. He had not eaten nor drunk since he had left the lake; anyway, the hornets blocked his retreat. He checked his bracelet. Mounting the next ramp, he climbed.

The second section of tower proved no different from the first, his practiced eye passing over panels of the same black glass, the same topics portrayed within them. He looked down and felt giddy. Glancing up only increased the sensation–the tower loomed higher than he had previously supposed, and he was thankful that its designers had made the ramp as wide as they had. Ten feet separated him from the walkway's knife-like edge.

He walked.

Towards afternoon he came to the second landing. He found it, again, no different. An avenue flanked by sculptures led to the next threshold of tachylite. The ramp about the third section wound more tightly than before, though the diameter of the tower remained wide. Soon he had circumvented the tower several times, enabling him to view the dome on all sides. Only toward the southwest did dome and landscape vary, the roof forming an inverted V, stretching into the distance to encompass the far plateaus.

Another night came. The next day Flores found that the diameter of the pillar had shrunk enough that he was able to mount the remaining sections in one supreme effort. Although he had brought another fish, and now consumed it, the lack of water had again begun to scourge him.

At last he stood on the final stretch of tachylite and gazed up in wonder. Overhead was a vast field of white. The slab of irsrem spread outward from the tower in all directions, till, succumbing at last to the pull of the earth, it arched downward to form the vast dome. He was in an inverted bowl, standing upon his head. His eyes focused upon a detail. What he had supposed were portals he now perceived to be enormous tubes that penetrated the edifice. Ahead, at the end of the ramp, one opened onto a darkened cave that led up. Flores noted that the selks had gone, though he could not recall the moment that had occurred. Their whirring and droning still echoed in his ears. The mist had also vanished.

Flores fingered his sword, and plunged in.

The tunnel was a repetition of those within the pits, and Flores soon forgot that he walked level with the clouds, only a refreshing drop in temperature to remind him. His nose twitched as he fancied that he again smelled corpses; but it passed. A glow broke through from above, and without warning he stepped into sunlight. To his left the tower continued up; now devoid of sculpture and ramp, the dark mass running perhaps two hundred vertical feet before piercing the next level of irsrem. Tower met roof flush. A rotunda surrounded the tower, uniting three immense corridors. One of these met a far window through which the suns, setting in the west, cast their glare unmuted. Another window was visible to the northeast. The third loomed to the south, a fresh breeze from the latter engulfing him. Toward the end of each thousand-foot hall, the floor–of still more irsrem–was rent by a series of holes. He walked south, and paused by the first of the vents. Far below at the edge of his sight shone a shifting patch of yellow–altheas. His stomach churned with giddiness. The yellow turned suddenly grey, and Flores moved swiftly back.

Bodies streamed forth.

Unconsciously Flores felt for his bracelet as he retreated to the edge of the hall. The chamber, spacious as a basilica, filled with wings. Gradually the malkops settled while he watched in silence. They bore a variety of objects and the creatures separated into groups according to their cargo. Some bore lozenges, red or purple. Some bore branches from the orchard. Still others carried a moss-like substance. And many bore small globes which they handled like putty, and which shined with perpetual wetness. Essence of irsrem, observed Flores. Of course, he nodded–how else could they construct the glass? A series of wide ramps intersected the hall, and the malkops walked onto these and ascended.

Throughout this activity the malkops spoke no word, and Flores decided that the rumors had been correct–malkops were incapable of speech. They were creatures of habit after all. The constant clicking, however, left him uncertain. At any rate, none of the selks seemed to notice him standing by the side of the hall, and he began to think that he would soon again be alone as the last of the creatures left. But before he could continue his exploration, a new clutch flapped into the chamber, with more booty to distribute. And more. As these trickled up the rampways, one, bearing essence in its hands, cocked its head at Flores. It stepped near, wings folded.

This was the test. Should his disguise fail now, or should his surmise turn out to wrong, there would be no escape. He could never descend the length of the tower with the selks in angry pursuit. Certainly not fatigued and thirsty as he was. And he could not hide within their city; the chambers were designed for them. Flores noted the sharp claws that adorned the selk's fingers. Thinking of the damage they could do, he held his gaze, and waited.

The creature paused. Looked him over. One hand reached up and behind his head as if to touch a wing. Flores stepped back in case the illusion did not extend to touch. It lowered its hand and peered into his eyes. Its tongue clicked; Flores raised his brows. Another click brought no further response and the creature gave a little smile and moved to rejoin the others. Those with essence began to mount the ramps.

Flores rejoiced–the illusion was complete! They must indeed regard him as one of their own who had injured a wing and was thus unable to fly. He felt giddy with joy. Then steeled himself. He resolved to turn the situation to his advantage and press on.

Apparently the emptiness of the chamber had been but a temporary condition for now a steady flow of selks emerged from or dove within the tubes. All ignored him, and Flores mustered his courage. He traveled the length of the northern hall and found that its window possessed a balcony that gave forth upon both southeast and west, being, as it happened, at the terminus of the entire Island. Flores smiled. The brazen suns rushed toward the blue sea; the creamy surface rippled in anticipation. It was good to see the world clear of the domewall again. His eyes wandered to the east side of the balcony, and he started. The rocky isle with the Grest was visible. From here it looked not distant, only a few miles intervening. He could see selks above it. To the south of the crag a dense belt was suspended–selks bringing corpses. They entered the pyramid at a point far below where he stood, on the third level he supposed. The one leading to the pits. More malkops patrolled the shore at the base of the dome. From his apex, Flores gazed up at the exterior of the domewall—balconies and courts studded the flanks of the city, so many that little wall was left. They were alive with wings.

The suns winked out and broke his concentration. He had to hurry. If he was to satisfy his needs, he would have to do so quickly, before the suns clothed the dome in blackness; he had seen no sign of artificial lighting and feared the return of night. He winced. He looked down; he had stubbed his toe on a rill in the floor which ran the length of the balcony. A culvert for draining water. Pain rose from his midriff, and he forgot his toe. His hunger had again become urgent. Joining a stream of malkops, he entered the nearest ramp, and climbed.

The ramp led to an orderly layout of corridors and chambers. None was large enough for a malkop to fly. Flores was taken aback. Somehow he had expected the creatures to take wing whenever possible, and to place impediments in their city to block pedestrians. Instead he found he walked about as freely as in his own palace. Indeed the similarities between these creatures and Vensor-sa was notable at times, as when they devoted themselves to their work, or strolled casually once work was done. They smiled as from joy. Or frowned as in disappointment or pain. Aside from the lack of play, or examples of civilized arts, he might almost believe he visited a new city of Vensor-sa. Except their numbers were far too many. The complex teemed with selks, though—luckily for Flores—the corridors were wide and, due to the size of their wings, the selks did not crowd, but allowed sufficient space to avoid brushing against each another. This was useful. He joined the flow, and, to escape undue interest, stayed continually on the move, striving to look as if he were on some urgent task.

He fell in with a band of moss-gatherers which climbed a series of ramps and arrived at a larger chamber. Here younger selks squatted amidst a welter of thread and cloth, weaving breechclouts from the moss with needles of bone. How Vensor-like they seemed, if less sophisticated. Almost human. But a little more muscle—and less breast—and they could physically pass for boys. But no, he corrected himself. The faces were different; slender, even delicate. They were not Vensor-sa, but malkops.

The chamber itself was unimpressive, at least to a Simet noble. The floor and sloping walls were unadorned irsrem, which was hard and uncomfortable, though not as cold as he would have supposed. Nor as dark, since their translucence permitted a soft glow to seep in from the surrounding still-lit sky. His initial awe was fading. The young selks, he observed, were far from efficient, and damaged or spoiled much cloth, and tangled the thread hopelessly. He shook his head. Could these be the same who had carved the sculptures? His hunger spurred him on without an answer.

Selks bearing lozenges passed by. Intrigued, Flores followed and traced them to a nursery. Here he found a chamber where young ones just hatched staggered and whistled, though he wondered why none was smaller than a Vensor child of twelve. They were born fully developed, the cocoons ripping open as he watched. Remembrance of what he had witnessed in the Temple of Ven at the hands of the Neset-sa induced a feeling of nausea and he left the chamber.

He glimpsed selks with branches of fungus, and his hunger and thirst leapt back to mind. They halted before a series of store-rooms. These were filled with food. The branches lay unattended, and after they had deposited their loads and left, Flores ate till his hunger was sated. Water remained a problem. He had not drunk in almost three days. He had seen no tanks or cisterns since he arrived in the city, and he began to fear that the creatures might drink on the run. Elimination was more easily solved. When within the city, he learned the creatures went to one of many corridors equipped with portals that were kept in reserve for this purpose. Their waste fed the meadows.

Next he encountered a vast chamber, cathedral-like, partitioned by a series of vertical walls. Both surfaces of each individual wall were covered with a network of hexagons, starting at eye level. A flood of malkops frequented the hexes. Flores nodded–a lattice of hexagonal chambers for rest and sleep. One selk to a cell. Stacked one atop another from floor to distant roof, most of the cells were presently empty, but he suspected that come dark the hexscape would be filled.

The pursuit of water became imperative. He eyed a band carrying essence, and he thought. In Ven he was familiar with the method smiths employed to produce the treasured glass. They mixed the essence, received from the Eunuchs' Guild, with corta obtained from the Mines of Maanus. This fused at high temperatures in a chemical reaction, which they then cooled in well-crafted molds. The result was the indestructible tear-glass–irsrem–bright, and both harder and lighter than iron. The process required water, to first mix with the corta, the substance remaining inactive till damp. Perhaps if he followed these selks and observed their creation of glass, he might find an opportunity to drink some of the fluid which they must have on hand for the process. He fell quietly in step behind the column.

The suns had long set and the light in the corridors was dying. Winding their way through the city, the essence-laden selks emerged on an open plaza. They assembled along a wall that lined the plaza on two sides; the outer wall of the dome completing the plaza's structure. Taking handfuls of essence in their mouths, the creatures spewed it upon the wall. Immediately the substance began to glow. Flores sat down to watch–and felt wetness on his hand. He turned: a cistern stood beside him. Praise Vensor for simple victories! He drank his fill, and life returned.

Reluctant to leave what he had sought, when night came Flores remained by the cistern. He lay upon the glass. Even after darkness had fallen, the selks continued to labor. Their work burned and sizzled, the wall flaring coldly in the dark. Like moths to flame his eyes were drawn to the steady glow, and for a time nought else existed. Finally, with the resistlessness of the tide, sleep came upon him. As he succumbed to its siren song, his final thought was to realize that the selks had used no water.

When he awoke the selks had gone. The parapet they had worked on rose two feet higher than before. Flores looked around. His initial thought was again to drink, and this he did. The cistern, he now saw in the light of morning, was part of a larger system of vats and channels that ringed the plaza where he stood. Designed to catch the rain, it diverted the flow so that the vats were periodically cleansed, fresh water being thus always available to whomever might be in need.

The vats, however, did not lift his spirits. Loneliness was beginning to tell. He had seen no human since the Vaw-sa departed and he longed to tell someone of his findings. He feared he never would. The dead do not return from Heaven. How long could he wander among the malkops? How long could he endure the eerie silence of the place, the lack of relief to eye and ear? Nowhere had he glimpsed anything to stimulate his mind or interest in aesthetics. Heaven–it seemed–was boring. And dangerous. How much time must pass, with strange chambers and stranger inhabitants, before he yielded to despair, or was finally discovered and killed? The execution-panels he had seen warned him of what lay in wait.

Flores sighed. He looked again to the northeast and gazed–now longingly–at the rocky isle. No detail was visible. What if some of his companions had evaded the malkops and returned? He had left specific instructions with Isav. He at least would be prepared. Checking his bracelet, and pausing to compose in his mind the image of the selk he had first met–a procedure rapidly assuming habit–he proceeded to the exit ramp and rejoined the flowing multitudes in the city. On the plaza he had sighted a structure of unusual shape that seemed to curve or bulge beyond the outer dome. This edifice apparently occupied the highest point of the dome, and, having had no luck in locating any structure that might imprison a human, he decided, after a quick trip to consume a branch of fungus, to investigate.

Hours had elapsed when he climbed the last ramp and emerged in the largest plaza thus far. The plaza was filling with malkops. Their numbers soon grew so large, in fact, that Flores became alarmed and sought to retrace his steps, but this proved to be impossible without brushing against the creatures, and he moved to a quarter where their numbers were somewhat less. From behind a bend of wall, he watched.

Much of the plaza was shielded by a stretch of partial roof that seemed to continue the outer wall and whose purpose he supposed was to shadow pedestrians in the square. For this Flores was thankful, for the tropic suns had climbed high and he found he disliked direct exposure to their rays. The underside of the roof was indented with a field of contiguous hexagons that were set to various heights. What purpose might they serve? Far from aiding audibility, they seemed to interfere, the movements of the selks returning to his ears as a steady hiss. His interest in this soon passed, however, for, as he gazed across the square, he found his eyes were drawn to another structure of unusual design. In contemplating it, his brows drew tight across his bridge—as if the muscles would infuse logic where none existed.

In the center of the plaza, and around which the throng of selks now gathered, circled a rim of black tachylite adorned with a strip of delicate carving. He had found the tower's terminus. The height of the black pillar was in itself a thing of marvel, but he marveled more when he came to realize that the entire structure of the tower was but an adjunct for something else. Suspended above the pillar, of similar diameter to the rim, was a sphere of solid irsrem, some hundred feet across. The sphere—like the partial roof—betrayed a network of hexes, a hexscape, here uniform in height. Curiosity eclipsing fear, Flores moved to view it better. Surely an unseen support upheld the globe. Near the edge he halted. Beneath lay only darkness. He recalled the tale of Macius, and Atasan's plunge into the Abyss, and through his mind ran another line from the poetic cycle of the Zeyd: I flee to the Lord of Dawn from the Evil He created. Could any still doubt the identity of the creator of the world? With a flash he felt he understood the meaning of what he saw, and his soul grappled with a dialectic of morality: Heaven in Hell; Hell in Heaven; Good in Evil; and Evil residing where one thought to find Good.

And he knew whom he would next see upon the plaza, and when the multitudinous face appeared, growing from a dot in the center of each hex, until reflected a thousand-fold, while the brazen globe crept slowly round in time with the turn of the planet, Flores involuntarily retreated into the shadow of the wall. Then He burst forth and was upon them, stiff wings darkening the suns. With a deafening buzz He circled. Like a meteor he drove at the underside of the roof, flipping on his back just in time to break his thrust. Limbs clasped the hexwork. Upside down, He surveyed His domain.

Flores was unable to move. Not that he wished to, absorbed as he was with the surprising apparition before him. Most surprising, however, was not the peculiar features the creature displayed, but the fact that–as he knew with certainty–this was not the first time he had beheld them. On that day, many months before, when chaos had reigned in the Three Valleys of Ven, and war had swung its scythe over the city, he had stood in the center of the inviolate Sacred Spring and gazed upon the remains of that which had brought his city life. And the Thing had come, as if to gloat over its handiwork, passing its inscrutable gaze over the maimed and the dead. It had paused only briefly before it left, but Flores had not forgotten–all knew the Heir of Vensor was the First Cause of Evil.

Green scales flashed. Compound eyes glared. Mandibles widened, then closed. Flores was so intense in his observation of the Evil One that he did not notice the human until selks pushed him clear.

It was one of the Vaw-sa who had tried to murder him, the one called Lesk. His arms were bound behind and his loincloth torn away. He looked dirty. Evidently he had wandered for some time as had Flores.

A thunderous buzz emanated from the ceiling. Then a series of random clicks, followed by clicks from several malkops. More clicks sounded from the thing–a long series that stopped abruptly.

Half a minute passed. Came a deeper drone. *"Adamul buyutta ^aam ra'allah limatha 'istaiqathta min hilm."*

The Vaw stared in confusion.

The drone–it could not really be called a voice–resumed. *"Mahboobal-lah lahabibta alnaum lahabibta alhilm laa^zhaba^ ainui^zhaz^ airu mashruu^ waladul mudunfi-ra'alla yuharrifu awadim"* clicks interceded *"yuharrifu awadim ^ainallah qaddisarruuh adamulbuyut qaddisalwahi."*

Flores waited. Had the torrent ended?

The Vaw shook his head. He forced an answer through fear-soaked lips. "I... I don't understand." Flores wondered what he would say were he in the Vaw's place.

Silence returned. A stretch of time passed, during which Flores began to fear they had been forgotten. Finally, though, the roof again hummed, the droning now clearly a voice.

"Earth bound of dwellings food of see face of God you see you hear why wake from dream beloved of God not please sleep not please dream food of see face of God not please source of miracle why see why hear converse false to order" clicks "converse false to order see face of God see eye of God not earth bound of dwellings restore breath earth bound of dwellings restore way."

The Vaw had said nothing. Suddenly his eyes widened. "You...you believe that I woke in the pits? You...you believe that I was dead, and I came back to life in the pits? No–no, I did not wake below! I live!"

The compound eyes shifted. "Not bring almala'ik through breath of God not sleep not dream not please source of miracle what child of cities bring converse false to order al-mala'ik eye of God bring earth bound of dwellings matter on water matter on water on matter that does not move earth bound of dwellings on matter that moves on water on matter that does not move on water."

The Vaw brightened. "Matter-on-water...yes...a...a ship–you mean our ship. Yes! The Grest! It is beached on matter-that-does-not-move, on the island. Yes, it was the ship that brought me here!" He looked suddenly urgent. "Take me back! To the island! I promise we'll leave and not return. Please. I swear we won't come back to bother you again!"

"Matter on water not on see face of God matter on water on matter that does not move earth bound of dwellings on see face of God converse false to order eye of God not bring earth bound of dwellings almala'ik not bring earth bound of dwellings matter on water not come child of cities through seed of God how come here."

"How?" His brow sweated torrents. "You want to know how I came here, since the boat is still on the island, and I did not wake in the pits?" Lesk swallowed, concentrated. "We...we...we came with Surge–and Flores–from Vaw and Ven. There were twenty of us, including Stalkin–one of the Vaws. As I am from Vaw. We beached on the island to the north and swam to the Island of Vensor and entered the pits–but we wished only to see the shores of Heaven! Only to look! We did know this was your land. There was no one but selks. We meant no harm. We didn't hurt anyone. We didn't mean to sin. It was a mistake! Let me go, Divine One, and we will take the ship and leave! We won't return, I promise!" The selks held him tighter.

Quiet again descended, but for the heaving of the Vaw's lungs. More time passed than before. Had the creature fallen into a trance?

Finally the mandibles moved. "Beloved child of Vensor..." The sound was slow, soothing, resonant. Flores was stunned, unable to believe that this deep and gentle voice had come from the same source as the previous harsh utterances.

"Why have you awakened from your dreaming? The dwellers found you wandering in the first level of Heaven. Were you not happy contemplating the Divine, seeing the Face of God? Were you not happy sleeping and dreaming, merging with the source of the miracle? It is not ordained that children of Vensor, who are beloved of God, should see, should hear before God has appointed them to join Him. This darkens the Eye, disturbs the Breath, disrupts the Hive. Twists what should be ordered. Tangles what should be straight."

Flores thought he detected a variation in the tone, and suspected the voice of having other flections, other moods.

"Did the dwellers in Heaven act in error? The dwellers in Heaven bring Essence, food for See-Face-of-God, and bring those dwellers soon-to-be-born. They do not bring wingless children of cities before their time. This is converse, false-to-order. Forbidden. Beloved of God, did you come to Heaven on the wooden ship that is beached on the island to the north? It has not moved. How did you evade the eyes of my dwellers? How did you come to Heaven without a ship?"

The Vaw trembled. His knees gave way, but the selks held him. "We didn't use a ship." His guilt burst forth with the force of a confession. "We came to steal." He wept. "We came with the aid of reven gills and swam below the water–to steal gold from your Island." He wiped aside his tears and grasped the contraption on his chest. The selks released his arms and he removed it from round his neck. "See! Here is one! The Vens–and Surge–made it with the aid of foreign scribes. We of Vaw know not how." He wept again. "I am sorry. I confess my sins. Have mercy! I beg forgiveness!"

The thing on the roof gave no sign that it saw either the Vaw or the gill. A minute elapsed and the Vaw, tears still streaming, let his arms fall to his sides.

More minutes passed.

The rasping clicks resumed. These were answered by the selks. A moment later a single malkop moved slowly to the forefront. The others gave way. No other sound came from the ceiling, but when the selk had reached the front of the crowd and halted, Flores noticed the multifaceted eyes of the thing on the ceiling move ever so slightly in the selk's direction. The selk breathed heavily in response. Its mouth fashioned in a moue, as if in a fit of petulance.

A click and the crowd descended. Before Flores'—and the Vaw's—horrified gaze, the crowd pulled the selk apart, their dagger-claws ripping through flesh and cartilage. The flock took flight, sped away from the dome. With their trophies, they plummeted, aiming, Flores guessed, for the third level of pits far below.

The Vaw had said nothing.

The gentle voice resumed. "Beloved of God. As it was God's will that determined the time of your birth to a maker-of-life, and God's will that determined the time of your return to dust, so it was not your choice to come to Heaven, but God's will that you be brought. It was God's will that decreed how you should come; God's will that decreed that you should pass through the lower levels without embracing the source of Heaven. God's Will. So feel no sadness. No pain. Who is there to question the wisdom of Creation? Who is there to contradict the dictates of what is? It is Life that brings unhappiness to you—as to all. Life that places burdens upon your shoulders. Life that brings suffering, and pain. Earth-bound child of cities—with me alone lies salvation. It is in my power to release you from the sadness and travails of existence; from the weariness of life. Beloved child of God. I have consulted the Divine. He has given His consent to bring you to the Eye."

The Vaw began to breathe as had the selk. He tried to speak, but could not. The malkops moved closer. The ceiling buzzed like a motor building strength.

It took him.

Above the plaza it paused, the terrified Vaw obscured by a tangle of wings. Flores caught one glimpse—the Vaw's face locked in grimace, skin pale with fear; then they they plunged into the sphere and were gone. Briefly the glass darkened, the facets reflecting the pair a thousand-fold. The thousand images shrank until the suns glittered whitely on the glass.

He could not explain how Vensor-sa had come to call it Heaven. Or why Vensor-sa revered the malkops. Just as he could not explain why the workers of the sky should bear the signs of Atasan's creation—femininity. But if gilas ruled the Temple, why should not their namesake rule the Island of the Sun-God, and the selks? Flores recoiled from the implication, then faced it. He had seen from childhood the coupling of all forms of life on Maalstrom. He knew that all animals but Vensor-sa were paired female with male. He had seen the Queen in Ven, seen the lozenges she birthed. He had seen the women—the priestesses of the Temple–place the lozenges on the tower for the malkops to retrieve. He had seen the panels on the black pillar with the flitting insect that visited bloated makers-of-life in many temples. He had seen the idealized conception of the predation rendered in exquisite mosaic in the Temple of Ven. Now he had learned that Atasan was flesh and blood. It was neither god, nor devil–but Thing.

Like a flash it was revealed. Thus it reproduced. Thus it laid its eggs. Thus it fed off the labor of the Vensor millions across the planet, and–with the cooperation of its slaves, the priestesses–imprisoned gilas for its use, transforming them into bloated swollen things, allowing them to give birth to Vensor-sa–but only so long as this did not interfere with the production of their precious lozenges. At what time in the distant past had they begun to prey on gilas? When had Vensor society become a caste of slaves for the malkops? How had they changed normal coupling with men so that the world had turned upside-down? And why had the eunuchs stamped this exploitation with an aura of sacredness? Had there once been a time when Vensor-sa lived as did the other species on Maalstrom? For Flores now understood that the panels had told a story–the sneaking into darkened windows, the raping of sleeping women, and their subsequent loathsome bloating as they gave birth to streams of eggs. This was what awaited Amina. The creature Atasan was female, and a queen of its hornet species. It had taken his consort Amina and planned to plant its eggs in her so she would become a Maker-of-Life.

He had little time to find her. He had begun near the edge of the city. He had worked his way inside. He had attained to the apex, and searched much of what lay between. What remained? He had found no chamber capable of imprisoning a human–no jails, prisons, or wards. He had indeed witnessed no punishment for misbehavior except the single execution, and he knew such would not be the fate of his queen–hers was infinitely more terrible. What was left? Chin in hand, he thought. Where would he keep a woman if he ruled the Island, what place was most secure? He sat up–of course. There was but one place he had not searched, and he shuddered in contemplation.

The Eye.

He nodded. He had seen Atasan take the Vaw within. Flores set his jaw, and instead of tears, felt anger. That an innocent would be stolen and taken to Heaven alive was bad enough. To know that Heaven was but a Hive under the control of a murderous parasite was worse. To learn that this parasite planned to use Amina for its reproduction–this was more than he could bear. He would do more than pull its beard. He would enter the Eye and strike it down.

There seemed but one way to accomplish his purpose. He must look like Atasan. He must compose his bracelet's image so that he looked like the creature. Then he could infiltrate the Eye, as none of the selks would dare interfere. With this, he left the busy plaza. He must find an empty room, as it would not do to be discovered. He searched. Every place he looked he found a multitude of selks. There seemed no end to them. At last he stumbled upon several rooms filled with branches of fungus; he moved to the end and began to practice the loathsome shape. Within a short time he felt confident of holding the bizarre image, and he returned.

The first chamber was empty. The second also. Within the third a single malkop loitered with its back turned to where he stood. In the hall beyond was traffic. No point in delaying—he must go forward.

He entered the threshold to the hall and paused amid a great throng of selks. It was time! Time to end the predation, time to terminate the Evil that conquered everything he knew and loved! He raised a hand—a tinny clink rang. Looking down he saw a circle of glass wobble like a toy. The bracelet had slipped off his wrist.

A hundred eyes turned. Fifty mouths writhed in rage. Scores of wings exploded in anger. Before he recalled that a sword hung at his belt the creatures were upon him. Hands pinned his arms. More seized his legs. His breath escaped under pressure from the bodies and he felt himself lifted in the air.

They did not fly with him, but ran, carrying him through twisting corridors. At length they halted and stood him erect and a greater crowd assembled. Lucky their claws are sheathed, he thought. Sudden pain followed ripping of flesh as the claws of one connected.

He was drawn suddenly aloft. A wall of hexagonal cells appeared, vertical, with a cliff-like face, the interior of each in shadow. Leather wings churned the air by the entrance of one cell and Flores was thrust within. He landed upon his side. A bruise would follow that as well.

The wings departed.

Flores groaned. Crawling to the lip of the chamber, he gazed out and down to the floor. Fear churned his gut. More than when he had gazed through the portals, the sheer drop to the floor frightened him. Some two hundred feet across loomed the next wall, similarly endowed with hexcomb. Above and below and to either side more cells of the huge structure lay. He hoped the southern sea had few quakes. No person could survive such a precipitous drop.

He sighed. Again all his efforts had been for nought. He had failed to find his consort; he had failed to kill Atasan; he had failed to save Revd; he had failed to return to Isav; he had failed city, Temple, clan. He had even failed to die, as he had at least hoped to do with honor. Moreover, he had lost the one device that had seemed to offer a chance. Slowly he pulled up his legs and crossed them, sitting and gazing disconsolately at the agitated malkops massed far below. There was nothing left but to jump. His mind ambled on with this thought uppermost, needing only to appoint a time for the deed. A small sound interrupted.

He blinked, and turned.

Through the translucent wall of glass that divided his cell from the next was silhouetted the form of a person without wings. Though half in shadow and clothed in black, the form's voluptuous curves were apparent. The face came close; feminine eyes peered into his cell and the soft voice repeated its heart-felt message.

"Flores. You have come!"

CHAPTER 12

"TREASURE FOR ALL!"

"Summon our murshid. We shall put to him the question." The King's Overseer of the south dock sat upon a trivet that his men had placed within the grove to shield him from the hot rays of the morning suns. The thin legs protested, but held. In response to a squeal from beyond the trees, where a reven was being butchered, his massive head turned. What better music to celebrate his triumph? He could feel his rage, nursed over the preceding month, begin to lessen, and–at last–turn to joy. He snapped his faded yellow cloak and straightened his faded yellow cap. Before him, outlaid on a sheet of canvas about his feet, were three strange contraptions of reven gill and rubber, and a pile of golden plates and trinkets inlaid with jewels. On one side stood a muscled giant, conceit upon his face. On the other a gaunt man, beside a third whose eyes gazed upon some object in the distance.

The two Vaw swordsmen returned. Surge walked behind.

Lips like octopus-limbs crept parallel across the expanse of Fish's jaw, and one hand rose affectedly in greeting–a strange gesture more at home with a nimble dancer than the squatting monstrosity whose blunt appendage it adorned.

Surge halted. He took in the trees, the Overseer, Stalkin, the guards.

The bullet head nodded.

"How quaint. How cute. How lucky we are to bask in your presence once more, dear Surge. May I say, your performance was masterful." The octopus lips completed their slow smile. "I see you have lost none of your old talent."

The olive face of the thief registered no reaction, but his eyes slid silently between the Overseer and the sentinels.

"And how lucky for us all that you succeeded in discovering the foreigner's plans." The smile settled into a smirk. "I wish to express my appreciation personally, my friend." Fleshy tent flaps rose in an enormous grin, lighting up the entire expressive face, and the hand rose again in its peculiar affected way. "And to inform you that for your role in the success of our plot, it has been decided that you are to receive more than the usual tenth claimed by the pilot of a crew. Of all that we seize, you will be given one-fifth. The royal fifth! Not King Kot himself can claim more." The grin settled into a caricature of a satisfied smile.

Surge bowed deep. "The King, then, knows?"

Fish and Stalkin exchanged glances. "Dear Surge," continued the Overseer. "It is not possible to undertake such an exploit as we contemplate without knowledge of our activity spreading."

"And he approves..?"

"Concerning our royal eminence, let us say... negotiations are pending." The round eyes blinked in noncommittal fashion. "Part of those negotiations, of course, will be the final level of compensation for all. And royal forgiveness for past...transgressions. But do not be concerned. What lies on this sheet beneath these palms is enough to interest anyone–even the head of the Order of the Sacred Cyclops."

The murshid arched his back in a slow move, catlike, as if his spine, and not his head, were reflecting on the matter.

Another squeal came from beyond the grove. A grey quadruped of slender neck broke into the trees, two men close behind. The Overseer sat up straight.

"Is this to be my evening meal?"

"Aye, master. We selected the least vigorous, as you instructed." The one who spoke glanced surreptitiously at his companion. "It slipped its harness when we raised the ax and prepared to block its head. Apologies, Initiate. We shall remove it at once." The servants took hold of the reven, and, the creature being small and sickly in comparison with most adult revens, were able to drag it without assistance. Its jaw was securely muzzled, but they could not stop its squeals. On Fish's command they halted.

"Do not bring me this scrawny creature. Look at its gut! Can you not see it is ill? You would poison me with its ailment! Select another and return this one to the pen."

They bobbed their heads and left. A minute elapsed and they reappeared with another, stouter animal. Fish nodded and they dragged the reven to slaughter. They had almost left when the first creature again bounded past, free of its muzzle.

"You blundering imbeciles! Does my dignity mean so little to you that you would constantly trod it in the dirt?"

Stalkin took a step toward one of the servants and raised his brows at Fish as if to ask whether punishment should follow. The Overseer waved him back. To the servants he called, "Let it go. We have no place in our ward for sickness." They returned behind the trees and moments later another high squeal was abruptly eclipsed.

Fish returned his attention to Surge. He thought a moment, then smiled. "I am glad that my murshid approves of developments and of our plans. However–before we discuss the details of the venture–there is something I must ask."

In preparation, Surge's spine straightened.

Fish waved his hand at the gills and he looked at his murshid askance. "Where, dear Surge, did he get them?"

Surge's ears shifted slightly backward. "The gills?"

"The gills," said Fish, lilting his voice on the latter word, another affectation that surprised his old comrade. Surge had not thought the ruler of the southern dock capable of pronouncing a word with such precision and delicacy. The massive lower jaw shifted in anticipation of the pilot's response.

Surge's fingers came together and began to rub. "Of Flores?"

"Of the foreigner. Yes."

He shrugged. "In Ven."

Fish took a breath and expelled it. "Why, Surge–as Stalkin reports–did Flores offer to give them to you?"

Surge's hands turned horizontal and moved casually through the air. "As a reward for my service."

"Why does he hold you in such esteem? Might there be some other..." the round eyes narrowed suspiciously, "compensation that you have failed to share with us–your oldest comrades?"

Nimble eyes moved like a butterfly, remaining nowhere long enough to offend. "None was offered. But the gills. Instead of pay."

"Why did you wish them?"

Again the shrug. "Mementos. Trinkets. Toys." His eyes wandered in the direction of the Island.

Popping drifted from beyond the trees, and smoke. Fish paused. His nostrils twitched. Another moment and an underling entered with a huge bent reven leg, newly severed, and scorched but far from cooked. The eyes of Fish bulged. He snatched the leg. In a frenzy the lips smacked, spraying red grease upon the canvas, and those unfortunate enough to stand near, like water from a sprinkler. Incisors ripped chunks of flesh from the limb, which, for lack of any distinguishable throat, passed directly to the stomach without chewing till only shreds of tendon remained on the bone. Fish threw it in the trees. Disgust, and horror, shone from the face of Stalkin and the other sentinels. The lips rippled and snapped, cleaning themselves of flotsam. A forearm finished the job.

Sated, the eyes again narrowed. Stalkin's demeanor reverted to its habitual sly contempt and Fish exchanged a wary glance with his smithy. He looked to his murshid.

"And who, dear Surge, is Yezd?" Fish waited sullenly for an answer.

The eyes roved. For perhaps a full minute the elastic body of the thief remained motionless beneath the stare of the bulk on the tripod and his weaponed guards. He broke into a multiplicity of movements, as energy transformed it from a dull slow thing to a thing in motion, the limbs rippling like sheaves of snakes. Then, as suddenly as it began, it stopped. He shrugged again. "A scribe." He fell silent.

Fish's fingers tumped impatiently upon one thigh.

Again the body exploded into movement, and the voice returned, music to the dance. "I came upon him by surprise. Unexpectedly." He froze. "He did not see me. The surprise was total." The head cocked, as if listening to something far away. The arms resumed snaking. "After a journey of many days I came upon him in the wilderness. His house was guarded. I entered. I was his guest—or he was mine. Then he journeyed to Ven where he met Flores. Flores of the Turlicum, who took the gills and went to Heaven," he looked to the ground, "and died."

His interrogators looked perplexed. Anger welled up from the just-stocked depths of Fish. His face swelled, struggling to contain it. Finally it passed. He sucked one cheek. "Ever the mystery with you, Surge. What I wish to know is *who made them!*"

The brown eyes looked up. "Yezd." And back down. "Perhaps. Or perhaps Flores. Or his employees. Or the scribal guild in Ven."

Fish leaned forward, shouted. "Do more of them exist? Can more be made?"

"No...and yes. Or perhaps not."

The gaunt man beside Fish interrupted. "We will learn nothing from this one—he hides himself from all!"

A fist like a hammer slammed into the gloomy face. "Shut up, Numtal!"

The gaunt man shuddered and grew silent.

"This is our murshid you refer to." The smile returned. "He whom each man in Vaw would follow anywhere, without question. We must show him the respect he deserves!" His quiet gaze rested on the pilot.

"Initiate," said Stalkin, "may I speak? It is plain, is it not, that he wished them for the Island? You see what is to be found there. And I heard the foreigner say that he stole all of the devices and that the scribe from whom he stole them disappeared. He must have died in their war."

Fish glanced at Stalkin and nodded. He snorted. "No matter. You said the arrows worked?"

"Indeed, Initiate. It is as I said. I swear to you that they bleed and die like us. If we had a hundred archers we would be standing on yon Island now, gathering its treasures, rather than cringing here on this deserted crag, fearing their attack. The treasures are great. Beyond belief!"

Fish gulped. He glanced at one of his guards who sported a bow and quiver. Scanning a patch of sky, he swore. "They watch us always. If we had even ten archers! But with only one, we cannot fight. And with only three gills we cannot bring out the gold. Especially if, as you say, they are ready, and now watch the beach for footprints. And if, as you also say, these gills were made by a single man who has now vanished, then we cannot get more." The extraordinary lips began to compress, turning slowly in on themselves like the subduction of fleshy plates. They plopped out. "That leaves but one way to gain our purpose. It will take time, and be risky, but sometimes the most direct way is the best."

Fish turned again to Stalkin. "What did you say he called the holy workers of the sky?" Stalkin looked at Surge. "He called them 'tools of Atasan.' The foreigner did not argue."

"And you say the Island is filled with dead? And bones? And the treasure lies among them?"

"Yes! In three levels joined by a tunnel that is too small for the selks to use. As is the first level. The selks cannot maneuver easily while within. There are many cave-mouths, so entry by a large troop would be easy. We have but to land upon the beach, haul our boats within the caves, then hold them off with arrows till we get away."

Fish looked at Surge. For several minutes he sat in silence, thinking. Finally he nodded. He motioned to Numtal. The assistant shook himself out of his gloom and gathered up the gills, put them in a sack and placed the sack at the feet of the Overseer, who counted them before tying the neck.

"Then it is agreed." Fish held up a fist and slapped his hand on the raised forearm in the Vaw gesture of power. "Assemble the men. I wish to address them."

The sailors gathered. The camp within the grove was small, but most managed to squeeze in, leaving a small space around their leader and the canvas with the loot. Fish stood and bestowed his most engaging smile upon them. The fact that few interpreted his expression as one of humor did not perturb him in the least.

"Men of Vaw! My children. Our associate and comrade, Surge of the Xotl clan, whose name you all know, but whose face few in recent times have seen, is with us." He gestured toward Surge and a chorus of bravos exploded from the Vaw-sa, bludgeons waving, those with swords clattering them on small round shields. Fish waited till they were silent. "It is my good fortune to inform you that Surge has requested our assistance in a new expedition, one that he himself has proposed, and that he backs to the limit of his abilities. We have discussed it. It has been decided. It will make us rich. I have given him...my full support."

The hurrahs rang forth again. The warriors circled their favorite son and began pummeling him with their fists, Surge striking back where he could. His blows evoked replies of such effusive gratitude that one might have supposed him a philanthropist distributing alms to the poor.

At length, the commotion ceased. Fish signaled to his smithy and Stalkin moved to the center of the crowd and pointed to the canvas.

The smithy's powerful voice boomed. "Men of Vaw! Look upon this canvas! What do you see?"

"Gold!" they shouted. "And mir!" Their faces shone with enthusiasm.

"Yes. Booty! But how much?"

"Enough to buy us villas and make us rich for life!"

"No. No, I repeat! Not enough. In fact it is nothing–a pittance only– and mere dross. But there is more. Oh yes, my lovelies, there is more! On yon Island from whence I have just returned by the grace of the merciful God–and from whence our murshid Surge has just come, having shown me the way, lies more! Treasure such as you have never dreamed! Treasure enough to buy eunuchs, cities, empires! More treasure than you can load in a lifetime–a thousand lifetimes indeed would not exhaust its mines! I speak to you, my lovelies, from my own experience, my own knowledge! I relate what I have seen with my own eyes! And I speak for Surge, our murshid whose skill has brought us here and who first discovered the wealth!"

The crowd burst out with applause again and clapped Stalkin upon the back till a small quiet voice from behind their ranks attracted their attention.

"Let me understand rightly what you wish, Stalkin. You wish us to loot the Island of God. And to take booty from our God Vensor." As his voice rose above the others, the men quieted and exchanged subdued glances.

They turned their gaze toward the stony ridge that blocked their view of the larger Island of Vensor to the west.

Stalkin shook his head. "Not from God. Not from Vensor. But from the selks. Creatures which are not divine, but have stolen all they have from you and your ancestors since the beginning of time. Look upon the canvas. See the brooch, inlaid in Vaw style. See the plates of gold, stripped from dead men–your clansmen! See the baubles fashioned by smiths who spent their lives in labor to produce them. What you see is not pilfer. It is not loot, or booty. It is yours! By all that is right–yours! Think, my beauties! Surge is not proposing a mere raid for profit, like others you know have done. He does not propose to violate the Holy Law or blaspheme against God. He proposes to take back only what is rightfully ours, even as the foreigners from Ven proposed–and who led the way for us–in the process exposing the truth of this accursed island, which has been a scourge to lost seafarers since the beginning of time. Is it right that the selks should keep what is ours?"

Silence.

The men looked at each other.

"You, Stalkin, would harm the divine workers of Heaven?" The man who had previously spoken, interrupting the celebration, pushed his way to the front of the band. His face was rugged like leather. In one hand was an old-fashioned iron sword. In the other, a small wooden shield.

"We intend to take what is ours. Surge and the Initiate have agreed."

"It is blasphemy."

"Did you speak, Telek?"

"I said: it is blasphemy."

Fish glanced at his smithy. Surge stared at Stalkin and Fish.

"And that is your opinion?" replied Stalkin.

"It is the opinion of all Vensor-sa. As you well know."

"Then you do oppose us?"

"I oppose only the ways of Atasan. I support the ways of Vensor."

Stalkin interjected. "And what if I swear that within the Island of Vensor the bodies of your ancestors lie buried, not open to the sky. Buried in dark pits where the selks have dumped them."

Telek frowned. "What proof have you of your words?"

"What proof do you need? I have seen the bodies myself. And you see what lies here before your eyes, proof that I have been there."

"Lies. And hearsay." Telek turned suddenly to the crowd of men and shouted. "This is forbidden! A thousand years of piety stand in danger of violation. Our grace, the grace of our city and temple, will be placed in jeopardy, the favor of God withdrawn, our sons withheld! We must put a stop to this talk and these plans before our souls are condemned. How can we go to Heaven if the divine selks refuse to take us?"

Stalkin grew silent. He had run out of arguments. His hard eyes rested on Fish. One of the Overseer's fingers moved and several armed sentinels gripped tighter their weapons. Surge stepped backward into the grove. Then the small man who had stood beside Numtal and still gazed into the distance edged forward and turned his glance on Telek. For the first time Surge noticed the depth of his eyes, eyes that seemed to swim in a sea of script, the letters even now bearing the boat of his mind like waves.

"Not all bodies are taken, Telek. We sometimes rot in forests. Then we burn our deceased on pyres, and with no danger to our souls."

Telek turned to him. "Because our priests allow it. But what is proposed here is against the laws of both men and gods. Men cannot enter Heaven till they die. Our priests have told us that as well."

"And why do you call this Island Heaven?"

His brows rose. "It is the Island of Vensor! All know it is Heaven."

"And what should Heaven be like?"

Telek shook his head, perplexed. He answered, "It is a place where the souls of the dead live in peace with God, and with themselves. A place where mercy and justice reign."

"Mercy and Justice–this defines divinity?"

"I believe so."

"Complete?"

"I suppose."

"You would say, then, that Vensor is a merciful god."

"Yes!"

"And the selks above us are also merciful, being Vensor's agents."

"Indeed! They treat our dead with kindness."

The smaller man paused. "And what if they did not?"

"I don't follow you."

"What if they were not merciful, but harsh and cruel?"

"How so?"

"Let us say they injured a child, a small and innocent child."

"That is their prerogative."

"Why?"

"Because the gods may do as they wish."

"You mean to say the gods are all-powerful and need not be merciful unless they wish it?"

"Indeed. Yes."

"Then you must change your definition of divinity. What you meant to say when I asked you if mercy and justice define divinity, was that they do not. Rather divinity is defined by power and justice."

Telek thought. "Indeed so. It seems I was wrong."

"Now. I would like to ask in regard to the injured child. If a man injured a small and innocent child, would you call such an act of cruelty just, or unjust?"

"Why unjust, of course! There can be no justice in injuring children."

"And would this man be guilty and deserving of punishment?"

"Without doubt. To the limit of the law!"

"And where does the guilt lie? In the injury, or in the deed?"

"I don't follow you."

"Could a child be injured by accident? Or is every injury presumed to be due to some man's fault?"

"A child may be injured by accident, that is true."

"And in such a case no man should be punished?"

"Yes. Because it was no man's fault."

"There was no deed, you mean. Only an injury."

"Yes."

"So where does the guilt lie? In the injury, or in the deed?"

"It seems in the deed."

"And, in theory, might any number of men commit such a deed? And each be punishable by virtue of having done it, since it is the intention that counts, not the result?"

"Yes."

"Including priests?"

"Without doubt! It would be even worse should one of God's representatives commit such!"

"And—since the crime is in the deed, and not in the injury—anyone at all may do such a deed, including selks?"

Telek thought, then nodded.

"Even though selks are God's representatives?"

He nodded again.

"And may we say that, in such a case, they would be deserving of punishment?"

He slowly nodded again.

"And if selks did such things to Vensor-sa, should we regard them as divine, or the place where they reside as Heaven?"

"No. We should not."

"Then the power to do injury to someone, for example to a child, must lead at some point to injustice. So power and justice are not the same, and do not go together. And we must change our definition again. It is not power to do a deed that defines divinity, but only whether that deed is just. Divinity, then, must stem from justice, and not from power, or mercy."

"It seems so." Telek thought. Then he said, "Let me rephrase my last statement. It is not necessary that divinity be good. The divinity of the selks may not stem from justice, but from injustice and evil. They may then do as they please, and still be fully divine."

"Power and injustice?"

"Indeed."

"And what is injustice?"

"I don't follow you."

"Is injustice something real? That one can touch, with dimensions?"

"No. It is something abstract."

"A deed perhaps? Like the one we mentioned?"

"Yes."

"And how did we determine that it was unjust?"

"There is no need to determine it! The harming of a child is unjust in and of itself."

"It is irreducible."

"Yes.

"An irreducible deed."

"Yes."

"And what if such a deed were committed by an animal?"

He thought.

"Would such an animal be guilty of intention to harm, and be punishable for such?"

"No. Of course not. Animals have no souls, they are not responsible for what they do."

"And Vensor-sa are responsible."

"Yes."

"Because they are men."

"Yes."

"Men with souls."

"Yes."

"And how are men responsible? Is there a criterion by which a man can judge what is responsible and what is not?"

"Indeed there is–the Holy Law."

"And animals are not punishable under the Holy Law."

"No."

"And on what is the Law based?"

"On justice."

"Now. What if there was no immediate injury, but the child was neglected out of spite till it starved. Is this an equivalent case of harm?"

"Without a doubt."

"Is the intention any different than if immediate injury had been done?"

"No."

"And the result is the same."

"Yes."

"So injustice is the absence of justice, but justice is never the absence of injustice?"

"Indeed!"

"Then may we say that injustice is not something in and of itself, but is defined as the absence of justice, which is incumbent on men with souls? Justice, in this case, being proper tending to a child."

Telek nodded. "It would seem so."

"Then for selks to be divine because they are both powerful and unjust would be wrong. Because as non-being is the absence of being, injustice is the absence of justice. And the selks, therefore, would be merely powerful, because divine creatures must have souls, and cannot act unjustly."

"I suppose so. But, on the other hand, power itself is divine. Whether it acts justly or unjustly."

"Oh? If you or I held all power, would we by virtue of that become divine?"

"No, we are not gods."

"We would still die when we became old and brittle."

"Indeed."

"And kings and priests the same. Each becomes old and dies, no matter how much power they may have while living."

"Yes."

"And those who wield power without regard for justice are simply overweening and strong?"

"No. You are right. Power is just power. It cannot be divine."

"And if the selks, therefore, were merely powerful, they would not be divine?"

"It seems not."

"They must, then, in any account, be just."

"Indeed so."

"Or they are not divine."

"Yes."

"And if not divine..."

"They would have no right to what is ours."

"And if justice did not reign on the Island–"

Telek thought. "Then it would not be Heaven."

"Divinity, then, it seems, is justice. The divine rule on Maalstrom because they are just. They are not just because they rule on Maalstrom."

"True."

"So it is a question of whether the selks have acted justly in taking what is ours."

"So it seems."

"And whether they have acted justly in burying our dead–if what Stalkin says is true."

Telek snorted. "That cannot be true. And he cannot prove it because we have no way of getting there without an attack from the Island's guardians."

Stalkin interrupted. "And what if the selks were mortal?"

The small man with the penetrating eyes turned. "That would not be possible. The surest sign of divinity is immortality. To be just is to be divine. And to be divine is to be incapable of death."

Stalkin smiled. "And if selks were capable of death, they would be neither divine, nor just? But as fleshly and corrupt as we?"

"Precisely."

"And we would be entitled to reclaim our treasure."

"Not only entitled. It would be our duty. And if they indeed bury our dead, it would be our duty to kill them wherever found. And what Surge proposes would be not a raid–but a crusade. A crusade to overthrow falsehood and lies. To overthrow those who claim to be gods–but in fact are as mortal as you or I–and whose lies and hypocrisy were thus worse than if they had been merely mortal."

Twirling, Stalkin stepped to the side of the guardsman with the bow. He seized it, then turned. "Follow."

Telek took Stalkin's arm. "If you do this, they will attack. Vensor will never let us live. His vengeance will come down on all our heads."

A snarl answered. Stalkin pushed Telek aside and marched to the edge of the grove where the noon suns shone bright upon the stretch of sand and soil. The bodies of the Vens had not been moved from beneath the palms. Stalkin seized one. He swung the stiff corpse across one shoulder. Coming out beneath the suns, he cast the body upon a boulder and returned to the grove.

He did not have long to wait. Like clockwork the familiar scene occurred–a scene as predictable and certain as the crossing of the suns. From the depths of the welkin, heretofore invisible to the men upon the ground, a selk shot forth and hovered. None moved, and in another minute the creature lit.

A sound snipped from within the palms. The creature stumbled. A shaft had sprung from its breast. Stalkin stepped forward. Advancing to the creature, he slid a sword out of its sheath–a worm-sword. The selk beat its wings in fright, but ceased when a torrent of blood spilled from its mouth. The smithy halted. He raised the sword. With a savage slash the sword clove head and neck from shoulder.

The men fell back. In a panic they took refuge beneath the palms. Stalkin dragged both bodies into the grove and buried them.

They waited.

Nothing happened.

When thirty minutes had passed, the men began to grumble. A hundred eyes settled on Telek, anger smoldering in each. Stalkin smiled–a sarcastic, confident smile. At a signal from Fish he turned to face the outcast. Confusion was on Telek's face. The sword struck once, then twice, a sideways slash cleanly removed his head.

Fish propelled his bulk to the center of the glade. "Is there anyone else among you who doubts the mortality of selks? Or questions the right of Vensor-sa to take what belongs to them? Or who believes that one's body must be taken to this island in order for one's soul to enter Heaven?"

With Stalkin's bloody sword before them, no one replied.

Fish grinned. "Good. Then here is what we shall do. We are going to collect a fleet. Summon your clansmen; tell your comrades; tell all who can float a seaworthy ship. We need sailors and soldiers and–above all– archers. And do not fear the displeasure of the King, or the vengeance of the Sacred Order. When he hears of the wealth that is ours for the taking–and the crimes of the selks–he will do nothing to stand in our way, but will address the kings of our neighboring cities and seek to recruit them as well. Now go! We leave at once."

The grove erupted in a chorus of shouts. The ruffians hurried to the beach, leaving Fish alone with Stalkin, Surge, the small man, and a few armed guards.

Fish turned and snapped a finger in the direction of the latter. Two men, led by Numtal, disappeared among the trees. While they were absent, Fish turned to the small unassuming man. He noted the far-gazing eyes, the short beard, the swarthy skin.

"Mens. I now understand why Kot expelled you from his court and has put a price upon your head. You are too clever for your own good. If I had no need for a defrocked scribe on occasion, I would not have you around either. Now say nothing. I wish my men to heed my sword more than their minds—or yours."

The men returned. They had Isav and the three surviving Ven-sa in tow, their hands bound in front.

The snake-lips curled in anticipation of the long-awaited moment. Fish settled his massive bulk again upon the trivet. He chewed the inside of a cheek. Then the huge jaw sprang open, the cavernous gullet yawning to such a prodigious extent that for a moment the weaponed guards around him feared they would witness a repeat of the earlier culinary display, but this time with a scandalous course. The jaw closed. They slumped in relief.

"Bring him forward."

The sentinels knew whom he meant. Isav was thrust rudely to his knees in the place where the canvas had been.

Fish maneuvered his fingers. More affectation? No—Stalkin, ever alert to the subtleties of his master's spy signals, strode to the side of the Ven. A massive fist slammed into the uplifted and unprotected face of the Turlicum chief. Hands grasped his shoulders to prevent him from falling, and the fist drove home again and again till the flesh had become an obscenity. Finally the hands allowed Isav to fall.

Numtal brightened and looked to Fish. "He squirms well. Let us beat him some more."

Fish, as little conscious of the incongruity—the incongruous absurdity—of his act after the arguments of Mens as would be an ungulate of the morality of consuming fodder, turned his gaze on his gaunt and gloomy comrade. He moved a finger. Several guards seized hold of him and Stalkin approached. He too was forced upon his knees and pummeled.

"I told you to shut up, Numtal."

Hands seized the Vens. On Fish's motion, Stalkin raised his scythe-like sword.

"Wait—"

Fish hesitated at the interruption from his murshid.

"Initiate. This grove is small. It cannot hold many bodies."

Fish's brows raised. "Is that of concern to us?"

"If the selks can smell them beneath the ground, it is."

The Overseer frowned.

Macius continued. "We do not wish to attract their interest, Initiate. Not yet, when we still have no way to defend ourselves."

Fish and Stalkin glanced at a patch of sky where the trees were absent. They had not thought of that. Several dots hovered over the cliffs, too far to observe their detail, too close to ignore. As they watched, more joined them.

"Would it not be better–for our own sakes–if we left these men alive on the island? Then we may be certain to get away without attack, while they, being marooned, will be unable to do us harm."

The smooth bullet head of the Overseer moved from side to side in contemplation of the proposal. He could feel his former anger rekindle at the thought that one of the two who had dared strike him on the dock should be permitted to live. His hand wandered to his jaw and rubbed it in a familiar way.

He slapped hand to forearm. "Take them to the beach. The tide is low. Within the hour we will put to sea and leave them. While they breathe, the selks will ignore them and thus we can make our escape; but when the tide returns–since they will be bound–their deaths by drowning will be assured. Now remove them!"

With the aid of well-timed blows and kicks, the ruffians dragged and pushed the four Vens out of the grove and across the sand. The ships, now four in number counting the Grest, had been swabbed and supplied and battened with oakum. At a cry from Stalkin, their crews pushed them into the water. The condemned were tossed in the shallows, where the water bubbled with heat. The remaining crew climbed aboard. Without a backward glance, the ships got underway in a northeasterly direction.

CHAPTER 13

ON THE LATTICE

His heart leapt. Flores leaned on the outward sloping wall of his hexagonal cell and peered upward through the irsrem pane that formed the lower wall of a cell adjacent to his own. Through the translucent greenish glass he could just make out the face of the object of his quest–Amina of the Temple of Vensor. She gazed down upon him, leaning with palms outthrust, her expressive brows and deep lashes melting in the shadows. The interior of both cells was dark. Sunlight hardly penetrated to the chamber of the lattices, the irsrem in the vast uplifted catacombs, where the malkops slept, having been imbued with some opaque substance to simulate night. He sought to discern details in her face. Perversely the image shifted, fading as she kneeled.

His mouth opened. How he had waited for this moment. How he had imagined what he might say when at last he once more embraced her. He reached out his arms, his heart aching. The planet longed to circle its sun once more, to clasp the center of the universe to its soul. His fingers felt cold glass!

"Amina." He gazed up. "I swore, no matter how far I had to go or however long it took, that I would find you. Now, come what may, I know that I shall not have died in vain." He drank in the curves of her torso, the lush inviting eyes, downcast and modest even through the intervening irsrem. Dark folds obscured the image excepting the clear bright eyes. She wore a Temple gown, an all-enveloping cloak. The image said nothing, but looked away.

"My love! Do not go!"

She glanced back. Wetness seemed to flash where her face was bare of cloth. She cried. But her eyes continued to smile.

He hesitated.

"Will you not welcome me? Have they not treated you well? Are you ill? Have they fed you poorly?"

Another smile seemed to shine vaguely through. But he could not be sure and squinted through another ripple of glass.

"Why do you not speak? Can you not hear me?"

She sat, raised her eyes, put a finger to her hidden lips, then glanced toward the entrance.

"You are afraid to attract the malkops?" He lowered his tone and whispered. "Or have they weakened you so from starvation that you can no longer give voice to your feelings?" He thought he detected a brief nod, but in answer to which of his questions? A repeat of his inquiry drew no response. She drew the cloak more tightly as if to protect her from cold. The temperature was warm, however. At least in Flores' cell. For a time he stood thus, palms upon the sloping side of the chamber, passing his eyes over the darkened form above. At length the pose grew uncomfortable and Flores straightened.

He began a more thorough inspection of his chamber. It was about twenty feet long by ten feet wide, composed entirely of irsrem. The walls, as he discovered by leaning out the entrance and feeling with his hand, were approximately two feet in thickness. Strong enough to support miles of lattice. By balancing on the slope he could reach just far enough that should Amina reach out and down they might touch. Urgent efforts on his part, however, failed to convince her to attempt it–assuming she understood his feeble signs as communicated through the irsrem.

There was no possibility of climbing up and entering her cell. Without holds to cling to, the attempt would mean death. The same with respect to climbing across the face of the comb. It was impossible without grapnel and rope–even should there be indentations to which a grapnel might fasten. There were none.

The other end of his cell was entirely covered with irsrem with the exception of a small gap that seemed to open onto a bottomless funnel or trench. For his bodily needs, he surmised. Beneath the trench he saw yellow–again he looked upon the meadows. The city of the selks was clean, beyond anything known in Ven. Flores returned to the slope and again sought a response from the elusive image on the far side.

Could fate be really as cruel as this? Could he indeed have finally found his love, only to be tortured by this inability to see, to hear, to touch? How she must also be tortured to see him while remaining imprisoned and unable to embrace. What could he do? He screwed his hands into fists and hammered the pane between them. The thought of those perfect eyes and lips at the mercy of the fantastic creature that ruled the Island sickened him, made him rage with hate. He felt revolted. How might Amina respond if she knew? Had she an inkling of what lay in wait? Somehow, he must change what destiny had laid down. In another moment he had determined not to tell her, to spare her the torment of contemplation, and decided instead to find a way to free her. But first he must look into those eyes again.

"Amina." She looked down. He thought he saw another eyesmile through more tears. "My love, a hundred speeches have run through my mind, expressing my admiration, my gratitude, my affection. Now they fail me. Permit me to say only that I love you..."

She approached, drew her veil more closely about her. Her lips pressed against the glass and she kissed it.

His heart shuddered and his speeches poured forth. For an hour he poured out his heart in the darkness, his ambitions, his hopes, his fears, his intimate restless stirrings, his appraisals of what they were up against spilling into the veiled eyes like milk into a newborn vok. When he paused and questioned her silence, he would detect a nod in reply, or glimpse eyes downcast in grief, or a sweet smile as he spoke with vigor on some point–or an occasional tear and stifled sob accompanied by a sigh.

His heart tore.

At length he grew exhausted and quieted. She lay upon her side, her face turned partly toward him, knees drawn up in a ball. A flapping of wings came from the entrance. The light had grown dimmer and several selks hovered in shadow. Bowls were in their hands. They seemed wary, and Flores soon abandoned the thought he had entertained of jumping on one and forcing it to take him to the base of the lattice. The creatures motioned that he was to retreat from the entrance to the far end of the chamber. Amina had already done so. The selks then entered and a fascicle of tree-fungus branches was placed upon the floor, tied together with string. One selk untied the string and released the branches. Another placed a large bowl of fresh water. They left.

Within minutes Flores had consumed half the food. A shake of the head from Amina warned him not to eat so fast. Apparently it was a ration and he could not expect more for another day. The water was delicious; Flores noted casually that even the bowl was irsrem–a casual use of the substance, though practical.

Flores gazed about his prison. All their domestic needs were satisfied. But why had he been placed within it? He knew why Amina's life had been preserved–to her misfortune. But his own? Why had he not been executed like the Vaw? As he thought, and wondered, the darkness grew complete. No moon or stars were visible through the lofty roof, no wind or noise intruded to disturb him. Amina still refused to reply to his utterances. Were it not for her first comment–which established beyond doubt that she was still capable of speaking–he would have believed that the malkops had committed some heinous deed to prevent it. But no. She lay upon the floor of the cell beside him, her body curled at eye level, relaxed in sleep. Her pain was in her soul, not her flesh.

Just before the last light died a great rush of wings beat the air in the chamber. He ventured to the edge of his cell and caught his breath. The chamber was filling with selks. Like bats returning to their cave, they were coming home to sleep. A considerable time passed and finally the beating ceased and Flores heard scratching and shuffling in the cells that ringed his own. At least he was being treated no worse than their own. He sighed, sleep overtaking him. What might they have in store for him? After all, he was no better than the Vaw, a mere thief in the end, in pursuit of something that they possessed. His eyes closed. He hoped he did not sleepwalk as it would be a terrible way to awaken, in freefall, dropping to the hard glass floor. But at least he had at last found his love and his thoughts wandered back to green and yellow meadows fresh beneath the suns, and two travelers on a reven, two perfect arms about him. At last those arms were again within his reach.

Morning crept upon the chamber of lattices much like it had upon the orchard beneath the dome. Flores awakened to a stir of wings and clicks and at first was startled, believing that they had come upon him unawares while he lay within the sheltering trees. He rose to one elbow and remembered. He glanced up. Amina still slept. He slid to the lip of the room. The light was greater than when he had first arrived, the lattice chamber apparently having been constructed to give greater access to the light of the morning than the evening. To moderate temperatures, he supposed. Rays stabbed between the tenements from some invisible vent. The sight was breathtaking. Flores speculated, imagining himself describing his experience to others. He shook his head. They would merely respond with knowing smiles, or suggest that insanity comes in many forms. He shrugged. It would be their loss. Though perhaps it would be a greater loss should they follow in his steps. Some experiences are not meant for more than one to have. He smiled. Alienation from others he could tolerate. It was alienation from himself that he could not.

Flores stood. After finishing what remained of the food and drink, and regretting that the water was insufficient for bathing, he turned his attention once more to effecting their escape. Again he thought to persuade Amina to link arms with him so that he could climb up to her cell. It was useless. On closer inspection of the slippery edges of the hexagons he realized that she had no means to steady herself or him. He would cause both to plunge to bloody ruin. He returned to the vent in the far end for his toiletry and gazed through. The domefloor stretched thousands of meters below. Two phalanxes of similar vents faced each other in a sheer drop over the gap. Even if he could wriggle through the vent, there was even less to cling to than in the front. The rest of the room was flawless, no hole or imperfection to be found.

His was the perfect prison. At the front of his cell he sat cross-legged, dejected, his bearded chin in his palm. Drumming his fingers, he watched. After the majority of creatures had left, occasional selks wandered in and out of the lattice so that, should he attempt to climb over its face, he could never do so unobserved. And he suspected that such would never be allowed.

Amina awoke. The curled ball moved and the dark arms stretched and the eyes turned toward him in sudden recollection. She re-curled, drawing the thick garment tighter about her and moving away from the glass as if conscious of the greater light that poured through. His brows furrowed. He leaned upon the glass. The shadow turned away.

"What have they done to you?" he demanded. "There is some reason why you will not speak to me, or show yourself." Only the eyes returned. He peered closer. There was something different about them, colder, harder, paler than he remembered. Anger rose within. He smote the glass. "If these creatures have done ought to harm you, I swear I will not rest till I have exterminated them from Maalstrom. It is plain what they do, how they choose to reproduce–" He checked himself–for her sake. "They have made you ashamed. There is no need. Whatever they have done, it means nothing to me. And will not to others. A captive has no control over her life." He leaned against the glass; she retreated.

"You will not speak?"

The eyes looked back to him, and lowered.

He twitched his lips, pushed out the lower as he often did when contemplating some problem. He sighed and returned to the front of his cell and turned his mind to thoughts of escape.

Lying prone upon the floor he thrust his head over the side. The drop was sickening. On closer inspection, however, he concluded it might be possible to negotiate the face of the lattice by hanging over the edge of each cell and swinging just enough to drop into the cell below. One mistake would mean the end. But that would be preferable to waiting for Amina to be taken for the grisly purpose of the malkops, leaving him to rage helplessly till they came for him. But climb where? He could never leave the city. He could not rescue himself, let alone her. He sighed. His chin again sank into his hands.

Something glinted. He let his eyes wander about the vast chamber. They took in the soft rays, the golden motes of dust, the amber cellwork, a soaring malkop in the distance, and returned to the floor by the high arching entrance. It glinted again. He focused his gaze and one brow shot up. A ring. A circle of glass far below, resting upon the floor near the entrance. There could be no doubt as to what it was. The bracelet– *his* bracelet. Dropped when they dragged him within. Suddenly he knew what he must do. He turned to Amina.

"My love. Listen. I am going to leave." Her eyes widened with fright and despair. She shook her head. "I must! Tonight, after it is dark, I am going to climb down the front of the hexcomb. I cannot explain but I know that if I can but gain the floor, I will be able to escape from the city of the malkops. I am still king of Ven, and the chief of the most powerful clan in the city. I am going back to Ven–but I will return with enough ships and swords to free you; and after what I have seen on this Island, I know I can persuade them to follow. Be patient. There is nothing I can do here to assist you, and I do not think they will kill you. But I cannot get you out without help."

She gazed through tears, saddened, but resigned. He sucked his lips and turned. He stood with confidence, now heedless of the drop, and watched the ring, its gleam burning in his eyes like a wheel of fire. The day was the longest he had ever endured, but at length the shadows began to grow, and the rays grew dull then vanished, and the selks brought the evening meal and departed, and the time came for him to act. Flores stretched and exercised his muscles. He used the water to clean feet and hands, to prevent losing his grip from grime. He would have to time his departure with care. He determined that he ought not to wait till the darkness was complete else he would no longer be able to see. The malkops saw well in the dark, and their hearing was good, hence his best chance was in semi-darkness.

The last light faded. The chamber was quiet. With a last tender kiss upon the cold surface of the glass and a tear from the blurred eyes of his consort, he strode to the edge of his cell and lay down. Backing carefully over the lip of the floor, he let his legs swing toward the interior of the cell below. He prayed that it would be empty–as each of the cells he would encounter. He lowered himself to his elbows, then to his forearms, then allowed his weight slowly to sink till he was stretched lengthwise over its front. He could now gaze upon the interior of the cell. He saw that it had no inhabitant. He began to swing. His scarred right wrist twinged with pain. Ignoring it, he concentrated. The slightest mistake would send him plunging. With an effort of will he avoided dropping his gaze the hundreds of feet to the floor. He swung–and let go. A moment later he landed within the cell, and breathed. He wore only his loin-cloth; he could now see how reckless he had been to propose to Amina to venture near the edge with her robe. It was perilous enough with only skin contacting the glass.

He returned to the edge. The floor seemed no nearer, and the darkness had grown. He had no time to waste. Turning, he backed over the lip a second time and let himself slowly down. With a twist he landed on the floor of the second cell. Again it was empty. However, the cells were each alike, none having any opening or variation that might offer another method of egress. He went on.

The next cell proved no different from the others, and the next. His progress was slow–agonizingly so. Each level a new stage for danger. He passed several more. In one he found an empty bowl. In another a trace of fungus branch. In another stray shreds of moss. He kept going. The darkness grew so that he could no longer see the floor, and the eeriness of his venture swelled, climbing steadily down the irsrem-comb like a spider down its web, except that he was the prey, whose soft flesh the owners sought, the malkops who perhaps watched from the safety of the night for him to exhaust himself or slip. He could see himself in his mind lying cracked like a melon, their dark shapes drawing near, claws sliding free, jaws opening... He paused in a cell to catch his breath. He had no notion of how far he had come, or how many levels remained. He had not counted them before he began. Now he regretted this over-sight and wished he could somehow gauge it. He descended to his knees to begin again–then halted.

Wings approached. Swarming from the dark they came, hammering the air in their haste, jostling, clicking. Wave after wave rose up to disappear in the maze of hexes. Flores rose to his feet. Had he his bracelet, he could block them. Make them think the cell was occupied. But he had not. He frowned, and waited, and hoped. Perhaps his luck would hold, perhaps none of those arriving lived within this cell. At the entrance wings beat, then folded. His luck had failed again.

Flores retreated into the deeper blackness of the cell's rearward section.

He knew he would be no match for the creature's strength and claws without his rapier or his dagger. He crouched, made ready to spring. If he could link one arm about its throat, he could silence it before it warned the others...

The malkop entered and shuffled forward. Its face and eyes were downcast, as from great exhaustion. Without raising its glance, it turned and reached for a bowl of water that lay by the entrance. It drank. A sigh filled the room. In the vague light by the entrance Flores thought he glimpsed a smile, the pretty features upended with joy. Placing its hands upon its hips, it wriggled out of its cloth and stood straight in the night. Its hands–claws now sheathed–ran over its bulbous breasts. Then along its inner thighs. Flores caught his breath. There remained just enough light to see the signs of Atasan. Again he wondered at the strangeness of his life that had put him here on this distant continent in a private cell with God's angel–or was it devil?–to glimpse what one should never see. Disturbing thoughts coalesced within and he found himself seeing the creature in ways that his more rational mind would never have allowed had he been less tired, or the night less dark. The wings half-unfolded, as much as the room permitted. They flapped tiredly. Flores thought he understood. It was exhausted, having just returned from a far journey carrying essence or a corpse. It wiped at its mouth as if it had paused in the orchard–the hand snaked again between its legs and Flores wondered where else it had delayed. It sat. One leg crossed the other and it lay across the cell, using the slope of one wall for a headrest. Flores chilled. Its pose prevented him from escaping.

What now? He reflected: he would have to wait till it was asleep, then seek to step over the sleeping form to resume his task. That would not be easy. Not only would the size of the wings make this difficult–they were still not refolded in their entirety–but he was uncertain as to whether he could move with sufficient quiet to avoid being heard.

He had no choice. In the shadows he waited, standing quietly, taking breaths in slow deep draughts despite his previous labor, the air passing through his open mouth to avoid any hiss from the passage of the air. For a considerable time he remained thus, long past the last whisper of wings or movement from the larger chamber beyond, and long past the last impression of movement from the creature that blocked his path– those in the chambers below must sleep as well before he could proceed. He chilled at what lay ahead. It was too late to return to his cell above. Yet he could not remain where he was. At first light the malkop would awaken and alert its companions to the fact that he had escaped from his prison–or perhaps kill him itself. Malkop or not, he must press on.

Stepping forward, he came to the side of the body. He gazed curiously upon it. It was beautiful. Somehow in the night it looked different from the day, when, like all Vensor-sa, he was accustomed to seeing the pendant breasts of the creatures without images of blasphemous seduction obsessing him. But now, in the night, with one of the creatures denuded of its clothing, lying supine as his own consort Amina had used to lie, he felt different... He found his eyes drawn to its breasts, and focusing on its loins, running over the smooth muscled abdomen. It had the figure of an hour-glass. The creature stirred and the wings folded behind it as it turned upon one side.

Flores stepped back–then took advantage of its new position to step entirely over so that he now had access to the entrance. Sinking to his knees, he prepared to let his feet slip over the edge. Then halted. His face was but inches from the face of the selk. He examined the creature's delicate features, unable to continue, unable to tear himself away. The face was so slender, so pale. The eyes, even in sleep, were large and round like those of Amina. The hair flowed, curving outward like its hips, flecks of gold interspersed among the blonde strands. Its forehead was high, intelligent, the lips full and sensitive. The cheeks moved, blowing air, and Flores realized that he had drawn even closer, his own exhalation passing over the creature's face, which was now flushed as if from passion. The creature moaned–a small sweet moan–and rolled towards him. The lips puckered, and, before he could let himself over the edge, moved forward and joined with his. For one moment he remained thus, eyes wide, lips fastened to those of the malkop, while the creature remained sedated, eyes still shut, its breath hot and restive from carnal memories and dreams, its lips moving seductively over his in a sensuous slippery motion. Flores chilled. He felt his body reacting in a manner that was as inappropriate as it was dangerous for the completion of his quest. This was not supposed to be; with a shock and a sense of eerie mystery he realized that he did not want to leave. Finally, with a delicious liquid squip his mouth separated from that of the selk and he lowered himself quietly over the edge, leaving the creature still asleep and smiling.

Observing the next cell below, he was chagrined to see it too was occupied. However, this selk was somewhat removed from the entrance so that he felt he could drop to the floor of the cell without much sound. He did so and found that he had learned to make even less sound than before. The deep slow rumble of the creature also assured him that all of the malkops had recently returned from a journey–perhaps the same journey–and that each was exhausted beyond what any casual noise could awaken. They might sleep thus for days, lost in their malkop-dreams. Flores proceeded, more confident.

The succeeding levels indeed turned out to be occupied by their complement of malkops, but the activity of Flores proved inadequate to alert them and after the passage of another half hour the bare foot of the Turlicum stepped quietly onto the smooth glass floor of the chamber. Elation seized hold as he swept his eye over the lattices. But a few more steps and he would have in his hand the means to deal with the creatures. To deal with the city–indeed to deal with the cities of all his enemies. He gazed into the darkness, which somewhere far above masked the prison of the object of his love–his queen–and his eye ran over the cells of her captors. He looked upon them as an eagle might look at monkeys, or, more precisely, as a snake might look upon birds sleeping in their nests. One more step and he would have them once more in his power.

He turned. Strode confidently to the vast arch that marked the entrance to the lattice-chamber. And paused. In his mind he counted off the steps that he knew would lead to the exact spot where he had seen the bracelet: first to the stanchion, then twenty paces to the left, and fifteen from the wall. He stopped. Frowning, he returned to the arch and counted again. Twenty paces along the wall, then fifteen out into the room. Nothing. It came to him.

The bracelet was gone.

He cursed, blasting his luck. Silently he condemned the god Gethos to perdition as well for the god's perfidy. After all of his effort, the risks he had successfully run, to lose once again due to the belated obsession of some selk with maintaining the cleanliness of its city. What could he do now? He dared not walk the corridors as himself–but he would die before he allowed them to return him to his cell. Die how? He had no weapon but his hands. He gripped them into fists and moved cautiously beneath the arch to where the lattice-room connected to one of the central halls leading to the tower. His foot kicked something. Turning, he saw a small glint in the night.

The bracelet! It was not taken after all, but had merely been knocked through the archway by careless feet, as it had previously been kicked into the lattice-room. With a sense of relief that brought tears to his eyes, he stooped, picked up the bauble...slowly, and with a deliberate sensuous move that was more caress than function, slid it on his wrist.

No immediate change was produced. Indeed, gazing upon his hands and body he could perceive no difference in his appearance at all, seeing the same grimy skin and breechclout as before. But his mind focused, and summoned the image of a malkop, and he knew that should any of the creatures stumble upon him now, he would not be recognized, but could walk away with impunity, go where he wished, observe what there was to be observed...

Flores turned back to the latticework for one last glance toward the cell that housed his love before departing. The upper reaches were lost in the pitch-blackness of the chamber. He was sad. After a journey of half a world, and untold dangers and harrowing survivals, he had finally found his love. Only to leave her. He needed warriors, and money, and–above all–weapons to free Amina. But at least he knew that it was possible, that if he had the will and the energy to do it, the deed could be done. He faced the corridor and his will set the energy in motion. He strode forward.

First he had to visit a certain spot, where a certain Vaw had stood before the inspection of Atasan. He found that his previous expectation that the city would be clothed in blackness at night was wrong. A subtle glow animated the corridors and chambers, just enough to enable one to negotiate the hallways. It could not be otherwise, he realized, since the physical needs of the malkops required them to travel the halls by night as well as day. Coming to a wide ramp–and passing several bands of malkops on the way, who ignored him as he had hoped–he mounted the passageway and followed it through several levels. He climbed the entire height of the city, staying as near the central tower as he could, though most of the passages were now familiar due to his previous explorations.

Before long he came to the place that he sought. He stood in the large plaza at the pinnacle of the city and gazed upon the auditorium that was not an auditorium and upon the sphere suspended over the pit within the tower. The sphere had moved, hanging somewhat higher over the abyss than he remembered. Or perhaps it was the light of the moons. Their red and green umbras lay draped across the plaza like flags upon a table.

Walking to the vicinity where the Vaw had stood, he halted. There it lay. As the bracelet had lain in the corridor where he had dropped it during his abduction, none of the malkops bothering to retrieve it, so lay the gill of the Vaw where he had raised it in his hand. Flores took it, brushed it off. He smirked. He needed nothing more. Without another glance he left.

More hours were necessary for him to traverse the many levels and return to the place where the tower intersected the lowest floor of the city.

His initial fears that the malkops might grow suspicious at one of their number carrying a strange device eased when he recalled that the bracelet had masked his loincloth. Why should a thing in his hands be more visible than a thing on his hips? He exulted again, realizing that even a sword and shield would be invisible should he possess them. When he arrived before the looming jag of tachylite he realized that he was tired. The climb down the lattice had in fact exhausted him; no more than nervous energy had carried him to the plaza. He must rest. Standing before the tower, he recalled the stab of light that had shone upon his face when he had first entered the city. He turned again toward the north where a faint breath of light indicated the dawning of the suns, and their illumination of the isle of the clashing rocks. But one glance upon the rock, nepenthe after his imprisonment in the lattice, and he would return and search for a darkened room in which to sleep. He set out for the light, ignoring the stream of laden malkops bubbling from the vents.

The speck of land was still there. Perched on the northeastern horizon it resisted the attack of the sea with the same tenacity as before, the great sprays of spume distinct, a perpetual mist of spoondrift about it. Through the coolness of the sea-wind, the suns warmed his face, sending a glow of satisfaction and humor filtering through his exhausted sinews. Flores sat. No activity could be seen in the distance. Only the steady movement of the malkops to the south as they arrived at the wall of the pyramid with their usual repellent baggage.

His mind returned to Ven and he tried to imagine what his reception might be–even whether the city still stood after his long absence. With no queen to guide them, his citymates had been incapable of action. Unwilling to defend or feed themselves, how did he suppose he could spur them to invade Heaven? He lowered his gaze in dejection. Now that he was prepared to depart upon his journey, the fantastic unlikelihood of its success seemed obvious. Why, even if he did manage to bring the army of Ven to the Isle, and somehow brought enough gills to evade the selks, they still bore little chance of surviving within the dome. The selks would be upon them like a storm.

His eyes fell on the bracelet and lit on a smudge of dirt. He pouted. Glancing about to ensure that no malkops watched, he ducked his head beneath the railing and removed it. A single wipe sufficed to clean the device. He moved to replace it on his wrist, when a sudden pain from his scar caused him to flinch. The bracelet dropped and bounced. He watched as it rolled within a small rill in the floor–by coincidence the same that had earlier stubbed his toe–and followed the rill down the balcony. Flores caught his breath. Lurched after. The bracelet picked up speed. At the end he glimpsed a manhole and with a merry ring the bracelet entered–and was gone.

For a moment Flores stared, frozen on hands and knees. Madly he scrambled, now oblivious to discovery by the selks. The network of gutters and rivulets he had previously observed, intended to channel the flow of rain so that the city would be free of floods, sprang into his memory with the force of a heavy blow. He stopped before the manhole, pale and shaking. His earlier curse of the deity Gethos became a eulogy before the white-hot vituperation he turned upon himself. Damn him for the fool he was! He gulped. Carefully intruded his head. The pipe turned outward; he could see it quite clearly in the penetrant light of the suns. Apparently it followed the domewall, and, pausing to listen with care, Flores thought he detected–from an incalculable distance–a quiet ring of glass on glass. It ceased.

He peered to descry the bottom of the pipe. Away it fell, plunging straight into the depths with neither turn nor crook for variance, and apparently within the domewall since it gave access to the first level of the city. On either side of the pipe, which was of sufficient width for a man, he glimpsed a series of small rungs, angled, and spaced every three feet. Also constructed of irsrem, they had been mounted with skill on the sides of the drain, presumably, as Flores noted, to prevent debris from accumulating and obstructing the flow. Lit as it was by the suns, the interior was not unpleasant and it came to Flores as he lay with his body half exposed on the balcony, that he had perhaps stumbled on a way to exit the city unobserved. He reversed and backed into the pipe.

For what seemed an age he climbed. Coming as it did close upon his previous demarche across the face of the web-like lattice, he was unprepared and already exhausted when first he embarked on the feat. In the best of circumstances the climb would have more than taxing or difficult. In his reduced condition it was torment. One leg followed another, his arms moved from grip to grip. At times he let his body contact the slick surface of the glass while he skipped monkey-like down the handholds. Often his pain rose to such levels that it required a supreme act of will not to let go–and let his weight take him down. But he had no notion of how far it might lead. Or to where. To some level of glass within the domewall, which would prove lethal for an approaching living thing? To the shore outside of the dome itself, where the malkops awaited trespassers? Or perhaps further, to realms deeper and unguessable, melding with that darkness within the tower? He must hold on, he gritted. He must descend at will, under control. He now praised Gethos–and all the gods–with the same vehemence, and more, as he had cursed them with during the night. If only they would intercede as they had for Macius, send him the strength and the courage to weather the trial...he would never again traduce their names, though he knew, even in his most trying moments, that he would not keep his oath, and that the gods knew he would not. The gods, he now suspected, did not exist. Except in the strength of men's minds, as aspirations for themselves, in their will to master themselves and a stubborn world.

Though the glass about him was thick beyond any in the city, and he could see nothing through the glass with clarity, nevertheless, the gloom was not complete, and, as he had discovered when he had first exited the pits, both suns and moons shone through. As the twin suns of Vensor rose higher in the sky, the glare they cast steadily increased his vision. Bathed in this light, he gradually became aware that within the angle of the wall a mass of shadow grew, a shadow that he surmised was the orchard. Outside the angle, in the direction of the suns–the orbs exuded dull and yellow through the irsrem–was a similar shadow, of a lighter complexion and more distant. The ocean.

A hand lost its grip, and he lost several rungs. He arrested his slide and groaned in pain. His shoulders could take no more. Placing his feet upon opposing rungs, he rested. He had not allowed himself rest because of his desire to regain the bracelet, but now he had no choice; the alternative was collapse. His head lolled back upon the drain. Glancing up, he hoped that no rain would appear that day as he had no chance of surviving the downpour. The power of the fluid in its crash down that culvert would be something to test the strength of irsrem itself. There seemed little reason to mount the rungs angled on the sides of the pipe, when the water alone would assuredly crush any obstacles in its path. But, he supposed, the selks wished to be able to clear the pipe by hand. He had already seen that what they built, they built to last. His mind traveled back to the wall-mounted plaza where the selks had fused the wall with their mouths. How had that been possible, he wondered? How had they accomplished such feats of engineering without tools, without equipment, even, seemingly, without rational intelligence?

A sudden sliding swam inside his ears. With a rush of adrenaline–which failed to counteract the mass of melatonin surging through his blood–Flores grew aware that he no longer clung to the rungs within the pipe and was falling through the culvert with ever-increasing speed. He sought to grasp a rung. His hand was dashed sharply aside. He accelerated, spun. He dared not lift a foot, as it would rip off a leg. There was nothing he could do–he fell. An explosion of light struck his eyes. He fought to keep them open but the susurrus of his contact with the glass was like a drug to his ear. Briefly he was conscious that his speed was turning, slowing. At length he stopped.

Flores struggled to one elbow and stared. Overhead swayed a pale thick trunk, its apex crowned with fruited branches. Others marched away in serried ranks, their endless columns reminding him of similar trunks he had once seen within pits. He was again within the orchard. Along either side ran aqueducts, or spillways, which paralleled grass-strewn peninsulas housing the trees. In one of the aqueducts he lay. And before him, not more than a few meters removed, was the bracelet. Quickly he crawled to the bauble. He put it on. Touching his chest to reassure himself that the gill was not lost, he clambered out of the culvert beneath the trees. He forced his eyes skyward–dark shapes hovered. He looked around, caught sight of a cave mouth. It was the way to the pits. Staggering within, he collapsed.

CHAPTER 14

THE GUILD

Ust passed a tremulous glance over the street, and waved his men forward with an impatient hand. On either side, scores of warriors moved from the shadows of tenements lining the avenue of Murfenmas to emerge in the bright light of morning. The king of Ven glanced to the suns. The day promised to be cool and clear, unusual for high summer on the Hedronmas. Good, he thought; I want no slip-ups. His eye followed the sunbeams to earth where they became lost in bas-reliefs, the phallic icons that studded the Guild's exterior casting obscene shadows down the road. Ust ignored them and focused on his task. It was long since he had visited the Eunuch Guild. Not since he first learned of the fates of Jaz and Clesp, who the previous year had criticized the Eunuch Lord in the Assembly–and were then found poisoned by consorts. In that sense he was like the Turlicum. He too did not wish to be next.

At the wide portal, he ordered a pause. At this time, just after dawn, the fewest patrons could be expected on the premises, and street and stoop were empty. Glancing to one side, he was gratified to see that the small garrison of slavers that had survived the siege of Neset offered no resistance to his warriors. He nodded to Revtal and Simlet, and directed a glare at Sendas. The portly noble of the Molersal, stripped of his personal guard, read his meaning and approached with haste.

"Simlet, stay close. Revtal, let your warriors spread throughout. I want every room searched, each chamber, each gallery. No cupboard or cubby will you overlook. And Sendas," the baleful eye fell upon him once again, "remain as close to me as my skin. If there are to be consequences to the deed, I wish us to face them as one. If I fall, or suffer at his hand–I will not fall alone."

Sendas glanced at the portal, thick with iron-banded rorewood, and swallowed.

Revtal spoke in low tones. "There is no need to worry, or for such talk. Before the day is ended, we will have Soorkrul in chains in the public square. Then let him pass judgment on what his king may do."

Ust nodded, glad for the reassurance. He felt less confident than the image he projected and his eyes flitted constantly about. "Right, Sir Revtal. It is I who am King–not he. Let none forget that."

"That foul cripple," added Simlet, unable to prevent sarcasm coloring his voice even when speaking to his overlord, "It angers me to think that the sightless whore hid like a coward all the while the city was being sacked. Only now, when the danger is over and the city renewed, does he come crawling from his hole. Such a one has the gall to tell us how to rule–Simet warriors and Assemblymen of Ven?" His eyes widened with violated dignity.

Sendas removed his hand from his pocket where he had been jingling trinkets to relieve tension. "We will show the blind braggart," he volunteered, joining the spirit of the venture. He had outfitted himself with a pike; it banged clumsily on the portal with the intensity of a doorknocker. Ust placed it more firmly in Sendas' hands. Sendas grinned apologetically. "Many thanks, Sir Ust–my king, that is. Just wait till I get my digits on him! Soorkrul will wish he had never heard of Ven, or that he had helped the Triumvirate before, when he was given the opportunity. And let us not forget his wealth! Despite his vow of poverty, I have heard he is rich beyond the average Simet."

"Just do not interfere, or inconvenience us." Sendas ceased smiling and looked hurt, and Ust softened his tone. "But I am glad you have chosen to come, Sir Sendas. When we are done, the throne will not forget who has helped–and who has hindered." Sendas broke into a smile again, and Ust continued. "Now, let us proceed before they discover us and have time for precautions." He glanced at Simlet and let his gaze tarry a moment longer than necessary. He rankled at Simlet's use of the pronoun 'us' but refrained from rebuking him as he had changed his tone with Sendas. All in good time, he thought. For now, Dos is right–even a king cannot rule without allies.

Ust slid a rapier from its sheath and paused to survey his warriors. About him a hundred Spandicum, Tumlefler, and Calomar waited with swords drawn and glinting. Though without their slavers Vensor's priests were personally defenseless, as befitted their roles as mystics, he had nonetheless insisted that his men wear armor. There was a mystery about the Eunuch Lord that, despite mutilation and blindness, made Ust wary. His predecessor had been in awe each time he had returned from his visits to the head of the Guild. Numsenmur had believed that none knew of his visits–but Ust had listened, and watched. Indeed he had known more about the Serclasler's dealings than he had dared let on while he lived. But now he was done with half-hearted measures. And with the keeping of secrets. He breathed deeply and set his jaw. When Soorkrul should fall into his hands, he would extract answers to many questions, only the first of which was the full extent of his conspirings with the Serclasler chief. He almost wished the eunuchs *would* resist. The first sign of violence on their part would be met with merciless and overwhelming force. Then, in the eyes of the Assembly, he would be justified in going further...

He signaled and felt a chill along his spine, as might a climber about to attempt an unscalable peak that had already cast many to their deaths, or a general crossing his rubicon, aware of the danger and the permanence of the act, but unable to forego his ambition. The portals squeaked. Due to the preoccupations of the eunuchs they were never oiled. Due to the constant traffic they were never locked. They swung wide. Ust relaxed. Their first goal was accomplished: their entry had not been forewarned.

Ust swept through the wide initial chamber used for the enticement of clients. The chamber was broad and low with corbeled torches guttering, the corners littered with salacious iconography, the walls worked in wainscoting separating a scarlet lower band from a pale blue upper. Graphicals obtruded from the blue, themselves painted scarlet, like heaven invaded. Along the walls, at intervals, vertical glass mirrors were inbuilt, here as in the private cubicles, Ust supposed, to provide further enjoyment for the clients. He glanced about the chamber filling with soldiers, and noted that they had indeed achieved surprise. No eunuchs were visible in the gloomy chamber, nor any men from the city itself.

He came to the center. Entry ways into adjacent rooms, where payment was customarily received from customers, opened up. The adjacent rooms gave upon corridors that led to a region containing a hundred cubicles. Steam floated just within sight. Revtal and Simlet began to enter; Ust blocked them with an arm. In one of the thresholds, a stout bald figure in encompassing black cloth had appeared, his garment hiding all flesh but face and hands. He yawned. Upon sighting them, his eyes grew white around the pupils and he turned to flee–a blade persuaded him to halt.

"Bring him."

Another eunuch stumbled from a side room. He too was seized. Ust waved his sword and his men rushed forward. Searches of the adjacent rooms produced dozens more, including a number of emaciated slaves, and a collection of prostitutes, the painted and feathered youths spilling from their beds with confused sleep-crusted expressions.

"Bring them all!"

Complaints rose from the disheveled crowd as they were herded to the center of the chamber. None, as it developed, were armed, though Ust remained alert to the possibility that weapons were cached secretly within reach.

He shouted and the captives grew silent. "I wish everyone in the complex brought to this chamber. There are to be no exceptions. I want all."

The warriors hastened to obey and crowded the eunuchs into one corner while they proceeded to inspect the many corridors and cubicles of the House. Baths and kitchens lay beyond, followed by series of private rooms more sumptuously furnished than the rest.

A group of Spandicum returned with another half-dozen eunuchs in tow. They were different from the rest, Ust noted. These carried less fat, their dress was more refined, and their expressions were more intelligent and less wavering. The others grew quiet as they entered. Eyeing them with redoubled suspicion, Ust's gaze settled upon the tallest who stood with hands in sleeves and watched him with a steady glare. A memory glimmered. It was the one who had insulted him in the Assembly.

Ust's eyes bulged. He could well remember the shame he had felt, his ears burning in recollection. Prepared to administer punishment, his gaze fell on the window-like mirrors and the sight of himself within one, eyes furious, pose agitant, induced calm. Instead he decided on a more cautious and indirect approach. Violence within the Eunuch Guild, after all, was almost as sacrilegious as violence within the Temple. "Approach. I wish us to speak."

Glancing briefly to either side, the eunuch he addressed parted ranks with his comrades and approached. His gown was soft. Unlike the first eunuchs whose garments were of muslin or linen, his was fashioned from indigo swansdown. Only his companions from the plush inner suites were similarly apparisoned. Their overall appearance was not much different from that projected by the lesser eunuchs, but the hems of each were stitched in red thread, which, before the stale mediocrity of the others, was a deviance to delight the eye. Ust gained inspiration from this. That red thread broke a million vows.

The king looked him over with interest, but was unable to entirely banish his nervousness. Before Ust spoke he swallowed. "Man, what is your rank within the Guild? Have you authority to command?"

The eunuch returned his gaze flatly. Beneath a black zuchetto his arrogant face was prismed with plates and angles, every bit as hard and precise as Ust recalled from his earlier intrusion. With a sniff the man glanced about the room. "There is no rank within the Guild. We of the order renounce power and wealth so as to serve God in equal fashion. You must know, King Ust, that I have not the authority to command the least of my peers. Nor do any of those you see." He smiled and briefly bowed, but somehow managed to insinuate condescension even into that act. The lips squirmed. "My comrades do, however, heed my opinion. Perhaps they even heed mine a trifle more than that of others."

Ust had difficulty restraining himself in the face of such insolence. He stepped closer, his sword between them, though he knew he would not use it, for an assault upon a priest would entail unpredictable consequences which he at the present was unwilling to risk. He could, however, still bully. "Be glad you recognized my rank, eunuch, or I might have shown you what command I do wield."

The eunuch said nothing, but defiance continued in his glance.

"Do you suppose you can oppose me?" Ust pressed.

The lips curled. "We oppose no one but Atasan, and then only in our prayers. The way of our order, my king, is nonresistance. It is well known among the corruptible of Maalstrom that no priest has ever raised his hand in violence against another, except in self-defense." He smiled, as if reciting a catechistic truism. "It is in the realm of the spirit where we wage our wars. Our weapons are sounds, words...talk."

"Sometimes talk is the worst of weapons."

A moment passed.

"Yes...both the weakest–and the most effective."

Ust snorted. Realized that the eunuch had understood Ust's meaning–and more besides. He refrained from asking why the Guild thought it necessary to maintain a garrison of armed slavers nearby. "Enough. It is apparent that you are the chief eunuch standing in this room, if not the chief eunuch of the complex. It is appropriate to make you responsible for the fulfillment of my instructions. What is your name, man?"

He paused.

"Sobol." The lips ejected the word, then snapped shut.

"Sobol. There is a man I want from within these walls. I know he is here. He must know he cannot escape. My soldiers have surrounded the entire complex and if he remains within I shall find him–it will go better for you if you produce him yourself. If necessary I will search the entire grounds, from baths to storerooms, without exception–and if I locate him without your aid, I promise that you and your colleagues will regret it."

Sobol slowly smiled while lowering his eyes. His voice turned silky and smooth. "The Guild exists only to serve, my King. Indeed we in the Guild strive always to be the best of citizens–though in truth we are international and have always placed Vensor above any man or city..."

Ust twitched. Was Sobol so bold that, after a direct threat, and before bared sword, he would make an open statement of defiance? A second glance at his image in the mirror brought Ust back under control and he calmed, still not ready to use force.

"Who might it be that you seek?" interjected Sobol. "As you can see we are open to your inspection, all of us, and our temple, for any purpose that the throne may wish." His face turned toward one wall and he directed a small smile at the imagery, seeming to forget that he was involved in conversation.

Disgust wrinkled Ust's face, mingled with irritation at being ignored by one he regarded as an inferior.

Sobol looked back to his king. "We ask only that you not disturb those preparing to meditate. The prosperity of Maalstrom hangs on their work in guarding this realm from the succubus–"

"–I shall disturb whom I like," interrupted Ust. "But perhaps it will not be necessary." He pulled up his chin, fortifying himself. "The man I want is blind–it is Soorkrul, your master and chief. Betrayer of all that you and the City hold dear."

An expression of disbelief melted the eunuch's face, and for a moment Ust thought he saw something alien shining in his eyes. But it vanished and the small smile returned. "Soorkrul, the master of the Eunuch Guild. Then you are not aware..."

"Aware of what?" Ust looked suspicious.

"That our Lord..."

Ust's eyes narrowed.

"–died. During the siege of Nesos. Our mourning was great. He was a famous teacher with many converts to his credit."

"Then perhaps I could see his replacement..."

He shrugged. "We have so lamented his passage that we have not elected one."

Ust frowned. "That cannot be so. I myself saw you enter the Assembly where you told us that–" Ust halted in mid-sentence. The man before his gaze whom he had believed was well-proportioned, with faceted skin and thin lips, preserved from the gross obesity of most of the eunuchs, looked suddenly darker, with lips thicker and bluish, cheeks more round, and the mass of the body greater than he had believed. When he had first entered, Sobol had seemed to be taller than Ust. Now, without a doubt, he was shorter. Ust shook his head. This was not the man who had interrupted him in the Assembly.

"No. No, you cannot be him. That fellow was taller, slimmer, and sharper. You, on the other hand, as I can see, have done nought but recline in pleasure-rooms and consume pastries."

"Forgiveness. The light, my king—it is poor. Worshippers frequently confuse the identities of the purified in the gloom. It is a pity. It makes for fierce jealousies among the patrons." He bowed, then pointed toward a corridor that led away from the chamber. "Are we ready to begin your search? If it pleases the king, I shall myself accompany you through every chamber in our complex so that you will see that what I have said is true." Ust felt another urge to combat, but there was something about Sobol's voice that, despite his manner, seemed to pacify his soul and encourage serenity. Before he had realized it, Ust found that he had suppressed his inclination for springboard violence and begun to trudge in Sobol's path. His guards following behind, he and Sobol entered the nearest corridor.

Sobol indicated one passage among several, and spoke to Ust while he walked. "It may please the king to learn that our teacher died at the hands of the Neset-sa during the sacking of the City by the barbarians. Some say by the hand of King Nesos himself. Along with the many dead produced by the invasion, the holy workers took his body to Heaven." He gently shook his head. "We now have no guide, no counselor in our work. Indeed, my king, after those troubled times, we have no initiates—no blind men."

Ust paused. "None?"

"None. Out of grief, all of our initiates immolated themselves when they learned of the death of our teacher."

"Then you did see his body?"

"Not I. But others did. We took our dead by night to the Fields where he was laid with the rest upon the altars. There was no special ceremony." He paused to look at Ust. "We do not accord our dead any more favors than we do our living. The next master—once he is chosen, or sent from the center of our order in Klopus—will depart Maalstrom in similar fashion: tossed in the fields to rot, or be removed, as the workers see fit."

Ust nodded, and resumed walking. With Simlet and Sendas close behind with their clumps of sharp-eyed warriors, Sobol proceeded through a maze of rooms and cubicles and hallways, filth and grime smattering their horizon at each turn of the twisted floorplan. Ust peered nervously down the narrow passages which offered any number of opportunities for ambush. He kept his sword free; everywhere he fancied he felt hidden eyes. His own shifted constantly between the dark form of Sobol, which moved with agile sureness, and the rotting walls that crept past. He was careful to keep him in view. Who knew how many secret passages or trip-doors lay among the walls and artwork? How could he be certain that what he saw was real? Or that the real did not lay behind it, unviewed and unsuspected? He paused on occasion to yank aside dustladen curtains, glare down rank wells, or test flooring. Constantly his wary eye hovered, each empty room they passed causing his fear and tension to mount, till his impatience became something tangible, like the fear which had turned to sweat.

The complex was larger than Ust had supposed and he found himself tiring. Several levels were traversed, each connected by wooden ramps like balustraded gantries, or gloomy helical stairwells of ill-hewn common stone. Descending a ramp, they arrived at the steam rooms of the complex. Here, overlooked by the first sweep of the soldiers, they found a score of slaves laboring in lung-destroying dampness and shadow, stoking a row of white-hot ovens with old refuse and wood. A few were chained. Recalcitrants, Ust decided, from the scars upon their backs. Several eunuchs, similarly overlooked, looked at them in surprise. They approached, unfurling great whips, and halted only upon seeing Sobol. Without a word they returned to their task. Ust squinted and glimpsed another stairwell. There were apparently lower levels still–Ust thought he heard groans from below. He turned away. Like all Vensor clans, the Guild judged its own. Its methods were no affair of the city. Still, he felt ill from confinement in the dark and filthy crawlways and wished suddenly for open air.

"Light," he coughed, "I wish light, and clean air."

Sobol shrugged, apparently unaffected, and climbed to the wing that led by catwalk to the Temple of Ven. Here on a walled veranda beneath the noonday suns, separated by baked brick panels and flanked by waving trees, five novices sat nude upon wooden palettes while gazing into the sky. As they stared, clothed servants attended their needs, both physical and mental, whispering into their ears verses of the Zeyd, and holy teachings from the Revelations of the Twelve. Ust was uncomfortable here as well. He shivered as he scrutinized the aspirants. What arcane arguments had the eunuchs used to persuade them to undertake such torment? Each was young, fresh from the orphanage; their eyes still tearing from the glare, unable to stand the pain for more than a few moments at a stretch. It was indeed as Sobol had said. They still could see, and would not be truly blind for months. Only then would the revelations begin, and in time–if they proved to be favored–might hope to add theirs to the Twelve, and become the Thirteenth. He hoped for their sake that they would remain believers. A few in the past had attempted to apostatize... He glanced once at Sobol. The chief eunuch smiled upon them, as if bestowing flowers upon children. Sobered, Ust resumed his search indoors.

In many of the chambers he had found displayed the same vertical panes of glass he had encountered when he first arrived. After an hour of useless scrutiny of gloomy and deserted passages, and fruitless dispatching of repeated squads of warriors to examine every crack and corner, who inevitably returned sullen and empty-handed, in the midst of a corridor Ust turned suddenly to Sobol and pointed to one of the panes.

"What is the purpose of this glass, Sobol? It seems too much." Ust eyed him with care. "Could there be some reason besides merely primping yourselves?"

The eunuch shrugged ever so slightly. He turned out his hand in nonchalance toward a door which stood two feet to one side–Ust smiled in triumph. He motioned quickly for his men to tear the glass free. "I suspected as much! A room from which you spy on each other and your patrons. Doubtless joined by secret hallways, and a chamber where Soorkrul waits laughing at our confusion."

Placing their swords behind the pane, the soldiers pried. With a splitting sound, it broke loose from the wall and tumbled to the floor in a thousand pieces.

Behind was unpainted wall and broken mountings.

Ust frowned. "The next!"

His men ripped loose another–it too clattered to the floor and broke. And another. Then several more. Ust turned to Sobol.

"You would joke with me on this? I'll have your nails torn from your hands!"

"I but invited you to do as you did, my king. There are no secret ways here. As I have said all is open. All apparent. I have not restricted your movements in the slightest, but on the contrary have escorted you myself wherever you choose to look. Our lord is as light, Sire–indeed He *is* Light. To crawl behind walls would contravene the highest teachings of our master and our order. It is light that we slaves of God worship–darkness and the flesh that we abhor." He gazed at the panes serenely.

Several more crashed to the ground and Ust signaled for them to stop. For a minute more he stood, then, swirling, strode away.

Next they came to storerooms and a central chamber–the heart of the complex–where the eunuchs stored the essence of irsrem until sold to the irsrem guild. Sobol produced a key and unlocked the massive rorewood that served as a safedoor to the vault. The interior of the room, circa fifty feet square, was in marked contrast to the rest of the complex. The floors and walls were of hard irsrem, glittering and spotless, great efforts having been made to keep it so. On a dais in the center was the Substance, compacted in a huge sphere of shiny wetness. The sides of the sphere, unsupported by any structure that Ust could detect, seemed to defy gravity. As Ust watched, Sobol picked up one of several sewn bladders by the threshold, apparently left when the soldiers had arrested the doormen, and opened it with a small knife. Ripping away the bladder, he gathered the essence in a hand, then tossed it upon the top of the sphere. Slowly, but quickly enough for the eye to see, the globe sank into the mass of the essence until the sphere had regained its original shape. The heart of the eunuchs' power, thought Ust. While we mine the corta from the Amanus-nama, they bring the globes of essence from their cultic center, and deliver it to the glass-smiths, who, with the aid of water, forge the tear-glass–irsrem–the seed of mortal empire. A single glance had sufficed to reveal that no man hid within the chamber, and Ust signaled to leave.

"I have seen enough, Simlet," he said in the hallway. "We will find no blind man here."

Sobol watched, and smiled.

Once more in the entrance chamber Ust halted to again inspect the eunuchs. At one end of the room, ensconced under a hallows' eve bramble of twisted erotica, they sat under guard. They seemed more bored than resentful. Several bore expressions, though, that Ust found unreadable, or vaguely impressive of...what? What was it that shone intermittently through their masked faces? Ust started. In a single glance from one of the eunuchs of red-threaded rank as he gazed upon Sobol, Ust read the first clear sign thus far. Fear. Abject, crawling fear. Ust glanced to Revtal and Simlet to see if they had seen. They had not and but folded their arms.

"No blind man." Simlet restated the obvious.

"And no wealth," added Revtal.

Sobol rejoined the priests, and stared quietly ahead with unshakeable confidence, the challenge that Ust had found so intimidating still present on his face.

Ust cleared his throat. "Heed your king, eunuchs. Sobol has told me that your 'teacher' Soorkrul is dead. I do not know if that is true or if he watches us even now from some unseen lair, but I am here to tell you that if he—or any of you—dares to interfere in my affairs in the future...know you that the lives of all in the Guild will prove extremely short."

The attention of several seemed to drift, whether from fatigue or boredom Ust could not tell.

The king shouted and stamped his foot. "I want Soorkrul's head! Or I want him never heard from—or heard of—in this city again! Elect a new leader in your way. And do not allow him to meddle in the affairs of his betters. For if I have to return to your building, or if I learn that you have lied and that your former master still draws breath within these walls, I swear to you that I shall not rest till this entire building is burned and the bones of every priest in Ven lie broken in execution square."

The eunuchs exchanged glances but said nothing, and with a last look of sweat-tinged disgust, Ust spun on his heel. Marching through the exit, he re-emerged into the clean sunlight of Ven. Though he looked decisive and strong, inwardly he felt stricken. Having invaded the sacred dwelling of the Guild, which was not only the fount of Ven's cult, but the source of its essence, a material resource the city could not afford to lose, he had gambled and lost. In his dispute with the Guildmaster, he had also squandered the element of surprise and could not now hope to catch him unawares—while Soorkrul, on the other hand, could now bide his time and plan his revenge in his own adumbrated way. That revenge would be, he suspected, both terrible and secret. Recalling Sobol, he felt desolate. His failure was virtual complete. Soorkrul's assistant had felt bold enough to defy him while he, unsure of himself, had blinked before the challenge. Indeed he found himself blinking before challenges more and more. He thought again of his vanished mentor and listed his attributes— if he desired to keep his throne, he must become even more like Numsenmur. He sulked as he mounted his reven. Being a king was less fun than he had thought.

In the avenue of Murfenmas, now at high noon and crowded with children and merchants, who halted to view the soldiers exiting the Guild, Ust looked around from atop his mount. He threw his hand.

"Sendas!"

His colleague came, brows raised.

"I have an errand for you—one of importance. I wish you to go to the dock and check on the departure of our friend. Make sure he is comfortable and that his boat lacks nothing in staples, for his journey will be long and tiresome. Then come to me at Vim."

Sendas nodded. At the bend in the street, Molersal warriors met Sendas and together they vanished in the direction of the docks, while Ust loped and hopped toward the plaza.

In front of the Guild, the avenue soon cleared of warriors and filled with the usual city traffic, among which were several slave-borne palanquins. Revtal and Simlet divested themselves of their armor, and the palanquins lowered to receive them. Their retinues began to move, then suddenly halted.

"Wait," said Revtal. "Simlet, I have just thought of something."

"Yes?"

"The Guildmaster..."

"Yes?"

"What if Soorkrul was *not* blind?"

"*Not* blind?"

"Not..." He turned and passed his glance once more over the imposing facade with its obscene gargoyles, which kept even the most oblivious and narrow-sighted from proceeding with their business unperturbed. "*...blind.*"

৯ৎ ৪) ৫৪ ৵

Evening fell as Sendas, trailed by footmen, plodded his reven along the broad esplanade that lined the southwest littoral of Ven. The waters of the Suma flowed sluggishly past. The far shore was invisible in mist. Some distance up the wharf, the galley he sought hove into view. It was small, but adequate. Still, he himself would not relish a month's confinement in its bow. Thank Gethos he did not have to endure such a voyage—but then he had not incurred the wrath of the king as had his unfortunate colleague. Sendas brooded on his perennial misjudgment of character. As he had misjudged his enemy Flores, he had misjudged his friend Ust, who, as it turned out, was not only more competent than he had believed, but was in truth no friend at all. How to judge? Did his errors spring from the subtlety of their characters—or reflect something within himself? A chill slowly spread, more from inner doubt than the mist. Was he really so different from other Simet-sa that, in the end, understanding was impossible?

The ambassador appeared in the growing darkness. He stood with a crew on the wooden deck, preparing to step onto the boat. Sendas appraised him from afar. A white surplice damp with fog could not hide his belly that protruded more than ever beyond the axis of his spine. He had only just recovered his weight after his arduous trip to Neset. How sad that he would now lose it, and return to his former ill health. Sendas looked to his own pendulous midriff, surrounded as it was by rolling regions of flesh. Like the ranges of an unexplored continent, the folds circumvented his gyrating body. Well, he thought, we cannot all be so healthy. Sendas looked again at his friend, and felt sad. He did not wish him to go. Before each meal I must toast his return, he resolved. He halted at the side of Dos.

The owl-eyes turned and peered. They seemed more resigned than defeated, staring up at him from the bland bald head that crowned sagging cheeks of taffy. The cheeks reversed the direction of their flow and curved into a hesitant smile. Diplomacy as innate as his could never be banished. Even with friends.

"Ust has sent me to make certain that you have all that you desire—since the trip will be a long one."

Dos shrugged. "My needs are met. There is nothing more I wish. Except more time to think and meditate on the ancients, and the Compendium of Sidros." He held up a work by a long-dead notable of the scribal guild.

"Your books keep you as food keeps others," said Sendas, attempting to inject lightness. "I think you will have time to read them—unless you lose them overboard." He laughed. "And this time do not start a war!"

Dos looked hurt. "That was not my fault. You know that."

"As you say. Well, I must go. I have other errands to run." He spoke but did not move.

Facing the galley, the ambassador swayed as he turned and negotiated the plank. He took a frail step on board. Settling on the benches, he slumped like some aged crow and fingered the bound palimpsest in his lap. The crew dipped the oars in the waters, and, with a last melancholy wave, the galley slipped away till it was no more than an outline in the fog. Sendas waited until it had vanished. Why did he feel he would never see his comrade again? Suddenly he was seized with the sensation that something tragic would happen on the trip, that if he were to yell or call for Dos to return that he may save his friend's life.

But the boat had gone. Slowly Sendas turned his reven and plodded

back toward the plaza, while his warriors, who had formerly trailed behind, moved now in front, then alongside. Only when they had entered
the plaza did the footmen again bring up the rear...

The night sank further into desuetude. In the sky above Ven, Gethos
bathed the city in blue, staining the river's mist like smoke. Sendas and
his party had long since entered the plaza and the wharf was devoid of
traffic when a lone figure materialized from the blue mist where the
Simet noble had been. The silence of the city flowed before it like the
first rumors of a disease. Quietly it approached the dock, leading a reven
by the reins. The darkness was almost complete and the water satiny
with moonlight; the figure advanced over the boards with a purposeful
air. At the edge of the dock it took form. It was a man, dressed casually
in clothing of a sort one might find on a summer day, though the night
was far cooler than the day.

Seeming not to notice the dropping temperature, he moved to the
water's edge. He halted, peered, listened. The eyes spun, taking in the
night. The mismatched organs, while discerning the path successfully,
were so rudely incongruous in their sockets, not to mention flawed in
themselves, that the face seemed fundamentally disordered. One–the one
on the right–was yellow. Not the yellow of the suns, nor that of polished
sand, but a yellow from deep within, and tinged with green, as if verdant
fronds stole forth hoping to snare with their stealthy growth. As in a
primeval forest, the young shoots harbored ambush and sudden death.
It was the hue of insane malice; the hue of the soul of a ros. Its mate,
with which it was doomed eternally to struggle, was the pale blue of ul-
tramarine. Far from dark seas, clear shallows swam in those pools, their
currents surrounding the pupil as quiet lagoons do a desert isle–but pools
of indefinable age, and, despite their clarity, still obscurant, dotted with
the effluvia of eons and stark limbs like frozen dead. What might one
find in those lucid depths? Denizens of a different world; predators of
old; elusive darting and crawling things with secret hungers that
watched. Swamping the conflicting orbs, which seemed at war with
themselves, was a landscape of soft puffy flesh white as dough and wet
as sweat, no stretch or particle of its unnatural slopes free of a glistening
that far outshone the mist. It was as if nymphs with jars hid unseen, pouring oil onto cotton, or a dermic film of glass had come to form a crust-
like patina. Beneath the verdigris, cells grew, became bloated, split.
White coils thicketed the brows; they sprang again from the masculine
forehead. No longer a compact nap, the strands ran thickly down his
temples, providing sufficient cover for any number of nymphs.

At the water the pumping legs paused. The man turned to a bag that was laid across the reven and withdrew a tangled thing of cylindrical tube and rubber. Placing the thing on his head, he inhaled. A hollow sound evoked a silent nod. He was ready. Taking the reins of the reven in hand, he began to lead it toward a ramp that gave directly upon the water, when he sighted something lying on the dock, and halted. There, on the boards before his feet, lay a circlet of shining glass, its flawless and unfaceted surface shimmering in the light of the moons. He bent to stare. Blue and scarlet and amethyst played about its rim, and without hesitation, though perhaps a subtle excitement did cause him to accelerate his movement, he slipped it onto a wrist. For a considerable time he stood as if rooted, the kaleidoscopic orbs focused statue-like on the bauble, his body unmoving, silent, breath itself not daring to impinge upon his thought. At last he broke the spell and moved, and revolved slowly in a circle. His eyes perceived: wharf, wares, ramp, stoops, galleys, rippling riverwater. Over all the fog hung like a cloak. He turned again to the stream and the bristled brows began to arch. With a sudden movement he removed the contraption from round his head and, drawing back his arm, let fly with surprising strength. Far out in the current the device slapped the surface and sank. He turned and, reven still in tow, prowled the length of the dock while his eyes combed the ground like a sleuth. He paused and nodded–the spoor led toward the plaza.

He too had long departed when more movement stirred ghost-like in the fog. Out of the midst of the Suma, the simple outline of a humble bark took form. It touched the dock. A broad man massively muscled climbed easily and silently ashore, where he planted both feet on the boards and extended a sure arm to a companion. Moving with less certainty, the companion clambered to his side. On the wharf they peered about and the companion carefully adjusted a voluminous black robe which, though threadbare and patched in places, still managed to hide all flesh and contours of the body. The companion whispered in the ear of the man. As if unable to speak, he replied by making signs with his hands. The pair slipped between two buildings and were gone.

❧ ❦ ❧

CHAPTER 15

MAROONED

Isav opened his eyes. He lay on his side at the edge of a pool that was filling rapidly with water. Sand clung to his face. Stubbornly the particles refused to drop off and the salt intermixed stung his wounds. Another wave tumbled and the small lagoon, separated from the sea by a brief lift of sand, swirled and raised the surface an inch. Summoning his last reserve of strength, he rolled up the shelf. He viewed a body floating prone in the surf–Meld had succumbed quickly. The suns had burned his pale skin without mercy and begun to shrink his bonds, driving him beneath the waves for refuge. Now they covered him. He himself had managed to roll his body to stay ahead of the tide while still keeping his bonds wet.

The suns hammered his back. At least his face was protected–the sand had seen to that. He twisted and looked beyond Meld. Toom lay on the beach. His companion had not moved or spoken all day. Of the four Vensa, after the departure of the Vaws, only Toom had said nothing, but had rolled up the sand and halted. He must have lost consciousness quickly. Zeydad had proved nimble. He had not only talked much and encouraged Isav–and Meld while he lived–but had managed to roll entirely out of reach of the waves. Still he had failed to overcome the first dune, and, after an hour of failed attempts, and groans from his shrinking bonds, had finally lapsed into silence. Isav could just see him by the hot white slope.

Zeydad and Isav were fortunate. They had worn full tunics when abducted and the cloth had protected their backs. Toom and Meld, however, finding them cumbersome, had tossed theirs aside. Isav felt no more pity for them than for himself. A slight advantage, perhaps, but a meaningless one in the end.

Isav twisted again and attempted to gaze skyward. He had once believed he heard wings. He knew what to expect. When the last had succumbed to thirst and the heat, the workers would come and fly their bodies to Heaven. Despite the tales of Stalkin and Macius, he still thought of the Island as Heaven, though he had listened well to what they had said. Habits of thought, he realized, were the hardest to break–far more than habits of deed. They in fact were the true reason he had evaded the surf; not because he wished to escape death, but because he did not want his body to vanish in the sea and the malkops be unable to find him. His neck grew tired and he let his face fall into the cup it had pressed in the sand. Nothing moved overhead. At least nothing he could see from this limited angle with the glare of the suns beating down.

He sighed, and let his mind go. It was only a matter of minutes. Or hours. Then he and Zeydad, and Toom if he still lived, would give in to the assault of the elements. He moved his tongue. It had swelled to such an extent that he could no longer speak to the others, just groan. If only he could roll past the pool and somehow make the grove. The tops of the trees waved seductively just within his field of vision. But he knew the distance was more than he could manage. If Zeydad could not summon the strength, what chance had he, being older, and badly beaten as well? He sighed again and tried to ignore his wrists. Though he kept them wet, the pain still grew. The heat of the pool was shrinking them.

Isav closed his eyes. Images from a thousand sources crowded his mind. He felt detached, separate, unconcerned. It was not a record of his life that flashed before his eyes, but scenes of his life intertangled with incidents he knew had never happened, remembrance mixed with fancy. And mixed with more recent scenes, scenes at once more frightening and more mysterious. One moment he labored in the great kitchens of the Orphanage; then a herd of rum-na trampled him. Next he embraced a creature called a gila; but it transformed into a squat bulk upon a stool. His mind recoiled, mesmerized by the horror, and he stared as the arms reached out and wrapped themselves round his own, and with terrible strength he was drawn near, closer to the mouth that yawned, to the teeth that snapped and slavered for its meal. He felt himself sinking, sinking, then started, and his eyes popped open and his sweat mingled with the sand and the salt which again stung his raw face.

He stared. A disturbance approached on the beach. The suns shimmered and burned and he no longer could tell whether he dreamed while awake, or whether he dreamed he was awake and dreaming. He tried to shake himself alert, and failed. The disturbance drew near and filled his vision. It was his dreams personified–incarnate. A multitude of faces and bodies, some feral and foreign, others familiar and intimate, flashed quickly before his gaze. From somewhere the pain ratcheted another notch and his dreams tumbled into a jar, each dream a pebble played with and placed, each night a further increment till the jar fell and broke inundating him, and the pebbles turned to salt and the salt mounted in waves and the waves crashed over him bringing pain and heat in their midst. He thought deeply, while the waves rose. He simply could not be lying on a nameless crag in a distant ocean drowning on the shore of Heaven.

Like a waterfall, the faces tumbled, each too quick to register, producing a whirlwind of illusion and imagery, the air around the whirlwind unaffected and calm. One took on substance and prevailed. On a background of dark flesh, a lip curled upward with conceit. Below the face, shifting images coalesced into a muscled body that bore scars as if burned from hot glass. Isav tried to speak, but could not. He could only open his eyes and glare, a last act of hatred directed at the man who had ended his life. The smithy stood calm and stared. He looked to the grove, then passed his gaze over the beach, his brows playing as if puzzled. The dreams returned and the smithy vanished and another face coalesced and Isav stared suddenly upon a selk. He sighed at its beauty and gazed upon the creature's delicate features and sought out its eyes as if to say 'I am ready, I am ready to die if you will take me to your master.' But the selk ignored his glance and dropped to its knees and produced a knife, and the knife cut through his bonds, and the creature lifted him and dragged him from the water.

He was pulled across the burning sand and over the little ridge that had hitherto proved more insurmountable than the highest range of the Amanus-nama mountains and he was taken within the shade of the pleasure-grove. Fruit was sliced, its juice squeezed into his mouth. His head was laid upon grass. Then it left. Within minutes Toom and Zeydad lay beside him, and a familiar face hovered over, and Isav wondered what had happened to the malkop, and was surprised that the dead should be permitted to leave the Eye and minister to the sick and the dying. The tide of his dreams returned, and his eyes shut, and the hot suns were replaced by cool shadow.

When Isav awoke, he first realized that his tongue had shrunk. For days his efforts to speak had produced only groans and croaks. He decided to try again.

"So. Macius...did not lie."

"Oh?" Flores glanced toward him while squeezing juice into the mouth of Toom. Zeydad was standing, staring out toward the horizon.

"He said he did not kill you. I didn't believe him. I was about to put him to the test." Isav struggled and sat up. He felt his face and grimaced.

"It will recover. You will soon be as ugly as ever, my friend." Flores grinned and placed a fruit into his palm. "Eat slowly. And sparingly. Once these are gone, we will have nothing but rainwater and fish."

Isav consumed it, tasting every bite.

Flores looked at Toom. "He is almost gone. I'm afraid my efforts will not save him."

"And Revd?"

Flores stared upon the ground. "Murdered–by the hand of Stalkin. Or all the Vaw-sa together. I was elsewhere in the pits looking for a rapier." He touched the blade at his side. "I found one." He sighed. "Too late to save him."

An inquiring glance.

"The 'pits'?"

"The pits of the dead. Where the servants of Atasan take the bodies of Vensor-sa. On the Island, which is not Heaven, but a monument of our slavery to the Evil One." The captain lowered his gaze. "And where Amina is held captive by the malkops." He glanced up. "I have seen her."

Isav brightened. "Then our journey was not futile."

"No. Unless I fail to return. For now she lives... But who knows if she will still live tomorrow?" He shrugged. "I must return to Ven. I need help to free her." He stared into the distance, one hand toying with a new bracelet, the other stroking a gill suspended around his neck. He had bathed and groomed his hair and beard and now looked something like the old Flores that Isav had known in Ven. But his expression was darker–more inured to hard deeds. "I had thought to find the Grest still here."

Isav and Zeydad shook their heads. "It was Fish took it. With a fleet of three ships he landed–Stalkin guided him with the campfire. He persuaded Fish to loot the Island of Vensor; the sack of gold he brought back was enough to excite them. Now they have gone. They plan to gather a fleet from every port of the southern sea; with Macius at its head perhaps they will succeed."

The Turlicum was surprised. "Do they not fear the guardians? How will Macius get ashore?"

It was Isav's turn to shrug. "Our friend has been as tight-lipped and evasive as ever. I am not sure what he intends."

Flores paused. He raised one hand to shield his eyes. "And here we sit on this rock, marooned and unable to do ought but wait for their return." He thrust out his lower lip and fingered the gill around his neck.

He stood, then passed his eyes over the grove. Without a word, he sprang across the clearing and plunged into the trees. Isav and Zeydad glanced at each other, and stumbled after. Coming to the edge of the oasis, they looked upon the north side of the crag and caught sight of their chief vaulting up the shelving plateau toward the isle's summit. Slowly they climbed behind him. Several minutes passed. When they came to the concavity where they had taken refuge from Stalkin's attacks, they halted in surprise. In the midst of the rocks, cornered by Flores between two large stones, was a young reven. An eating reven from Vaw.

"Good fortune! We shall not have to subsist on fish after all!" laughed Zeydad.

"Return your mind to your fish, man. This animal is not for anyone's stomach."

Flores coaxed the creature and made friendly sounds with his mouth till at last it permitted him to approach. He placed his hands upon its head and stroked. He spat upon its gills. With a yawn it bared its teeth, and curled its neck in satisfaction.

"With the gill in my possession, and a sword at my belt, this creature is my way of returning home to Ven. We shall feed it well with fish and make sure it is fat. And I shall fix a muzzle and reins to control it. Then I shall depart. Once I arrive in the city, I promise I shall waste no time in assembling a fleet for your rescue–and Amina's."

The weeks slowly passed. The reven, or Tha as Flores named it, grew beyond what they had expected, maturing swiftly into an adult and healthy animal. Flores found it responded to kindness and came to heed and obey him, as if it understood it owed him its life, and a bond of trust developed. It could often be seen at his side, whether on the shore, or behind him as he walked. When Flores removed himself to the summit of the rocks, as he did each day without fail, as if to practice some art, about which Isav and Zeydad were warned not to inquire, Tha would not be put off, but would follow and remain till he returned. The others said nothing, but waited. Their disappointment at losing a good meal was nothing compared to their fear of being permanently marooned and living the rest of their days on this crag; or–worse–awaiting the return of Fish. At times also Flores mounted Tha and trained it in the surrounding surf. The moment he first removed its muzzle and allowed it to hunt was a difficult one–would the bond that had grown between them hold?

Or would the creature take advantage of its freedom to flee, and disappear into the sea? When it returned and laid its head in its master's lap in a gesture that had become habit, Flores knew he would again see Ven.

At last the moment came. The suns rose in the east and lay their calm exudence on them and Flores led Tha to the shore. The creature curled its long neck and peered into his eyes. With calmness, if still not complete confidence, Flores removed the device from its snout. It snorted and lashed the water with its tongue. Flores mounted and urged it forward. With a whine of pleasure and a shudder of nervous exhilaration as if it understood that from this trip there would be no return, the creature lumbered into the restless water. Flores fixed his gill; touched his wrist. The tail began to snake. The body of the reven plunged forward...

❧ ৪৩ ☙

As the two black-clad figures crossed the plaza, the silence of Ven fell over them like mist. Scars littered the jaw of one, imparting to its thick hairless line the likeness of a pillaged landscape. About the waist, hung a short skirt of common Ven design, with a strip of reasonable right-angles bordering a cloth of white faded muslin. Oft-repaired sandals of lyart hide wrapped the feet. He moved quickly, surely; the muscles of his limbs coiled as if to spring at a moment's notice. Above the brows the hair had receded, leaving a broad and sloping shelf. Beneath were a pair of eyes that reflected a mixture of strength and caution. They peered this way and that; they squinted and roved across the wide cobbled plain. The lips, in contrast, remained small and still and may have been a spot of paint for all the use they got.

Tilsis turned and signaled to his companion.

The other, who responded with a combination of gesture and whisper, and whom Tilsis seemed to wish to shadow from observation, held his dark robe aloft to prevent its dragging the dirt. The power that lurked in the muscles of Tilsis had no reflection here. His companion's shoulders were slim. The amber-colored eyes that peeked from the encompassing folds of black linen peered hesitantly upon a wide world of unknown but rumored hazards. Yet in those same eyes lurked a strength of a different sort, a hardness that controlled the delicate limbs as efficiently as each hint or suggestion evoked an expected, almost predetermined, response from the larger, stronger man. Crestal nodded to Tilsis and together they passed swiftly down the avenue, Tilsis in the lead, but Crestal, as it were, leading.

Crestal spoke. "We must, we must." The youth peered ahead into the darkness. "He will welcome us, I am sure of it."

The servant paused and answered with an earnest series of gestures.

Crestal nodded. "I know that a man may act different when in the company of those whom he respects. I also know he has gratitude and that he will keep his word–come what may."

Tilsis raised his head and gazed down at Crestal with paternalistic concern. If you are certain...

The youth touched him reassuringly and they resumed their advance.

The plaza vanished in a tangle of sidestreets and the moons winked out like the orbs of slain giants. Crestal hesitated in the darkness and Tilsis led the way, moving as much by instinct as sight. Snoring and coughing escaped the surrounding flats as they passed. But for occasional wanderers and watchmen, all of Ven slept. After a short distance they halted. A pedestrian on some errand stumbled close. He passed, and the two increased their pace; it would not do to be discovered, whether by dark or light.

Arriving at a cross street, they again paused. The street led eastward, paralleling the Avenue of Murfenmas, toward the region of the Guild and a rough district populated by transients and ne'er-do-wells. Tilsis pointed in the opposite direction. He halted.

On the far side of the avenue, a clump of brown approached from the south. Moving quickly, they took the form of beggars, their clothing in tatters. Crestal and Tilsis waited until they had passed and Crestal made as if to resume their movement but Tilsis restrained him again. Another group appeared, now entering the street close beside them and turning to follow the first. More appeared from the south. Tilsis suggested they retreat into the shelter of the sidestreet. They turned, and behind them a shuffling sounded–still more approached, this time about to traverse the very spot where the two stood in the dark.

The mute servant laid a hand on Crestal. He began to pull, but the youth pulled himself free.

"Let us see what they find so entertaining!" Crestal whispered. An expression of horror stole over Tilsis' face as Crestal stepped into the boulevard and joined the growing band.

The crowd seemed not to notice but hurried on their way as before, whispering together, their faces hard and eager, anticipation upon them. Tilsis hurried to join the youth, shielding Crestal from the occasional glance of the others, and followed in lockstep. More groups joined from other sidestreets. Soon their band became a crowd; the crowd a mass;

and the mass a flood; and the two, caught up in its midst, wondered how the city could fail to realize that such a movement was in progress and still sleep. Their numbers did not become so dense that they were threatened with physical harm. However, their fear of discovery increased with the increasing throng and Crestal began to feel he had made a serious error in joining.

They came to the stretch of avenue which the crowd apparently sought. Opposite them, and offset a short distance, was a peculiar circular construction that rambled over an acre of ground. The structure consisted of large fans eight feet in height, concatenated in alternated twisting fashion so that they joined into a single morbius. The fans of the morbius were twisted in such a way that each offered passage to any who wished to penetrate the facade and stand within. The interior of the circle, like some prehistoric dolmen, was dominated by a flat irregular stone, itself surrounded by trees, hard and ramrod straight, with shaggy bundles surmounting them atop a circle of forty-foot trunks. The circle was in reality a tomb, or more precisely, a cenotaph–a monument to the many dead suffered by the city in its infancy from attacks by alien Mok-sa, the cruel slaves of Atasan, who had sought to strangle Ven at its birth and had continued their attacks till vanquished. Gold suns and barbells still indented the stone where victorious Ven soldiers had given thanks to Vensor in those primordial times. Now the circle had filled with their descendants, and the inscriptions were obscured by their numbers as they surrounded the dark stone and the circumvening trees.

Crestal stepped into the avenue. Tilsis forcefully shook his head. Crestal glanced once to either side to ascertain whether any paid concern to them, and found that all eyes were focused on the stone. He crossed. Tilsis followed, and together they slipped beneath the morbius and entered.

Upon the stone a glittering appeared. Then a flash. Without warning, the glowing figure of a man took shape, red flames sparking in the air. The crowd sighed and sank to their knees and for a time thereafter Crestal and Tilsis thought they heard a peroration or monologue emanating from the figure. Minutes elapsed and the flames began to weaken. Swiftly, Tilsis grasped Crestal and pulled him into the open street. A moment later the figure vanished and the crowd began to disperse, but not before the two had progressed far down the avenue, and resumed their search for their destination.

They entered the Avenue of Murfenmas and in another minute the insulae lining the street gave way to a series of elaborate many-storied chateaus bordered by high impregnable walls and topped with variate splinters of glass. Tilsis pointed to a high wall running along the southern walk that framed a chateau of several levels crowned with a newly installed dome of irsrem. A massive iron grate gave ingress. Tilsis ventured near. A sentry materialized and, after a moment of hesitation, the three quietly conversed. The grating opened to admit them.

CHAPTER 16

"DO YOUR DUTY"

On the far side of Ven, a clump of figures in dark robes crossed the avenue of Sish and approached a high wall. Two attendants held open a gate. The figures entered, crossed the grounds, and entered a yellow-roofed four-storied chateau. Here they were met by more attendants and armed sentries who escorted them into a chamber resplendent with decorative arms and armor. The attendants left. In a hard wooden chair by the inner side of an oblong table of similar make reclined a youth, his face sporting the first hairs of manhood.

The figures removed their robes. While several held back and peered furtively about, three advanced with smiles.

"Nidrenmor fathered a fine line of warriors–none can deny."

"Indeed! The clan of the Serclaslers will always be a jewel in the Assembly's crown."

The third was heavier than the others, and sweated as if the visit were physically arduous. As the youth rose, he caught up with the others.

"You are welcome in my household Toosel...and Nilsit. And you Mosum of the Kalikum." Though the voice was friendly and responsive, the face was sedate and reserved. The youth bowed. "It is kind of you to say such of a clan that greatly oppressed the city and was outlawed for its deeds. I hope my own deeds have helped to restore the respect and trust in which the city once held my kin."

Toosel and Nilsit exchanged glances and relaxed a trifle.

Mosum mustered respect and displayed it in the direction of the youth. "We have known of your efforts, Lirsus-Numsenmur. It is not a simple matter to serve one's city as well as one's own clan. If their interests are not the same, then one is torn asunder by divided loyalties. I can appreciate the agony you must have felt."

"My loyalties are not divided."

Mosum pushed out his lips in surprise.

"They belong to Vensor–above both city and clan."

"That is good–" ventured the Kalikum.

"My father sinned against God. It was for that reason that he died."

Again the exchange of glances. Toosel and Nilsit looked to Mosum, who cleared his throat and continued. "Dear Lirsus. We know that you mean what is best for all: our city, our clan, and our God. We know also that you are young. Perhaps you have been confused by what you have seen. I wish to convey to you the advice to examine carefully on which path your future lies."

"How so?" The Heir to the Serclasler clan stared in puzzlement.

"You must be aware of what is happening in our fair city. True, your father no longer reigns. His rule–if I may speak boldly–was doomed from the start. The Assembly has no tradition of single governance, no tolerance for kings and despots. But this may change: power is now slipping rapidly from our hands. Your comrade–Ust–who learned at the feet of your father, is following in his steps. He has already ruled longer than did Numsenmur, and shows every sign of extending his scope."

Lirsus said nothing, but turned his gaze to the rug.

"Whether Numsenmur ruled justly or not, he was not removed by the hands of the Simet-sa. It took the army of a foreign king to depose him. It was during a time of despair that we granted to the Turlicum the throne. Had we believed the city would live, we would not have given it to him, but would have kept the power where it belongs: in the hands of the Simet-sa. Now we are under the heel of a new tyrant, one who cannot point to war as an excuse for his tyranny, nor did we put him on the throne ourselves."

The youth looked up. "But the oracle–"

"The oracle," interjected Toosel, "placed him merely upon the throne. What power the throne wields is up to us!"

"That is so," added Nilsit. "The rightful government of Ven is the Assembly of the Simet-sa. The throne is whatever we make it–strong if we wish it so, or weak if that be our desire."

Mosum glanced surreptitiously about. "And we wish the latter," he whispered. He looked into Lirsus' eyes for some sign of agreement. "Are you not aware that Ust is becoming more powerful? Thanks to the former supporters of the Triumvirate–"

"–the Loyalists–"

He paused. "–the Loyalists. Thanks to them the Calomar grows stronger each day. His men have used the wealth of the Lurenmurg to recruit hundreds from the Orphanage, all the very best. They train on his estate without pause. I even hear he intends to merge his militia with those of the Tumlefler and Spandicum and perhaps even the Molersal–another cue he took from your father. Both Nilsit and Toosel have recently lost important officers to assassins. Ust has even invaded the Eunuch Guild and attempted to seize the Guildmaster and put him in chains. The worst sacrilege! He does all this, and, due to the oracle, none dare complain! He is only beginning to exert his strength. In another year his weight may crush the city!"

Lirsus turned, drummed his fingers upon the table. "Unless..."

"Unless we join together. Now! While resistance is still possible!" Mosum gestured with animation, while his colleagues watched and nodded.

"What do you propose?" The youth stared coolly, immune to their emotion.

Mosum took a breath. "We need your assistance. Your help. We need your warriors to restore the balance against those who support the throne. And if fighting does break out...they could then show truly that their loyalty lies with Ven." Mosum risked a sideward glance to his colleagues. "So let's have no more doubts. Join with us, Lirsus. The other neutrals look to you. If you throw in your lot with us, Ust would not dare to initiate a struggle. It is the surest way to keep the peace!"

Lirsus strode casually around the room, gazing at his father's paraphernalia upon the walls. The martial traditions of the Serclaslers reached back as far as the Turlicum–further, if clan tradition be true. When Ven was no more than a camp between the Suma and the Hedronmas and the Mok-sa had wished to destroy it, a Serclasler had defended the first primitive huts and the first bricked hexagon. After the victory, his son had built the first spire in order to celebrate, placed the cornerstone of the first wall of the Temple. The oracles had begun soon after, and Serclaslers had been among the most zealous. The first crude spears and daggers were suspended even now upon the wall before him. Kept free of dust, their permanence was a testament to the incalculable age of Ven, to its eternal presence, to its potency in battle.

"There is something else I wish to discuss as well," said Toosel.

"Yes?"

"You have absolved the Turlicum from responsibility for the defeat at the Twin Peaks. But you have never explained yourself. Now it seems to me that if the Turlicum was not responsible, then someone else was. Do you see, Lirsus? If Flores was responsible, then Ust was not. But if

Flores was not responsible, then there may be grounds for the impeachment of..."

"Impeachment? For what?" Lirsus looked shocked.

"Treason. Connivance with the enemy."

Lirsus frowned.

"Did Ust cause the defeat of our army?" Toosel pressed.

No reply.

"Then did the Turlicum?"

Opening his mouth, Lirsus almost spoke, but then thought better and said nothing.

Toosel exhaled harshly. "Why do we waste our time? He is not with us."

Mosum and Nilsit turned apprehensive faces toward their comrade, and gestured.

Toosel waved them aside. "I will put it bluntly, son of Serclasler." He stepped closer. "Do you side with us against Ust, the latest tyrant of Ven? Or do you–as some have said–plan to betray the city as did your father, and join Ust?" The stares of his guests were suddenly sullen and hard, belying the many compliments they had delivered.

"You wish to depose Ust from the throne?"

The others nodded. "He cannot remain."

Lirsus folded his hands. "In violation of Vensor's decree?" He stared at the floor, and Nilsit spoke.

"Can we count on your assistance?"

Lirsus seemed hurt. He frowned. Flexing one arm, he loosened strong biceps that had tightened from exercise.

At length he answered. "No. You cannot."

A moment elapsed and the three Simet-sa moved subtlely away from the youth. Without a word they turned. They signaled their bodyguards to open the door. Passing through, they departed the estate of Lirsus.

"He is not the man his father was," said Toosel, while the others nodded. "Numsenmur may have been a tyrant, but he was at least a man in all that he did. This whelp is no more than a eunuch, a slave to the example of his father. He dares not violate his memory, or the oracle, even to save Ven."

❧ ଡ଼ ଓ ❧

A week passed. Midnight arrived and at the Hall of Vim, where the busy reconstruction ordered by the king was nearing completion, a dark-clothed man exited a side-gate, saying less than he had on the previous such occasion, but communicating more than before. This time he was not alone, but enjoyed the company of a pair of young bodyguards whose tongues had been excised. More mutes shut the gate behind them. King-ship was assuming a pattern, Ust noted. All kings had affairs they wished to keep secret.

Ust and his silent guards slipped quickly across the plaza and dove into the maze of dwellings that flanked it. The apartments passed by swiftly and without event and soon they emerged by the Temple. Ust paused. He always paused at this stage. Something about the way the clouds framed the merlons and the upthrust menacing spire sent a chill rippling through his spine. Gooseflesh accompanied the feeling. He calmed himself; glanced at his bodyguards. Their impassive demeanor obscured a fierce brand of loyalty to his person entirely at odds with the fact that it was Ust ordered their mutilations. If they knew it had been he and not the trainer whom he had had butchered in alleged retaliation for the deeds, their loyalty would vanish in a flash, with horrific consequences for himself. But Ust knew in the meantime that they would defend his life with their own, and that had been his purpose in the matter. He was satisfied. Finally his scruples had become as few as his mentor's.

Tumsenet was again overhead and spread His ghastly green over all. The constellation Barazaggar the Eunuch, the perfect image of God, hung above the battlements; its unclouded Eye, never-changing with the seasons, was bright. Other constellations could be seen: the Gila, which portended autumn; the Rum of summer; the Maker of spring, though the meaning of the last had been lost in remote antiquity. And more constellations. All dense; all smeared; all difficult for the unpracticed eye to discern, wide-spread over an exaggerated expansive ecliptic. Ust shook off the spell. Ordering his companions with a word to watch—but see nothing—he hurried to the familiar wicket and scratched. In a moment the expected response came. He waited. He slipped inside.

A few minutes later Ust entered the room of candles. Their flickering light revealed no change from his previous visit. He gazed at the familiar table, dusty arras, the carven posts, soft bed. A sensation of actual pain stole over him. The pain was not physical or due to a sense of shame from his previous failures to satisfy his paramour, but was an expression of unutterable boredom. The offense that she had committed, the crime that in his private thoughts evoked his worst rages and contempt and re-mained forever unforgivable to him, even more than for the petty insults and the personal violations, and the lust, hatred, and envy that she had brought into his life–was her towering, inexpressible boredom. For boredom did he hate her. The thick-laden dust of the room, the lay of the lines on her face, the peremptory nature of her dull arrogant stare; the whole crushed his soul like a stone.

The handle turned and reluctantly, slowly, he restored the mask of nails.

The old woman entered, turned, and stood. Her eyes swept his form with unseemly ease. The downturned mouth turned what might have been a caress into an intolerable intrusion. It had not been meant as a caress, however.

"You crawling maggot. You mewling pathetic creature of a man!"

Ust tensed. This was extreme even for Wijah.

"Do you realize how much time has passed since you last visited?" She threw a hand in irritation. "You were to return in one week, but it has been a full month. Did I not tell you my time is precious, that I cannot wait any longer for results? Do you think that I am young like the slatterns that I supervise and but need the right moment to achieve my goals?" She stalked toward him, waving a miniature fist in his face like a club.

"Don't worry. I will make it up." He tried to restore the truce but his inner disgust surfaced and the mask crumbled.

She reared back as if struck. "What is this look about you? You come here not only late but with a poor attitude as well? Do you think I will accept this? Do you think I will let you enter me and enjoy my fruits when you scowl so?"

Ust suppressed a nauseous heave and with some difficulty recomposed his expression.

"Indeed no!" she laughed, and, turning away, folded her arms. "So you think you are necessary to my plans... Well, think again! I can find another, you barrow, you shoat, you swine!" She shook her little fist again. "As the voice of Vensa to the city, I have but to whisper to any who stands upon the golden platform and he will take your place beside me– here, in my chamber." She smiled and twisted her hips and her voice became silky.

It was Ust's turn to be horrorstruck. The emotion that followed was genuine. "My love! You cannot mean what you say! Think of the danger to yourself in such a deed; with me at least you are safe! You said as much the last time that I came."

She narrowed her eyes. "Which, I remind you, you did not!"

She lapsed into silence and Ust approached. Steeling himself, he took a deep breath, and placed one arm (which was exceedingly slow to respond) about her withered shoulders. It rested too heavily and she shook it off.

"Dear Wijah. Come, let me bring you to your bed." He replaced the arm and she relented. "Even as yon creature descends into the arms of his gila." He nodded toward the dry arras which hung over the mattress. A small smile stole across her face.

She spat. "Not that you could fall within a league of his ability! The incubus makes all else feeble in their efforts to please. Atasan is the very definition of pleasure for a woman." Ust looked puzzled; shook his head. "Anyway," continued the old woman, unconcerned, "we shall try. Lie down."

It soon became apparent that Ust would do no better than before. Wijah halted in disgust. "Man, must I remind you of your duty! Have you forgotten what will follow any failure on your part?"

Sweating, Ust redoubled his efforts and finally managed to accomplish the act–but interrupted it, soiling both him and his partner.

A screech followed. "You imbecile! You have done worse! Why do you not listen?" The aged beldam threw her hands to her face and shed a torrent of tears into dry palms while perched on the edge of the bed. This time she showed no sign of ceasing. Ust grew agitated. His mind traveled to the defenses around his new palace and he wondered whether they might withstand the attacks of a populace enraged by the oracle. Would even his new mutes remain loyal if such meant disobeying the Word of God? He sought to place his arm again over the ancient hag's shoulders, and halted in surprise: the limb would not obey. Instead it rose silently above the shuddering figure and to Ust's horror his fist closed as if clutching a knife. He sighed. Oh, how he wished to release it! To see the shocked tear-stained face frozen in terror as his steely blade drove home! His soul drank in the scene, his mind weaving a vivid scene of vengeance...a small noise brought him back from his reverie.

Someone rattled the handle of the door.

At first Ust suspected that Wijah had placed an accomplice close by to watch and warn her of just such an attempt on his part, knowing as she did of the inherent violence of men, but the white fear displayed on her face soon dispelled this notion.

"Away!" she whispered. "Get back into the tunnel, and depart! None may see you here: it will mean death for both of us!"

Frantically she pushed him across the room and through the entrance, leaving him to secure the panel, and he witnessed through the crack her sere form snatch up a black scrabble of clothing and vanish through a side-door. No other sound had escaped the first threshold, which he knew as the entrance to her chambers, and Ust let the cover close and shut, though he had no means of securing it from his side. His own clothes were bunched in one hand, and, after penetrating the tunnel a little way, he paused to replace them on his body.

The nexus of corridors followed. The small candle still glowed where he had placed it.

He raised the holder, turned left, and without a backward glance headed toward the place where he knew another awaited–one whose allure and perfect sensuality was to Wijah's as a sun is to a lump of coal. His mind rose in anticipation; his feet could not move quickly enough to bring him. His successful interruption of his act with the old woman and the lucky brush against the handle by some passerby had ensured an exquisite experience with the true object of his visit.

Ust hurried the length of the tunnel. He turned at the familiar projection of soft light, smiled at the cloud of steam. Crossing the spherical chamber and ignoring the lattice on the right which disgorged great bursts of steam into an adjoining chamber, he arrived at the head of the stairwell. He descended. Caught sight of whom he sought. Heard what he wished to hear: a squeal of pleasure at his coming. Now, he thought, now was the time to request a new oracle, and to assert the fulfillment of his rule and his independence.

CHAPTER 17

REVERSAL

Several days passed, and a new Ust gazed across the Assembly upon his subjects. An Ust invigorated. An Ust restored. An Ust with a new confidence in the outcome of the struggle that he had initiated–unwisely so as he had for the past month suspected. But a struggle which he now believed would lead not to an ignominious death, but to a grand end, hitherto unguessed, something not formerly experienced by any son of Vensor, but was reserved in the tablet of Heaven for him alone: Ust Terenol of the Calomar, Emperor of Maalstrom, Irsrem-lord of the Valleys, chosen Progeny of God. His heart lifted in contemplation of his destiny. The next calling of sons was imminent; the oracle would speak on his behalf. Vensa had promised. Soon he would no longer have to grovel before...the hag.

In the meantime, however, he had still to govern these unruly peasants before him, his erstwhile comrades who adorned their bodies and disported themselves with unsufferable pomp and arrogance, as if they were his equals. His lip curled as he gazed upon the crowded biers and benches where their throng perched like crows waiting for his guard to drop, waiting to snatch their spoil from what belonged to him. The usual sprinkling of his enemies was there, and in their midst the empty seat of the reven clan, where the crippled vagabond had blustered. The very sight of the bench inflamed him. Once I complete my rule, I will obliterate the structure and all that is on or near it. Even the kindling will I burn!

His eye moved to the near side of the chamber where two rows of warriors stood between him and the Assembly benches, with a band of well-armed mutes surrounding the throne itself. His anger eased. The ranks of his followers had grown, while the number of neutrals had thinned. Endel, Misenta, Kal, Fursel and Hama–the last still not deceased but living on like a family curse–had taken note of the expanded size of his bodyguard, and glanced frequently at the throne for cues on when to speak. And on their fringe sat Lirsus. Ust nodded while he observed the young chief of the Serclasler clan. The youth's allegiance would seal his victory.

Still Ust squirmed on his throne. Despite the promise of Vensa to use the oracle, and the report from his spies that Lirsus had rejected the proposals of his enemies, his mind would not let him rest, but sent his nervous eye roaming and peering over each robe and vest, looking for hidden menace. In each face he saw the white-crowned eyes of Osis, in each hand a ghostly blade poised to strike. More and more he thought about the attempt that had been made on his life. What had been Osis' real motivation? How could one so decrepit plan and carry out such a plot? Did he in truth act alone? Or had he been but the tool of another? From white bushy brows his mind wandered to a face of sharp prisms and angles, and to Soorkrul... It was obvious: only the Eunuch Lord could have planned such a crime. Only he was so elusive, errant and subtle. Only he could have slipped through his alert warriors in the raid on the House. And he would strike again. There was but one way that he could be absolutely certain that he would survive the Guildmaster's next attack. He must master all Ven. More than Ven–the world. Only then could he relax, only then could he embrace his destiny, only then could he become something more than human...

"Give your attention to your king," the high voice of Simlet interrupted his reverie. "And to me, his appointed voice."

The noise of the chamber abated, and Simlet continued.

"It is apparent that there are some within this Assembly who still register dissatisfaction with our king's beneficial rule, some who still doubt the wisdom of his judgment, and the high destiny that Heaven has appointed for him. Can there still be doubt?" The noble directed a disingenuous visage to his colleagues. "Our Lord proved correct in his faith in Ven. This came about because Vensor had faith in him, because of all His sons in the largest of His cities only Ust the Seer, Ust the Wise, kept faith in the continuance of Heaven. Our Leader has now consented to do us an even greater deed, one that shall make our city shine in the Eye of God; he has agreed to perform the Communion that the oracle has demanded. And the Assembly, in its usual ignorance–"

"Has not agreed." Mosum stood and leveled a calm gaze upon the throne.

Simlet gazed upon his colleague with exaggerated shock. "Our man from the Kalikum does not agree?" His lips twisted in a wry expression. "What a tragic outcome for our proceedings! Hold all, we must abandon our plans and hasten to beg his forgiveness!" His eyes narrowed. "It is not necessary that the Assembly agree! Our Lord, King Ust, has merely to state his desire, and it is for us to agree and seek to implement them."

A noisy ripple of opposition swept the benches.

Toosel stood and joined his comrade. "You well know, Simlet, the rules of the Assembly. We have not given our consent for any such change in the rules."

"Does the Tooselwat object as well? Oh, well let us rush to beg his pardon too. Sit down, you oaf! Vainglory becomes you outside these walls, but this body of men values virtue–not ego."

The guards around his opponents drew more tightly together.

Ust silenced Simlet with a hand. "No, dear Simlet. Our opponents have a point. Indeed there is no call to force anything upon them." The Assembly directed puzzled stares at the throne. In what ill-thought direction did their ruler lurch this time?

Toosel rejoined, "We do not seek to be mere critics, sire, but to 'advise,' as we are duty-bound."

"Critics or not, it is Our sincere desire to bring a consensus to this chamber. If it is more acceptable to your faction–"

"Faction, my Lord? We wish only to discuss–"

"–which you may do to your hearts' content. And in the end I am sure you will come to Our viewpoint."

"Which we shall–if it has merit."

A dark pallor spread from beneath Ust's collar. "If it has merit?" Ust breathed deep, caught himself. He glanced again at Lirsus. The youth with his guards sat on the fringe of the neutrals, staring to neither right nor left. Ust reflected that he was allowing his enemies to divert him from his purpose. Ust motioned to Simlet to come near. He whispered in his ear, and the thin aristocrat nodded.

Simlet turned to the Assembly. "If our dear colleagues Tooselwat and Kalikum are content for the moment with having accomplished their purpose of interrupting the chamber, then we shall leave the matter of Communion for the moment and direct our attention to another matter. A matter of the utmost importance–a matter of heroism, loyalty, and betrayal. Let us speak of one whom this Assembly abused unfairly. Let us speak of one whom this Assembly betrayed, though he had devoted his life to Ven. Let us speak of a man who was a master of the sword, accomplished with the reven, steadfast in his devotion to his God...."

Several nobles yawned and summoned servants to bring them drinks.

"–Numsenmur of the Serclaslers."

Mosum and Toosel exchanged glances. A worried look settled on their faces. Lirsus remained impassive, like one who expected no less than panegyrics to his line.

"Loyal as a clansman, pious as a eunuch, strong as a lyart, but his own man."

His eyes on Lirsus, Mosum whispered to his comrade, "We must prepare for the worst. His enmity for us may dominate any regret he feels for his father." He shook his head. "If he joins his clan with theirs, we shall lose in both Assembly and street."

"Let us consider the line as well," said Simlet. "His father Nidrenmor was equally virtuous, the pride of the entire city. Defender of his Spring, leader of his peers, champion of the long struggle with the venomous subversions of the reven clan. And let us speak of his Heir, who, by sitting with us today, honors us with his presence."

Lirsus looked up.

"Numsenmur's son: victor of the Battle of the Twin Peaks in which our brave warriors defeated the vulgar Neset-sa. Faithful to his father and his tradition and his memory; loyal to all he stood for, and unafraid to say so openly; but, again, like his father–his own man."

Mosum snorted. He at least had possessed more dignity when he had courted the youth. He glanced at the throne where Ust sat quite still, for once untroubled by his glass seat.

"And let us speak of his enemy, who sought to steal from him his victory, as his father once sought to steal from Nidrenmor his own."

Mosum sought to rise, but Toosel held him back.

"And let us speak of our enemy," continued Simlet, "whose machinations and devilish intrigues have kept the empire in turmoil for an age. Whose assassins made a plague upon this land. Whose hand struck down the noble Sruk, and injured our comrade Sendas. Who pilfered the city's coffers, purchased a war from the tyrant Nesos, and threw open the Temple gates to the enemy. Who, indeed, it has now been discovered wielded the very hand that struck down Numsenmur himself. Flores of the Turlicum–the epitome of all that is evil and perverse in the civilized world. A name that has become synonymous with Atasan himself."

The gathering sucked its breath. Slander was one thing; sacrilege another.

"–for which analogy I extend my apologies to all. But the seriousness of the Turlicum's deeds, and the moral questions that his intrigues have raised for all right-thinking men have demanded a new level of alertness, and new precautions against their recurrence. It is well that he has gone, again deserting his city in its hour of need–as he was always wont to do. And his son as well. I daresay we shall see neither again. May fortune grant us that."

A frustrated and angry Mosum finally succeeded in rising. "And may fortune grant that he does not return to challenge your speech, Sir Simlet!" Simlet returned a snide expression. "For each one of us here knows the untruth of what you say."

The expression melted into a feral and predatory gaze. "Untruth?" Simlet ground his jaw. "Would the kind Sir Mosum be willing to defend that comment like a Simet?"

The Kalikum put a hand on his poniard and took a step. A host of cries erupted.

"Sit!"

"Desist!"

"We must have no violence here!"

"Gentlemen! No duels!"

Simlet gradually lapsed into a sulk and sat.

Mosum, flustered, sat also and was replaced by Toosel. "Dear colleagues. Are we to be subjected once again to the pointless harassing of the absent? The Turlicum has vanished."

"Precisely," replied Revtal, "he has vanished. Which is why the next motion submitted by our King is so reasonable, and why no right-thinking Simet could oppose it."

The chamber quieted in expectation.

"The throne hereby decrees–but consents to allow a canvassing of Assembly opinion–that the office of Public Commissioner, the chief manager of the internal affairs of the city, be removed from the absent–eternally absent it appears–chief of the Turlicum, and be awarded to the infinitely more deserving and responsible Lirsus-Numsenmur of the Serclaslers!"

A chorus of bravos erupted from the ranks of the throne's supporters. Several stood and shouted encouragement to the youth over the grumbling from the aisles of the opposition. Mosum and Toosel turned to Nilsit and their comrades. A look of defeat came over them.

Ust nodded to Revtal and he continued. "The Assembly is granted permission to take a vote and decide whether or not they 'agree' with the throne's decision on the status of the Turlicum and the Commission. Once and for all..."

"It is too soon for a vote, we must discuss the matter first," called Toosel.

"Enough talk!" shouted Simlet. "The throne has called for a vote!"

"Indeed," echoed Endel. "We have concerned ourselves too long with this question."

Ust looked to one side and let his gaze fall on Sendas. The recently chastened Sendas, who had taken no part in the debate, turned his rotund face about. He peered earnestly at Ust, awaiting a deposit of royal will like a blank slate awaits chalk. "In view of his unrestrained enthusiasm," pronounced Ust, "I have decided to allow the noble Molersal to supervise the proceeding."

Sendas stood. He gulped and began to speak.

"The King–our king–has moved that the office of Public Commissioner be declared hereby vacant and that the Serclasler Lirsus-Numsenmur-Serclasler–of the Serclaslers, be declared the rightful Public Commis-sioner...in charge of the Public Commission." He looked to Ust for approval.

Ust smiled. It was good enough. He moved his hand, and the Assembly groped for their voting blocks.

"I do not wish it."

The groping ceased. They looked up to behold the youth Lirsus stand-ing alone.

"I do not wish the position. My father Numsenmur strayed in the eyes of God. He sinned and he paid for it. Not only did he violate the most sacred law of Vensor in the midst of his own household," the Assembly puzzled over this, "but he betrayed the city by dispatching his servants to help Neset. His servants, who lost the war, and then sought to blame it on the Turlicum. His servants–the Triumvirate and its allies: Simlet, Revtal, and Ust."

The Assembly gasped.

The dark pallor emerged again from beneath the royal palatine of Ust. It spread across his neck and face infecting all with a scarlet blush, the tide collecting around his eyes until they bulged. Two bulbs like onions seemed to protrude and stare upon the youth.

"The Turlicum was falsely accused," continued Lirsus. "God decided that he become king of Ven. And God has not said that we should remove him from the Commission–despite having given us a new king."

The youth stared calmly upon the throne. He said nothing more but continued to stand as the opposition rose and shouted, overcome with joy at this sudden revival of their fortune. With the Serclaslers on their side, the balance had been restored.

An arm slammed the wing of the irsrem throne. Ust rose. He stepped to the edge of the dais. His head twitched as he contemplated the small figure of Lirsus almost hidden among the neutrals. It mattered little that most of the latter continued to take note of his guards and made no move to endorse the defection. His eye roved over the chamber and in a sweep that was both habitual and deliberate halted on Flores' seat. Had the Turlicum again managed to foil him, even from the grave? This was more than a matter for oracles. His pride before the city was at stake.

"A vote!" Ust exploded. "I wish a vote! I hereby move—I command!—that the Assembly remove the Turlicum seat from the chamber! And that all privileges of the Turlicum and all reference to his clan and person be eliminated from the Assembly, on the grounds that he is dead!" He slammed the throne arm.

Several rose to object, but a quick gesture from Ust brought the entire row of his warriors forward in their direction. The chamber, never so close to mass violence within its walls, fell suddenly silent and wary. Ust motioned for the vote to commence.

"Take your blocks," sputtered Simlet.

Again the body groped for the symbols of their will, and a sharp clattering of wood on marble rang. Ust glanced at Sendas. The Molersal had cast his black board correctly, his white board still resting on his lap. Ust grunted approval. On the floor both colors were represented, however, and in so close a proportion that it was not obvious which side had prevailed. Black blocks intermixed with white to such an extent that it soon became apparent that one of those rare moments had arrived when the official Numerator would have to be employed. A man dressed half in black and half in white entered the chamber with two assistants. Approaching the stack of boards, the assistants began to separate them into two orderly piles, one for each of the two colors, while the official loudly counted. Several minutes passed.

"Sixty-eight black."

"Sixty-seven white."

"Sixty-eight white."

"Sixty-nine black."

"Seventy white."

The tension grew with each utterance. So close was the balance, fear of Ust's legions countering the popularity of Lirsus, that it became apparent that a single vote might decide the issue. Ust needed that vote; a tie would defeat the resolution. Clear-headed individuals had already polled the number of Simet-sa present and come to a total of one hundred and forty-nine, making a tie impossible.

"Seventy-one black."

"Seventy white."

"Seventy-one white."

"Seventy-two black."

"Seventy-three black."

"Seventy-two white."

"Seventy-four black."

"Seventy-three white."

"Seventy-five black..." But one block remained.

"Seventy-four white."

The men about the throne exuded looks of triumph. Ust emitted a sigh of relief; his lip at once reassumed its old curl of arrogance. He had finally–after months of maneuvers and threats–imposed his imperious will upon the Assembly. He had won a vote against his enemies. And in his own right. When the oracle did speak, it would only endorse what he himself had done. His intuition had indeed been correct: he was destined for something more than mere mortality; he was destined to join the gods. He let his gaze wander over the crestfallen, worried looks of his opponents. The youth Lirsus alone stared ahead without emotion, unconcerned as to what may follow.

The youth looked up.

A block had fallen.

Removed a short distance from the ordered stacks of wooden boards, another voting block had appeared. As the fact of its presence became known, a movement spread among the Hall traveling from one end of the chamber to the other with the swiftness of a quake. Ust looked as if he had been struck with an ax. Simlet stumbled and almost fell down the benches. Mosum was induced to leap to his feet, a sudden joy about him, relief and happiness likewise transforming the faces of Nilsit and Toosel as they eyed the bright, vibrant thing before them. Like a fallen gull the board rested, white as the light of day. But it was not only the sight of the board that had wrought the change of mood in all, but the figure that had plainly cast the vote, the figure that had entered the Assemblyhall, and now stood beside it.

By the entrance stood a man. He was tall and slender but with a dense net of thick muscle. A black beard covered his chin above a worn tunic of blue. Soiled moccasins dressed his feet. Knotted calves and sun-burnt skin attested to his having spent much time beneath the suns. On one hand was a modest ring; the other hand conspicuously touched it as if to make sure it had been noticed. A quiet smile took shape upon his face. Calmly he crossed the Hall. He climbed the benches to an empty dust-laden seat. It was the seat of the Turlicum. He paused. Nodded at Mosum and several others. Then sat. Stretching his long limbs before him, he sniffed.

"As head of the Tribe of Turlicum I disagree with the proposition to remove my seat from the Hall, and with the motion to remove me from the Commission. I hereby register my objection to the view that I am dead. In fact, sirs, I was not aware that I was even ill. I feel quite well." Flores chuckled. "The day is, in fact, a fine one."

CHAPTER 18

A BANQUET

"Your rooms, sire, are as you left them." The thin soft-spoken man with the balding pate and bowed back indicated with a roll of the eyes the direction.

Flores followed his gaze. Opening a door densely carved in ornate patterns of Vensor-script, he passed two rapier-equipped guardsmen and entered his private quarters. He hesitated. He let his gaze, quiet and calm, turn about. A wide elongated chamber with rough-hewn pilasters alternating with plain stretches of whitewood covered the walls that surrounded him. Through a section of the irsrem dome overhead shone the softly glowing suns. The short day was rushing to its terminus. In the wash of light, stood a massive table with tastefully carven chairs, and depressions in the surface for palimpsest, inkpot, and pounce. Flores nodded. In the Turlicum's clan, literacy was not left to scribes. Narrow exits attested to a pair of antechambers that adjoined the conference room. Flores glanced knowingly at the planks that barred them shut. Though guardsmen were within earshot, none would violate the Turlicum's privacy without the consent of the Master of the clan.

None but he was present in the chamber, and Flores passed through to the next. Here he found his toilet. It was meticulously clean, not only from lack of use, but due to daily cleansing by factotums, with a spread of cloths hanging along one side. Flores glanced over the articles. Most were undistinguished, spare, many in need of mending; only the few elaborate costumes present seemed unworn. Flores snorted. His eye continued its inspection, passing over divers materials stacked in the corners. The chamber was less ornate than the previous, if that were possible, and, being partly roofed, lacking somewhat in light which fact Flores also found displeasing. It reminded him too much of dingy polluted cubicles. He passed through the far door to the next room.

The third chamber was somewhat wider than the previous two and permitted a greater complement of furniture. In the center was a rambling oblong couch with cured vok skins piled at one end, evidencing that it doubled as a bed. On the floor was a thick-napped golden rug. Testing the nap with one sandal, Flores smiled. He ground it with a toe. The feel of the nap, worn though it was, was pleasant. He crossed to the couch and sat. His gaze wandered about the chamber, seeking relief from the austere atmosphere. On the wall opposite the couch his gaze paused. Half-way up hung the Turlicum escutcheon, and Flores peered, a growing gleam in his soft-brown eyes.

The escutcheon consisted of a single round shield with a pensile fringe of cured reven claws, a tilted spear projecting from behind the flanges to upper right and lower left. On the shield's surface were two registers: the upper bore an erect lingam in red-figure above swelling barbelled suns; in the lower a squad of warriors pursued creatures of apparently mythological intent, for, though they defended themselves bravely against the onslaught of the muscled soldiers, their chests displayed the bared breasts of the slaves of Atasan. Gilas routed by Zeyd in the dawn of time. Some of the gilas had fallen. Beneath their bodies was a black-figure yoni and animals giving birth–symbols of the Fallen One and His ways. Flores again smiled, as if he found the panels not only entertaining, but of unexpected interest.

To one side of the escutcheon a narrow door opened. The aperture revealed another antechamber and two short busy fellows of serious expression who walked rapidly toward him. Flores briefly recoiled. He glanced once toward the exit–then relaxed. The men had paused with their arms outthrust, presenting articles of clothing for his inspection. Flores laughed. They wished merely to assist him in dressing. One made a move to remove his master's tunic.

"No." He withdrew several paces, then said, "Place them on the divan. Then leave."

They exchanged puzzled looks. "And your bath, my lord?"

Again he recoiled. "That won't be necessary...today. You may go. I shall not need your services again for a while."

Shrugging their shoulders, they turned to obey. One halted. "My lord! Your hand–it has grown worse?" The shorter of the two looked with empathy and concern at Flores' right hand where the bare wrist was exposed to the light.

Flores moved the arm behind him. "It is nothing..."

"Strup," said the first, the puzzled expression on his face increasing.

"And Gorl," added the second. A tad taller than the first servant, his face seemed entirely expressionless.

Flores bestowed a reassuring smile. "Strup. And Gorl. It comes and goes. I have discovered a new sap that eases the pain."

Their faces brightened. "That is good, my lord. If you need nothing more..."

"No. Nothing more."

Once the bodyservants had departed, Flores examined the back of his hand. The scars traveled across his wrist and forearm forming a nexus of white lines. The lines were quite thick and Flores found that if he squinted he could trace the entire network in the sheen of a band of irsrem from across the room. He frowned. Returning to his wrist, he traced the many paths with his eye, clenching and unclenching his hand. A moment later the scars could no longer be seen in the irsrem, and he was satisfied, and stood. He grasped the sandals, twisted, flung them. No pain from the scars could he feel. Turning, he examined his new tunic. It was a dull thing of plain muslin. His look of satisfaction gave way to a wry expression tinged with disgust and disappointment. But he donned it and placed a fresh pair of sandals on his feet, hooking the latchet.

He entered the next room. He found himself in a broad chamber of bright light positioned so as to cross the T of the previous three, which had formed an unbroken line. Fused plates of irsrem formed three walls of the wide sunroom, enabling him to view with ease most of the estate that unfolded three floors below. He looked through the southern pane. Below him ran a lush park with meandering stream and stone benches, a high wall encompassing the grounds rendering unto the whole the air of a mountain fastness, or a desert-bound oasis in need of defense from jealous neighbors. Flores gazed upon the garden and nodded at specific discoveries as if he had known the whole but had forgotten the details of the scene. He turned to the west. The longest stretch of pane paralleled not the garden, but the clan's wide exercise yard, a simple fact whose significance did not escape him. Though lacking the Serclaslers' numbers, the Turlicum were no less martial. Dust from the stick-figures below rose even as he watched. Beyond the yard slumped barracks and a pergola-structure for the reven-na. He nodded, glad that the strength of the clan had not suffered from their master's long absence. He stepped to the northern view. Here the vista was greatest, the entire city unveiled below. Mountains rose in the distance. The Nether Fields lay on their first small rising. Beyond them his eye continued to the steady uplift of the Amanus-nama, and back to the bulk of the city where a dark mass occupied the acropolis, in the center a sharp spire brushing clouds.

Flores returned his attention to the room. Along the fourth wall, in the middle of which was the door that led out of the flat, he found a variety of writing instruments, a latticework library containing a number of scrolls, and a large block of slate with several expressions chalked. He looked them over with the disapproving stare of one who mistrusts what he sees, though the astronomical scheme he had to admit did attract his interest and for some moments he stood and silently examined the diagrams, repeating the addenda to himself. He found of particular interest the path assigned to the body inscribed 'Maalstrom' and its proximity to a clump of bodies labeled 'Teknos (Atasan),' and a spot on Maalstrom termed 'Source: Eye of Maalstrom.' Upon reading them, his expression clouded and he turned away. The scribblings were clumsy and pale copies of an original that rested open beside them, an ancient tome of peculiar make, durable in itself but poorly preserved. Ancient tinkerings.

A buzzing rose from one corner. He looked, and pressed forward in surprise. What he had at first glance mistaken for a container or box low against the central pane he now perceived to be a distortion in the irsrem, an intrusion modeled directly in the glass itself so that a portion of the pane formed a sealed enclosure within the sunroom available for inspection by observers. It was from this enclosure that the buzzing had come. He sat on the adjacent stool and peered within. Inside the box, which was equipped with a sliding panel so as to enable access to its interior, was a nest of leroo-sa, the species of hornet common to Maalstrom. Flores inched back–their sting was not to be scorned. But his brows drew into a nexus, and he peered more closely.

The nest, like all leroo structures, was of irsrem–not the Guild's variety, but the denser, natural type–produced by a mysterious process which they alone of creatures (besides, of course, the enlightened children of Vensor) could implement. The insects ignored him and carried on with their affairs, coming and going with brachs full of nectar, from which they made their nest, and tending their young. Standing, he checked the panel to ensure that it remained tightly shut. He shook his head. The enclosure and what it implied disturbed him.

Footsteps from the conference room drew his attention away. A knock followed.

Unhurriedly, he walked through the bedroom, and opened the door to the toilet. Before him stood the balding old man again–Sandol. A rapier-equipped bodyguard accompanied him.

"Forgive the intrusion, sire. Storl of the Bandabok begs your indulgence. He is in the first antechamber."

Flores arched his brows in surprise. A brief smile took his lips.

"I hope I did not err in letting him in, my lord. I know how you feel about his visits, but after your long absence I thought you might wish to decide for yourself whom you shall entertain."

"You were right...Sandol." Flores gazed at his long-time advisor with an evaluative eye. "I do indeed wish to decide for myself whom I shall entertain. And I desire to see my old friend Storl without delay..."

Flores walked into the conference room, then paused. "Which...?"

The old man directed a puzzled stare at his master. "Why, the northern one, sire. It has always been termed the first antechamber."

"Of course." The noble took a step. "How soon one forgets the mundane after a long and pleasurable absence."

He took a step.

"Sire—"

"Yes?" Flores turned expectantly to Sandol.

"It's good to have you home. Ever since the ships returned without you, the clan have feared for your safety and longed for your quick return."

The Turlicum smiled again, this time a wider, more genuine smile. No trace of the long journey seemed to cling to mind or body, but every nuance and inflection were as fresh and genuine as the old Flores whom Sandol had known. Even the pain lines about his eyes, lately acquired in the Neset war, had vanished. Flores yawned. "You have my eternal gratitude. Now you may go."

The old man hesitated. His brows lifted.

"But you," Flores said to the guard, " shall stay and remain always in an adjacent room for when I may need you."

Brows still raised, Sandol retired.

Flores opened the sidedoor.

"Flores—ah, Flores, my friend!" Storl entered. "Do my eyes play tricks? Do I really see the same Turlicum who saved me from my vulture-like creditors? Could it really be he standing before me in all his temperance and health?" A stout man with a moustache like a black broom grinned and lay a playful reproving stare upon him. "And they told me you floated in the sea somewhere—of all the absurd things to imagine!"

They clasped hands. Flores took Storl's hand solidly and clapped the other hard upon Storl's back. "Storl of the Bandabok! How pleased I am to see you."

"Not a whit more pleased than I am. I held vigil upon hearing of your disappearance, and sang with joy when I heard of your return. I wasted no time at all, but hurried to your estate to congratulate you on your venture–whatever it may have been–and to rush to offer my services..."

"And to deliver your excuses of why you still have not repaid me?"

"Repaid? Why, I, uh..."

"First, however, what is this you have brought with you?" Flores gazed beyond Storl to the far end of the antechamber. There, seated about a table, were three dull-eyed youths. At Storl's signal they rose and approached. Their bodies were indecently clad; bright feathers were in their hair; red and blue paint on their faces and hands.

Flores passed an approving eye over them. "The House has improved its lot since the Tyrant of the East invaded, which it appears to me did but cleanse and purify the city. Even the youths of the Orphanage seem invigorated and ready to labor for the state. Do you not agree, Storl?"

The noble looked at him in surprise. Storl peered at the youths as if suspecting strangers to have taken their places behind his back.

"Why, if you so believe, Flores." For a moment he looked closely at his host, his gaze passing subtlely over him. "These...'invigorated youths' as you say, are a gift. Trained by the finest in Ven. Obtained from the Eunuch Guild, but also, I hasten to add, inspected and certified by the city."

"Inspected? For what reason, Storl?"

"Why, inspected for...for, but you know quite well why they are inspected."

"No, I don't, Storl. Why?"

He shook his head. "I do not wish to speak of this–"

"But you will speak: because I command it."

Storl blinked. He looked Flores over again, now measuring his earnestness. Finally, he glanced to either side, and motioned the youths out of earshot. He whispered, "For weapons–for disease. For in case Soorkrul, the Master of the Eunuch Guild, instructed them to...'go beyond their duties,' while we sleep." He glanced toward the youths as if he himself did not trust them.

"And have you obtained any for your own harem?"

"My own?"

"Yes," said Flores. "Listen to me. I asked: have you placed any of Soorkrul's eunuchs in your own harem?"

"Well...well, yes. Or rather, no. That is, almost. I will soon, I mean, when I have scratched together the money to buy them! Yes, indeed! It takes much money to buy such!"

Flores put his lips into a peculiar set that outwardly had the contours of a smile, but that in truth bore not the slightest resemblance. "That is not necessary. I will give you one myself. Here, you may have this one."

"Oh, no, Flores. That is not necessary. I cannot accept gifts from you; you who have done so much for me. Besides, Soorkrul told me to make sure that you–" Storl choked, turned red. "I mean, I heard that the Eunuch Lord–"

Flores ceased smiling. "That's enough. Be quiet. I know what you meant to say. I know perfectly well. And I also know that you are a great oaf and a fool and that the world would be better off without you. And I know that you have already fallen into debt once again and that powerful Simet-sa are demanding payment, and that if you do not pay, this time you will have your title stripped from you in the Assembly. And I know that Soorkrul offered to pay your debts provided you persuade Flores to accept one of these whores and start a harem, like every patriotic son of Vensor ought, so that sometime soon in the dead of night one of these upstanding young men will reach over in the dark and pour the substance in his drink that will spell his doom..."

Storl turned white. He staggered back to the table where the surprised youths made room for him to lurch onto a seat.

Flores advanced.

"How...?"

"How is unimportant." A quick gesture from Flores and the guardsman entered the antechamber. Another gesture and the guard escorted the youths into the conference room and shut the door behind them.

"Now listen to me, you pig. I wish to be repaid. That is what is important. I wish you to return the money I lent you one year ago this week, and I wish no delay in its repayment."

"But, Flores–my lord–I am in debt as it is!" His eyes suddenly lit. "What about the consorts: surely they count for something. They are worth a great deal of money!"

The Turlicum permitted a contemptuous turn to settle on his lips. "They were a gift. I shall keep them for myself. But as for you," Storl staggered to his feet, "you have two days to deliver what you owe, or I shall send my clansmen to that filthy sty you call an estate to extract from you what is mine. Now, am I perfectly clear and comprehensible? Or must I deliver a further promise– 'promise' since I make no threats but merely predict what shall indeed happen to those who dare to cross me?"

Storl opened his mouth. "Soorkrul–"

"–Soorkrul," Flores cut him off, "no longer exists. He has been missing since before the invasion of the Neset-sa. Is that not so?"

The Bandabok, equally poor in name, wealth, and spirit, let his eyes fall to the floor. He nodded.

"He will be of no help to you." Flores observed his crushed demeanor. "On the other hand, there may be something else you can do for me to repay the debt you owe."

Storl momentarily brightened.

Flores moved closer. "Listen closely. First, you will obtain the regalia of a Calomar, the warrior clan of Ust. Then..." They whispered together for several minutes. Finally Storl turned and left, and Flores returned to the conference room. Here he gazed with interest at the half-clad eunuchs.

"Enter my private rooms and remain there–I shall return later."

To the guard, "Search them and watch them well. And stand post by the door. If ought happens to them–or to my rooms–while I am gone, it will go ill with you."

The warrior swallowed, and obeyed.

Flores opened the door that led outside his private chambers, and halted. Beside the two guards stood Sandol and a further trio of warriors in partial carapace, their right hands on their weapons' helves. A brief chill like a hand of ice caused his heart to skip. Sandol saw him and smiled. The others brightened and raised clenched fists in a martial salute.

"Flores! The Turlicum has returned! *Selenevnía Flores wa Turlicum!*"

The chill passed. Flores smiled and raised his fist likewise. Two more clansmen appeared at the far end of the corridor which traveled the length of the main wing. "Flores! Now we are saved!"

Sandol stepped close. "Word of your return has spread. Your clansmen are as glad to see you as I–"

Flores interrupted. "I wish to inspect the estate, Sandol–to see what changes have been made in my absence. You will explain them to me in detail."

"No changes, sire. We knew you would keep your word and return when you were ready."

"Nevertheless, we shall inspect everything, and you shall explain."

"As you wish. And may I say, sire, that that is most like you."

"You may. However, I find...this noise unsettling. I wish no unnecessary distractions–my trip was arduous, you know. I was lucky to return at all."

"I quite understand, my lord." Sandol turned. He waved the warriors away. Soon only he and Flores remained, and, with two bodyguards as an escort, they exited the Turlicum's private chambers and descended a flight of stairs.

For the next hour they walked the estate, Flores examining all he encountered in the smallest detail, and what did not seem familiar he motioned Sandol to explain. During the inspection, Flores would often pause to listen, or peer into small poorly lit rooms, and showed an interest in all the activities the clansmen of the estate undertook. Observing him, it seemed to his companions that he sought something in particular, and each inquiry that failed to reveal what he sought, and each room that failed to provide the quarry, imparted a greater impatience to his manner. At last, in a large chamber below ground packed with bales and hogsheads and ceilinged with raw unworked timber they paused. Flores motioned that the trio of guards should retire to the far side.

Flores turned to his majordomo. "Sandol."

"Yes, my lord?" The expression of curiosity and puzzlement which Sandol had displayed since the beginning of the morning acquired an element of apprehension as his brows contracted.

"You have been in the Turlicum clan for a long time, have you not?"

"Why, yes, my lord. As you well know."

"If something were to transpire on the grounds of the Turlicum estate that you thought I might not approve of, you would realize, would you not, that the proper course of duty would be to immediately inform your lord of what had happened?"

Sandol gazed about the chamber a moment without speaking. He blinked as if holding something back. "Without doubt, sire." He resumed his errant gaze.

"Sandol. I believe you have hidden something from me."

The majordomo hesitated, fumbled for the words. "You have learned–already?"

"I have known since I arrived. Where are they?"

"I did not know how to tell you–or whether I should simply return them to the street." He sighed. "The gateguard let them in a week ago. They claimed to have known you well, and begged the protection of the clan. When I heard what had occurred, however, I seized them. I saw at once what it was, and knew that it is by its nature a liar. And now that you have returned, my lord, I will throw them out at once before the city learns of its presence."

"You will do nothing of the kind, Sandol. I am, in fact, very glad that you gave them refuge. In truth, the consequences would have been dire had you refused them. And not only for them. The opinions of others, you see, do not matter anymore."

"Dire? Opinions do not matter? I am sure I don't understand."

"That also is of no consequence." Flores raised his chin a trifle. "Now where do you have them?"

"In our best keep, my lord. Properly guarded."

"Which is..."

"Why, the Winkling turret. Next the Gallery. By the Officers' Stable."

"I wish to see them–but to see them only. I am not prepared to speak."

"As my lord commands. And, as you know, the keep permits of casual observation without knowledge of the observed."

Summoning the guards, Flores and Sandol set out at once for the Gallery, and soon arrived in the main hall of the eastern wing, balustraded stairways rising to adjoin juxtaposed mezzanines. Behind the highest mezzanine was a small unobtrusive stairwell that led to a narrow corridor. At the end of the corridor was a small door. Flores approached its peephole, and looked down. Ten feet below were two figures. They stood on the floor of a small wall-turret whose only access was attained by a rope ladder lowered from the threshold of the door. For a time Flores watched, observing the dark clothing of a eunuch-priest, and the worn tunic of the eunuch's escort. When he was satisfied that all was as he wished, he withdrew, having made no noise audible to those observed, and Flores motioned Sandol to another tete-a-tete on the mezzanine.

"Sandol, you have done well. Now. Listen well. The gateguard who first let them in–and all those who have glimpsed them on this estate– you are to transfer. Remove them to some distant province where the Turlicum clan holds sway. With whom have you shared knowledge of their presence, Sandol?"

"Few, my lord. No more than a half-dozen, besides myself."

"You will remain, of course. But the others must go. Including those who serve their meals. From now on you yourself shall serve them. Is all clearly understood?"

"Yes, my lord."

"And prepare a meal for me–indeed, prepare a feast–and summon all of my officers and the best of my soldiers–and its youths. I wish to celebrate my return. I will sample the best that the estate has to offer."

"As my lord commands. But–"

"But what?"

"Sire, may I say that you have never voiced such desires before." His brows slipped down the bridge of his nose. "I am not certain that I can locate the makings of a feast. There have been none in this clan since the death of your honored father."

Flores directed a peremptory glare upon his servant. "Then buy them. Or steal them! I care not how it is done." Flores let his eyes wander about the lofty ceiling of the hall. "I wish entertainment to free me from my boredom–to free me from a lifetime of boredom!" His shining orbs flitted over the tapestries and statuary and vaulted pendentives as if having stumbled on a wonderland, his face lit with new warmth and yen.

"My lord–"

"Yes?"

"Might I inquire...the one said it was a friend of yours..."

The stare turned sharp–a warning. "How little you know, Sandol. And how wise you are to follow my instructions to the letter without demanding explanations, or putting questions to me concerning matters which you are better off not knowing." Flores stared at his majordomo with a steady observant gaze. "I will say this, however. We were companions for a time, and even traveled together. But," he glanced back at the small iron-backed door which had allowed him to watch the prisoners without being seen, "it does not follow that we were therefore friends..."

Flores resumed his seat in the Assembly amid a cloud of silence. Again there was a full quorum and, news of his return having permeated the city, even Simet-sa who had not attended a session in years found the time to occupy their customary seats. Beside him the former friends and allies of the Turlicum smiled and nodded. When Flores ignored them and stared straight ahead, the smiles ceased. Across the chamber the stick-king ensconced in his expansive throne frowned down upon him, and counted the number of imperial guards between the throne and the newcomer. Ust's hand shook from nervousness each time he sought to gesture. At length he abandoned the attempts and touched Simlet on the arm.

"Flores of the Turlicum."

Flores continued to stare ahead, seemingly without interest.

Simlet continued. "Fortune has been kind to allow you to return. Not only to yourself, but to us. As we noted in your absence, the city has need of your clan, and of your experience and judgment. Vensor himself has need of you."

Mosum, Nilsit and Toosel eyed Simlet carefully. Would he slide again into the kind of shameless courting as he had done previously with Lirsus?

"And since Vensor has such need, who are we to argue with such, or to fancy we could dispense with your many talents? The mere fact of your survival in the wilds for many months without men or reven-na is testimony to your worth to sit here among us here."

The Kalikum began to nod knowingly.

"Therefore, the throne wishes to welcome you, Turlicum, back into the ranks of the subjects of the Calomar–"

Toosel began to rise, anger upon his face.

"–back into our ranks," added Simlet, "the association of equal and ennobled Simet-sa–"

With a look of relief, Toosel sat again.

"–over whom rules Ust of the Calomar, the head of the Empire of Ven, Irsrem Lord of the Three Valleys, elected as our King and Ruler by the divine intervention of Vensor Himself through the mechanism of the oracle." Simlet paused while Ust leveled his gaze directly on Flores. "Which act plainly rendered inoperative any prior act or election of the Assembly itself concerning its leadership."

All eyes rested on the quiet figure in the Turlicum chair. Flores still made no move, but stared upon the marbled floor that stretched its oval between the benches. He sighed. The effect of the prismed light pouring forth upon it was entrancing.

Ust looked to Simlet. Then back to Flores. "May we conclude then, that the Turlicum accepts the dictates of Heaven, and does not wish to endanger his soul? One would think that prudent for the least of us, and the wise and ethical choice for the great Flores."

Mosum and his companions exchanged looks. The inflection of Simlet had turned provocative–even insulting. Why did Flores not defend himself? The noble sat calmly, voicing nothing, not deigning to glance toward his allies. Could he have harmed himself while away? What could have happened to render the combative and disruptive opponent of all the Triumvirate's plans as docile and amenable as a pet targan? They peered closely. Flores opened his mouth, and they leaned forward in sudden vigor and enthusiasm for the coming argument and debate–then collectively groaned. Flores had put his hand to his mouth and yawned.

He waved the hand briefly. "You have my consent." Flores glanced at the throne. "You may do as you wish. It is no concern of mine."

The Assembly lapsed into stunned silence. The silence indeed was shattering in comparison to the quiet that had foreshadowed it. The former allies stared open-mouthed; consternation upon them such as they had not experienced, all the stronger in impact due to its unexpected nature.

Ust, on the other hand, and his friends as suddenly found themselves without an enemy, like some who have prepared long to battle a mighty opponent, and at the last moment, though girded and equipped with fortitude, dour intention, and stolid weapons, their enemy failed to show, or died in the night, leaving a vast sunlit vista before them waiting but for an advance to conquer.

The King sensed the change of fortune, saw it in the eyes of erstwhile neutrals in the chamber. Their gazes wandered to him, looked to him for guidance now. He would waste no time in providing that guidance. He rose and gestured. His hands had recovered their strength.

"Good. Good! The throne is pleased. Not to mention Vensor, who must be shocked as well as pleased as he looks down upon this, his most fractious of cities, and sees order, and law, and piety, for the first time in a generation. A vote! I wish a vote!" A secret signal to Revtal, and the row of soldiers before the throne stepped forward. The neutrals hastened to give ear.

"The oracle," continued Ust, "commanded on the last occasion that we resume the war with the city of Neset before they are able to recover from the defeat we handed them when we drove them from our city. We are to carry the battle to them. Who would shrink from such a duty? Who would not wish to volunteer himself and all his clansmen for such a noble task, that of ending this age-old threat to the well-being and prosperity of Ven, and destroying the mortal enemy of all present in this chamber?"

Mosum sought to rise.

"Sit, windbag," yelled Endel. A chorus of voices from the ranks of the neutrals echoed him, drowning Mosum out.

Ust continued. "But our army cannot fight a war without a leader. It needs talent and strength to do the deed. And I know precisely whom to nominate for the privilege of saving Ven forever from the eastern scourge. The throne proposes that we amass as large an army as we can muster, with supplies and reven-na for six months, and that we appoint Lirsus Numsenmur of the Serclaslers to lead this army until victory!"

"Bravo! Lirsus of the Serclaslers!"

The Assembly broke into a chorus of shouts as they showered compliments and accolades upon the youthful leader of the chief clan of neutrals, who was to be rewarded with such an honor, despite having recently disappointed the King. The King, however, gazed upon the youth with a sly and triumphant eye. Lirsus had been sitting quietly. He now stood and looked upon the shouting multitude in surprise. Before he was fully aware, he found that his arm had risen to accept. He sat. Looking to Mosum, he was again surprised when he saw the rotund noble return his stare with a glare of disapproval.

Mosum let his gaze pass on and finally alight on the clipped blue beard and olive skin of the chief of the Turlicum. Lirsus followed Mosum's gaze. Soon most of the chamber had quieted, emulating Ust, Mosum, and Lirsus. The same thoughts crossed through the minds of all. What would be the reaction of Flores? Allowing Ust to retain his throne was one thing–to oppose Ust would mean violating the word and message of God. But would Flores allow Ust to send away his most important ally, whose support was both essential and sufficient to drive Ust from Ven? Or would Flores consent to Lirsus' exile and allow the throne to split the resistance–perhaps permanently?

All eyes settled for a second time upon Flores.

Flores opened his mouth. "Let the vote be taken. I think perhaps we should avenge ourselves on Neset."

His former allies groaned aloud, now regarding the old alliance of interests gone as if it had never existed, and diverted their gaze away from the meek bore in the Turlicum seat. Nor did they again look his way, or at the throne where a new Triumvirate of Ust and Simlet and Revtal basked in the admiration of a new Assembly, while a long series of white blocks tumbled to the floor in their support.

Mosum took the arms of Toosel and Nilsit. He whispered. "Not only is Lirsus not the man his father was, but Flores is not the man he used to be. What happened on that trip to the distant south? Does he not understand the weapon he has placed in the hands of Ust? Does he not understand the danger we all are now in?"

❧ ಐ ಲ ☙

Behind him the twin doors to the King's inner chambers thumped shut and Sendas paused. Somehow, despite his haste, he had managed to be the last to obey Ust's summons, and he jingled trinkets in his pocket to relieve his embarrassment. Simlet and Revtal were already present, and several assistants along with Ust's Calomar chieftains. Ust sat in the chief adornment of the private quarters of his palace–a royal swing, appended by two lengths of chain to a horizontal lintel overhead. He swung, and sulked. Sendas noted that the latest oracle of the Temple had pleased him no more than had the previous ones. Since the first, which had made him king (and Sendas still could not comprehend how his erstwhile colleague, certainly something less than the bravest or most stalwart of the aristocracy of the city, had foredivined the knowledge), Ust had greeted each pronouncement of the oracle with undisguised anger and disappointment. He glowered as he swung. The lieutenants in attendance said nothing, but waited. Ust glanced at him in irritation. Sendas ceased his jingling and entered.

Ust signaled to a servant. The man depressed a crank to slow the swing. A moment later it halted. The servant turned and exited the room.

The King suddenly smiled. "It is too late. It is a boon he has granted us–which Vensor himself has granted us. We would do well to accept it without complaint or examination."

"Flores–" interjected Simlet.

"–missed his chance. Had he but pressed the issue he could not only have resurrected a solid opposition to the throne–around himself–but rallied the Simet-sa to question the validity of the oracle. Even called for its repetition to verify it." Ust leered with contempt at the imagined image of his foe. "Now, it is too late." He nodded. "He preferred to sit and convalesce while his opportunity passed. And we moved! And Lirsus accepted. And the army gathers. And the Neset-sa are aware. And the disloyal faction in the Assembly is shattered and under the pressure of war, and any complaint concerning my leadership would now embarrass them."

"A wise move it was, my king, to have nominated Lirsus to head the army." On a nod from Ust, Revtal relaxed into a chair. The others followed his lead, selecting from a variety of soft armchairs and divans. Sendas headed for a particularly lush and compliant one, and soon sank deeply into its recesses from whence, like a sloth in its bower, he observed the others.

"A fortunate move in that Lirsus accepted it. Now we must lose no time in ejecting him from the city. Let him go where he will do us some good–to fight our enemies!"

"Even though the oracle did not actually say to destroy Neset, but only to attack it."

"The distinction is meaningless. One will lead to the other."

Simlet spoke again. "But what of the Turlicum? You wished not merely to coexist, but to eject him from the Commission, and remove his seat from the Assembly. He may be content to observe for now. But in the future...will he remain so?"

"No. You are right. We must find a way to eliminate the Turlicum. And soon. But without driving him into the arms of our enemies."

The chieftains put their hands to their chins and thought.

"Assassination!" called Revtal.

"Good. At least we can always fall back on that if necessary. But we have tried that before, and have never succeeded. His clan is numerous and alert. And cannot be corrupted."

"Rumor and gossip!" said Sendas, rising momentarily from his bed-like support.

Ust let fall a withering glance on the Molersal. "Words have never yet caused the healthy to cease breathing."

Sendas released an appeasing smile and sank again into the chair.

"Send him along with the army," suggested Simlet.

"No!" Ust shook his head. "We wish to divide our enemies, not unite them at the head of the strongest force in the Three Valleys. We would cut our own throats, should they decide to march on Ven instead of Neset."

They sighed. "Indeed."

"Our enemies must not be allowed sufficient time to rejoin against us. If Flores should link up with Soorkrul..."

"It will have been wasted effort to rid ourselves of Lirsus."

Ust brightened with an unexpected thought. "There is another alternative which we have never seriously considered."

The others perked to listen.

"Although I, in fact, did at one time suggest such to the Turlicum, more than a year ago. He refused my suggestion. But he had the upper hand then, not to mention a sword within it, and perhaps did not see the merit."

"What is your suggestion, my king?"

"That we invite him to *join us*." Ust grinned, disingenuousness emblazoned on his face like a tattoo. "Here. In this room. And there, in the Assembly. We shall form a new ruling coterie: a Quadrivium. Good Simlet, and Revtal, and Flores, and...myself." He did not even glance at Sendas who sank deeper into the couch in an effort to avoid the contemptuous glances of the others.

Ust smirked. "And once he has joined us, and learned to expect a share in the power and privileges of rulership in Ven, then he may encounter one night, perhaps here in this very room, in our very presence, a sudden blade whose edge has been forged with the greatest skill–for him alone." His eyes gleamed with a special wickedness which Ust reserved for those times when he contemplated the destruction of his enemies. "A day I await with impatient joy."

The others nodded, wrapt with the rawness of their king's emotion. "Let the day approach," they echoed. "A plan without match in the annals of Ven. A scheme worthy of you, O king."

"Now depart. Prepare the army. And call another session of the Assembly. And Revtal, I leave it to you to make contact with the Turlicum's representative."

The King's entourage rose and filed out, with Sendas bringing up the last. He again had his hand in his pocket and Ust halted him at the door. The King stared angrily, his eyes shot with red. His hand held the noble firmly.

"Molersal! For a span of months you have annoyed those in your presence with this infernal jingling. What is in your pocket that you would offend your betters so?"

Sendas, surprised by the vehemence of Ust's reprimand, withdrew his hand. It clutched a glass bracelet: translucent, pure, clean. He almost dropped it. He recovered, and held it aloft for Ust to see.

"I don't know what it is, my king. I found it in the southern wilds last year along with several of its kind beside a dead malkop that had gnawed off its foot, before the workers retrieved their own. I have not yet found a purpose for them, though they do make a pleasing noise when bumped. In truth, they are burning a hole in my pocket and I am tired of them, but they are so pretty I cannot bring myself to throw them away."

Ust passed a quick glance over it. Dismissed it with a sniff. "Well, get rid of the things at once. The noise is not pleasing to me, but puts my nerves on edge."

Sendas shrugged. "Accept one as a gift from me, dear Ust–I mean, my king. I will dispose of the rest elsewhere."

"Very well. Now go. And prepare for the next session of the Assembly. I wish a quorum to get our business done."

Sendas replaced his hand in his pocket and left. When he had gone, Ust wandered about his apartments for some moments reflecting on developments, his eye enjoying the many comforts and luxuries with which he had had his palace outfitted. Several large mirrors adorned the walls, and Ust approached one and reached below it to where a small cupboard stood. Reaching inside the cupboard, he touched its bottom in a subtle manner and the bottom unfolded to reveal a small secure safe for valuables. Ust took the bracelet and approached. Just before placing it within the safe, he chanced to catch a glimpse of himself within the mirror, and paused. The thing seemed just the right size for his wrist. He slipped it on. Gazed admiringly into the glass.

An hour passed.

Outside the portals to Ust's private rooms the half-dozen sentinels who stood perpetually on guard became suddenly alert as the doors were jerked open. A disheveled and excited Ust stood panting before them.

"Sendas...*get Sendas!* Bring me the Molersal. And everything on his person! Go! Quickly, I tell you. *Quickly!*"

CHAPTER 19

REVELATIONS

Another tap and the warrior no longer embraced the eunuch. Despite the seductive charms of the youth, and the visible excitement of the soldier, the split that traveled the length of the rhyton broke their embrace, thus ending their affair forever. Flores tapped the drinking horn upon the marble surface of his drink-stand and it shattered. He gazed upon the pieces morosely. They flickered many colors in the twisting shadows. Timbrels rattled, and his gaze turned up to where a dozen dancers, hastily summoned from the Guild to an unprecedented engagement at the palace of the Turlicum, cavorted before Vensor warriors. Occasionally a Turlicum glanced surreptitiously in the direction of his chieftain, as did Sandol and Sedrech, seated on either side of their master. Could this be the Flores they had known?

The chief of the Turlicum clan occupied a low-stooled soft-backed couch, on which he reclined at leisure in a gown of voile and moiré. At his feet rested half-nude slender youths, also from the Guild. His beard reflected now yellow, now red. The yellow came from firebrands in iron poles that had been placed beside him; the red from the midst of the chamber, where thundered a wide open pit, roasting a pair of huge lyarts skewered on gargantuan iron spikes. Greasy assistants pierced and sliced. Pikes distributed the meat to two half-moon tables where sat the most important of the clan. Lesser ranks sat behind. Along one wall performers plucked strings and blew into reeds and hollow pipes, the notes reverberating wildly.

Flores tapped the drinking-stand with his finger. Although the servants hastened to replace the rhyton with a new one and to fill it and his plate with more delicacies, they entirely misread the gesture. Sandol had disappointed him. All that he had formerly heard of the celebrations of Vensor clans had excited, enticed him to view the same tonight. Now he learned that this was the best his clan could do, and the affair held his interest less than he had hoped. The Turlicum clan was poorer than he had realized. In fact, it was an unlikely springboard to the fount of Ven's power. He had spent too much, recruited too many, preserved too little of what remained from the Neset-sa. A servant brought a fresh platter of sweetmeats and steak. He chose the most moist and the tenderest he could find. After passing a few to his taster, he slowly chewed them and spat out an unexpected chunk of gristle, and grimaced. His gaze still rested upon the dancers. Although the eunuchs had been trained from birth for their role, and an occasional salacious glint of admiration crossed his visage, he still was disappointed. He tapped again, confusing the servants, his stand lacking nothing. His mind was elsewhere.

In time with the dancers a crash of timbrels reverberated through the chamber, and Flores stood. At once the celebrants grew quiet.

"Sandol–Sedrech. I command you to continue. I wish all to enjoy themselves in celebration of my return. And now I must absent myself. Let the evening wear itself out of its own accord." With that, Flores turned and exited, followed by his perpetual clutch of bodyguards.

He knew where he was heading. He breathed deeply in and smiled. For long he had awaited this moment–longer than he had realized. No more would he pretend. No more would he hide himself inside an empty shell. He had had his fill of playing and scheming–now he would go where he wanted, see whom he wished...take what pleased him. He had tasted forbidden fruit before. Now fortune had favored him and he would taste the fruit again.

But first, he must be free of his guards. He turned toward his private chambers and instructed the guards to remain by the entrance along with the two sentinels who were always by his rooms. Inside the conference chamber he let a few moments pass. Then he strode into his bedroom.

Another sentinel approached.

"Your consorts are ready and waiting and your rooms are in good order, as you commanded, sire." The guard he had assigned to watch over them stood proudly beside the two languid youths that Storl had brought.

Flores nodded. "Well done. Now do not leave this room. I wish you to remain with them through the night. And I desire privacy in the conference room for a time."

Again in the conference room, Flores paused. Carefully, he examined the inner and outer doors to ensure against eavesdropping. Then, once convinced there was no one to see or hear, he curled one finger about a wrist and permitted himself a smug smile. With a flash his appearance changed and the chief of the Turlicum, black-bearded and olive-skinned Flores of the renowned reven clan, vanished to be replaced by the image of the guard whom he had left behind in the bedroom. The guard, who had but a moment before been Flores, withdrew a small mirror from his pocket. He gazed in it, inspecting his face.

The outer door opened and the guard emerged from Flores' apartments. Flores' bodyguard perked.

The newcomer cleared his throat. "Our Lord has retired with his consorts. He has commanded me to tell you that he is not to be disturbed under any circumstance but that the lot of you are to remain on guard here, by these doors, till dawn. I myself have been ordered to leave."

The warriors shrugged.

"Well, enough, Lenec," said one.

They began to disperse. Lenec attempted to pass and the one who had spoken halted him with a hand on his arm.

"One moment." He winked lasciviously. "Are the Turlicum's consorts, Lenec, really as beautiful as Frel and Mot here insist?" He nodded toward the original pair of warriors who still stood by the Turlicum's doors.

Lenec froze as if insulted. Casually he removed the speaker's hand off his arm and a brief glow within his eyes sparked before submerging. "Indeed, yes." His steady gaze sobered the expression of the other. "Ask me when I return and I will tell you just how beautiful–and more." His audience's brows lifted. To broach with the harem of a clan's chieftain was more than a bold courting of danger–it was a betrayal of the clan, and could place them all in danger. Saying nothing more, they exchanged glances and let him pass.

Lenec descended by way of several ramps till he came to the central hall. Here the celebrants roared and drank, with decidedly less inhibition than when Flores had been present, and Lenec made a mental note of the fact. It was just as well. He intended to change things greatly anyhow–it was best that they should be inhibited in his presence. Soon they would be not only inhibited, but frightened. He moved on, ascending more ramps until he came to a stairwell. He climbed, and emerged on the mezzanine.

"Sandol! We thought you were at the banquet!" The pair of guards whom Sandol had posted to guard the wall-turret snapped to attention.

"I was. And now I am not, am I?"

"Indeed, no, sir." They glanced apprehensively at each other. "None have approached, as you instructed."

"And have you repelled all curiosity seekers as well, and without arousing their interest, as I commanded?"

"We assure you, sire, that we have done just that." One brightened. "Placing the prisoners in this portion of the estate was wise, sire. There have been no curious to turn away. None have come near."

"That is well. It is indeed as I wished." Sandol lifted one hand. "Now do as I instruct once more... Both of you are to lower the rope ladder into the turret and summon the man to you. You are then to apologize to him for the way he has been treated, and escort him to the mezzanine on the promise of meeting the Turlicum. You will guard him well, and take him outside on the grounds of the estate. There in the moonlight, by the back grating, you will meet a band of slave merchants and their drivers. You are then to seize him and bind him, and turn him over to them. They will take him away–far, far away where he can do us no harm, yet still bring us revenue. No need to waste good muscle." Sandol smiled a sickly smile that was so unlike his own usual expression that the pair blinked to reassure themselves of his identity.

A few minutes passed, and Sandol gazed upon the athletic form of an experienced warrior approaching in the darkened corridor. The warrior paused to stare upon the majordomo. The cessation of his movement brought the two guardsmen up so abruptly that they briefly stumbled. For one moment the warrior, whose beardless face was scarred like that of a ruffian, stared hard upon Sandol. Distrust hovered about him like a cloud.

Finally Sandol spoke. "Proceed. Have no fear. He awaits you upon the grounds. He has even asked for you by name, dear Tilsis. I am sure you understand quite well the need for precautions and secrecy. You of all people are not new to the facts of the matter."

Tilsis exhaled; let his glance drop. Acquiescing, he allowed the two guards to lead him away. He turned the corner and he and the guards were gone.

Sandol breathed. Dipping within his pocket, he again pulled out the mirror. A moment passed and he stared again upon Flores. Quickly the noble walked the length of the corridor and halted to gaze into the wall-turret. He kicked the rope-ladder and it tumbled down. He descended into the turret.

Fear...fear such as he had known before. At length the eyes calmed and relaxed.

"I knew you would come, Flores. But must we be shut up here forever? Like before?" Crestal struggled to control the tears, then lost. They broke into a flood, and the youth collapsed into the pillows of a soft couch.

"No," Flores replied. "No longer. You shall leave with me–now." The youth's wet eyes gazed up, encouraged. "But you must swear to be silent–utterly so. Nor question what I now must do. We must not risk discovery. We both know why that is so."

Crestal did not argue, but gazed upon the floor without comment.

"Now take my hand." Together they climbed the rope-ladder, the green emanations of Tumsenet shining in through the narrow mullions, just as it had on the night of their first meeting so long ago. At the top they paused, Crestal surprised by the lack of escort. Flores merely smiled. Reassured, Crestal followed.

Moments later they stood in the avenue outside the estate's wall. Minutes more and they threaded narrow alleyways in Ven. A half-hour and they came to a ponderous spreading stoop, whose pediment and rim were alive with gargoyles, each sculpture a travesty, an affront, an obscenity. Not even the questing darkness spared their eyes the violations of its presence. Planet, moon, and star refracted brightly on its multitudinous surface, the gods alone indifferent, a ghastly green sheet over all.

Beneath the stoop, Crestal hesitated.

"Why?" Fear bordering on panic shook the frail body, folded though it was in its dull unprovocative black sash. The youth sought to pull away as if some terrible memory resided within the building. The eyes gazed up in confusion.

"Come! Follow! And speak not." The chieftain turned and again flashed the confident smile upon his companion and watched the fear grow calm and relinquish its hold. "Be bold–you are now with me. I promise that no harm will come to you from Flores."

Swiftly the noble pulled open the twin portals, and together they entered the red-painted room with its cerulean upper panels and misshapen forms looming in the darkness. The room had none of the relieving starlight of the exterior. The chamber was empty. Flores pulled the youth across the foyer and down an aisle. Descending a helical stairway, they paused before an oblong glass mirror, and stared in silence upon its reflection. They saw nothing more than Flores and a young delicate-featured eunuch. Flores reached out a hand and touched a place beneath the glass. Immediately, the mirror opened to expose several tubes within the wall. Grasping one, Flores pulled it out. He twisted. At once the wall began to grind and move and did not cease until a passage of sufficient size for a large man to pass had yawned.

Crestal turned and stared at Flores in shock. "How did you...?"

"Oh, I know, dear Crestal. Indeed, I know." Flores merely smiled, and indicated the passage.

Dumbstruck, Crestal obeyed.

They followed the turns of a corridor till they arrived in a chamber that was equipped with a worm's-tangle of verticillate tubes, branching and joining and multiplying on all sides. The walls and ceiling of the chamber were a comb of glass tubes and refractors, and in the center, focused round an ancient swivel seat stained with dirt and gore, were arrayed their terminae. Crestal peered, incredulous. On each terminus was a small representation of a room within the Guild enabling any who sat in the swivel chair to see all that happened in the House simultaneously and in safety, and without the knowledge of those seen.

Crestal's eyes swept rapidly over the exposed secrets of the House— how could Flores have known? Crestal glimpsed one tube that led into the lowest dungeons.

"What is happening below? What are they doing there?"

Flores merely smiled. He indicated another open passage, this one behind him, behind the swivel seat. "Please. All will be explained. Now obey, and walk before me."

Crestal stood, staggered, hands covering face. A minute later they entered a dark cell, a single flame corbeled in one corner. Upon the far wall hung manacles. Crestal glimpsed them and again halted. Turned, stared again at Flores, eager for the accustomed reassurance.

Flores merely smiled. He pointed. Behind him, obscured for a moment by his body, two figures entered the cell. They halted in front of Flores, and stepped to one side.

Crestal looked. And moaned.

One of the figures was young. A youth of no more than thirty-six, in the short Maalstrom years. He was soft, fleshy, putrid. He wore the greasy robes of a eunuch, and scratched at his loins as if to relieve some persistent pain. The other was older, shorter, and more vigorous than the other. He wore not the soiled dress of a whore, but the leather straps of a slaver. Oddly shaped ears like huge palms drifted from the inertia of his movement. A look of recognition came to him as he viewed Crestal, rendering his face both sullen and crafty.

"Dear Crestal. Have you made the acquaintance of Mesret? I understand you have heard of him often, and believe you came quite close to meeting at one time." Flores grinned. "Oh, you cannot know how much happiness it gives me to abuse the Heir to the Tribe of Turlicum." He nodded. "And I abuse him often. He is one my favorites—and the favorite of many others in the House. Too bad for him that he resisted the operation. He could have come through less affected than he did." Mesret scratched again and glanced morosely at Flores. He showed no surprise at encountering his father in the secret chambers of the Guild.

But Crestal was staring at the other.

"And Malag, of course, you know well. None who had been enclosed in a copper and wooden litter traveling across the desert in high summer can forget the driver and guardian whose task it was to ensure their survival–and who was charged to ensure their obedience and their silence by any means necessary." Malag unfurled a short whip. He cracked it upon a stone.

Flores gestured to Mesret and Malag. Advancing, they seized Crestal by the wrists, and, ignoring the high-pitched shrieks, clamped the manacles down.

Flores merely smiled. And laughed. Let loose gales of laughter. The three turned and exited the cell.

An hour elapsed.

Flores returned. He bore a torch and swung it thunderously in the small enclosure, and let it pause close to his face so that his features were illuminated. Crestal's eyes lifted, looked in shock. Where a moment before the chief of the Turlicum had stood, Crestal now looked upon something less precise, something smeared, obscured far more than the weakness of the light could explain. A blur passed before Crestal's gaze. It coalesced and Crestal gazed suddenly upon Tilsis.

"Tilsis!" the youth screamed. "Get me out, please, now!"

But the servant had gone, to be replaced by the erstwhile dictator of Ven–Crestal's former lover. Numsenmur of the Serclaslers glowered upon his errant consort, his huge hand raised to cuff the youth back into line.

Crestal again shrieked.

Numsenmur vanished. The features distorted, swirled, disappeared in a maelstrom of color and shape till they collected suddenly anew. Now was the First Born of the Vensors, Nesos of Neset, as clear and convincing as if the Emperor himself stood in the room. Again it blurred and a host of images followed, each appearing just long enough to allow of recognition before being swept away. Mosum of the Kalikum; Sruk of the Nevsonhet; a eunuch with red-threaded robe and face angled with prisms; Mesret; Nesos again. Then a series of others, till Crestal grew tired of the deceit and bored with the blurs and the trick lost its brightness and wonder, and Crestal looked away and would not glance back. Then the image returned to Flores of the Turlicum, and Crestal now knew it was not Flores at all, but someone else–some*thing* else–unless the Flores Crestal had known had never in fact been Flores at all, but had always been another masquerading as the man who had once visited the moonlit tower. Flores reached one hand over the other and removed a bauble from his left wrist. In a span of time too quick to measure, the illusions vanished and a slender man of medium height and auburn hair gazed with arrogant and quiet interest upon the youth.

The youth responded with a word. "Soorkrul."

The man merely smiled.

"Yes, dear Crestal–*Soorkrul*. Soorkrul of the Brotherhood. Soorkrul of the Light, whose sacrifices and ministrations have gone unrecognized for so long by the inhabitants of Ven and the Valleys. And whose efforts and interests have for as long gone unrewarded by you, dear Crestal. My dear, dear, Crestal." Soorkrul's lips turned the phrase over like the sweetest of fruits. "Words cannot communicate how pleased I am to lay my gaze upon you once again, and upon your flesh–your beautiful, sweet, sweet flesh." He sighed. "So much pleasure in life." He raised his arms. "So much joy! On seeing you again more words wait to fall from my lips than there are thistles in the spring–so many that I can scarce restrain my tongue."

He stepped close, the torch casting a violent yellow umbra. He breathed deeply–and began.

"So much has happened. So much there is to tell. It was near a year ago today when fate interrupted my meditations with the Divine and awakened me to a greater destiny than I had hitherto imagined. I had grown tired of sitting; tired of dreaming. The revelations came poorly–always had, since Vensor had revealed to me that I was not to undergo the conditioning of the suns, but to wear a mask when I viewed His glory, thus sparing my eyes His divine torment, even as He had revealed to me that I was not to be cut like the others, but left whole, to serve his special, his mysterious, purpose. Then it was–in the midst of my private meditations, wondering what his purpose might be–that my spies brought me news, and, eager for a chase, and my soul straining to be free of the confines of the Guild, I acted forthwith. Hastily I summoned my brothers and hastily we embarked. Into the wilds of the night we plunged, backed by the swords of our slavers and their cohorts. We arrived early by a day. We found the palmate rock, and encamped. But we were too late, for while we slept, from the darkness around us that night came weapons, and men, and reven-na of the Turlicum, and we were taken down and butchered and the survivors pursued into the bush. Only I escaped. Yet

I cannot call it ill luck. Luck it was, of course, but luck in truth of the best kind–for it was the hand of God behind it. Having fled from the scene and survived the sly assault by Flores' men, I became lost in the wilderness searching for the road back to Ven, and glimpsed the back of a Ven on a limping reven as he disappeared over a hill. It was then I found...the *Jewel*."

Deftly Soorkrul removed something from about his left wrist. A bracelet. He held it high in the light. Its translucence rendered it almost invisible in the shifting flames of the torch. Replacing it on his wrist, he continued.

"No more than a bauble it was, and for some time to come I did not understand its significance nor what powers it imparted to he who wears it, so, though I had had the foresight to place it upon my wrist, I did not know how to focus it, or to concentrate its powers and use it to its maximum, so that before I was able to take another step, I was caught and seized by a band of rude Neset-sa. For miles I was hauled, slung ignominiously over a reven, till I arrived at their camp in the midst of the southern wilderness."

The yellow face paused. Took another breath.

"They dragged me to the tent of their ruler. Although I knew enough not to reveal my true identity, my feeble efforts to control the device and throw a fog over myself only attracted the attentions of their King–the Neset king–King Nesos. He was entranced. He was enthralled. Like a child with a new toy he kept me close at hand, examining me, taunting me, abusing me, and when he discovered the extent of my talents he clamped a chain about my ankle lest I change into something unforeseen and vanish. Then...he told me to dance."

Soorkrul's voice turned sad and he turned red eyes upward.

"I at first refused. Yes, I refused–for several days remaining obstinate, till..." Soorkrul's hand touched various places on his body as if in remembered pain, and his jaw began to grind, "till finally I learned to listen, and learned that relief from torment was more important–but then he would not let me to dance, and at last I begged for the privilege of dancing rather than undergo his displeasure again."

He released a breath. Sucked another. "And so I danced. Humiliated, I danced–for the King, for his nobles, and even for the vermin Simet-sa from Ven, among whom was the man you esteem so much that you would enter the den of your enemy for no more than his smile. I danced. And bided my time."

A sudden light came to his eyes and he gripped his hands into fists.

"The beast! The fool! How little he knew of my true powers! How small he was in comparison to the scheme that took shape in my brain! How he wasted his time, and mine! Yes, I pranced and cavorted for his entertainment, but I swear that not a moment passed that I did not use to my advantage in plotting my move against him. I swore that I would at last take my revenge!"

The Guildmaster's eyes glowed with passion.

"Finally, when his vaunted ambition and his towering arrogance had brought him to the edge of defeat, as I knew it must in time–he came to me. To me! His whipping boy–his footrest. And begged my help! *Me*– who for so many months he had scorned and cuffed. He asked me to enter Ven and open the gate in the guise of the dictator Numsenmur, who had resisted his worst assaults and blandishments." Soorkrul shook his head, chortling with deep satisfaction. "And I was ready. And when the soldiers came and broke the chain about my leg, I lost no time in imitating one, and–despite Nesos' warnings–the fools at once fell into confusion, and allowed me to escape!" Soorkrul laughed, tears rolling on his cheeks. "What a simple matter it was!"

He grew suddenly more serious. "And into the hot night I escaped, and I made my way to his tent, to his blue and white pavilion of the stars where on many a brazen night he had forced me to grovel for his pleasure, and in the darkness I approached, slipping silently across a jungle of rugs, with an irsrem dagger poised to strike, having already taken on his guise, needing only his royal ring to deny any proof of the identity of the corpse, which I was prepared to condemn as the illusionist whom I, Nesos, had killed–with his last illusion frozen upon him in death."

Soorkrul's eyes dropped.

"But he saw me. From the glinting of the blade in the light of a single star shining through a smokehole he saw me, and leapt at once to his feet, and he pummeled me with his great fists, and when his guards came from the entrance, threw me bloodied at their feet, warning them of my illusions, and again had me put in chains. And when the city fell I was dragged without pity through the streets of Ven with a dirty bag about my head, laughed at and abused, because even then they did not know the secret of my illusions. I still looked and spoke like the Emperor! And they hauled me into a dungeon below the Hall of Vim where my piteous cries for forgiveness which my despair drove me to utter were met with ridicule and for many days thence my pleas were ignored and I was forced to endure the spittle of the King and his imbecilic Heir. I was put into a pit from which no mortal could escape without the help of one from outside, and there I shed many a bitter tear and at length was re-duced by my regret to leaping like a beast as if that alone might free me. I even began to hope that I might be injured and die in my attempts. The boredom of the Guild I had traded for the lot of a slave–and the lot of a slave I had traded for the confinement of one condemned."

He paused. Suddenly his voice uplifted.

"Then it was that my fortune turned. Attracted by my leaping, the Turlicum came to look, having been freed by Nesos to do some foul deed of his. And Flores–yes, your Flores–gazed upon me, and I saw my chance–and took it. He believed he saw his son, and turned at once upon his guards–and murdered them. The fool killed them both! And lifted me out with a harness, and delivered their weapons to me, before himself departing. To escape from the palace then was a matter of the greatest ease, for from the beginning of my enslavement to the end, Nesos had never guessed the secret of my illusions! The cretin!" Soorkrul gazed wildly about the cell. "I still possessed the bracelet!"

Maniacal humor wrung his features.

"So I was free. At last–free to go where I might. Free to do what I had contemplated for close on a year, free to attempt again what I had sworn, no matter how long it took! No longer had I to wait! No longer must I prolong the satisfaction of my hate! But I must not repeat the mistake I made before, when I had thought to use mere darkness to cover the deed. Not at all. I learned from that mistake, you see. Not darkness, but light! The light of glass! The light of day! That is what the bracelet loves! That is how one uses it to its full potential! Hence when I entered the Assem-bly grounds in the guise of a common Neset soldier, and glimpsed Mes-ret departing the Assembly room, knowing as I did that the putrid youth had joined the Neset King's harem, it was the simplest of matters to ap-pear before Mesret as Nesos and order Mesret to remove himself from the city, then to take on Mesret's guise and rejoin the King in the As-sembly before the eyes of all. Came my chance–and I drove my blade home. And was rewarded when I looked into his eyes while I still held it. For one moment Nesos looked back–and knew. Before he died, *he knew!* He knew that it was not Mesret that had killed him, but *me*–his despised illusionist–his crow, his worm, his dog, his lowly entertainer! And before his body hit the floor I had already become a Neset guard, shouting with all my might to seize and hang his assassin!"

Triumph shone from his eyes. Soorkrul sighed and refocused again upon the youth chained upon the wall. The Guildmaster breathed deep.

"Then I left. For a time I wandered in the wilds. Not wishing to again endure my castrati colleagues and their petty intrigues, I walked among the Valleys and the deserts seeing what real life was like. Till I finally realized–it came to me one evening like a storm–the miracle God had placed in my hands, the vistas which had thus opened before me." Fire seized his eyes. "And I hurried back to Ven, and announced myself, and resumed my place in the Guild. And the revelations came–in torrents, in a great river of light and passion, and I could not contain them, and I began to speak to the brothers, then to all who would listen, then to the masses of Ven in the Morbius at night, telling them of what the future holds, as I shall tell the fathers of my order in Klopus when I return to them–after the instructions of God concerning Ven have at length been fulfilled."

He returned a calm gaze to Crestal.

"And now I am overcome with pleasure to have my favorite whore back from Numsenmur, who was becoming troublesome, and whom I would have had also to kill had Nesos not done the deed for me. And how pleased I am that the upstart Ust of the Calomar–whom I shall soon deal with as easily as I would a fly–did not get his grasping hands upon you. My child, my spies saw you the first night you arrived. But I did not have you seized because I knew why you had come, just as I knew where you had gone, and I know where you have been, and know the company you kept during your long absence away from me. But I did not hurry. Because I also knew that I would soon have you by my side once more.

"And so that has come about. And now you must know that you can never leave my side, for the same reason that Numsenmur did not wish you to leave his tower. Because the Order cannot permit you to corrupt Ven with your energies, and because your presence contradicts the plan of God. And why did you not slip the poison in the Serclasler's brew as I instructed when first I delivered you to him two years ago? It took much time to find a gila; the Serclasler was cautious of me. He would have no eunuch that was trained within these walls–only a gila from abroad would he accept. So I had to bring you from far away, from the land of the Mok-sa. And when you declined to do as you were told, and after he refused to let you return to me, why did you not take the secret escape route and return anyway, the route that I had arranged for you when the deed was to have been completed? Numsenmur was to join Jaz and Clesp in death. Instead he became king and frustrated all my plans."

Soorkrul shrugged.

"But now they are all dead. Dead and gone and vanquished: Jaz and

Clesp, and Nesos, Sruk and Numsenmur, all who have rejected my commandments–all but Ust, whom I shall soon sweep aside with the crook of my smallest finger. And Flores–should he return from his exile. He resisted not only my offers of eunuchs, but of gilas as well. And now you must do as you are told, and submit to punishment for your disobedience. You would resist? That only makes the road more thorny; it still leads to the same destination. Or would you rather return to those from whom I brought you? You know what that would mean–a long trip by barge to my stronghold in the forest, then a hundred miles in a sealed litter in the hot sun, escorted by my ungentle assistant, Malag, whom you know so well. No–you need us. Without our protection, neither you, nor any other gila, could survive!"

Crestal raised her tear-stained face, relieved to learn that her sojourn in the forest had not been with an impostor, but with the real Flores. "Why do you wish to kill Flores? He has done nothing to deserve death!"

"Deserve?" The predatory glance returned, mixed with incredulity. "And who are you to say who deserves what? None deserve, and all do. We are born deserving of death. Why? Because we are free. As Atasan is free, but will never choose the good, so men are free, even though, as God Himself knows, they will never choose the good. Free–but damned. They may be pilots of their souls, but they cannot escape the flesh of their own bodies. You might say we have choice, but that the choice was chosen. By Vensor Himself at the beginning of time when He begat His son, and allowed him live out of His boundless love–out of indulgence– out of kindness. By His choice we are doomed. Doomed to evil because God loved. Doomed to evil because He allowed His Son, Atasan, to live. Why Flores? Because he is flesh; because he is bone; because he *is*."

He turned his gaze upon Crestal's body.

"Even so with you, dear Crestal. Now, I have spoken enough. And my dreams are returning. My dreams, which have grown strong with the memory of your flesh. With the fond memory of your cries, your screams, your tears."

He approached, brought the torch close so that the heat caused the sweat on her face to bubble. "Now my lust shall once more fall upon you like rain; and your hot tears shall bathe me with their drops."

Placing the torch in a socket upon the wall, he grasped her robe with both hands. He ripped it. Breasts like inverted bowls shook free. With a jarring motion he tore the remainder of the thick cloth away.

She cried.

"Cry, my dear. Cry. I have not heard the music of a gila–your music–

for an age. And I long for more than memories."

CHAPTER 20

DRAGABONDS

His heart raced. Again, as he had the previous autumn, Flores felt the steady pressure of the resisting current against his face as a reven propelled him forward. Around him, the sunlight seeped into the watery depths, illuminating the lower reaches of the ocean as through the colored panes of a cathedral, its greens and blues gradually muting into blackness.

The reven had changed greatly from its former starved, skittish self. It now accepted his mastery without recalcitrance or fear, bearing him effortlessly along with strong strokes, indeed, from its occasional pauses to glance back at him, seeming to take genuine pleasure in his company. Well, he thought, it was raised to be ridden and likely had never been long out of the company of Vensor-sa. Good. They would have to spend many weeks together.

Flores exhaled, spilling bubbles from his gill, and relaxed his head on the gently throbbing jugular of Tha's undulating neck. The time passed—as it had during his descent through the hollow wall of Ra'Allah—as in a dream. But now the dream was awash with pleasure, no longer the nightmare of discipline and effort that he had previously been forced to endure. The water was deliciously cool. Soon he had forgotten the island's beach and the suns that hammered down as on an anvil.

Moving away from the island, he lost sight of the submarine landscape he had come to expect in the shallower areas. The coral phantasms. The leafy weeds. Within a few moments the seabottom that bore these had dropped away and vanished. They floated in the womb of the ocean. Weightless. Motionless. Suspended between earth and sky, he flew, or rather drifted on the breeze. Flores held out his hand and the illusion broke. They moved swiftly through the current, Tha giving every sign of knowing his destination.

Flores again lay his head, lulled by the monotony. He found he could shut his eyes and, after pausing to loop his hands around the creature's neck to prevent inadvertently slipping off, discovered he could catnap without losing his seat, though if he fell into a deep sleep the gill would begin to leak forcing him to surface to clear it. How to rest in the coming days without losing time, and with no land in view?

This bore some thought. Indeed soon came to dominate his thoughts to the exclusion of food and water. His mount proved adept at snatching fish enough for the both of them–Flores consuming his share raw. His thirst was assuaged by the constant influx of moisture-drenched oxygen through the gills, hence, to his surprise, he had no more need of drink than did the creatures of the sea. Sleep, though, was another matter. No matter how many catnaps he took, no matter how he sought to conserve his energy, he learned he could not sleep without awaking suddenly in a panic, his gill filling quickly with water, requiring urgent signals to Tha and a trip to the surface. Attempts to sleep while the reven swam upon the surface proved no more successful, as the constant wash of waves and dipping of the animal in its locomotion dislodged his gill with equal frequency. Tightening the straps produced only chafing which was worsened by the salt. If only the contraption of rubber tubes and leather straps could be exchanged for the natural gills of the reven!

Finally, he could endure it no longer. He had to find land–and to sleep. He had no notion of how far they had come in the several days and nights they had traveled, but he knew he could go no further without deep rest. Then–just as he was on the verge of giving up hope, and the despair he had felt when descending the shaft on the Island had begun to return, he glimpsed it...a briefest wisp of cloud. Denoting, through its discoloration, something beneath its wing besides sea. Land–and greenery.

An hour later they arrived. Struggling ashore on a coastline that bespoke a mass considerably greater than the small island where he had left his comrades, Flores dragged himself onto the hot sand to collapse beneath the overhanging eaves of a grove of tropical palms. He paused only to remove his bracelet and gill before losing consciousness in the lee of a high bank.

He slept as he had never slept before. Dreamless, in the shade of the drifting palms, with the calm undulations of the sea in his ears. When at last his eyes opened he was immediately aware that he had no recollection of ever having had so refreshing a respite, so complete and perfect a rest. The morning was bright and sunny. A smile broke as he turned toward Tha.

Where was the reven? His eyes searched the sand and spied an imprint indicating the reven had slept beside him. From the imprint to the water's edge was the slithering track of the quadruped. The beast had gone. Once beyond the control of his master, the natural pull of nature had prevailed.

Flores sighed. Again he was marooned. But at least he still had his bracelet and that marvelous work, the gill. He looked about, his brows furrowing. He stood and scoured the ground in ever widening circles. He swore, fighting a sense of rising panic. Finally he located the spot where the devices must have lain while he slept. Their imprints were smeared, but plain enough. A dim memory returned of his having laid them here, on the other side of the bank, before he sought the shade of the palms. He berated himself again–then faced the truth. The devices had vanished! After all he had endured, after all he had overcome, once more he was stranded and helpless! Had he still not learned the lesson? He must never remove the bracelet from his person!

He glanced down. The impressions in the sand were altered, smeared. The bank was covered with tracks. A chill rose within–some creature had apparently stolen the items. The tracks were almost, but not quite, human. They were bipedal, but there was something about the width, and the depth of them, and their stolid march that ignored every thorn or impediment that suggested an owner different from any son of Vensor he had ever encountered. Plainly visible in the sand, the tracks paralleled the sea, leading along the shore just behind a line of bank.

Flores followed.

An hour passed. The twin suns reached zenith and began to decline and still Flores followed the spoor. He came to a bluff. Here the tracks turned upon themselves, and merged with several similar prints that approached from a different direction and clustered behind the bluff. Remnants of crustaceans' shells and nut fibers lay strewn below the rock as if the unknown creatures had stood for a time, hidden from the sea by the rock's crest. Flores had no time to climb the bluff. Ven called–and Amina had only days before her fate took her.

Into the bush he plunged. A great mass of brown trunks and shaggy foliage formed a canopy, and he began to worry that he would lose the spoor, but as he progressed he realized that he was on the trail of a large number of the creatures, and the track they left was unmistakable, broken branches and crushed grass abounding, as if an irresistible flood had passed. Contemplating the numbers of his quarry, he began to fear he would be unable to defend himself should he succeed in overtaking them, and Flores paused to select a stout branch from a brake for a cudgel. He wished now that he had brought a blade on his journey, and not relied solely upon the bracelet to protect him.

A complete lack of abandoned weapons or clothing in the wake of the creatures, together with the occasional remnant of food reassured him somewhat. Whatever manner of creatures they were, it seemed they lacked the refinements of Vensor-sa, and presumably therefore the intelligence. Still, even animals were known to use weapons, and to be able at times to outwit the average Vensor. Flores slowed and took to pausing in the darker patches of shade to listen before he advanced.

Pressing through a bower, he halted.

About a broad clearing lay a score of Vensor-sa sprawled like ripped dolls. The hairs on Flores' neck rose. The bodies of the victims were not merely wounded, but were rent in pieces, every limb dissevered. The scene was beyond what one might find in a slaughterhouse, and left Flores nauseous–he who was as familiar with carnage as a butcher. Every skull was crushed; every limb broken; even the torsos had not been left unmolested, but bore the marks of rending as by the jaws of some animal of ferocious strength. He stared, shocked. What manner of creature could surprise a band of armed Vensor-sa in daylight, and annihilate them without weapons, and without losing a single one of their own?

He shrank into the shadows. Vensor prepared to bed–the suns, invisible behind the canopy of trees, were sinking, and the scarlet shadows deepened as Atasan rose in the sky. Flores did not relish an evening in such a forest. And did not wish to be near when the workers of the sky came to claim their right.

From within the shadows, his eyes spied out every fact to be had. He had learned much from Macius. Now he employed the best of what he knew–caution. And stealth. If his adversaries–for such they must be–might ambush men by day, might not their night capability be even more pronounced? Peering into the bush, his hairs rose with each rustle.

But the darkness was not complete, and would not be for another half-hour. And the victims had not been unarmed. Taking up a discarded rapier, Flores penetrated the far side of the clearing. Again in the jungle, he was relieved to see that the trail was no more difficult to follow than before. The creatures apparently took no caution, but regarded their land as perfectly safe from invasion. He glimpsed a dark stain on the blade–at least one of the dead Vensors had scored. So the creatures bled like men. Therefore, they must die as well.

He breathed deep. With his hand around honed glass, he was again the ruler of his fate. Let them come. Whatever they were, they had yet to meet an irsrem lord.

The half-hour passed. The last of the spoor had gone, and Flores slid silently through the bush, a year's journey in the forests outside Ven returning in an instant. When he heard the thrumming, he realized he had been hearing it ever since he left the clearing, and knew he no longer needed a trail. Like the primeval heartbeat of the forest, now more distant and quiet, now closer with a change of wind, a dull, echoing reverberation imbued the trees around him. Every few minutes the drumming increased again, drifting from far ahead, and seeming to bear in its midst the staccato of a higher-pitched shrillness whose tones sent chills down his spine.

The drumming grew. Around him the forest sank suddenly into a morass of swamp with sphagnum moss trailing in the slime. His feet splucked as he plodded forward. Again a drift of wind–and again the thumping. This time the piercing sound was plainly a voice–high and shrill, alternately harsh and threatening, then thin with terror. He strained to discern words, and failed. Only the tones could penetrate the dense mass of jungle. At length he approached the last line of foliage.

He peered through.

Red flames from a gigantic pit bathed his face. The crackling of wood obscured his gasp. Never in his deepest nightmares–not even when he dwelt in the pit beneath the Hall of Vim awaiting death at the hand of the Neset king–had he imagined that death could come so horribly. Who could deserve such? He had killed, certainly, and with his own hand. He had even extracted information for a purpose, and with warning. But not in the span of his life, or that of his lineage, had he known of the torture of flesh without reason. In time with the groans of the damned, the drumming thundered upon him without pause. Circling the great pit, which had been dug in the midst of a village of raw stone, were the remaining victims of the party of Vensor-sa, all of whom had not been murdered in the ambush in the forest. A few had survived–or been seized–and were now undergoing a fate far crueler than mere murder. The creatures–or devils, for Flores had never seen their like, and took some minutes to properly order his impressions–had crucified each victim with his face to the flames and a large bowl placed behind. The victim's lower extremity was then flayed, and–while yet living–his skin fixed to the bowl in such a way that the devil might beat upon the improvised drum before the uproaring flames, which seared and burned the gory flesh of the wretch.

At least a dozen boiled thus.

Flores turned–retched. Shaken, he steeled himself, and gripped the rapier. He would not stand by idly while such occurred. Not even enemies, and such the Vensor-sa must be since they were obviously not citizens of Ven, could be left to such a fate. Whatever sort of creatures these were, they would taste the anger of his blade amid a stench of ozone.

While the irsrem sword warmed and began to hum, he spied the authors of the deed. They were unlike any he had seen. They walked upright–or rather shambled, for they were immensely large, and handled their captives with ease. They had no clothing, which led Flores first to suppose that they were on a level with Talon's animals as regards intelligence. The expressions on their dull and placid faces indeed indicated that this was the case. But apart from a thick beetling look about them, they seemed humanoid, and wielded stone tools. Even as he watched, one gripped a dull obsidian blade and partly cut, partly ripped more skin from a victim. The Vensor shrieked. The creature showed no reaction, but concentrated on the primitive drum, stretching the skin to tighten it with the aid of another of his kind, leaving Flores with the impression that the whole elaborate ceremony–shocking and fiendish though it was–was in fact nothing more than a method devised by the creatures to produce better drums. Flores frowned at the mindless deception, the callous and stupid devotion to their craft. With a wave of revulsion and contempt, he swore to burn every drum after he had dispatched their makers.

A twig snapped.

He turned. A trio of shapes shambled from the darkness. Instinctively, his blade thrust–without effect. His limbs halted in their movement, struggling against massive arms that embraced him with irresistible strength. His sword was plucked from his grasp. In another moment his hands were secured with vines and he was being carried over stone roofs. He dropped off a precipice into the midst of the village, then was carried to the entrance of a large stone hut and his captors tossed him within.

"Does he yet live? Could they have relented and spared him?"

A deep rumbling echoed from the darkness that encompassed the interior of the structure. "I know not. All I said was a body had come."

The first voice spoke again–not as deep as the second, but strong, and edged with a sarcastic quality. "Does it move?" A rustling arose as if the owner of the voice sought a less uncomfortable pose in the dark. "I wish to know whether I will survive their attentions or not."

"You will not–nor will I–so cease your egoistic prattling." This from across the room.

"Keep speaking, Numtal," replied the sarcastic voice. "Ha! How like you to find your voice only when all your betters are bound and unable to put you in your place as they should."

"What? You, Stalkin, are capable of a sentence that does not have *you* as its subject? You, at least, I note, remain true to form–bound though you are. You are as obsessed with your own fate as ever."

The deep voice rejoined. "Fear not, my little foul-mouth. If ever I manage to release these bonds, I myself will teach these dragabonds a thing or two. They will regret having imprisoned an initiate of Kot. If only I could loosen these bonds...and find food for my gullet." The rumbling of Fish, the king's Overseer, was unmistakable.

"Gullet?" replied Stalkin. "It was your gullet landed us here in the first place!"

"So how can we sail to Vaw when we are starving?"

"*You* were starving you mean! I was quite content. Can you not think of something besides your stomach?"

"Surge warned us to avoid this land–you ever ignore our murshid's advice. Three weeks we spend repairing our ships, because you take us over shallow reefs! And no sooner do we put to sea than you insist on stopping at these forbidden isles!"

"Enough!" shouted Fish. As Flores–who had yet to speak–twisted his face above the row of supine bodies he glimpsed several faces similarly twisted, grimacing in the shadows of red flame visible through the entrance. Apparently the victims of the dragabonds' attack were an expedition from the ships of Fish and his Vaw-sa, who had come ashore to replenish their larder. The living lips of the Overseer writhed in the dark like a snake in a trap. "We must find a way to get free. Look–these are but vines. We must find a way to break them." The tone of his voice was less certain than his words. "Surge! Have you had luck?"

The murshid's voice rose from a sack dumped in one corner. "Have I had luck? No. I have had no luck..."

"But..." inquired Stalkin.

"But what?"

"But what does this mean, 'I have had no luck?' Does this mean that you are still bound? Or that you have managed to free yourself, but not by means of luck?"

" 'What does this mean?' "

"Don't echo my question. Are you free? Or are you still bound?" cried Stalkin.

" 'Am I free?' "

Several captives rolled and shouted at once.

"He ever evades plain Vensor speech!"

"Shut up! We must not attract the attention of the dragabonds!"

"You shut up, for you are the one shouting!"

"We are doomed whether we attract their attention or not."

"Do not abuse our murshid; we need him to get home," said Fish, his powerful voice dominating the others even in a whisper.

The doorway grew black—the voices ceased. A giant ten feet in height lumbered in, flames hot behind him. He leaned over a body near the door.

"Not me!" screamed the unfortunate, apparently selected to be the next victim. "Take *him*—*that* one—the one you just returned! He wasn't supposed to come back! Take him again!"

Realizing the Vensor meant him, Flores said nothing as the giant bent at its low-slung waist and effortlessly lifted the Vensor with a single great fist. The giant turned and halted. Several younger versions of itself had appeared in the entrance.

"Lum want?" growled the first in a voice deeper than Flores had thought possible in a humanoid. He felt relieved. He had begun to fear they were so primitive that no communication was possible.

The tallest of the newcomers, eight feet in height, spoke. "Lum want eat. Lum want eat food." The others echoed this. "Mig want eat." "Gab want eat food." The first youth glanced past the giant at the Vensor captives. "Bak give food Lum." The eight-foot giants made slow finger motions toward their mouths.

"Food hut Bak," replied the first dragabond. "No food hut Bak."

Lum pointed to the interior. "Food hut Bak."

Bak swung a ham-like hand. It struck the chest of the largest youth. The youth lurched backward.

"No food hut Bak! Food hut Bak!"

Flores shook his head. It was Vensor speech, but so degraded and simplified that it was fraught with ambiguity, and useless without gestures to accompany it. He could barely comprehend it even with the gestures.

The youths' brows beetled more than formerly, and Bak—as the largest giant apparently was named—lumbered past with his victim, ignoring them.

The youths loitered a moment. Then they entered the hut. Producing several sticks, they began slowly to poke at the nearest Vensor-sa, whistling dull laughter. A stick jabbed Flores. Though the effort exerted by the first dragabond seemed little, Flores felt as if he had just had his ribs cracked. The youth was a good eight feet tall and as solid as any three Vensor-sa. Desperate to prevent another jab, which might inflict real damage the second time, he blurted out in his most stern and authority-drenched tone, "I food Bak! No touch food Bak!"

Dully, and with agonizing slowness, the youth lowered the stick. He raised his gaze. He peered through an unkempt mass of dirty blond hair.

Thinking that he must not have made himself clear, Flores repeated, "I food Bak! No touch food Bak!"

For another minute the youth thought. Calmly he directed his gaze around the darkly flickering room and met the puzzled looks of his comrades.

"I food Bak," repeated Mig.

"No touch I. I food Bak," added Gab.

The first looked at the others blankly. His brows raised as if a thought had just occurred to him. He stared. "Bak no here."

The others raised their brows to look at each other. "Bak fire. Bak no here."

"Lum want eat. Lum want eat food. Bak no here."

The others nodded agreement in their slow dragabond fashion. The facts were indisputable.

Lum again raised the stick, and looked as if preparing to club his meal into submission. Flores opened his mouth to shout for help from Bak, though he wondered if this would itself be wise.

One of the other youths put a blockish hand on the shoulder of the first. Lum halted.

"Bak strong."

"Bak strong-strong."

The first lowered the cudgel. A frown seemed to cloud his expression, rendering it even duller than before. Slowly he turned his gaze to the other Vensor-sa scattered about the interior.

"*I food Bak!*" chorused every throat. A row of shining Vensor faces looked in amazement at Flores, though he could not discern whether their expressions were due to relief at not being eaten or surprise at encountering the Turlicum in this most unlikely of places.

Disappointment seemed to overtake Lum. Or confusion. The distinction was exceedingly difficult to tell, even with the full radiance of the flames upon him. Another moment passed, and the trio lumbered out, muttering.

A low laugh rattled in the darkness. "So the gods are just after all. So they have brought you to me–a mere slave of the Golden Cyclops–to do with as I will. And bound so you cannot resist. You, Flores of the Turlicum of Ven. Ha ha!" Fish squirmed with jubilance, the laugh deepening till it merged with the thundering tom-toms.

"How? You are bound as well as he!" Stalkin called. "Who's to say he will not slip his bonds and escape you once again, as he did before!"

"You had best wish that does not happen, lest I blame you for giving him aid and support."

"Blame if you wish! It was your folly that landed us here, and we shall not live to see Vaw, much less take revenge on anyone."

"Enough!" rumbled Fish. "You always boasted of your strength before, fair Stalkin, now I command you to use it. Break your bonds and free us at once. I wish to kill this Ven without delay."

The sounds of strain rose from where Stalkin lay. They soon ceased. "It is useless. These ropes are like iron–or irsrem. Not even these dragabonds could break them."

Numtal snorted. "Weakling."

"When I break free I will show you who is the weakling!"

"You will not," answered Numtal.

"Then when I am returned–"

"Oaf! Have you not realized? It was Flores captured and tossed in among us. Spew was taken and doubtless dies even now." The others grew silent and sighed. "There is no succor for those whom the giants choose."

Stalkin exhaled. "If I could break my bonds I would take up my sword and slay the lot. See! It lies still in the corner where the first dragabond dropped it."

"And what good would that do?" sneered Numtal. "We all struck home when they first attacked us–to no good. I swear I ran three of them through with my rapier and they did not notice. Have you not perceived that they feel no pain? They haven't the intelligence to know when they have been stabbed!"

The others' silence lent credibility to this statement, thought Flores. His own experience certainly reinforced the impression he had received of imperturbability.

"Such creatures! Talon be damned."

Silence ensued.

At length it became apparent that no more of them would be taken that night, and the lot of them, Flores included, sank into exhausted sleep. The few questions directed at him concerning how he had come to join them–being answered with evasive replies or none–soon ceased. In another hour the cries and groans from the village firepit ceased as well, and Flores once awoke and believed he heard the sounds of a grisly feast. On what, he could only speculate.

Dawn came.

A grunt like that of a ros announced the return of Bak. The giant, now bedecked with a snake tied around his neck, and carrying a cudgel fashioned from a small tree, staggered beneath the lintel, making the floor shake. Behind him trailed a group of lesser dragabonds. Flores surmised Bak was their leader and the snake his badge of authority. He stared harder–the snake had moved. It reared its head and bit. Bak took no notice. A finger scratched the bite, then ignored it, and he continued on his errand.

Flores sighed. If even the bite of a venomous reptile could not harm them, what promise had he? It was no surprise therefore that the creatures, armed only with stones and sticks, and presenting a solid front of bodies, had been able easily to subdue the Vaw-sa.

Bak continued past the rows of captive Vensor-sa. Nearing the far side of the hut, he halted. He reached down. He retrieved the sword that Stalkin had so wished to grasp the night before.

Stalkin groaned.

As the other dragabonds crowded the interior, Bak staggered slowly around the room. He gathered all the items which the Vensor-sa had brought and which lay inside the hut. At least they are no longer hungry, thought Flores.

Flores eyed Bak with a strange look. There was something different about the chief that seemed to put him in a different category than the other dragabonds. A glint that bespoke superior intelligence, however slim the margin. And more than normal curiosity.

Bak turned the rapier over in the air. Fish and Stalkin looked at each other. No other dragabond had showed an interest in the object. Another moment passed and Bak let it drop. He picked up a casque of irsrem armor that one of the fallen had discarded. He peered at the strange material, then also let it drop.

"The moron wishes only to find more to eat," whispered Numtal. "If it smells not like food, he throws it aside."

"No," called Flores, "can you not see? What is remarkable is that he knows these items are not food. He wishes to learn what they do–"

The Turlicum fell silent. Bak had lifted something new, and unexpected. It was a contraption of tubes, bag, and slits like those of a fish's gill. Flores sucked his breath. So the dragabond who had stolen his gill had placed it with the rest of their pilfer! And if it had retrieved his gill, perhaps it had retrieved his bracelet as well.

Bak raised the rapier again. He cut the air. Then halted and ran the blade across a palm. Red blood appeared. Flores shook his head. A minute passed and still the giant did not respond. At last, after two full minutes he grunted and peered at his hand. With a shrug he ignored it– the blood was slight, and the wound not deep.

He grasped it by the helve and let his gaze wander about the room.

The Vensor-sa chilled and made no sound.

The floor shook. Pausing, the dragabond pointed the weapon at a hor- rified Vaw. He drove it home. The Vaw shrieked. Bak pulled it out, al- most cutting the Vaw in half with the force of the movement. The shriek abruptly terminated.

Again the giant's gaze wandered about the room. Mumbled prayers rose from the doomed captives. But this time Flores noted the dragabond's gaze rested chiefly on his own kind. A peculiar fascination took hold and Flores found he was unable to look away.

Shambling forward, the giant approached the dragabonds attending his investigation of the prey. One–a giant almost as large as Bak–and evi- dently harboring similar ambitions, as one might suppose the carcass of a lizard draped upon his temple signified–stared dully upon his chieftain as he advanced.

Bak halted before him. A low rumble issued. "Stug throw neg. Neg no Stug. Neg Bak. Neg Bak neg." For emphasis Bak raised a massive hand and plucked the lizard from Stug's forehead.

Stug raised his own hand and seized Bak's before he could drop the lizard. "Bak bad. Bak no neg. Stug neg."

"Stug no neg!" roared Bak. "Bak neg!"

Like a pantomime the two giants locked arms as each strove to throw the other down. Bak seemed to have forgotten the rapier he held in his right hand, but in another moment he recalled it and slowly pressed the point into Stug's chest. The wound widened, and deepened. Stug fought on, oblivious. Minutes passed. The two still contended, the other dragabonds seeming to have belatedly realized that a struggle was on and they began to file out.

Another moment and Stug noticed that something was amiss. His gaze lowered to his chest where the blade was now half buried and a river of blood gushed over him and his attacker. His eyes grew puzzled. Dark- ened. More seconds passed and he staggered. A great hoot escaped his throat. He ceased struggling, and fell backwards in the entrance, shaking the ground.

Bak stared. He raised his eyes upward and opened his mouth to give forth an eerie silent gasp in lieu of a victory howl. Outside, the tribe of dragabonds watched through the entrance.

One of the items that the Vaw-sa had discarded and which the creatures had retrieved and placed inside the hut was a small sack. This sack Bak now took, and, after a few minutes during which he learned in his stumbling way its purpose, he laboriously placed each item inside.

"Can you believe it?" whispered Flores. "He is a genius among his kind."

Numtal snorted. "I'll teach this 'genius' more than he ever wished to know if I get loose."

"My limbs are numb. I must get loose soon or die."

"Ssssh!"

Bak slowly looked up and searched the hut with his eyes. He resumed filling the sack.

"You won't get loose. They will eat the rest of us tonight."

"Macius. Any luck?"

The murshid responded. " 'Luck'? Have I had any?"

"Shut up!"

"Don't annoy our murshid!"

"You shut up too!"

"Who said that? You'll regret your words when I get loose!"

"You won't get loose."

"Ssssh!"

Bak again looked up. Grasping the sack in a bloody hand, he turned and shambled from the hut.

"Great! Now what do we do? He has the only sword, and all else besides!"

"We must find obsidian, as they use!"

"I have had luck."

"When I get loose and find a weapon you will regret your actions here."

"You won't get loose."

"What actions? I have spoken words only. Why do you always protest mere words?"

"Luck?" Fish's deep rumble erupted. "Macius—you spoke?"

"I said 'I have had luck.' "

Stalkin snapped. "But what does that mean? 'I have had luck.' In what way?"

"I mean: I have cut my bonds."

Silence.

"You've cut your bonds?"

"Quite so. During the night. On the blade before the giant took it."

"*Selem-na!*"

"Up with our murshid! He has saved the day again!"

The captives exploded with joy and relief. "Get us loose–without delay!"

"Yes," rumbled Fish, "I wish to cut the throat of the Ven at once!"

"I'm afraid I cannot permit that," lamented Macius. "If that is your plan then I cannot release you." Macius slowly stood and rubbed his arms and wrists. The electricity that animated his soul jerked and stretched his thick muscles.

A moment passed quietly. "Ah, as you say, dear Surge." Fish was suddenly calm and his voice soothing. "It was but a fleeting notion. Nerves. No more. Why I wouldn't harm the noble Ven for all the gold on Maalstrom."

"I am glad to hear that. For we really must be leaving if we are to survive another day. I do not think we will live long if we remain among the dragabonds."

Macius found an obsidian blade and freed the rest.

Stalkin pressed his sculpted muscles against each other to bring them back to life. Numtal jumped to shake out the sleep. Fish heaved his bulk onto his stubby legs, then sat and rolled, his feet flopping momentarily in the dust. Another four Vaw-sa had survived–and Flores. Two more Vaw-sa breathed shallowly and did not respond to the urgent summons of the others.

"They cannot make it," whispered Macius. "We must not delay."

"But how to escape?" hissed Stalkin. "There is no back exit. We will have to walk forth in daylight."

"You are right. We cannot run after such an ordeal. And these creatures swarm the village like rum-na. How can we make the forest and the ships? A single blow from a dragabond hand is enough to crush a skull."

Numtal stood by the entrance. "Look! They are departing! The way is clear!"

Fish grunted.

"Now!" hissed Macius.

As one, the surviving Vensor-sa emerged from the hut and limped past the scene of the previous night's butchery, their legs still tingling. Traces of the cannibal feast littered the grounds amid a selection of empty crosses and new skin drums. And–to Flores's relief, another rapier–or was it the sword which Bak had taken the prior night and inadvertently dropped after dispatching his rival?

Flores snatched it. In reaction, Fish bit his lip. Stalkin looked to the latter for guidance, and the Overseer exhaled a brief frustrated breath. Let it go.

They hurried on.

The central clearing of the dragabond village was surrounded by stone huts, all of which were interconnected to form a single stone wall twelve feet high. The forest was visible above the huts, but the great height of the dwellings made it impossible to scale them. Only a few avenues gave egress. Glancing nervously about, the band made for the nearest of the avenues, where a ramp led upward to ground level. Another moment and they had reached the end of the avenue.

A six-foot dragabond blocked them. It was Lum.

Flores crouched to leap upon him.

"Wait!"

Lum pushed past, shoving them aside.

"Look!"

They followed Numtal's gaze and gasped. Beyond the stone huts was a second clearing that served as a courtyard for a stone edifice larger and more imposing than those they had viewed thus far. In the midst of this clearing moved a mirage. Alternately comic and vicious, it floated and lumbered in the midst of a crowd of hooting dragabonds. Slow and dull as they were, they managed to convey an impression of fright and horror as they moved away. A series of images was suspended in air, none of which was striking or terrifying in itself, but taken seriatim unnerved the observers.

The first was a large tropical fruit. The yellows and reds were vivid and Flores' stomach growled. It was replaced by a half-eaten Vensor leg, a vestige of the dragabonds' feast. Next came a grey lump of flint. Then black obsidian. Then vines–a waterfall of milk (the ground remained dry), and the horrifyingly large groin of a female dragabond (the Vensor-sa recoiled at the symbol of Atasan.) The vision turned toward the firepits. A drum floated before them. Then a Vaw upon a cross, strangely unconcerned. Next a wisp of cloud; then a tower of termites. A long pole appeared and intruded into the mound and a monstrously huge disembodied tongue licked it clean. The vision was obscured by smoke.

The tower of smoke turned toward the Vensor-sa. A new series replaced it, images of sky and forest and domestic life dominating the litany. Suddenly a rapier appeared, and pierced a dragabond whose chest gushed red life–it was Stug, although they had just left the dragabond's body in the hut. Then, inexplicably, a Vaw galley joined the scene, complete with stick-figured Vensor-sa working the sail. Another moment passed, and the half-eaten Vensor leg returned.

Stalkin frowned. "Does it seem to you that yon leg bears the burns of glass?" His hand wandered to his own leg and rubbed it.

Fish wiped beads of sweat from his brow. He grunted. "Now it is a torso. Is that not my medallion upon its chest?" The beads grew into a stream. He wiped his purple face with a greasy forearm. "What manner of magic is this? Surge, how do we escape this demon's trap?"

Macius said nothing but eyed the vision closely. Once he glanced sideways at Flores, a strange look about him.

The yard was now clear of dragabonds and only the eerie vision continued to move hesitantly about. Beyond it another avenue led visibly up to merge with the forest. They had only to pass through to win their freedom.

"We must find another way," rumbled Fish.

"No, wait. And watch," said Flores. "I will clear the way."

"Do not–"

"Do as he says," said Macius, a hand blocking Fish. "This appears the only way out and the other dragabonds will return soon."

The others stared as the Turlicum brandished his rapier and strode boldly forward. The vision changed. Suddenly Flores faced an enormous dragabond–larger than any they had seen thus far–but which was somehow misshapen, asymmetrical, and floating a foot above the ground. A tree magically appeared. Huge arms uprooted it and brandished it at the puny Ven.

Flores gazed calmly.

The tree swung. The Vaw-sa gasped as the cudgel passed harmlessly through Flores.

The Turlicum cut the air once, then stepped back.

A minute passed. A great hooting arose from the vision, which became more misshapen.

The Turlicum swung the rapier again.

Soon the noise repeated.

A third time.

The image shrank and became less imposing. Parts of it became translucent, and the chieftain's hut could be seen through it.

Flores swung his blade several more times, with each cut or thrust the image becoming less fearsome. Finally, he stepped in close to press the blade home, thrusting it into a large bed of straw, turning it as it sank. He released the helve.

The hooting ceased. Bak the dragabond, returned to his normal size and constitution, took a single lurching step. By his feet lay a severed hand. His left arm dangled by a shred. Flores' rapier protruded from a gaping hole in his chest, the last of his blood joining a sloppy pool.

Bak collapsed.

The Turlicum knelt and grasped something that seemed to glint. He placed it on his wrist. He looked up to find Macius staring hard at him, expressionless as always. The Vaw handed him the gill and Flores retrieved the device while his city-mates watched dumbfounded.

Flores waved the others forward. "It is time," he said. Fish took a step back rather than offend the Turlicum–and grunted assent.

Soon they had gained the forest. In another hour they stood on board Fish's flagship, its oars dipping as the four galleys, replenished with food and water, headed for open sea.

CHAPTER 21

THE DOOM

Flores smiled. Much had changed. No longer did the Vaw-sa gaze upon him with supercilious gloating as on his previous trip across the ocean. Some watched with curiosity; some with puzzlement; still others with fear–all watched with respect. Even Fish. The corpulent Overseer of Vaw's southern dock, third-degree initiate in the cult of the living Kot, slave of the Golden Cyclops and domo of the eternal whirling sceptre– Flores wondered at the meaning of the terms–was the most changed. Fish watched him from the poop where he stood rooted close to his mur- shid, his stubby arms folded, his dirty yellow flag whipping in the wind, his lackey Numtal at his feet. Flores knew he but bided his time. Hatred such as his could not be denied. But he was not worried–so long as he had...the item.

Flores glanced at his wrist. He had no need of practice. The illusions had become second nature, the atoms in his brain ready to configure ac- cording to his need, to control perfectly the image he wished to present. He had felt no need to demonstrate his power. Though they knew not the source, the Vaw-sa had seen his confidence and his sword. And were afraid. For now, that sufficed. No longer must he hide beneath cowls, or skulk in back alleys. No longer must he accept insults from the vermin of the seas. Breathing deep the salt air of the ocean, Flores' breast swelled.

Fish whispered with Macius. The murshid leaned upon the flagship's rudder, his eyes on the suns by day, and the constellations by night, un- erring in his guidance of the fleet back to Vaw. Macius alone seemed unimpressed. The pilot's hard body wielded the boom with ease. Like the ship's wooden gargoyle, 'Surge' seemed other than human–an alien presence among them. What did Flores truly know of him? How many names did he sport? Was he of Vaw, or had his presence in that city in the end been as calculated as his presence in Yezd's castle? Flores on occasion caught him gazing openly at his wrist, and its shiny bauble, which Flores had seen no reason to disguise. He wondered: what had been Macius' purpose on the Island? That it had been something more than merely serving Flores, he was now certain. And finally–why had he saved Flores from his city-mates?

Flores pondered deeply as the wind threw his jet-black hair and beard. A hundred yards away, on the Grest, a nauseous Stalkin huddled near the stern. A heaving sea was the one thing with which his body could not cope. On a third ship stood Fish's aide Mens, still and quiet, staring with veiled eyes at a world invisible. Flores was occupied with a private world as well–Ven, and shining through it, the gorgeous face of Amina. Once home he would equip a fleet to free her. True, his rule had been no more than symbolic, and his townsmen may object, but with the bracelet he could change all that. He could try it now, in fact: commandeer the ship and direct it to Ven–except for the strange looks of Macius. And the fact that with each day his captors brought him nearer his goal despite themselves. He nodded to himself. Patience–and subtlety. Yes, he would continue to use the thief's own tactics against him, and against the others. Fortune is the slave of the patient. And when the moment came, his power would overcome all–perhaps even Vensor Himself.

A week passed, and the vessels approached Vaw. None had molested Flores, even while he slept. As he had done nought to avenge himself on those who had murdered his men and even now defiled his ship with their boots. A truce. Which could soon expire.

With the east dock approaching, he touched his sword. The gill. The bracelet. Gulls wheeled and dived. A rough sea threw sprays upon a dock packed with roustabouts.

They touched. Flores leaped onto the boards. Fish, Numtal, and the others descended and stretched their legs as assistants cleared the deck for passage of the treasure. The Overseer was in an ebullient mood. A hundred feet away Stalkin's boat pulled in and the smithy struggled ashore. Macius had already vanished.

Remembering his previous debarkation, Flores glanced warily about. Should he have need of his device, he preferred to use it in secret, and alone, rather than amid a crowd of onlookers. Still, he was confident.

"Knight of Ven; noble from the brow of Vensor; I wish to extend my apologies." Flores looked in amazement at the bullet-head of Fish bent in obeisance. He had not thought it possible. "And my thanks. Upon con-sultation with my colleagues, and with Surge–may the peace of Vensor be upon him–I have decided to recommend that you be awarded a special commendation–a citation if you will–for your part in freeing us from the filthy dragabonds. Surely if not for the quickness of your sword-arm, we would not now be enjoying the favors of Vensor." Beside him Numtal bowed even deeper.

Now Flores had heard everything. This was surely something new.

"Could my deed have amounted to more than that of Macius?"

"Macius? Oh, yes, our friend Surge."

"It was he cut your bonds. I but cleared the way."

"But it was your courage, and foresight, that saw through the phantasm that blocked our path, and made it possible for us to escape!"

"Luck–and a sharp sword. That is all."

"Some think a bit more than luck. But no matter. Numtal!" The Overseer's voice boomed across the clapboards. "An escort for our friend! Stalkin! Clear the pier! Let our guest from Ven lead the way to the palace!"

Before Flores could object, a full score of armed guards and sailors had collected around him, and, scarcely before he knew it, he was marching in their accompaniment across the esplanade that circled Vaw's harbor in tune with a drum while a mass of spectators assembled. Any thought he had of resorting to his trick and slipping away was soon banished.

The city of Vaw shelved upward before him. Within the hour they arrived before a sprawling irsrem edifice halfway up the slope whose gates lay open. On all sides was evidence of fabulous wealth, as befit a busy trading nation. Yet, intermingled with the gold and irsrem, in a curious melange, were rotted walls and faded paint and other signs of neglect and deterioration, surprising in the residence of a king.

Fish directed the booty be carried within and deposited on the floor of a wide poorly lit lobby. While this occurred, the palace guards ushered Fish and his officers into an antechamber. The darkness and dinginess of this chamber contrasted markedly with the splendor of the palace's entrance and facade. Cobwebs hid the corners. Flores peered into the shadows. At length he espied a wizened figure ensconced in a broken and rusted armchair, giving forth a loud snapping. A dirty cushion leaked entrails onto the floor, and an odor of unwashed flesh hung in the air.

"My King!" announced Numtal, his eyes upon the floor, "O glory of God, whose magnificence pales before your own! I bring you–"

"–*I* bring you!" interrupted Fish, glaring at Numtal.

"–*we* bring you–"

The Overseer thrust Numtal aside. "Your servant brings you the booty of a world. The treasure of a lifetime. The result of a month in far waters, your reward for having sent–"

"Eh?" The paleness on the throne moved. The old man set aside a tray of sticks he had been splintering and looked up. Dust fell as from a corpse. His clothes were as patched and decrepit as the throne, and, as he moved, threads detached themselves from his worn cape and floated in the air. Had he encountered the apparition on the street, Flores might have mistaken him for a beggar, except for the large golden medallion that hung from his neck, the sign of Vaw royalty. "Did someone speak?" A fogged eye detected the massive bulk of the Overseer. "Oh, so it is you, Squawk. Well, speak your mind. I haven't all day. And shut that door. There is a draft in here." A sour grimace settled, which, had he been standing on his head, might have been taken for the grandest of smiles.

"I said we bring you–"

"Eh?"

"My King, we have been across the ocean and have brought–"

"You'll have to speak up. There is a draft in this room. It causes a whistle. The repairmen did their work poorly, despite the princely sum I paid them."

Fish paused. Took a deep breath. "O King Kot!" he shouted. "Look what I have brought from our expedition to the south!" At Fish's signal the guards hauled into the anteroom the treasure from the lobby and lay it upon the floor for King Kot's inspection.

The King seemed not to notice. "You don't have to shout, you imbecile. I am not deaf you know." He reached for his tray and resumed his breaking of twigs.

"Sire, look what I have brought–"

"Eh?"

"I said look what I have brought."

"You'll have to speak up! This room is quite noisy!"

The Overseer cupped his hands and shouted. "I have brought–"

Kot recoiled. "No need to shout. I can hear quite well."

"I said I have brought–"

"Eh?"

"–brought treasure!"

"Pleasure? Yes, it is a pleasure to see you. Have you been gone?"

"I have brought TREASURE!"

"No need to shout–"

"Gold and mir!"

"Yes, I have a mirror. Do you need one?"

"I said gold!"

"Old? Of course I am old. Rude of you to mention it."

"Gold!"

"Eh? What's that?"

"Gold! Sire–*your sticks!*"

Far from putting them aside, Kot tore at them with renewed energy so that the throne-room fairly resounded with their popping. "My what?"

"GOLD!!" Flores thought the Overseer would pop a vein.

"Oh, GOLD! Why didn't you say so? Yes, I have gold. But you'll have to earn your own." He paused in his snapping to shake a reproving finger. "I am too poor to give you any. Why in only three months' time I will have to pay my attendants their salary. Twenty-five mir it will cost! Can you believe it? As if a poor man like me can afford to pay anyone a salary!"

Fish signaled to a pair of attendants who flanked the throne. One produced a horn.

"No need for that," Kot said, refusing it. "I'm not deaf, you know." He turned his jaundiced glance back to the audience. His good eye lit on the abundance of treasure that had been laid before him. The eye grew large. "Wait a moment. My attendants have left my property lying about." He waved a hand, and within seconds the treasure and ingots had vanished down to the last ring into the depths of the palace.

"Now what do you want, Squawk? I have already said there will be no raises this year. I am a poor man. Times are bad." The aged shoulders shrugged. "Being a King is not what others suppose, you know. Not like I can just snap my fingers and become rich like my spoiled lazy subjects. Come now. I am busy. I have much bark to strip and cannot be bothered with your constant trifling problems."

"King Kot!" Fish shouted, the chamber booming from his great voice which on a normal day could make itself heard the length of Vaw's longest wharf. "We have returned from the South with much treasure!"

"What's that? From the South, you say?" He reflected. "Yes, you did go on an expedition, didn't you? Well, Squawk, did you waste my time and money, or did you bring anything of value back? I could use some cloth. My store of cloth for patches is almost gone." His good eye inspected his caftan, which bore so many incongruous patches that the original cloth had entirely vanished.

"I said: we brought back much treasure! We placed it on the floor. Your men have removed it!"

"What's that? Removed treasure you say? And why not? Why shouldn't they remove my own property?"

"We brought it from the South!"

"*You* brought it you say? What my men removed? Are you certain? No...no, that cannot be. I recognized several of the items."

"Perhaps you did, Sire. They came from the Island of Vensor!"

King Kot lay a skeptical glance upon him. "You are mistaken, Squawk. What they removed was plainly mine. This is my palace. These are my sticks. This is my throne. And this is my room." He shrugged. "Besides, if you left some of your gold on my floor and my people picked it up, I think in the future you had best keep better track of your things. Serves you right, leaving valuables lying around." He shook a fist in the air and began to rock. "But don't think you will get it back! I ought to deduct it from your paycheck for losing it! Hi-ho! That would teach you a lesson, wouldn't it? What's that, you say? Yes, I know you are a spendthrift! I saw you spend a coin last year with my own eyes! How easily you let it slip! And only a month after I paid you your fat salary!" Kot rocked with glee, spilling stale dust in the air. "Hi-ho! Yes! A fat man with a fat salary! I shall put you on a diet, that's what I shall do! Maybe then you will learn the value of money. You and all my fat lazy subjects!"

"The Island, my King! The Island of Vensor!"

"Eh? What's that?" He stopped rocking. "The Island of Vensor?" The ancient brows knitted. "What has that to do with my subjects' spendthrift ways?"

"The Island of Vensor, Sire! We brought the gold from the Island!"

"The forbidden Island?"

"Yes!" Fish sighed with relief. Finally he was getting through. "Your expedition has returned! We have brought you much wealth, my King! And there is more gold! Much more gold!"

"Old? Yes, I admit I am old–"

"GOLD, Sire!"

"Oh, GOLD!"

"Yes, gold! There is more on the Island!"

"Eh? What Island is that?"

"THE ISLAND OF VENSOR!"

"No need to shout. I'm not deaf you know."

Fish stepped near. "O King, might I suggest you put aside your twigs for just a moment so we may address affairs of state..."

"Eh? What's that?"

"We have important matters to discuss! Will you put aside your twigs?"

Kot looked indignant. He shook his finger again. "I can strip bark and talk at the same time. I'm a busy man and have no time to waste." His thin fingers flew and the room echoed with a renewed splintering of wood. "Let me tell you, nothing is more important than thrift. Nothing!" A moment later, however, he laid aside his tray. Irritatedly he asked, "Now, why do you interrupt my important work with foolish talk of the Island of Vensor?"

"I wish to go back, my King. To retrieve more treasure. On the Island lies enough gold to make the city rich! But we need a fleet, and an army, to obtain it!"

"A fleet, you say? And an army? Ha-ha! You think I am rich? Is that it? You think I am rich? Why, I cannot afford even these few servants you see here. An army, you say? Ha-ha! I am but a poor man. And very busy." His palsied hands stretched again toward the tray.

"Sire! Only a small fleet is needed. Think of the wealth to be had!"

"Oh, but boats! Boats are not cheap! Will they walk there? Ha-ha! No, your plan will not work, Squawk. It is like all your others, and you had best forget it. They must have boats, and I cannot afford them. The ones that we have needed repair just two years ago! Here, I have the record with me." Kot fumbled beneath his throne and pulled out a stack of foxed and stained parchments that had been scribbled upon and erased so often that parts had become translucent. "Let us see...yes, it was during the month of Gogol, on the fourth day. I remember it well. I had to spend six mir out of my own pocket. And now I hear they are already in need of repair. Oh no, I do not wish to buy more boats. Boats spring leaks, and leaks must be repaired! Boats are too expensive for a poor man to own."

Flores wondered silently how a port could survive without boats, and saw in his mind the fleet of Vaw rotting in mire while Kot wrestled with his servants over six silver coins.

"We will not be alone. We can invite the kings of Ud and Spelf to contribute."

Kot brightened. "And well they should! If we are to allow them to accompany us, the least they can do is pay for the expedition themselves." He sat up suddenly. "But we must still get all the booty! It is, after all, our expedition!" He thought a moment. "Squawk, what expedition are we discussing? I thought you already left on one."

Fish nodded. "Indeed I did, my King."

"I don't suppose you brought back anything really useful, like bottles, or twigs, or old clothing?"

"No, sire."

Kot frowned. "So you failed. And wasted my money just as I expected." He shook his head. "Wait. Didn't you go after some wanderer from abroad?"

"Indeed, my King! And here he is–Flores of the Turlicum of the city of Ven."

"Ven...Ven...Where have I heard that name?" He looked up and squinted. "Is this him?"

Flores stepped forward. His sword had been taken at the entrance, but his fingers confirmed the presence of the bracelet. He bowed deeply, saying nothing. He had no wish to add to the confusion. Best to wait until the medal, or whatever they had for him, was bestowed.

"And what did you want with him? He was going to the Island of Vensor, as I recall. Well, young man. Is that where you have been?"

A sly look stole over the Overseer who cast a sidelong glance at Flores. "Indeed he has, O King. Just as did another who stood before you some years ago. Might I suggest the same reward?"

Kot shrugged. "Why delay matters? You know, young man, that what you have done is a very great evil. You have not only trespassed upon Vensor, but you have insulted us and Him by returning to tell of it. Your boastful and selfish attitude cannot be permitted in a civilized and god-fearing city such as ours. It wasn't so long ago that we condemned another for the same crime. He only narrowly escaped execution for his deed."

The Turlicum's jaw opened. He turned to Fish. Both the Overseer and Numtal were gloating. This had been their purpose.

"Well, let me ask you: did you bring back anything of value, or did you also return empty-handed like Squawk and the others? No? Nothing of value? Well, then. There is little that I can do for you." The fingers closed. Snap!

Flores had had enough. He took a step forward and shouted through the spears that intervened.

"King Kot! You had best think twice before you pass judgment! I stand before you as the reigning King of Ven. My people will extract a great revenge should you detain me here unlawfully. I had not wished my identity to be known, but your attitude forces me to speak thus."

Incredulity and humor wrought the visages of his audience.

The twigs grew silent. "Eh? Did he speak?"

"He claims to be King of Ven, Sire!" boomed Fish. "He threatens us with war!"

"War? Wars are expensive. Perhaps we should let him go. But King of Ven, you say? No. I know that he is not." Flores cocked his head. "Because I have recently received word from the *true* King of Ven, and from the lips of his own ambassador." Kot clapped his hands.

Behind him a portiere was drawn aside and a tall slumping man with belly round as a bird's egg, and a face as pale, entered. His bald head crowned eyes like those of an owl, and his hands, burned from tropical suns, clutched a sheaf of papers emblazoned The Compendium of Sidros.

"Dos!" shouted Flores.

Dos made no sign of recognition but attended to Kot with his usual imperturbability.

The King twisted to view him. His throne's cushion extruded more lint upon the floor. Crack! A throne arm broke. Quick as lightning, Kot produced a wooden twig, buttressed the arm with its body, then used the bark to tie the stem in place. The rickety structure again took his weight–for one more day.

"Ambassador Dos," Kot peered at him closely as if not quite sure he had the right person.

Dos bowed.

"Do you know this man, who claims to be from your city of Ven?"

The Ven noble curled his beak-like head in the direction of Flores and gazed silently for a time. "Yes, O King of Vaw, though he has greatly changed."

"Is he king of Ven?"

Dos took a short sharp breath. "No, King Kot."

"Who is king of Ven?"

"Ust of the Calomar. Who dispatched me to Vaw to represent him."

"Ust!" expostulated Flores.

Kot looked back to Flores and blinked. "Well, that is that." He reached for a broken fixture held by an attendant. It was a royal sceptre fallen into disrepair and the attendant handed both pieces to Kot. One piece fell and broke into a further two. The attendant produced a roll of tape which Kot used to carefully reconnect the pieces–for another day.

"I hereby pronounce, by the grace of the Golden Cyclops, and the Will of Vensor, that the one Flors Lurticum of the Sum of Vim be condemned to die the Doom at the next session of the Whirling Sceptre. Now, Squawk, tell me what else you wish. Quickly–I have much to do and I am now behind schedule thanks to you!"

"O King, our expedition must begin at once–"

"Expedition? An expedition would be expensive." He shook his head. "I am a poor man. I cannot afford expeditions. And I have much bark to strip. Did you know that there are a hundred chairs in the palace in need of repair? If I strip ten sticks a day, and it takes ten strips to repair one chair, then it will take me a hundred days to repair all the chairs in the palace. And that is only the chairs! There are beds, and tables besides! Yes, I am a busy man."

"Sire, might I suggest this be left to others. There are affairs of state that need your attention. The sea kings of Ud and Spelf are fishing in our grounds and taking trade from our merchants. There is corruption among our officials. I cannot collect what is owed us on the docks due to a common disrespect for the law."

Kot threw up his hands. "Hi-ho! I have heard all this before. But thrift begins at home, I say! And if I provide an example of waste with my time and money how will my subjects have faith in me?" He redoubled his snapping, then paused and held up a broken stick. "To you, this may seem a mere twig. But I tell you it is a wonder of engineering. A product of nature's genius. Why, with the proper attitude, and a little ingenuity, I could run the palace–perhaps the city–on this one twig. This twig is as important as anything you could bring me, I tell you, and far more worth my time."

"Then, O Sire, perhaps if you appointed a vizier to attend to affairs of state."

"Ha-ha! I have tried that. But I cannot afford to pay what they ask. Besides if you want something done right, you have to do it yourself. No, I do not want another Mens to argue with. You talk and I will listen–" His thin fingers flew.

"Your father–"

An evil glance cut him short. "My father! But you knew not my father. He was a poor king–and a worse man. He left me to rot in exile until just before he died–only then sending for me–he on his deathbed! Too late to change his spendthrift ways. Too late to make time for me." A look of grief stole over him. He rocked sadly in his chair. "If only he had saved his money. If only he had left something besides debt so that when I inherited the throne I could have enjoyed my life instead of having to live like this, saving every penny. A curse on him and all his tribe, not one of whom cares a whit for his Leader." He snatched a piece of lint from the floor and stuffed it into the depths of a ripped pocket as if it were a nugget of gold.

"But, Sire, your palace is huge. And the city is not poor."

"Eh? What's that? The city's poor? Let them get their own money! I have no money to do them favors. Now, enough! If I do not complete my work today I will fall too far behind ever to catch up. As it is, I will have to spend the entire evening stripping bark in order to regain my schedule. And I have you to thank for that! On my expeditions I expect profit. Ask me how. I have been making money since before you were spawned. Take my word: scour the beaches for sticks and bottles as I often did when I was young. Then your trip will not be a complete waste, as this was!"

Kot produced his yellowed papers again. "Now. I paid exactly thirty-six mir to you for this wasted 'expedition' of yours. I expect you to pay it back from your salary. And don't forget the forty-four mir you already owe me! That makes a total of eighty-two. And that does not include the interest! And do you smile Numtal? You owe me seventeen mir. I expect you to pay me also. But don't worry. I don't expect such lazy fools as yourselves to actually have the cash. You may continue to work it off. Of course, you are all sliding deeper into debt all the time, thanks to your spendthrift ways–your three meals a day–your new clothes every year–your constant wearing of shoes. Since you are finding it difficult to live up to your obligations, I suggest you vacate your current sumptuous quarters and stay in my workrooms. They are small, but dark, like my own rooms–no annoying sunlight or distracting views of gardens to bother you. Plenty of time to sit in the dark and think about how nice it will be when you finally pay me what you owe. Which reminds me–we must raise the wharf tax. Collections are down again. I cannot understand why. But I have no time today. If you take up any more of my time, I will have to add it to your bill. My time is not free, you know. Now, be off. And, you guards, lock the door behind them when they leave. I cannot have any remaining to sneak into my treasure room and steal my property." Kot huddled over his tray, and the room soon filled with such a frenzy of snapping as to drown out an army of crickets.

Disconsolately, the Vaw-sa began to file out. Fish and Stalkin exchanged a long silent glance. The Overseer cleared his throat. "Sire–"

"Eh? Still here, Squawk?"

"Sire... And what if I were to tell you there was a way to recruit men and ships from many cities without costing you a cent? Yet still provide us with most of the booty?"

For once, Kot paused without prompting. He narrowed his one good eye. "How?"

Fish took in his breath. Turning, he stepped to one side to reveal a small man, formerly obscured by the Overseer's entourage. The man made no sound but approached the King, his eyes seemingly fixed on some distant object that remained invisible to the others.

"Mens!" The single eye lay a baleful glance upon him. Kot nodded. "I sensed the presence of another behind this talk of expeditions. Squawk hasn't the brains."

The scribe bowed.

"Well, Mens? Is it as Squawk has said?"

Mens showed no emotion. "It is."

The king wheezed. "Clear the room. I wish to consult...with my vizier."

Before another ten minutes had passed, Flores stood within a cell deep in the palace of Vaw with nothing for company but rats.

❧ ∽ ⳩ ⳨ ∾ ❧

Blue mist dissipated before a wall of stone and a locked gate. Beyond the gate, the footsteps of sentries sounded to echo off a pale blue and yellow facade several stories in height. The colors were muted–as were the footsteps–by the lateness of the hour. Nantifus was at zenith. The moon cast a plague-light over the land, bathing all in a spotted whiteness that entirely failed to reveal the arrival in the street of a man.

Moving slowly and silently, the man presented no more substantial an image than would a spirit. He glided rather than walked, and made small sniffling noises as he progressed. Bent as if searching the ground, he snorted and reversed direction. Then reversing again, he resumed his path southward through the alley. He paused. Looked up. Before him rose an iron portcullis, signaling the estate of one of the wealthier and more powerful nobles of Ven. He turned; peered. Taking a breath, he drew itself up to full height, and seemed about to rap upon the plate when his eye caught a dull glimmer in the street.

He turned a yellow eye upon it, then a blue. It was a simple clasp, the kind that might have once held a number of keys, or bracelets, but now held nothing, being merely an old rusted hulk. He sniffed. It was without lettering, but bore darker stains that induced him for some time to stand, and to think. Finally, he smiled and slipped the clasp into a pocket. He gazed at the cloudy facade beyond the wall, and whispered the inscription: 'Molersal.' Breathing deep, he fingered a glass bracelet on his wrist. At last! For the first time since he had left his stronghold in the western forest so many months ago, he was within reach of his goal.

They came for him at night. The squat bulk of Fish overshadowed the lone guard who manned the small anteroom to the dungeons. The Overseer said nothing, but grunted. Flores followed. They had stripped him, but they had not placed him in cuffs, and he saw no reason why he should use his powers to delude his captors. There would be time for that soon enough. Now, his curiosity held sway. Some minutes later the three entered an audience chamber which Flores conjectured was another room of the palace. The dirty figure of the King was there, coughing thready filaments from polluted lungs.

"Why? Why? Why must I attend the ceremony? I am already so far behind with my work that I shall never manage!" The aged Kot turned his one good eye upon his vizier and kicked an attendant in petulance. "My twigs pile up! My piebald raiment awaits!"

Mens stared placidly ahead. "You are the ninety-ninth Master of the Sceptre, O King. None other is qualified. The initiates will accept no less than perfection. You possess the throne because your grandfather attained the ninety-ninth level. Should you neglect your functions..."

This seemed to have an effect. "Humf!" Sullenly he rose. "If we must..." With a vicious wheeze he lurched toward the exit.

A half dozen guards flanked Flores and swords prodded him forward. Exiting the palace, they emerged onto a walled terrace open to the Maalstrom sky. Nantifus hung above, spreading its message like a contagion, a gong suspended above the swelling ocean that stretched darkly to the west. Behind, Flores glimpsed a cleft in the mountain-slope of the city. Torch-light revealed a throng of cultists filing into the cleft. The King and his party entered.

The passage wound deep. A splashing of water carried and they came again into the night, as a gigantic amphitheater opened around them, a smell of salt in the air. A natural platform of pumice served as a sort of stage, squarish in shape, around the circumference of which loomed the high jagged lip of a volcanic crater. At the eastern end rested a seat of polished obsidian. Flores took this to be the cultic throne. Toward the west was an enigma–an enormous black-red lump of worked iron enclaved in the side of the crag, with a strange complex of sword-like horizontal blades fixed to its upper side. These blades, Flores observed, were in perpetual motion, spinning beneath an outthrust of the crater's lip under the force of a constant stream of water. The stream gushed from an unknown source, gravity supplying the blades with their energy.

Flores nodded. Here was the cultic center of Vaw. Here the eternal whirling sceptre. He was puzzled–the lump of iron was obviously of artificial construction, a product of will and intelligence. It had an interior compartment large enough to hold several individuals, and seats apparently designed for such. All of the device was rusted, a relic from time long past.

Kot sat on the throne and let a bored stare fall upon the proceedings. Mens took the seat opposite. Two nobles whom Flores did not recognize occupied the north and south positions. The night matured while a throng of cultists filled the arena.

Flores was made to stand in the center between the four seats. A sneer of contempt–mixed with a sullen disinterest in the details of the ritual–surfaced in his visage. Behind all glimmered the face of Amina and a monster planning to impregnate her. All else was dross and delay. Another minute and he would depart. But first, he would speak...

A loud banging of wood rang out. As in response a second man arrived in the center to join Flores, from his appearance a native of Vaw. Neither was he bound, but from his nudity, the stiffness with which he moved, and the cold stares Flores believed he detected on the part of the man's compatriots, he concluded that his companion was another convict condemned to die the Doom.

The King's new vizier rose. "Who comes?"

"A poor blind beggar who seeks entrance."

"Who goes?"

"A rich seeing man who has betrayed his comrades."

"What is our purpose?"

"To transmute God's Word to Flesh."

"What is the Law?"

"Man with man."

"What is the Law-breaker?"

"Man with animal."

"What is the reward?"

"Fortuna, Hap, and Kot."

"What is the punishment?"

"To broach with Chaos."

And so it went for what seemed an eternity, meaningless phrases accompanied by symbol-ridden rituals of no obvious significance. Despite himself, Flores took in some details: only a few wore the yellow skullcaps of third-level initiates. Possessing these, Fish and Mens were high in the pecking order. Their yellow caps, in fact, designated them as nobles–high-ranking cultists being the Vaw equivalent of nobility else-where. Blue skull-caps were more numerous. Flores sighted Stalkin wearing one. Green caps more numerous still, being the predominant color in the arena, and the color sported by the remainder. Only one wore purple–the King himself, on his obsidian throne. And, Flores noticed, each color was subdivided into multiple shades that were not immediately obvious, presumably indicating degrees within degrees.

At last, when midnight approached, the droning ceased and Kot rose and signaled to Flores and his companion. They approached the whirling blades. Behind was a cave accepting the flow of spent water, leading perceptibly down, and some minutes later they emerged in an underground grotto whose chief feature was a shallow pool, the black surface of which rippled with reflected torch-light. From a raised walkway overlooking one edge, Kot, Fish, Mens, Stalkin and a dozen soldiers peered into the cave's recesses.

"Flores Sumvensor Turlicum–"

The noble noted that Fish now knew his full name by heart. He had been right–hatred such as his could not be denied.

The liquid lips flowed and rippled like the pool before them. "–I have waited long for this moment. Tasted it in anticipation!" The cavernous lungs rumbled until something akin to a laugh escaped.

"It first strips what it plans to kill!" smirked Stalkin.

Floresf raised one hand. "It matters not. Thirty minutes hence I will no longer be in Vaw." Flores raised his black-bearded chin. "I remain only to satisfy my curiosity."

His captors paused, incredulous. Their eyes opened wide. They burst into laughter. "You may have tricked us elsewhere, and used whatever sleight of hand you possess to deceive us into thinking you have some special powers...but here you are under our control. We have searched you, and know that you have no weapon on your body. No, Flores, you cannot escape. You will never leave, but will die the Doom!"

"Eh?" coughed Kot. "Did the prisoner speak?"

"He declares he will escape in thirty minutes time!"

"What? What? Ha-ha!" Kot tittered. "No one escapes the Doom! No one!"

Fish rubbed his bullet-head with one scabby paw. "You are arrogant to the end. Your presumption has finally undone you." The appendage wandered to his chin. "Now watch!"

Vaw soldiers jabbed at the other prisoner with pikes and forced him into the pool. One produced a flute and blew.

Several minutes passed. The attendant blew again. Finally, from the depths of the cavern emanated a sloshing clearly audible over the trickle of the waterflow. The pool itself was not stagnant but was constantly renewed by the fresh stream that spun the blades, and emptied into dark recesses where the light of the torches failed to reach. Out of one of these recesses a tawny body materialized, with struggling limbs. Moments later a massive, slug-like creature, the mass of twenty men, rolled and arched toward them. The head—and Flores started as he noticed the resemblance to another such creature he had once encountered—was absurdly small, being only a little larger than his own. A grunt escaped the muscled lungs. The tiny limbs kicked. With difficulty they propelled it through the shallow water.

"What is the reward?" shouted the onlookers in unison.

"Fortuna, Hap, and Kot!"

"What is the punishment?"

"To broach with Chaos!"

The head twisted. At some time in the past, its face had been injured and one eye gouged, leaving it hideously scarred. Flores suppressed a nauseous heave. He noted the golden skin typical of Vaw. This, then, was their Golden Cyclops. The Vaw Queen—for such Flores understood it to be, wondering what oversight or error had led the Vaw-sa to mistreat their Ruler in such a way, and why She allowed it, and he further reflected with a chill that such could be the fate of his own Amina should he fail in his task—caught sight of her victim. The watchers held their breath.

The creature inched forward. Its mouth curled into what Flores took to be a smile, beneficence and lust in its curve, and the tiny arms rose and clumsily pulled at the Vaw's tunic. The Vaw shuddered. Stepped back. In response, the One Eye screwed shut and a roar shook the cavern to its depths as the smile transformed into a glare. Rearing up, the creature flung itself upon him, and, seizing him in a grip of surprising strength, pulled him below the surface.

"It has him!"

The water boiled. The blackness changed to red.

"Now, Flores! Let us hear you crow!" chuckled Fish. "For you are next!"

"It is no matter. I tell you I will be beyond the city in one-half hour."

Fish was crestfallen. He exchanged a worried glance with Stalkin. This was not what they had desired. Where was the groveling? Where the pleading for his life? Could the Turlicum really possess magic after all, magic that he knew would save him?

When the noble of Ven spoke again, none interrupted. "I wished only to see what manner of foolishness you Vaw-sa occupy yourselves with, before I resume my journey to Ven." Flores snapped a finger in Fish's face. "I will deal with your Cyclops just as I dealt with the Dragabond–and just as I will one day deal with you. If I wished, Fish, I could strike you as I did before, I have only to move a finger to accomplish this. And there is nothing you can do to stop me. Or to punish me. I have only to wish it to make it so."

Like embers in a slag-heap, a pallor spread beneath Fish's skin, penetrating every cranny until finally it burst forth in full flame. He raised his massive fist and shook it.

"Aaaagh! No one speaks to me thus! You dare to refer to your prior offense, and to use that insulting name in my presence? You dare to threaten me yet again? Do you not understand that you are about to be torn apart by the Golden Cyclops? Have you no sense at all? Is your arrogance so deep and wide that you would spit on your betters even as they end your life?" Beside himself with rage, Fish whirled to face Kot. "Your permission, O King! Your permission to remove this impudent criminal for a week of torture. And to burn what remains of his body before his eyes. My king, I beg you to let me deal with him in my own way!"

Kot glanced at Flores and at Fish, then peered into the recesses beyond the Cyclops as if expecting to see something obscure. "No. He will die the Doom. Now get on with it, Squawk. My time is worth more than the last moments of this criminal's miserable life."

Pikes prodded Flores down the steps, forcing him into the water. The Cyclops withdrew its head where it had been occupied with its victim. Flores grimaced. Shreds of flesh hung from its mouth. Had the Queen's treatment by her irreverent subjects reduced her to such a state? Or was there some insanity already embedded in the creature that led to this? Flores shook his head to clear it. It was time.

Turning to the alcove above him, he put his fists on his hips.

"Your attention, kind gentlemen of Vaw, your attention, I beg! Yes, even you, King Kot! You see, sirs, that I have no weapons. Nevertheless, I assure you that I am able to impose my will on you all. First I have to close my eyes. Then I have but to think the correct thought. And then, upon opening my eyes I will have transformed into something altogether different from myself, something that you will find utterly unrecognizable, or perhaps something that you will find recognizable, but that you cannot detect, never realizing that what you see is actually I, Flores Sumvensor of the Turlicum, former King of Ven–future king of Ven– and of more..." He smiled. His audience was frowning. They had not expected a speech of triumph from one about to be torn apart and consumed. This was less fun than they had hoped.

Flores turned to view the Queen. She fixed her one eye upon him, and let loose a deafening roar. Confidently, Flores felt the bottom of the pool with both hands. It was hard and firm. Should he have need, he could maneuver. He raised high his arms.

"Now watch, O fools of Vaw! Watch how your better teaches you, how I will evade your little trap! Prepare to flee, slaves! Prepare to run shrieking from my presence!" With that, Flores shut his eyes. Though he could hear a splashing directly behind him, and he knew that the Queen was approaching hungry for another meal, he fixed in his mind an image of the largest dragabond that ever lived, with sloping head, massive muscles, a tree trunk in one hand, hairy pelt and legs like columns. He tossed in breasts to add to the shock.

Slowly he opened his eyes. There! They were looking–any moment and they would throw down their weapons and flee... They smiled. Behind him the Queen reared up. He turned to confront her and willed the image in her direction. Her claw-like hands opened. With frantic haste, he swiveled, glared at the Vaw-sa, directed the image to appear in their eyes. The smiles broadened.

"Ha-ha-ha!" Fish and Stalkin exploded with hilarity, "Well, Flores? Are you king of the world–or just *king of fools?*" The latter elbowed King Kot, who seemed to be enjoying the spectacle as much as the others. "What were you saying? You will send us away shrieking from your presence?" The band convulsed with laughter. "Perhaps you should turn yourself into dinner, the better to please the Cyclops! Are you capable of that?" Again they guffawed, slapping their thighs.

Flores spun on his heel. The flickering from the torches was such that he could detect no shadow, so there was no way to determine whether he had been successful in transforming himself. His illusions had never been solid enough to block all light. Here, in the darkness, he was at a loss to understand what had happened. Enough to know the bracelet had failed. His fingers sought it. It still remained. He would inspect it later– assuming he escaped with his life. For now, it seemed he was truly to die the Doom.

The bulk of the Queen loomed, then crashed. Carried by the wave, he found himself momentarily beneath the water and beyond her grasp.

Lucky for him her first attempt to seize him had missed. Before those appendages could close, he took advantage to swim further, without surfacing for air. His long days in the sea had left his muscles toned and conditioned for swimming and not till he encountered the rocky edge of the pool did he allow his head slowly to emerge from the water and suck a breath.

He was bathed in shadow, treading water just beneath a jutting crag, some twenty feet from the Queen. She beat the water in rage. He could not see the Vaw-sa due to the cropping which hid the upper region of the steps and the walkway from his view, but he could hear the laughter still ringing, mocking him, the Vaw-sa vastly amused at his discomfiture. Apparently, they believed he had been taken under and drowned. How close they had come to being correct, they could not know.

Flores narrowed his eyes–bit his lip. He, not they, had been the fool! Not to take advantage when it had been presented, but to delay for the sake of vanity and petty boasting. Another hard lesson that he determined to learn. A sparkle of light attracted his eye. From deep within the darkest recess, hidden from the walkway by a turn of the passage, he glimpsed it. He needed no more invitation than that. In another moment he was swimming.

He paused in total darkness. The water was now deep and he had to tread it to stay afloat while he inspected the latest puzzle. The light emanated from beneath the surface. He dove deeper. Before him emerged a chamber carved out of the stone and faced with irsrem. Inside was a bench, a table, and the remains of a meal, with utensils, a cup with drink, and a flickering candle. It was the candle whose light had attracted him. An opening indicated a way back to the surface, presumably the amphitheater with its cultists. The room was apparently a box for viewing the Queen in her vat. One more item within the chamber betrayed itself to Flores–a large arrow pointing one way with the following alongside scribbled in chalk: "TO VEN."

Flores surfaced. Gulped another breath. Then swam. Perhaps his escape was not so fortuitous after all, he thought. In another moment he found himself in a circular vat with starlight gleaming through a port hole far above. Black figures moved along its edges, some carrying eggs or lozenges, and, rather than risk discovery for having committed what was doubtless the most heinous crime a foreigner, or any man, could commit–violating a city's Sacred Spring–he embraced the instruction of his unknown benefactor and dove again into the stream. A fine-meshed grill separated the vat from another tunnel. He found a latch. Opened it.

Passed through and locked it again. Soon Flores staggered along the bank of a nameless cove, beside a stream that emptied into the wide gulf of Vaw, with the Maalstrom night about him. Another arrow mounted on the cave-wall lent him confidence in its safety.

In the moonlight he paused. The strangeness of his interlude–indeed of his entire quest in the southern ocean and the mysterious vistas it had opened–induced him to shake his head. Would he ever probe its myster-ies? Penetrate to the core of the riddle? What had he learned about his home, his world, about Maalstrom itself, and the spider's web of rela-tionships that seemed to hold him fast? Who had been his benefactor? Macius alone he had not seen since touching dock in Vaw. But the mur-shid had given him little cause to trust. No longer could he doubt that Macius had been in league with Fish from the beginning, and he must bear some responsibility for the deaths of his comrades. Then who? Flo-res sighed. The constellation Gila embraced half the sky and moved slowly in an eternal dance with the Eunuch. Was that the explanation? Did the material plane reflect the spiritual so precisely that one had but to consult a horoscope to become privy to the secrets of the Universe, the Gnosis that held the keys to the future? Nothing he had thus far dis-covered led to such a key, and he resolved to place his trust in Gethos, the god of luck, as Macius had done. He could no longer accept any force on Maalstrom but the blind god of Fortune. After all, what had led him to the bracelet but luck?

Flores glanced down. Touched his wrist. Without delay, the shadow of a dragabond played upon the sand. He flashed a wry grin. Luck indeed. Only luck could explain his previous failure...unless... His eyes nar-rowed. Stepping to the shore, he dipped the bauble in the water. Imme-diately the images ceased. He stretched his arms in exultation. Water! The bracelet functioned only when dry! The realization came to him like a shot that the vat of Doom had been his first attempt to use the device when wet.

An hour passed and the king's Overseer strode upon the Grest. The flapping yellow cape and cap–smeared with dirt from long use–testified to his identity. His gruff threats ensured swift obedience.

"The Ven captive's reven! Bring it at once. And his belongings, and saddle." Fish folded his arms. "What? You would delay? At once, I said! King Kot himself demands them!"

When his servants had obeyed, their Overseer ordered them off the dock. Before they had departed, and while their backs were turned, a loud splash sounded beside the moored vessel. Both Fish and reven had gone.

❧ ✿ ❧

CHAPTER 22

"ARREST THEM ALL!"

The Morbius glowed red. The Eye of Barazaggar shone calmly from the spotted illness of Nantifus. Taking no heed? Or unable to divert its gaze from the shaky flame in the ring of pines? The flame grew, flickered, and faded, rising with the emotion of the Speaker, and again dying as the emotion was spent.

What message did it portend? What Word irrupted from the trance of God to course like arrows into the hearts of the Locuter's audience, Ven's rabble that spilled from its rabid warrens? With rapt expressions and quiet guard the rabble listened till midnight approached and the flame extinguished and the river of revelation grew silent...

The gate to Crestal's cell creaked open.

A eunuch one could describe only as nondescript observed the gila as she sat on one thigh, nude, her hands manacled. A guttering torch from the sweating tunnel silhouetted him.

"Yes. This is how you shall be with me. This is how I prefer you. How I prefer all my slaves." Soorkrul pursed his thin lips into a smile. He produced a cane. Crestal whimpered, and a red welt appeared on her bare flank. "Good! But I expect a louder squeal, and begging...abject, sincere begging." His expression brightened. "I might even make you dance!"

Crestal felt like burying her face in her hands. But did not. She could not tear her eyes from the gaze of her master.

Soorkrul began to pace. "I have use for you, you know. You are going to assist me on a very important task. Before the multitudes of Ven! Yes, my dear—I am not surprised you should have a panic-stricken look about you. But have no fear. Soorkrul will be beside you at all times, and I promise no harm shall befall you." He paused to meet her gaze. "Unless you disobey." He resumed pacing. "Tonight is the palace celebration for the Divine Communion. At midnight tonight, the toady Ust of the Calomar hopes to Commune with the Divine for three days. But before the Temple raises its portcullis to allow him entry into its Sacred Spring, our Leader plans to violate it on his own terms by entering a secret sidedoor and conferring with a collaborator inside the Temple. Does this knowledge surprise you? Why should it? I have known of his visits from the beginning. You forget: I hear all; I see all. His visits occur always at the same time, on the same night of the month. Tonight it will recur. And after he has departed I will enter the palace of Vim and put my plan into effect... He will face a surprise when he returns.

"Why tell you of this? Why does it matter? Because during his absence–in the interval of time between his presence in the celebrations and his entry into the Temple at midnight–I am presented with an unguessed opportunity! Yes, I could murder him in some alley. But another cur would simply take his place. I could imitate him and replace him on the throne. But he is too unpopular, and his unpopularity would come down on me. So I have decided that in one blow I will complete his ruin...humiliate Ust, discredit him so fully, so completely that when I am done, the people of Ven will come to me and beg me to govern them. *Me!* Not an image or an illusion, not another corrupt Simet noble, but *Soorkrul!* The populace is prepared. It remains merely to convert their betters, the Simet-sa. This, my dear, is how I shall do it. Give ear to how you shall help..."

"He has not been found? You're certain you have searched everywhere?" Ust clenched his fist. "Search again! Summon soldiers and scan his estate! Bribe his clansmen! I don't care how–just find Sendas of the Molersal!"

His clansmen made haste to obey.

Ust's visage relaxed. Shutting the door to his anteroom, he pulled out a small hand mirror and stared. "My fortune! The future of the city! All lies now within my grasp!" He hugged the mirror to his bosom. "Free at last! No longer will I have need of Wijah, for it lies in my pale to finish her–and all my enemies–at once! Soorkrul...and the Turlicum!" A supercilious grin settled. "No more need to delay. When Flores enters the palace and is seen murdering Lirsus; and Soorkrul is then seen by the Assembly assassinating Flores–I will have nought left to do but to keep my appointment with Wijah...from which appointment only one shall leave alive. A foolish utterance on the part of Soorkrul will then suffice to enrage the Assembly against him, and support me when I call for his destruction." He put the mirror away. And smiled.

An hour later, with Sendas still unaccounted for, Ust sat upon his throne within the newly completed throne room in the Palace of Vim before the assembled Simet-sa of Ven. A wave of his hand cut short the droning ritual. With a grunt he summoned his bodyguards. He nodded to Simlet to make excuses for his absence.

Returning to his private rooms, Ust stood before a large wall-mounted mirror until he was satisfied that he gazed upon the image of Flores. Too bad the Turlicum had not attended the evening's celebrations. He had wished to study him in detail. But no matter. The image was close enough that Ust had no concern that his deception might be discovered. He turned. Paused. In his mind he saw the upturned face of Wijah, her eyes popping as they glimpsed the plunging dagger in his hand. He relished the scene. Repeated it often in his mind, each time with more cruelty and gory detail. Yes, he would keep their usual appointment, but only after he had executed his plan.

The minutes passed and as convincing a replica of Flores as Ust could muster stood in the shadows outside the entrance to the Hall of Vim, watching the celebrants within. Two mutes in disguise escorted him. He had of necessity revealed his new powers to them–though of course not their source. He couldn't take the chance that one of his own assassins lying in wait for Flores might mistake him for the real item! Calmly he entered. Now would he, Ust, take revenge on the youthful leader of the Serclaslers for his humiliating defection, thus eliminating two gadflies at once. When the army left to attack Neset, he would appoint his own man to lead it. Uncanny–and glorious–how all the pieces were falling into place...now that he had the bracelet.

Ust-cum-Flores nodded, acknowledging with a smile the profuse and vehement greeting of Ultem. The former gate-guard now commanded the palace detachment, having been promoted by the real Flores before the latter vanished. Without ado, the fakir penetrated the milling crowd of Simet-sa. He found the sensation intriguing–to wander and mingle with persons he had known for decades yet to be mistaken for another! Individuals who knew him well said nothing; strangers approached with smiles of recognition; friends suddenly glared hatred; enemies beamed affection; unknown consorts approached as if by accident and whispered seductive invitations. It was intoxicating! Ust strove to resist the temptation to approach Revtal and Simlet and share his secret with his cronies. They would not understand, but would think him Flores gone mad. Which was precisely the hope, and the expectation!

A commotion induced him to look...

"Speak not, but obey." In the shadows before the entrance to the Hall of Vim, Soorkrul hissed. The palanquin in which he rode, escorted by slavers reinforced and alerted to prevent further violations of the House by Ven's king, lurched to a halt. "Wait till I call. Make no move till then." Before her anxious face, flashed again the miraculous transformation that Crestal had witnessed often enough to realize lay at the beck of her master. Ust of the Calomar, prodigy of statecraft, progeny of Zeyd, slipped out.

The King of Ven addressed a squat slaver with enormous ears and malignant expression. "Surround me, Malag. If any approach, your lash will remind them to keep their distance." He chuckled. "Have no fear! The more offended are the Simet-sa, the better! Now come!"

Ust's eyes focused; and his skin crawled. Entering the Hall of Vim was...himself! Indistinguishable to the smallest detail from the real Ust–and, beneath the gown of his silver lameed vest, he nearly ripped his flesh to assure he was awake and conscious–the King strode into the midst of the Simet-sa, whips clearing a path for a litter borne by armed slavers. In a flash Ust-cum-Flores comprehended what was transpiring, what more would follow. He was ruined! But one further cut and he would have nought to return to but an Assembly in revolt.

The King mounted his throne. Motioning to his Calomar soldiery to move aside, Ust nodded for the slavers to take their places. They deposited the litter while Ust smoothed his delicate robe and smiled.

"My subjects." His lip curled for emphasis. "So you thought to resist me. What contemptible creatures you are. Has the truth not sunk in that I am favored by God?" He shouted. "Has not the realization taken hold that I am one with Vensor? That Vensor Himself consults me?" He smiled at the buzz of outrage circumnavigating the chamber. "That I myself am progeny of the Divine Twin, in truth a second Atasan?"

"This cannot be tolerated, Ust!" called a dozen voices.

Simlet hissed through the blades of two slavers who blocked his approach, "Ust! What do you? You will destroy us all!"

The King stood. "Now I command! It is my wish to take a consort. Whom I take shall be my affair only, and I decree that the Simet-sa accept it at once and without discussion. Behold my consort whom I intend to add to my harem on the conclusion of my Communion with the Divine!"

Ripping aside the curtains, Ust pulled from the litter: Crestal the gila. Her nude body glistened with anxious sweat as she shuddered before the crowd of shocked and angry faces.

Flores staggered. The blade had cut home.

"Atasan is among us!"

"To arms! Its energies shall consume the City!"

Suddenly Ust-cum-Flores believed he understood. This was the real Flores on the throne, who had deliberately played the dunce to lull him, Ust, into a false sense of security, so that he, the real Flores, could lay his own plans and execute them. That Flores also possessed a bracelet, even as he, Ust, possessed one, and was playing at being Ust even as Ust played at being Flores, was inescapable. That Flores intended to ruin him beyond hope of recovery by his antics, was obvious. Damn that Sendas! He had not found the Molersal's bracelet in time!

"ENOUGH!" The voice reverberated through the Hall with such volume and such a tone of grief and desperation that for a second all noise abated. In that second Flores pushed into the center of the chamber, and jabbed a thin finger into the air. "I...*you*," he fumed. Regaining his breath, he attacked the only way he could. "That is *my* gila! You have stolen her from me! I demand that you return her at once!" He smiled inwardly at his cleverness. Let Flores on the throne recover from that! If he, Ust, was ruined–so now was the Turlicum! To possess a gila was a capital crime, even for a Simet noble.

This, Soorkrul-cum-Flores had not expected. The Hall slithered with the sound of rapiers sliding from their scabbards. Briefly he closed his eyes...think... Think! This was someone who possessed another bracelet, of course–but who? A cry from Crestal distracted him.

"Flores! My love! Soorkrul has had me chained in his dungeon for weeks! I want to return to your estate!" Her arms stretched out.

The King glared–and for a moment the illusions stopped. A stranger sat upon the throne, neither Ust nor Flores, but one clothed in the raiment of the House of Prostitution.

"Soorkrul!" several expostulated.

"Do not speak, I said!" Soorkrul's fist slammed into Crestal, sending her prostrate. "But obey me!"

All eyes upon him, Soorkrul turned to glare at Flores, the latter's accusatory finger still pointing. Suddenly, faster than the eye could detect, Soorkrul vanished and Flores of the Turlicum sat upon the throne, every bit as convincing as the Flores standing on the floor. The Flores on the throne stood and shouted: "That man is an impostor! Seize him!"

The other Flores caught his breath. His finger rose higher. "*That* man is an impostor! Seize *HIM!*"

The hall exploded. Nilsit, Toosel, and Mosum shouted together, "Seize them both!" and their clansmen surged forward and clashed with the slavers and Ust's Calomar, who had no notion whom they were defending, but flung themselves into the fight nevertheless. Nilsit burst through, strode up the steps, and leveled his blade at the throne. It was empty. He turned, motioned to Toosel, and together they searched the dais till driven back by Ust's mutes. Soorkrul had vanished. The Simet-sa returned to the floor and examined the area where the other enigma had stood. Vanished as well! Swearing, the three joined with Simlet and Revtal, who, having managed to dissuade their own followers from joining the struggle, surrounded Crestal. Soon the fighting ceased.

"We hereby decree that the persons Ust of the Calomar, Flores of the Turlicum, and Soorkrul of the Eunuchs be arrested on sight and dragged before the Assembly in chains!"

Ten minutes passed. On the nether side of the palace, being the flank nearest the Hedronmas, a warrior of weathered appearance, with muscles sculpted as from marble, and skin tanned from many months under tropical suns, stepped quietly from the darkness. He paused. Had any stood close to see, they would have glimpsed in the merest fraction of a second his face transform into that of a pale nervous shorter man with wispy beard. Ust approached the guards at the gate.

In shock they stared.

"Well, sirs, why do you not part and allow your king entry? Do you not recognize me?"

"Sire...King Ust–" The pair grew tense, tensed their brows. The tone of their voices alerted several more soldiers from the interior. "Apologies, Sire, but the Assembly and the Magistrate have directed us to...arrest you on sight! You are no longer king!"

The Calomar hesitated. He did not seem in the least upset at the news, but stood silently in thought.

"Do not resist, sir. You will have to accompany us–" About to place their hands upon him, they hesitated.

Someone entirely different suddenly stood before them.

"Ust did you say? What foolishness! How could I ever be mistaken for the Leader of the Calomar? Do you not recognize your former king– your real king–Flores of the Turlicum?" The tanned warrior had returned. He raised a hand bearing the ring of the Turlicum as evidence.

"That is worse, sir! The Turlicum is equally wanted by the Assembly for similar crimes as Ust! Do not resist but come with us now!" They raised their blades again.

Without warning, the figure dissolved, melted, was sucked into a whirlwind of light and smoke. A giant stretched its tentacles to embrace them, the tentacles giving birth to shrieking ros-skulls that snapped their jaws in the air. It advanced upon them–the guards broke and ran. From nowhere another guard joined them, running as they ran, as panicked as they, calling for help as loudly.

Flores searched for the throne room. Locating it, he noted a small clot of Simet-sa in close inspection of some object of curiosity, more tending to recent wounded and corpses. He would deal with them later. Now he had other concerns. Before the night was out he would once again be King. This meant finding Ust, and deposing him. With his cooperation, if possible. By taking his place if necessary. But, one way or another, even if it meant taking his life, the Calomar must be deposed within the hour. No more opposition and hindering from the remnants of the Triumvirate; no more compromising with self-absorbed and corrupt Simet-sa. No longer would he brook interference in his plans for the first City among Vensor-sa.

He climbed several ramps. Turning a corner, he sighted outnumbered Calomar defending a doorway from a band of Serclaslers. A Serclasler soldier appeared and plunged into the fray. The others blinked confusedly–the new soldier was not a Serclasler, but a Calomar, and had switched sides. The warrior spun on his heel. Diving into the doorway, Flores was gone.

He strode confidently. Due to unfamiliarity with Ust's new palace, it was some minutes before he found what he sought: Ust's private quarters. He was not sure what he would say, what arguments he would use to persuade Ust to abandon the throne. But they were not important. He possessed on his wrist the most persuasive argument of all, the only argument that he needed in the end. Nearing a double-door that bore Calomar insignia, he slowed. A familiar figure stood within, listening to voices.

Meanwhile, the guards whom Flores had dispersed at the back entrance to the Palace recovered their nerve. They had resumed their post when another vision came upon them. A lyart leg floated in the air like an apparition. They were speechless. So unexpected, so unexplainable was the vision, that the guards made no move even as the leg transmuted into a keg of mead and floated past them into the palace. A voice rang out.

"Greetings, friends! Had a devil of a time avoiding the crowd tonight! Don't bother to announce me, I'll find Ust myself." His pockets no longer jingling, Sendas climbed the ramps to his king's apartments, taking no notice of the amazed stares that followed.

In Ust's private suite, a worried Ust stood before his mirror. Lost! In a span of moments he had plunged from pinnacle to pit. He no longer dared walk the halls of his palace as himself. Should he take on the guise of Flores? The Turlicum appeared in the mirror. Sadly he shook his head. Flores' cause was lost as well–he himself had ensured that. Association with a gila had ruined him. Unnecessarily, as it turned out since it had not been he on the throne after all. Soorkrul? He peered into the eyes of a nondescript eunuch in the mirror. No...although he had been responsible for the catastrophe, Soorkrul had revealed himself in the throne room and was now, like himself, hunted by the mob. Who else might still command in Ven? What other image lay within his repertoire? He broke into a sweat–seconds remained. He must assume that soon the palace guards would break in and throw him in manacles... An unexpected face in the mirror caused him to turn.

"Ust."

The voice was silken. Soothing. The face peaceful. One of his own Calomar guardsmen stood just within the double-doors to his quarters, the doors open behind him. Ust needed no evidence from his eyes to know that it was the one from the throne; the one who had wrecked all his plans. A smirk twisted his mouth. At least he had the satisfaction of knowing that he had wrought similar destruction on his rival.

The guard nodded.

Guard? No. Ust blinked, and, too quick to measure, a man with prismed skin and upraised chin stared upon him.

"Sobol...or rather Soorkrul."

Soorkrul smiled. A simpering indulgent smile. "Sobol. Yes, one of my many identities. Oh, you have seen me often. And I you." The vision clouded, spun like a twister, settled into the features of one of Ust's most trusted mutes. Ust shuddered. He had not guessed. "Yes, Ust. I know of your plans. And of your desires. And of your midnight skulking. And even...the gate...and the *assignation*." He smiled broadly at Ust's sudden paling. Soorkrul's mouth opened in mock alarm, then grew serious. "But you still managed to foil me. Upon your wrist...what you possess... Where did you find the bauble? I had thought mine was the only one on Maalstrom. I glimpsed it on a lonely path in the midst of the southern forest a full year ago. Suddenly you appear in Ven with another. How could this be?" The illusions stopped and for an instant Soorkrul–the real Soorkrul–was visible, deep in thought.

Ust screwed up his courage. "You stand here, in my rooms, and insult me? Do you believe it will be easy to bring me down? I now have the same capability as you!" He spoke stiffly, trying to appear braver than he felt, but realized that Soorkrul had practiced for months, whereas he had possessed his bracelet for but a day. Still, that day had proved sufficient to throw an empire into confusion, and evade a dozen traps.

"You cannot escape me, Ust. I know all your refuges. All your needs. You can never know where I might be lying in wait, anticipating your next move. Perhaps as one of your guardsmen! Perhaps as your advisor! Perhaps...the lover by your side." Ust chilled. "Should you continue to oppose me, the dagger will always be ready–"

A scratching sound caused both to face the doors.

They blinked.

In the doorway stood two figures: both were Sendas of the Molersal. One of them grinned and stretched out a palm, sparkling with glass. "King Ust! I heard from my servants that you wished the remaining bracelets. Here are two. Funny thing, my King–greetings, eunuch, pardon the intrusion–they impart the strangest sensation when placed on the wrist, like so–"

"Wait!" shrieked Ust.

Sendas slipped one on.

The other Sendas snatched the remaining ring from his grasp.

"Make no move, sirs! Or we'll run you through!" A phalanx of guards rushed into the room, brandishing pikes. They stumbled to a halt–the room was occupied by four exact copies of Sendas of the Molersal.

"Why the excitement, Ultem? Have the hors d'oeuvres all been eaten?" the first Sendas chuckled.

"You must jest, Ultem!" echoed the second. "The celebration is still early!"

"A thousand figs on you! I need a drink!" added the third.

"Patrimonialism be damned!" exclaimed the fourth, "I'll take yon servant for my own!"

As one, each Sendas directed a look of total surprise at the others. Each scratched his head in puzzlement.

"I am indignant, sirs!" the first pouted, "One of you is impersonating me. I demand redress!"

"In front of Ultem, no less! How can he know that I am really me?" added the second.

"An insult, sirs! Next you'll be taking my place at banquets!"

"Guards! These others are impersonating me, a Simet noble! I demand that you arrest them!"

Ultem took a step. Paused again. One Sendas had changed to Ust.

"As your rightful king, Ultem, I command you to arrest these others!" The Calomar chief stood before him, fists on hips, his chin outthrust, frowning.

The Sendas to his right flickered. Ust now had a twin. "Pay no attention to this swine, captain! I am your real king! Arrest the others!"

A third one appeared, Ust in every detail. "No! I'm your real king. The rest are impostors!"

The room filled with Usts. Fingers and accusations jabbed in all directions.

One of them changed again, this time into an old man with white hair who leaned and lectured. "I have warned you of these conspiracies! Atasan is plotting against our empire!"

"Sruk! Tell these fools who I am!" begged Mosum.

"I'll crush you with my bare hands!" threatened Numsenmur.

"I had nothing to do with it!" shrieked Dos.

Faces and images alternated like fireflies in a darkroom.

"You are all under arrest! Don't move!" Ultem started. He was now staring at himself.

"Guards!" his counterpart shouted. "Arrest everyone but me!"

Too stunned to act, the soldiers retreated.

A third Ultem appeared and was about to speak when a guard appeared at his side and clamped hands on him. "I arrest you in the name of Ven!"

The second Ultem changed into Flores of the Turlicum. "Are you blind? Can you not see these are all impostors? Arrest everyone but me!"

Immediately the room filled with images of Flores, each commanding that the guards arrest the others.

One figure had said nothing for a while, but merely watched and smiled and changed in response as the others changed. One of the four Flores' now reached out, gripped this silent Flores and slipped something off his wrist. Instantly the silent Flores was replaced by Sendas. The first Flores turned to Ultem.

"I swear to you, Ultem, by the Eye of Vensor, that I am Flores Sumvensor of the Turlicum, former King of Ven. And that I speak the truth when I tell you that each illusionist in this room gains his powers from a bracelet placed upon his wrist. Remove that bracelet and you will learn the identity of each. Let none leave, but search every arm, by force if necessary, till all the devices are accounted for!" He held up Sendas' arm. "You see? We two weave no more illusions. As I am truly Flores, this is truly Sendas."

Sendas waxed indignant. "Of course, you insolent man! Who else would I be?"

Still clutching Sendas' arm, Flores raised his own hand with the ring of the Turlicum on it. "Ultem, you owe your career to me. I now call upon you to back me as any client backs his patron. Block the doors and search the others!"

The captain concentrated his gaze. "In truth, I believe you. Shut the doors! No one leaves this room till I have searched each man." Aided by Flores, who now drew forth his sword, the guards confronted the two remaining illusionists. The first was switching repeatedly between images of Flores and Numsenmur.

"Give it up, Ust. Your identity is apparent." Flores nodded in satisfaction as the guards felt his wrist and removed a bracelet. The Calomar suddenly appeared, disheveled and shaking. The guard handed the bracelet to Flores, who now counted four of the devices.

They shifted their blades to the remaining enigma. He looked as much like Ultem as his own reflection, and the guards hesitated. Then, without warning, he erupted into a whirlwind of images that grew toward the ceiling: a dragon's head spat flames of ice; a skeleton ros sprang upon them its paws sprouting roots; suns flashed and swirled about their heads burst into fireworks before coalescing into a densely muscled demon that reached to crush their bodies—only to vanish as Flores plucked the bracelet off his wrist.

Soorkrul stood before them. Calm as tea, and placidly smiling as if nothing more had occurred than a chat between friends. He shrugged.

Flores spun about. "And now you, Ultem. And your men as well. There can be no exceptions."

The captain's jaw dropped. He smiled a shy smile. Reaching into one pocket he produced two silver spheres and with a swift gesture cast them to the floor. The room exploded with smoke and flame. When its occupants stumbled out, coughing and rubbing their eyes, Soorkrul, Ust—and Ultem captain of the guard—had vanished.

Flores swore. Thank Gethos, he still held the bracelets. Five remained in his possession. Quickly sliding one on, he assumed the guise of one of the guards, and watched the remainder wander off in confusion, accompanied by an outraged and bewildered Sendas. Flores then strode the halls of the palace, peering, thinking, trying to hide his agitation. Without the bracelet, Soorkrul was no longer a threat. Flores could not explain the episode with Ultem, but since he now possessed all of the bracelets of which he was aware there was no reason to expect any danger from him. However, he could not rest while Ust remained at large.

Somehow he must apprehend him. There was no telling how many se-crets and hidden allies he might have accumulated while king! Secrets... He snapped to a halt. Returned to Ust's apartments at a run.

Upon entering the doors, Flores crept inside–and waited. Soon his pa-tience was rewarded by the sound of a creaking joint. Slowly he inched forward. Peered around a corner. Ust emerged from a hidden niche in a wall, and glided past flickering torches to a thick door studded with locks and knobs. Noisily they surrendered to his touch, thus explaining why he had not taken this route to escape while the room was filled with smoke. One last stealthy glance and he descended a steeply angled flight of stairs. Flores followed like a ghost.

At the stair's terminus, a second thick door barred his progress, and Ust hesitated, muttering. Finally he flipped the locks in spite of the noise, and opened it. He let his breath go. No guards were there to stop him. The Brother of Moons advanced into the darkness.

Flores trailed him through a tangle of Ven alleyways. On the edge of the Temple plaza, he lost him. He doubled back, turned up one alley, and another, then returned. It would be a shame to lose his quarry at this stage, just when he was about to discover the Calomar's destination. Back at the plaza, he stopped and swept the expanse with his gaze. By the Temple wall something moved. Flores fixed in his mind an image of a shadow and threw himself into the moonlight, trusting to his new pa-tron Gethos that his skill at weaving illusions would make him one with the night. He neared the wall. It was Ust. The noble stood by the massive pylon as if wishing to merge with the stone, peering nervously about. At one point he turned and gazed directly at Flores. Flores froze until Ust at last relaxed and looked away.

A section of wall collapsed inward. Ust crawled within. He attempted to bar it shut, but Flores slipped a sliver of wood in the joint, and after a moment Ust gave up the attempt–as Flores had hoped–and continued on his way. When his footsteps had grown silent, Flores crawled after.

Ahead flickered a tiny pinpoint of light. Flores paused. Memories of his harrowing struggle beneath Soorkrul's lair in the wilderness flooded on him and Flores shuddered at the possibility of a repetition of his or-deal; other memories of his incarceration within Ven's Temple made him think twice about the wisdom of following Ust within, since the noble obviously had sympathies among its inhabitants. But he shook off the deadness, seized control, and returned to his task. After all–he had the items! He plunged ahead.

The light turned, attenuated, and reversed. Rapidly it grew. Flores felt in the dark for some niche that might offer a refuge and avoid detection. The light approached swiftly. Ust's visage shone in the light of the candle. Just when Flores gave up hope that he could avoid a confrontation, Ust suddenly halted and placed the candle in a holder on the ground. He moved away at an angle, and disappeared. Some twenty feet away a panel opened, momentarily framing a rhombus of light, then shut.

Flores followed.

Moments passed and he crawled into a room of candles. A door on the far side stood open to reveal a dimly lit corridor. Flores shook his head. Did Ust possess such privileges that he could walk the corridors of the Temple in safety? Or was desperation driving him to take unwise measures? He paused beside a gleaming plate of copper, assumed the guise of a priestess, and strode boldly after his quarry.

Soon he caught up with him. Face taut and beading from the strain, Ust scurried from one sheltering turn to another, taking advantage of every shadow. He seemed to be calculating distances, constantly throwing his glance over the walls that he passed. At last, having negotiated the pathways to his satisfaction, and having successfully avoided detection by the Temple priestesses–leading Flores to decide that desperation was his rival's chief motive–he arrived at the head of a spiral staircase. Cautiously, Ust descended. In the stairwell, Flores saw a portal open; heard voices within; watched the portal shut. Hurriedly he advanced and pressed his ear against it–he could hear no more than two voices mumbling, though something about the higher of the two seemed familiar. The deeper voice seemed to be pleading, begging. At one point it rose in anger. But it was answered by cold unconcern, and peremptory orders. A rattle on the other side sent Flores rushing back up the steps.

"What do you here?"

He almost ran her down, he stopped so suddenly.

"Don't you know this is the hour of Vespers?" continued the voice.

Flores was shocked–very nearly the greatest shock he had ever felt. Before him stood an old woman in worn black cassock, whose sere and wrinkled face burned in his memory like no other: Wijah. "Do you not know that in one hour the Queen will take a man from the City to dally with? Divine Communion is about to begin, the event that will ensure the Queen's immortality, and the City's immortality as well! After tonight the Goddess will live for a thousand years, spawn a million young! Long after priestesses like you and I are gone, Her glory will continue to shine across Maalstrom! Come with me at once. There is much to do."

Flores breathed in relief. He had forgotten his priestly disguise. Thank Gethos he had said nothing. He was careful now to merely bob his head. They turned to go when at the bottom of the stairs, the portal opened. A man backed into the stairwell. Wijah drew Flores into a dark recess to watch.

The face of Ust was illumined by a torch. He had the look of the hunted. Gaining the corridor his eyes darted. He hurried back the way he had come.

Wijah gasped. Such turmoil and inner struggle Flores had not witnessed before. In her face he read recognition, disappointment, love, grief, anger, blinding hatred, and thirst for a terrible revenge, one emotion flooding to the fore only to be strangled by the next irresistible wave. But she said nought. Flores turned his priestess gaze to the floor. If Wijah had ought to do with Ust, it would be best not to let on that he knew.

"A child of the City is within our Temple," she wheezed. "He violates the sanctity of our sanctuary. Go to the room of garments and summon the guardians. I will wait here for your return." Flores nodded. He strode off in a random direction, having no idea where his destination may lie, but at the end of the hallway he looked back.

Wijah had gone.

Of course! Smiling with sudden understanding, he returned. She had merely sought to put the other priestess, himself, off the track. Her black cassock moved in the distance, and he hurried to keep her in view, and saw her take a different route than the one Ust had taken. It was apparently a shorter route to the room of candles and in another minute Flores stood again outside its door. He resumed his shadow-guise. Peering inside, he saw Wijah hugging the panel which had admitted Flores and Ust. Rage and grief contorted her face. Her hand lifted to a bar set in an alcove above the panel and something about the raw emotion which the bar seemed to evoke from Wijah lent an evil significance to the device in Flores' mind. He frowned.

She grasped the bar and pulled. A thump carried to his ears, followed by a muffled peal of terror. Wijah hurried into the adjoining room to return a moment later bearing a flaming torch and an axe. She entered the tunnel. Her shadow followed.

Just behind Wijah, Flores halted. The priestess stood without moving. Instead of firm ground such as Flores had traversed when he had earlier passed through the corridor, an open pit now yawned, dank odors curling from its depths. The old woman stooped. Her torch illuminated the face of Ust, who hung by his hands from the ledge, cold terror exuding every pore.

"Wijah! Thank god you have come! The ground seems to have betrayed me," he grinned. It was a grin of panic.

"Shut up!" Her face contorted with scorn. "I am sorry, my mistress," she mimicked, "I will do better next time. None other loves you as I do! I swear I will never touch another I have sworn it is only you I desire!" She glared. "So you thought to deceive me...believed you could visit the Queen and leave me barren and alone to die in a few short months. Did you think that I would not learn of your deceit? Such a man you are! I knew from the beginning that you would do this you males are all alike not one of you can be trusted for a moment!" She waved the torch menacingly above him. Stamped one tiny foot.

Ust sucked his breath. "No, my love...it is only you I live for...give me one more chance—" A sloshing emanated from the pit, and Ust glanced below and paled.

"Silence!" Wijah screamed. "I gave of myself to you—violated my oaths to Vensa—condemned my soul to perdition so you could have your pleasure with me! Now you beg me to take you back?" Tears of rage gushed. She brandished the axe.

The grin vanished. Ust's fingers gripped a protuberance, caught a firmer grip. "Wait!" With his free hand, he drew forth a dagger...

Flung it.

His mark was wide.

Wijah jerked back. Thrust the torch into his face. "Ha!" She seized his weapon. "What did you imagine would become of you, betraying me so? Do you not recall the oaths you swore? The oaths we swore together?"

Ust streamed sweat. A growing hissing from the pit failed to distract him.

"Do you not remember what I swore should you betray me by looking upon another?" Raising the dagger, she plunged it through his hand into the floor. Her voice mingled with his shriek. "Your hands will be cut from your arms! The eyes will be gouged from your head!" She leaned forward—the axe did its foul work. Flores almost retched hearing the low moans. The torch thrust forward. The walls echoed with crackling; danced with flames from burning hair and skin. The axe swung and in another moment nothing remained of Ust but an impaled dismembered hand.

Wijah trudged into the room of candles. Sat heavily on the bed and lay the bloody axe beside her. She started. "You, priestess? You are here?"

Insanity snarled in her eyes.

Flores dropped his guise. A moment...

She shook. Sanity was not so far removed after all. "So it is you. I suspected you would return. What man, once tasting the fruits of the Temple, can resist the urge to taste them again? You did not find life with a gila in the outside world so hospitable, did you?"

"It is hospitable or not as I make it." He glanced toward the tunnel. "Ust did not deserve that."

"He was only a man."

"He was already deposed. I am now King–"

"The affairs of the City do not concern me–"

"This affair *does!*" He stepped closer, fixed her with his eyes. "You see, I know of the oracle. I know it is your voice that speaks to the masses, and that you do not always communicate your Queen's desires with precision."

She took a breath. "The secrets of the Temple are not for mere men to know! Or to judge!"

"I not only judge, but command as well! In the future it will be I–or my intimates–who will mount the golden path to receive the Word of God! If the oracles are not to my liking, I will search you out and show you the error of your ways." He slipped forth his own dagger and spun it for effect.

Wijah looked indignant. "You cannot. I have only to bar the hidden panel in the wall, and you will be exiled forever. The Queen will seal the gate, and the children of the City will tear you to pieces!"

"One word from me to the Queen, and She will order you torn to pieces for meeting with Ust!"

She started, then recovered. "You forget. Ust is no more!"

"Oh? Behold...Ust returns." With a blinding flash the image of the dead noble leapt into Flores' mind and Wijah reared back in horror. Then burst into tears. She buried her face in her hands. Flores said, "His image is with me always. And not only his." The priestess from the hallway returned, followed by a series of faces and images. "You see that you can never again be certain that the person by your side is who you believe it to be. You can never know if I am not the Queen Herself on a particular day." Flores returned to his own image. "Now. I have a question... I have traveled far for an answer. And returned..."

"The malkops," she said.

"Amina–"

"The malkops took her... as I intended. Unconsciousness deceives them, you see, as they believe the unconscious dead, and they fly away with them to Heaven. So she is gone! You will never see your gila again, and I am glad! Glad! They took Amina to Heaven and left Nara–who hates you no less than I do. Nara is now Queen in Ven! You should think twice before you imagine addressing her."

"Then we shall have silence. I will keep your secret of Ust. But the oracle will henceforth repeat what I direct from the platform, and initiate no request but food without my permission. Any attempt to use the oracle to depose me shall be met with overwhelming force–either from me in secret, or from my subjects when I direct them to climb the Temple walls. My first instruction: at first light tomorrow, the oracle shall proclaim me King of Ven." For emphasis, Flores recalled the image of Nara.

Crushed, Wijah nodded. "As you say."

Flores motioned to the bar above the panel and Wijah flipped it back into place. A loud grating of stone on stone followed as the floor resumed its place over the pit.

"Precede me through the tunnel. If ought happens to me, we die together."

Morning broke on a completed Revolution. From the throne of Ven, and with the blessing of the oracle, Flores drew all power to himself. His allies welcomed his return–now that the deceit of Soorkrul lay exposed. His enemies either swore allegiance; or were exiled. Flores was glad to find that most preferred the oath as he was anxious to avoid new conflicts, needing, as he did, all of Ven's strength for his War against Heaven. On his command, the entire city began to work on a fleet. From a single underwater breathing device, and mounds of corta, its scribes went to work with the purpose of replicating it into hundreds. On his instruction, the army was recalled from defeated Neset and headed for Asan to rendezvous with the new fleet. However impossible it seemed, however quickly the Island faded in his mind's eye, no matter how the difficulties might multiply upon contemplation, Flores persevered. All the resources he could summon he focused on his one task: invade the Island of the Sun-God, and bring Amina home.

Noon of the second day approached. Flores stood in the Nether Fields, Sandol by his side. They had come in secret so none might witness the sacrilege but his own, his trusted Sandol.

"I have placed the bracelets in the safe in my own private rooms, the safe beneath my hive of leroo-sa. All but one. This one." Flores bared his arm to show a gleam of glass. "You are to tell no one of their location.

And you are not to touch them yourself. I have left Mosum in charge in Ven; Lirsus and Sedrech, the army and navy. You will continue to guard the House of Prostitution–and watch for Soorkrul–as you have done thus far. When the expedition is ready, all are to depart, and search for the Isle of Vensor. My commanders know well the constellations–and the plan."

"By the way, my King. Crestal has returned. She was not injured, and now resides on your estate."

" 'She'?" Flores looked confused.

"I took the liberty, knowing as I did of your acquaintance with her."

"Crestal...a gila."

"You knew, of course..."

Flores shrugged. "I had guessed. I did not want to believe it. No matter. Let it wait till I return. Protect her. Do not let the mob harm her in any way, and grant her whatever she wishes." Approaching a rough-hewn rectangular altar rudely cut from the hardest ashlar, the newest king of all the Vensor-sa disrobed but for a loincloth.

"Make me yellow."

Taking handfuls of yellow altheas freshly plucked from the meadows of the Nether Fields, Sandol rubbed their pollen-laden stamens over Flores' body and legs.

"You are intent on this course, my lord?"

"Not you or Atasan Himself could dissuade me."

As a humming grew in the distance, Flores lay upon the funeral altar of the Turlicum, on which generations of his clan had been laid in death and from which endless generations of corpses had been retrieved by the workers of the sky. The hum grew to a buzz. The air darkened with winged messengers–both insect and selk.

Wide-eyed, Sandol stepped back. Before his gaze a cloud of leroo-sa collected about Flores and settled upon his body. A hundred probosces flicked. A thousand compound eyes focused.

The soporific chemical penetrated his skin, flooded the synapses of his brain. Flores breathed deep. His eyelids grew heavy; the strangeness of the situation stole over him, accepting death as it were on his terms, awaiting the denizens of the sky to transport him to Heaven in order to bring one long-dead back to the realm of the living. Dropping into the Abyss, a question struggled to surface. "How, Sandol?" he muttered. "How did you know that I knew Crestal since I have never mentioned that to you?" Before he could hear the answer, the illusion of death swallowed him.

A minute elapsed.

Two.

At length, the yellow had vanished, consumed by the insects like locusts consume a harvest. Sated, the leroo-sa drifted back to their meadows.

As the last flitted into distant dots, Sandol stepped cautiously foward. The smile on his face faded. He adjusted Flores' arms, smoothed a fold in his loincloth. Glancing once about, and seeing no one, the servant shifted his jaw and rubbed his thin lips with glee. He reached forth. Taking Flores' hand, he pulled the bracelet free.

"How?" repeated the silken voice, dripping with sarcasm. "Have you still not learned that I know all? See all? You wretched creatures whose egos guide you around by the nose. Do you imagine you can rival Soorkrul of the Suns, He of the Light of Revelation?" His illusion dropped, and Soorkrul stood in unadorned simplicity, examining his find in the suns' rays. He pulled another bracelet from the wrist of his left arm. Laughed. "Slow, clumsy Flores. It didn't occur to you that I might have discovered a *second* bracelet in addition to the first, on that far day a full year ago! Next time, inspect both my wrists if you want to truly strip me of my powers!"

Without a backward glance, Soorkrul departed. Within the hour Sandol stood within Flores' apartments, his private safe open, counting six glass bracelets. Putting them all on his wrists, he walked out.

☦ ☦

CHAPTER 23

SINGSONG

Of all the adventures that had befallen Flores, of all the spectacles he had witnessed, the secret splendors and hidden gardens he had glimpsed–whether one considered them privileges, or afflictions–none, from the audience chamber of Atasan to the depths of the southern ocean, rivaled the breathless sensation he felt upon gaining consciousness from the effects of the drug. Implicitly he knew, and his inner nature would have directed him to do so anyway, not to move a muscle nor show the slightest sign of animation till he was fully awake. When he did open his eyes, it required all the self-discipline he could muster not to tense in response to what he saw.

He saw the planet Maalstrom. Outspanning the horizons, weald and wilderness replicated in every direction into the distance. Rivers, forests, mountains, clouds repeated to infinity while he drifted among the heavens. He could well imagine he was already there, except for a tightness about his chest. Bands like iron gripped him. He lay prone with limbs hanging loose so that he could see no more than the pinions of leathery wings as they oscillated. They seemed enormous. He calculated the energy expended was not great, though. The creature depended mostly on updrafts of air to carry them both to its destination. Ever so slyly he peered at his bearer. No more than its legs and arms could he see, but the creature's hot breath purled continuously on his neck. The sensation, and his situation, were unique. He and his bearer–alone among the clouds.

Hours passed. Flores became aware of acute pain that grew in several parts of his body and spread. His notion of remaining motionless during his trip to the Island was beginning to seem foolhardy–the equivalent of suicide. How much longer could he remain still? How much longer resist the urge to flex his stiffening muscles? The consequences of showing signs of life in what was supposed to be a corpse were more than he cared to think about. The urge swelled. Became overwhelming. A monumental struggle launched in his mind, spreading to every niche, drawing every mote of energy to resist. At last he knew he could hold out no longer and prepared to grapple with the selk. The ground rushed forward and a dense copse of trees enfolded him.

He was dropped unceremoniously on a bed of leaves. The impact wrenched a cry of pain that was quickly overarched by a wash of pleasure as his limbs broke free from their former restraint and resumed their natural movement. He groaned with relief and rolled. Before the gaze of the selk? He no longer cared. Now that the journey had ended and he had come to the Island, he had no need of the creature–except, he had seen no Island. Nor ocean.

He jerked up. Where were the pits of the dead? He sat within the overhang of a grove of trees, beneath a temperate sky strewn with scud, early autumn breezes rushing in periodically among the limbs to cool and invigorate him. The landscape reminded him in no way of the Island of the Sun-God, but was a completely different clime. The selk had left. Or at least was no longer within vision, having deposited its burden and gone about other business. Flores shook his head. Yet another puzzle. So the creatures did not fly direct to Ra-Allah with corpses, as he had assumed, but at times detoured or delayed their passage across the ocean. But why? And how might he resume his flight, now that the drug had worn off? One chance remained–use the bracelet to deceive the malkops as he had deceived them before in Ra'Allah. It was risky, and he had no confidence that he could remain motionless for the distance, but he had no choice. He reached for his bracelet. And caught his breath. Vanished! A quick search revealed it was nowhere in his environs.

How his difficulties multiplied!

Despondent, his gaze wandered to the surrounding fields. Numerous selks glided about. Some entered or departed other stands of trees that interspersed the fields, some burdened with corpses, but most seeming preoccupied with some obscure activity in the fields themselves. He had been placed in a dense stand of wood and Flores stood and loosened his limbs until all trace of the tortuous trip had vanished. He stepped closer. The fields, he decided, were not natural, but were a result of cultivation. The individual plants were too distant to discern much detail, but their general appearance was more pale and light than the green he would have expected. The individual specimens, being evenly spaced, provided sufficient room for a selk to touch one with its wings half-unfolded without fear of entanglement with neighboring plants.

Flowers, thought Flores. For the malkops apparently were greatly attracted, and no sooner did a selk part with one, than it flitted rapidly to a second, then a third, and so forth. The entire expanse of meadow, in fact, was alive with vertical movement as the malkop-sa touched a multitude of the plants in succession, never seeming to tire of the dance. Which was his ride? Luck of Gethos! he cursed. What chance had he now? He had not the slightest notion where this country lay in relation to Ven. Drugged as he was, he had been unable to note even the direction they had traveled. What's more, hunger and thirst were beginning to dominate his thoughts and he realized he could not remain hidden. Before long he would have to search for food.

The day was late and the suns moved swiftly toward the horizon. At the far end of the field that lay directly before him something disturbed the selks and they took to the air with a ripple that soon left the field bare of them. Flores peered. In the distance, several objects moved among the plants. They came closer and he decided they would soon come quite close to his little stand of trees, and then the suns plummeted, the shadows lengthening so that all became grey. He turned around and all was shadow. He turned again and the swift Maalstrom night covered all with blackness, except for a sprinkle of lights that moved among the plants.

Children of Vensor! That meant food.

Venturing forth, he approached the edge of the field and came close enough to one of the flames to hear it sputter. From somewhere a vast sighing or soughing emanated. He stepped to the nearest plant, raised his foot to proceed, and halted. It was staring at him. He glanced at the others. Nantifus had sunk far in the nightsky but still cast a sickly white tinge over the land–the moonglow illuminated a host of faces and unclothed masculine bodies.

Men.

What he had assumed to be plants because of their regular spacing he suddenly realized were children of Vensor, standing in perfect silence, each in his own space, waiting patiently as if for some imminent apocalypse. Their eyes roamed freely, however, and Flores felt his skin prickle with the impact of their cold glare. Why did they not move? How long had they thus stood? Why did the malkop-sa touch them and not flee as they always did with living persons?

His questions were cut short as the torch broke into the open. The sighing swelled. The bearer of the torch was a man in plain tunic, sandals, and broad sunhat. He bore a sack across one shoulder and from the sack withdrew what to all appearances was bread and meat. The 'plant' that Flores had first seen lifted human-like arms. Slowly and with poor co-ordination, but apparent relish, the creature accepted the food and devoured it. Meanwhile, having distributed the ration, the cultivator stooped and scraped what appeared to be clear jelly from about the creature's legs and ankles. This he deposited in a bag tied about his waist, and moved on.

At first Flores prepared to flee, fearing the creatures might prove to be hostile, and would cut short their contemplation to pursue him. Soon, however, he concluded that they either would not, or could not, move. Or perhaps they simply had so little interest in him that they cared not whether he departed or stayed. Despite the eyes that focused on him whenever he moved, Flores resolved to inspect more closely, taking care not to come within range of their grasp. They were to all appearances human, down to the last detail, excepting that, what he had initially assumed were feet, were in fact a harder substance that had merged in some fashion with the ground. To his relief, Flores realized they were incapable of departing from where the cultivator had placed them.

None had made any attempt to touch him, aside from the sighing he had heard, and, his hunger becoming paramount, Flores determined at last to satisfy his need. Walking among them, he noted one had dropped a portion of its meal. It appeared older than the others and had lost much of its hair and its skin was dry and shriveled. Flores retrieved a piece of the bread and took a bite.

"Does it speak?"

The noble looked up in surprise.

"Does it feel?"

He resisted the impulse to reply with his own myriad of questions. As the creature clearly was discussing him, even if addressing itself to another, he replied. "I assure you, sir, that I both speak and feel."

The creature, for Flores still had reservations on whether it was a true child of Vensor or not, made no sign that it had heard.

"How does it survive without roots? Why does it breathe without the possibility of loving the Divine?" It broke its glance and gazed skyward. "A mote lost in the cosmos, without place or belonging. Why does it bother to struggle?"

"You speak as if I were an insect, sir. I not only speak and feel but have a soul as well."

"Soul-as-well... Yes, without belonging invention is essential... Without love, true life is impossible. Does it love? How can it without roots, without skin to touch the Divine? Does the Without know it is Without?"

"Skin? Of course I possess skin. My clothing hides it."

"Soul-as-well has 'clothing'. Hides its love. Hides its skin. 'Without' invents 'withs' to fill its emptiness."

A shadow passed swiftly across them. The sighing rose, ecstasy and passion imbuing every voice. Flores noticed several male members grow in response. The moonglow returned and the eyes refocused on Flores.

"Soul-as-well has no sustenance, fails in its duty, knows not its place. How can it come to know itself–to know Love–if it wanders lost like the wind."

Flores raised his eyebrows. "I admit that I may not know my place, and even that I don't know myself as well as I would like, but I assure you that insofar as I know my duty, I have always striven to perform it."

" 'Eye' admit– 'eye' know– 'eye' assure 'U'..." The man–which Flores now was forced to admit he was–returned Flores' puzzled stare. "Soul-as-well tears out eyes, splits organs from Loving, splits mind from SingSong. From pain, lack of place, lack of belonging, not touching the Divine. Soul-as-well knows not why it breathes, why it waits. Even grubs in the soil know why they breathe, why they wait. Have no soul. Need no soul."

Shrugging, Flores took another bite of bread. He sampled the meat. "So you don't understand the words 'I' or 'you'?... Okay... Does SingSong know why it breathes, why it waits?"

The old man brightened. "Life knows! Life knows love! Knows why it breathes, why it waits. SingSong waits for Love, for caress of the Divine. Loving knows why it breathes. SingSong knows why it sings. Soul-as-well has no song, hides its love with clothing, its voice flat, dead. Waits for nothing. Dreams nothing. Does not feel, but thinks and talks *of* feeling."

Another shadow flickered above and the soughing rose again. All eyes turned heavenward and Flores followed. To his surprise a malkop hovered some distance away. It descended into the field. He had supposed they only visited during the day, likely from the parallel he had drawn with real flowers. But malkops frequented Ven at night. Why not here as well? His musings were cut short by the swelling of the voices into a cacophony, an orgy, of pleasure. Every man-tree in Flores' vicinity seemed transported into a realm of ecstasy, their full attention drawn to the winged creature that moved among them. Flores hid behind one man-tree to watch.

The selk landed, folded its wings. It stepped close, pale in the moon-light. Sighs enveloped it, accompanied by a high-pitched trilling that Flores took to be invitations. Concentrating on one man, the selk cocked its head. Chirped. It raised its breechclout and in response the man's member rose fully erect and his arms extended, reaching forth to em-brace the visitor. The selk accepted the embrace. Lifting one leg, the selk wrapped it around the man's buttock and together they moved their hips in a slow caress, their lips and arms locked together. Flores was shocked. He was witnessing yet another violation of what he had until recently believed was the purely spiritual nature of the divine. Heaven had turned out to be as material as Maalstrom; Hell no different; now he had dis-covered that the angels were as carnal as any eunuch!

Before the act was consummated, the selk withdrew. Deftly and as if from long practice, it ran one hand along the inner thigh of the man while he ejaculated, scooping the quickly solidifying ejaculate into a ball. When it had collected the bulk of the substance, the malkop spread its wings and ascended a short distance into the air only to descend beside another object of passion. The procedure repeated. And afterward yet again until the selk had collected a large mass of ejaculate that shined and glittered with reflected moonlight. When it had accumulated a suf-ficient quantity, the selk flew into the sky and vanished.

Flores returned to his bower, munching on the bread while he contem-plated what he had seen. He nodded with recognition. *Essence of irsrem.* So this was the source of the most valued commodity on Maalstrom, the building material of Heaven and of the Domeworld, the substance that had imparted to Ven its empire and upon which the martial civilization of the Vensor-sa, the dominant civilization of Maalstrom, rested. It was bewildering! And obscene. Going against a lifetime of religious training and genteel education, and violating every precept of morality, his every assumption about the world and how it functioned, he could not help but feel a wave of revulsion. But it made sense. Like the ros that takes the new-born reven, or rum-na that bolt over a cliff. Like the spring floods that drown the farmer even as they water his crops. Each was made nec-essary by the requirements of life itself. The collective of Singsong lived for no other purpose than to satisfy the selks. To satisfy the physical lust of the malkops' collective body—Loving. The men, rooted to their Place, wished nothing more, lived and breathed for nothing else than the visi-tation of a malkop. They could no more wish a different fate, imagine a different life, than could the grubs beneath their roots, or the selks that they embraced, or the other Vensor-sa who spent their turgid lives in conflict and war and, by pursuing this–their own passion and interest–thus served the Queen in Her Temple, and Atasan. But the question remained: *why* did the Queen allow Herself to be preyed upon by Atasan? How could the world of Vensor-sa allow itself to be exploited by an insect creature that used Vensor queens for their own selfish reproductive purposes? How did it serve Nature for Vensor-sa, which these man-trees apparently had once been, to be exploited by the servants of Atasan, as he had witnessed? No, he still did not possess all the answers. And but a short time remained–if indeed it was not already too late–for him to rescue Amina before she was impregnated and suffered the same fate as Vensa.

The days passed while Flores fretted in his stand of trees, resenting the passage of each hour. At night he ventured forth for food, and on the second night discovered a clear stream and was thereafter able to slake his thirst. Before long he ceased to stay in one place, but–true to his rootless status–slept in a different grove each night. Wherever he wandered, the fields extended, with their cultivators appearing each afternoon with their torches and sacks of provenance, feeding the SingSong collective and scraping the remnants of ejaculate from the night's activity.

Some days later he found himself in an isolated meadow, some distance from the other fields, and surrounded by rising hills. Here the plantmen were different. Though they also were unclothed and obviously masculine, there was something about them that left Flores uneasy. Perhaps it was their mesomorphic build and the many scars about their bodies. Perhaps the element of alienness in their eyes when they glared at him. Or their large jaws with massive temporal muscles that bespoke unusual power. Or the fact that Flores had not seen the cultivators' torches in their vicinity and could see no remnants of meat or bread or drink. Nor for that matter any trace of ejaculate. Flores paused.

Before long a selk arrived and began its customary task. Upon touching the first plantman, whose behavior heretofore had been indistinguishable to Flores from those in the other fields, the selk was seized in an unbreakable grip. Ignoring its high-pitched chirping and frantic attempts to take to the sky, the plantman ripped one wing from its body. The selk puckered its mouth. Out shot a length of white rope. The plantman howled in pain and hastily scraped it off, and the selk's claws ripped red streaks–to no avail. In another moment, the plantman had torn it limb from limb and fell to devouring the carcass. With malicious cleverness, it tossed the bones and remnants into neighboring shrubbery so as to deceive its next victim. Flores avoided the meadow thereafter.

Three weeks had passed when the idea came to him. He was about to venture forth in search of the city of the cultivators when he realized that another method to gain the Island lay within his purview. It was a plan that involved more risk than his former plan, but, if successful, he would have no need to feign death.

In the early hours just after midnight when the moons were full, he entered the nearest field of plantmen, ate and drank his fill, disrobed, and took a position between several old and unattractive examples of Loving. If the cannibalistic plantmen could successfully attract selks with the worst of motives, and the malkops' natural instinct in the face of danger was to take to the sky, then it should be possible for him to attract one as well, for his own purposes.

He had not long to wait. In the light of rushing moons that advertised his charms, one of the creatures flapped and lit before him. Sighs of ecstasy rose all around punctuated by trilling invitations from rivals and Flores could well imagine, with the magic of the night in his eyes, and the exotic whispering in his ears, how this image of Atasan–the god of flesh and lust–might dovetail with his desires, answer his hidden longings, fulfill all his unspoken and unthought cravings. He had imagined he would be detached when it approached. Was concerned he would betray himself by a lack of interest. But now, with the Thing upon him, its sweet breath moistening red lips, its firm breasts swelling before his eyes, a slim hand raising its breechcloth while it delicately smiled, and lifted one leg to press its heel against the small of his back, now he found himself taut with energy, electrified, transported, struggling vainly to control his irrupting passion that surged with life and a power he had not suspected, as when he had been briefly kissed on the lattice. His soul cried out to plunge his member into the womb of the selk and release his passion in a spasm of bliss...then his lifetime of Simet training asserted itself and–not without an inward whimper of protest–he suppressed it. Placing one arm around the creature's neck, he spun it around and clamped both his legs about its midriff. It jerked with fright. With Flores astride, it launched itself into the sky.

To Flores' surprise it neither deviated from its course, nor sought to land, but flew with the greatest speed in a singular direction. But one brief attempt to shake him free, which failed, and it resigned itself to him. Soon the coast appeared. Islands passed. Then the ocean opened before them like a blue tide and the hours elapsed eventless. Daylight came and went and the moons returned and still the creature did not pause. Flores leaned forward to peer into its eyes and glimpsed a flow of tears and wide-eyed panic. Well that it was so. That meant there would be no more interruptions in his journey.

Another night passed and he saw a black cloud in the distance. Nearing, he discovered that it was a belt of malkops that stretched from horizon to horizon. They soon surrounded him. To his relief they were ignored, evidently believing him to be merely another corpse en route to Heaven, and they flew on without respite, remaining in the company of the others.

With the passage of another day, the last rays of the setting suns gleamed on a distant mountain of glass. The suns vanished. Another hour passed and a vast wall aglow with the red light of the moon Atasan expanded before him. Another hour and they were even with the third level. An endless procession of selks were entering the aperture with one branch splitting off in the direction of another aperture that yawned a mile to his left.

Before Flores was able to mentally prepare himself for the pits–though immensely relieved that his journey was about to end–his bearer plunged into the gaping aperture. The smell of the charnelhouse engulfed him. Again he glimpsed the pillars awash in patchworked light; the hexagonal cells of bricks; the strewn bodies of the dead with their strange tectonic putrescence. Finally, his bearer halted in a recess of the cave far removed from the other malkops, where it descended and folded its wings and waited as if all life had gone, and Flores realized what he had done, that by forcing the creature to bring him to Ra'Allah he had ensured the selk's demise. To bring an earth-bound-of-dwellings, a wingless child of cities to See-Face-of-God before it had truly expired was perhaps the worst offense a malkop could commit. Its life was over.

Flores soon located a rapier, and a small buckler for protection. The selk still had made no move. Approaching, he took its hair between his fingers and stroked it. It glanced up, eyes streaming tears. Moodily he left it, still motionless, and wondering why he felt like a criminal.

He ascended the ramp. Destiny waited. True he had not the bracelet, but he knew a way to gain the Hive without exposing himself to discovery and the rage of the selks.

In another hour darkness was complete and he found the entrance to the nearest of the domewall's drainage pipes. The same he had previously traversed. He curled up at its base for a night of rest–without doubt his last. Once more he glimpsed the soft glow of the night sky through the domewall; felt the delicious tropical warmth of the vast terrarium; wondered what Mind had conceived the whole, what Divinity had built it. His last thought as he slipped into oblivion was, come what may, whether death or life came with the dawn, no matter whether he possessed magic trinkets, or whether the fleet arrived from Ven, he would not falter or desist from his purpose until he had regained his love, and the dark splendor of Amina, priestess of Vensa, lay once more open to his passion.

CHAPTER 24

RA'ALLAH

When he awoke the suns had not yet returned and Flores took advantage of the remaining minutes of darkness to prepare. A quick investigation of one of the orchard's spillways yielded a branch of fungus. The lake quenched his thirst. Returning briefly to the uppermost pit, he located a bow and clutch of arrows and a pair of daggers. Dawn found him within the culvert, ready to begin his climb.

His plan was to ascend in one quick effort, then to wait just inside the lip for night to return, when he hoped to steal forth and penetrate as far as he was able before being discovered. His object was the room of lattices where Amina had been last imprisoned. How to scale the hexwork he had no notion. He would think about that when–and if–he found it. So far he had seen few selks. Those within the Hive generally rested at night, and those burdened with corpses usually waited until light to bring them into the cave. Hence he was surprised to feel, while in the cave, that something, or someone, was observing him. His gaze detecting no one, he dismissed the feeling.

At last he was ready, and, as the muted discs of the suns rose in the sky, he began the ascent. Being well rested and fed, and knowing beforehand the impediments and utilities that awaited, Flores felt equal to the task of negotiating the rungs in the passageway. Still, the climb strained him to the utmost. Whereas before he had been exhausted when he began, gravity now opposed rather than assisted him. Thus he found he had to pause frequently to rest. An hour passed. Then another. He could have climbed more quickly, but, given the enormity of the task ahead, and the unlikelihood of success, he chose to conserve his strength as much as possible.

During one of his periods of rest, with his irsrem rapier propped against opposite rungs as a seat, a small noise carried to him from below. The noise ceased as soon as it began and was not repeated for the duration of his climb, however Flores could not help but recall his earlier impression, and was forced to conclude that, one way or another, he had already been discovered. He sighed. Likely due to his mercy with the malkop that had transported him, his chances of surviving to midnight were now even less.

Finally, as the Twin Suns headed once again for their rendezvous with Chaos and the duskline enveloped the vast dome of Ra'Allah, after an absence of what seemed to Flores an immense span of time, though he knew it could not have comprised more than a month, the noble of Ven, Heir to the Reven Clan, defender of the Temple of Vensa since the dawn of time and descendant of the warrior Zeyd, skulked just within its egress, and plotted to overthrow everything he knew. No more gods. No more malkops. No more Heaven. No more Hell. An end to the network of lies that served Atasan and its nest of insect predators. Termination. With Amina by his side.

He waited till midnight. Then, when the Hive was darkest, illuminated only by the scarlet umbra of the Adversary of Men, he stole forth. In the night he knew the stream of incoming selks never ceased, and that they continued to arrive with their usual burdens, but the balcony which formed one end of the great hall leading to the rotunda and pillar of tachylite, was clear and cast in shadow. He walked free on the balcony, stretching his muscles, sucking in the brisk clean night air. It was hard to believe that violence and the deception of ages surrounded him.

Molded irsrem defined a doorway between the balcony and the hall, and Flores paused to inspect the latter. The incandescence of the substance exposed a band of selks emerging from the nearest tubes. Flores took out an arrow, placed it in his bow, glanced down. His hand shook. Earlier, the trinket had protected him. Now he realized how much he had depended on the bracelet for his courage.

Not far from the balcony lay the opening to a ramp which he knew led to upper levels less frequented than the hallway, and which offered access to the chamber of the hexcombs. The selks departed and for a moment the hall was empty. He slid inside. Gained the ramp...thus far success. A thudding of wings on air signaled the arrival of more malkops in the hallway behind him, and Flores wiped his brow in relief.

Quickly he turned the corner.

He gripped his forehead, dropping his bow. A malkop jerked, holding and shaking its head. A second stumbled, crushing it.

They focused.

Screeched.

Damn his luck!

Twisting to avoid the swipes of their claws, Flores fell back in headlong retreat, tripping and rolling into the darkened hallway, where the band of selks emerging from the tubes set up a wild hissing. Tossing aside their burdens, they threw themselves in his direction.

Seconds after he had left the balcony, he found himself again on the platform, defending the threshold from an onslaught of the winged creatures, keeping them at bay with his sword and buckler. The suddenness and finality of his reversal attested to the folly of his ambition and his plans. Curse him for the dunce he was! How could he imagine that he could scale the heights of Heaven, and challenge God in his lair? How could he suppose that his puny plans might successfully oppose a civilization, a world, of superior beings? What induced him to think that hasty instructions to a few boatloads of men sufficed to overthrow a mechanism set in motion at the dawn of time?

A selk lurched forward–he ran the creature through. More surged from the corridor and he lopped off limbs and wings, in the gloam barely able to see the results of his mayhem. Several puckered their lips and shot forth ropes of acid as had the malkop Flores had seen butchered by the cannibal plantmen. His buckler took the fluid; his riposte cut their jugulars. Soon the bodies piled so deep they had difficulty approaching, and the creatures paused to drag away their dead. Flores peered past. The shadowy corridor was filling with angry denizens like ants whose nest had been crushed. He began to fear they would come at him from behind, and it was not long before he detected the flapping of wings in the darkness. If they came at him from both directions he was done. Where was the Ven fleet? Where were the Vaw-sa? Had the latter already come and gone, having stolen what they wished? Had Sedrech and Lirsus made their thousand gills? Trained their men to use them? Taken to sea in time? Located the Island? His hopes faded. Impudent fantasies unworthy of a sensible man.

The flapping drew nearer. A horde of hissing malkops took shape in the night, and the masses in the hall surged forward to renew the struggle. Flores calmed and let the training of a lifetime take over. From deep within, the automaton of the Simet cult of violence sprang to life, the last and perhaps the truest element in his soul, and he found he needed no whirlwind, or ozone, to evoke the bloodlust. He saw only gore. What was more appropriate than that the Ritual of Atasan should rule in Atasan's own abode while his moon above imbued the whole with blood? Twirling and slashing he brought down a half dozen more before he felt the first claw rake a thigh. A clutch more he slew. He bounded forward and drove the front rank into their comrades, gutting several in their confusion. A strand of rope touched his arm and burned like fire. Hurriedly he scraped it off with his blade.

The selks surged forward again. Two fell pierced. He glimpsed the reflection of a selk in his shield. Slashed backward. The selk tumbled from the air, bounced off the railing and plunged out of sight, taking a second with it. A blanket of red spread over the balcony. It seeped into the rill and flowed with ever greater force down the drainage pipe.

His sword wove an impenetrable net between him and the malkops, and for a time they paused, having learned to respect his blade, giving Flores a moment to reflect on his encounter, on the strangeness of his end. At some level he relived the legends of the past, when Ven warriors resisted the attacks of the Mok-sa and massacred their gilas. Like gilas, the selks bore the signs of Atasan and with every slice through a fulsome breast or gutting of a female abdomen he chilled, knowing that he both fulfilled the dictates of Vensor, and at the same time committed the ultimate sacrilege against Him by murdering his messengers. And again he wondered how to undo the knot of his emotions, how to straighten what was tangled, make the converse true to order. Not forty-eight hours previous he had been making love to a malkop. Now he was butchering them. How events had turned!

With a tide of hissing and chirping, they pushed forward once more. Again the claws connected. Red streamed down his sides. The blood began to interfere with his footing. He slew several and succeeded in pushing the rest back, but at last Flores felt his arm tire. The selks were not as skillful as Vensor warriors, nor as strong, and fell to his blade more easily than most other opponents he had fought, but their numbers, and the unfamiliarity of their weapons, at last threatened to triumph. Without succor, or respite from their unrelenting assaults, with their disregard for their own death, Flores calculated his last breath was but a moment away.

He slipped.

With hideous cries, the creatures crowded upon him, bursting through the threshold and descending from the sky. Claws ripped off his buckler. Tore his rapier from his grasp. He pulled free his daggers—lost those too. Stunned, he fell, his eyes closing with pain.

He had not forgotten the sounds in the culvert. Now he heard them again.

It was the end.

The end did not come. When he opened his eyes, he found the nearest selks sprawled about him. A whirring shaft buried half its length in the breast of another. Followed by a second. A third. As the creatures recoiled in surprise, he gazed behind him.

A stocky man of dark amphibian features stood with one leg still within the pipe. He brandished a bow and a thick quiver of shafts. While Flores watched he notched several more and with practiced swaths loosed the bolts into the bodies of the malkops. In rapid succession they fell, till the remainder fled into the hallway, or sought the cover of the night.

Macius showed no emotion. He could have been engaged in mere exercise for all that his face showed. His body, however, was in constant movement. Never pausing, he scurried across the balcony scanning the darkness, and whenever a red-tinged wing materialized in the moonlight his arrow unerringly found its heart.

Flores stood. Recovered his weapons and his breath.

"You always knew, didn't you, Macius?"

"I could have employed greater subtlety, I confess. But there was little chance I would find the bracelets without your cooperation. As it was, I failed to complete my quest. I only hope you can complete yours."

"And Fish?"

"Apologies, my chief." Macius shot another bolt into the night. "I believed you dead in the pits and was forced to side with Fish or be stranded with the rest of your crew. I assure you I had no role in your betrayal. It was all I could manage to prevent Fish murdering Isav and the others before we left."

"Our thanks to you–the both of us." Flores smiled. "I freed him. He is even now on the clashing rocks."

"Yes...I saw him two weeks ago."

Flores looked at him in surprise.

"I have been under the domewall these fourteen days. Searching. But they are gone." He glanced inquisitively at Flores. "Why do you not use the bracelets against the selks?"

Flores thought before replying. It was the first time he had heard anyone mention the items. "I haven't any. The last was lost just before I arrived."

Macius nodded. "So I thought. Else you would have no need of my assistance. How...?"

"I commandeered a malkop. Without the bracelet."

The dark man paused. His blank stare communicated total astonishment better than any expression. "And I spent a night swimming in total darkness."

It was Flores' turn to be impressed. "But how did you know they were on the Island?" he continued. "And where did the bracelets come from?"

"You remember the tale of the sailor?"

"Who was none other than yourself..."

"I never finished it."

Flores raised his brows, the better to hear.

"You see, after my boat gained the shore, during the great storm, I entered the cave–the very same entrance through which we later entered with the Vaw-sa–"

"–thus the torch and tinder–"

"I penetrated the caves; found the pits. I was rich! Provided I could avoid the selks and return home with a few choice treasures. But that wasn't all. I climbed the ramp and discovered the orchards and lake. Saw the black tower. Glimpsed the city far above. But I was cautious. Returning to the orchard, I hid to rest and refresh myself with food and drink such as I had seen the selks consume. Then He came."

Flores gazed at him. The selks buzzed angrily in the hallway, replenishing their numbers, massing for what must be a final assault, but for now left them in peace.

"He?"

"Yezd. The Master of the Portal. The bracelets are his. With the bracelets he controls them when he chooses to visit Maalstrom. While I rested in the undergrowth, he arrived on a selk, landing beside me. I watched him practice his illusions. Then he washed himself in the lake, and while doing so removed and washed the items. I saw how he lost control without them and became vulnerable. When he was done, the selk became refractory, and with a curse he replaced the bracelets on his wrists and swore he would make it take him to his castle by the Suma. It obeyed and he flew off unmolested. It was then I conceived my plan–here was a treasure greater than any other!"

"But I found you in the forest..."

"It was a long journey; a quest in itself full of adventures. Eventually I found his castle. Watched for weeks. Saw how he made men into beasts, and, like the selks, controlled them with his bracelets. I slipped among them without his knowing and pretended to be under his spell, but never gave him cause to use his power against me. At last my chance appeared. He retired early; the others were absent; the bracelets unguarded. I slid them into a pocket. Slipped into the courtyard–but I was discovered. His beast-men saw me and I was pursued out the gate and into the guard tower where Yezd confronted me. In the tower he was accustomed to experiment on the selks. One selk remained alive. The bracelets were on an iron ring. As he challenged me, I placed the ring on the leg of the selk and broke the chain that confined it. In his desperation not to lose the bracelets, he sought to seize hold of the creature, and instead fell through the window to the ground while the selk flew away. Yezd departed, doubtless intending to follow the selk to the Island of Vensor to recover his bracelets, and left the beast-men to guard the castle–their former instructions which Yezd could not have changed even had he wished without his bracelets."

"Hence you could not leave, and thus we found you."

"Yes. I assumed the selk would fly to the Island. That had been my intention, and when you arrived I thought it a grand opportunity, sent by Gethos. The gills were all I needed to beat Yezd to the Island and get ashore and obtain the bracelets for myself." Macius glanced at Flores. "But, when the Vaw-sa were in the cave, you instead found them."

"I found one in the clutch of a selk."

"With the remnant of a bag about its neck," added Macius. The dark man glanced up. Cocked his head. "Only one?"

"Only one. Four more turned up in Ven and are now in my safe. My colleague Sendas claimed to have found them in the southern forest on an iron clasp beside the body of a malkop. Apparently the selk chewed off its own foot and died."

"But the pits..."

Flores shrugged. "All corpses end up in the pits. Whether malkop or man. It clutched one bracelet in its hand. That is what I retrieved. Sendas must have taken the rest."

"I stole seven."

Now Flores was puzzled. "Four in my safe–plus one that I found and then lost–that's five." He thought a moment. "Ultem, captain of the guard, who vanished before our gaze!"

"Yezd!"

"Numsenmur's favorite scribe. It was he fashioned the original gills. Now we know why. He wished to continue his journey to Vensor's Isle."

"That's six!"

"And the seventh?"

Both thought deeply but found no answer.

The buzzing swelled. While they had been speaking, the first light of dawn had stolen upon them.

"Macius. If you knew I had not the bracelets, why did you emerge from the culvert and rescue me?"

He shrugged. "It seemed you could use my help."

"Why did you not show yourself earlier?"

"How was I to know it was really you? I last saw you on Vaw, escorted to the palace under guard. None who have been to the Island return from the palace alive." He looked at his companion. "But only you would travel to Hell for a gila–even as you said you would."

Flores nodded. "You should go. This is not your fight."

"Friends do not desert each other in their hour of need." Macius glanced at him. "Besides, what better way to die than with a friend at your side?"

Flores smiled. At last he understood. "And what better time to die than now? My thanks again for the flame and the signs in the grotto. They saved me from the Golden Cyclops and the Doom."

"Flame? I gave no signs. I departed Vaw the very hour I arrived. I saw no way to assist you in your predicament."

"But–"

"Look!" Flores followed Macius' glance and caught his breath. The balcony gave upon the south, and from that direction they now glimpsed a seething and rippling in the waters. A host of white dots reflected the rising suns and glittered as on straining canvas and the wet backs of ocean-going reven-na.

"Ships!"

"They move fast. They are of Vaw."

This explained the selks' long delay. A number of the creatures had separated from the main mass and these now disappeared into adjoining corridors and ramps or plunged into the tubes. Soon they streamed from a hundred apertures and balconies on the southern flank of the domewall. The remainder threw themselves on the two warriors with renewed fury. With Macius defending his back from those who were airborne, Flores struggled to keep those in the hall from breaching the doorway. Again the corpses piled up so that they had to pause to drag away the dead.

"They attack the ships. Such a fleet! The ocean has never seen larger."

Flores gazed down upon the surface of the ocean. The Vaws, advancing on a broad front from the clashing rocks to a point opposite the south-ernmost point of the Island, were turning aside and marking circles. Some drifted aimlessly. One burst into flame. Others followed. From left and right dark clouds gathered. Selks massing to attack. Flores did not know whether to despair or celebrate. He had no love for the Vaw-sa, but without help his own life would soon be over. The clouds darkened. Circled the Vaw fleet, fastened upon them like ill luck. Flores could almost hear the screams of the stricken; see the selks swoop down, snatch them aloft and drop them into the sea. In a short time nothing was left of the huge Vaw fleet but flotsam.

Flores and Macius had no time to discuss the defeat. The selks poured forward with renewed determination and they soon were hard pressed to preserve their lives.

Macius pointed to his quiver. "Almost gone."

"At least the breeze is good." Flores handed him a dagger.

A feint deceived two opponents. Employing his old tactic, he switched his rapier from left to right, and drove forward, murdering both before the remainder adjusted to his new strategy. More white rope struck his buckler. A fragment flung across his chest and sizzled. Macius warded off the selks while Flores scraped his skin clean. Next Macius took some and contorted with pain.

"We cannot last long, my friend."

"I fear you are correct." Macius spun. Opened a red valley in a selk's leg. "It would have been nice to experience the power of the bracelets. But I have seen much in my life. One cannot see everything. Nor wander forever."

"Aye. All lives must end. And all deeds, good or evil, come to nought."

"To the present!"

"And the skill of a warrior!"

With that the hissing returned and a tide of bodies burst upon them. Flores was a scarlet robot of death, whose horn impaled all that approached. Macius shot his last bolt and brained one with the bow. Flores' rapier locked in the torso of a victim and was lost when the selk tumbled over the balcony. He drew his other dagger. Ripped two more. Recoiled at the silent screams.

"Perhaps the worst is not over."

"How, Macius?" Flores' eyes wandered to the horizon.

"It seems we are doomed to die only after witnessing the deaths of all whom we know," added the Vaw. His eyes fixed on the far horizon. "More Vaws..."

Flores stared. "No. Vens!"

On the horizon a new fleet hove into view, on either side of the clashing rocks. The sky had cleared and few malkops remained from the battle with the Vaw-sa. The Vens were somewhat slower than the Vaw fleet, and soon a great mass of them swept from Flores' right and moved quickly to the attack. A repetition of the previous disaster played out before them, except that the Vens, having witnessed the fate of the Vaws, managed to extricate themselves before they were destroyed and took refuge on the beaches of the clashing rocks. Flores watched the dark cumulus re-gather and settle about the isle. Macius exhaled. There was nothing more to say.

The selks pushed forward yet again.

Flores had slashed and killed for so long that he could hardly lift his weapon. Macius strove to keep his eyes free of blood. He broke his dagger and Flores gave him his last. Each was covered with a dozen slashes, every limb burned and blistered. Flores staggered; his eyes dimmed. Friend and foe moved through a mist of red that seemed increasingly unreal and remote, and, as in a dream, he saw his sword arm thrust, glimpsed himself from outside, no longer part of the automaton that propelled and thrust, no longer animating it, but watching from a distance with the detachment of a spectator. Time ceased. Lost all meaning. The struggle on the balcony became remote and irrelevant and he found his gaze wandering skyward unable to summon any interest in the fate of the doomed warriors throwing their lives away in a frenzy of destruction. The fate of three men mattered not a whit to...three? No, not three, but four...then five. Then a dozen.

The air split like lightning.

Flores stood in the hallway of Ra'Allah, panting over the butchered remains of a malkop, its claws still buried in his forearm. A familiar face restrained him with arms covered with glass armor. "My King! Cease fighting! No need to continue! You expose yourself needlessly!"

Flores blinked in surprise. Lirsus of the Serclaslers stood beside him, sword in hand. On either side two dozen Ven soldiers loosed arrows into the selks, driving them back. Several men lay dead–more took their place. The Turlicum sat heavily and stared until his breath ceased coming in hard wheezes. His eyes questioned Lirsus.

"We made half the distance before the malkops came," said the youth. "Enough time to send two thousand men with gills into the water before our ships were forced to return to the clashing rocks. My men penetrated the caves, climbed the ramp. Half under Sedrech made for the pillar. My half are emerging now from the culvert; we found other culverts besides; some are ascending those. The malkops cannot stop us. Your instructions, Sire, were flawless–as was the work of our scribes in Ven. The discovery of the caves, and the corpses..." A hard look settled on Lirsus, "violates all that the oracle teaches us. The men wish to destroy all they see."

Flores stood. But one thought occupied his mind. He forced his muscles to submit. "Fight through to the pillar and take the ramp. That will help Sedrech. See these tubes? Guard them and block them well or the malkops will surprise us from behind. And give me twenty men with bows. And a bow and quiver for me. I wish to find the chamber of the hexcombs."

With the men following, Flores set out at a run. After a month of forced delays, of imposed postponements, not even the punishment of his long struggle on the balcony could make him delay the fulfillment of his goal a moment longer. Twice he was ambushed by enraged selks. Each time he paused for a brief, bloody engagement until the way was cleared. Finally, cutting down a last pair of spitting hellions, he burst into the chamber of the hexcombs. Only five archers remained.

Empty.

Whether the selks had all left to join the battle, or had purposely evacuated the chamber for some other reason, he couldn't say. Repeated calls for any prisoner to show himself or herself, that they would be protected during their descent by the arrows of the archers, yielded nothing, and finally Flores departed heavy-hearted. Listlessly he led them back to the central pillar. The ramp came into view.

Flores sucked his breath.

He took off at a run leaving his men with surprised expressions and, upon arriving at the ramp, sped up the spiral in pursuit of some object. No selks appeared and at last he stood on the upmost level of the city in the same plaza that had witnessed the murder of the Vaw cutthroat while he had skulked behind a crowd of malkops, protected by the bracelet. To his right the Eye now rested level with the wall of tachylite.

No selks stood upon the plaza. However, in the center stood–Amina, struggling, like Flores, to catch her breath after climbing the ramp. She was clothed precisely as he remembered, in enveloping dark cassock, which did nothing to mar his memory of the glories beneath, and thick veil covering her face.

He advanced.

She stepped back.

"Amina! My love! I have traveled over half the globe to save you! You need have no fear. Have they imprisoned you for so long that you no longer wish to be free?" He advanced again. "Let me embrace you and you will soon forget all that has happened!"

He became aware of a soft hissing and clicking, and paused. A host of selks emerged from all about. They surrounded him. Lost or too slow, his own men had failed to appear, and he realized that the numbers of the enemy were too great to vanquish, but the image of his love squarely before him, after so long a period of absence, bolted him to the spot and made him dismiss any thought of retreat.

The sunlight faded. Amina grew scales and turned green.

Atasan.

In shock Flores stepped back.

Ommatidia inscrutable as ever, wings gold with transluced sunlight, the creature stepped closer, brushing aside several selks that sought to protect him from the intruder. A loud buzz sounded.

"*Adamulbuyutlimathaantahunahlimathataqtulumala'iky?*" A minute passed. The mandibles clicked. "Earth-bound-of-dwellings why make See-Face-of-God converse false to order why kill al-mala'ik?" Three seconds passed–much less than on the previous occasion which Flores had witnessed–and the voice resumed smooth, resonant. "Child of Vensor. Why do you disturb the peace of the Hive? The sight of the Eye? Were you not content dwelling in your earth-bound city? Why do you kill my angels? Are you not aware that they are essential to Maalstrom?"

All the anger and frustration of a month–a year–of exile and violence and growing disenchantment with everything that Atasan was and represented boiled to the surface at once. Flores spat venomously. "I don't know what you are, or why you act thus, but I am aware that you live only to prey on my city! As your slaves prey on all Maalstrom! I have come here to put an end to your rule and to kill all those who would stop me."

The rumbling in Atasan's chest deepened. His tone grew sharp. "Then you do not want the woman? On your previous visit, you would not rest until you found her."

Flores swallowed. "You...saw me?"

"You stood there," a clawed hand pointed, "beside the containing wall, a little behind my subjects. Apparently you believed that because your toy made you invisible to them, it made you invisible to me."

A chill crawled up his spine. Atasan saw through the illusions!

"Oh, yes! I saw your bracelet. When the execution of the other intruder did not deter you, I allowed you to see the gila." The green head moved. "If I had known you were spying and intended to invade my home, I would have killed you outright. I do not allow wingless ones to violate the serenity of the Hive." The voice buzzed like a motor building strength.

Flores raised his blade. Suddenly a barrage of arrows showered the selks, throwing them into confusion, and Flores lunged at Atasan. The ramp disgorged a hundred Ven warriors, Sedrech at their head. To Flores' surprise, Atasan turned and ran. Flores flung himself in pursuit. The creature made for the Eye and, before Flores could overtake him, plunged within, disappearing instantly from view, several shafts clattering harmlessly off the surface of the glass.

At the edge, Flores hesitated. He glanced down the shaft. It plunged a minimum of half a mile. He suspected its depths went much deeper. Indeed if legend be true it literally had no depth, but penetrated to the planet's core–and beyond. Five feet distant, the multi-faceted face of the Eye gleamed. No portal was visible.

Flores closed his eyes and leaped.

He blinked. He was in a glittering tunnel. The translucent hexagons that formed its walls replicated in all directions, making it difficult to ascertain in which direction the path lay. Like a hall of mirrors, or more precisely windows, the glass tricked and deceived with every step. Flores pushed forward. He halted in surprise. The entire globe had shifted in response to his step, instantly and without warning. His hand felt cold glass. Blocked. He decided to test another direction. The Eye flipped ninety degrees and pitched him on his face. He stood and shook himself. Somewhere far ahead, refracted through a dozen panes, the dark mote of Atasan shrank.

Flores swore. How could he penetrate the maze? He could not break it. Irsrem was indestructible. He could not proceed. With every step the ground lurched as from an earthquake. Dare he go back? He turned and discovered that the gyrations of the sphere had confused that as well, the exit being already lost. His hopes again faded. If the answer to Amina's location, and Atasan's manipulations were to be found, they would be at the center of the maze; in the very Eye of God. He had no choice but to persevere. If only he were an insect like Atasan! Then he could crawl about the walls and let instinct take over.

He snapped his fingers. Perhaps that was the answer! The sphere was not moving in response to his steps, but he was walking along the walls, the change in perception making it seem that the Eye, rather than he, had shifted. An instantaneous change in gravity reinforced this delusion. He breathed easier. Suddenly his mind flew back to another sphere of hexes, in another chamber in a distant city and the tripod that he would often sit upon, his hands upon the sphere of the leroo hornet nest. He had often practiced thus, closing his eyes and letting his mind penetrate to the interior.

Now, here in the Eye he shut his eyelids again, and placed his hands on the sides of the tunnel and let the images flood into him. Hexagons enveloped, beckoning, blocking, opening, closing about him as he sought the inmost chamber. The obscure tug began and suddenly he saw the exact route to the center. He reopened his eyes. Recklessly he launched himself on the path, anticipating the bewildering shifts and jerks of the sphere, avoiding what he knew were cul-de-sacs until, with drawn sword, he sprang through the last hexagon.

He paused before the latest conundrum. He stood at the bottom of a spherical chamber, with every step remaining always at the bottom, the peculiar forces in the Eye creating the illusion that it was the Eye that moved, and not him. In the center, suspended in air as it were, was Atasan. The Adversary stared down at him, its legs and arms folded as in meditation. His body was not at rest, however, but moved and crawled with life. A closer glance revealed a blanket of green and red hornets on his greenish scales. More flew about the chamber, avoiding Flores–for the moment.

Flores looked closer at the hexagons that composed the structure. They opened not upon the interior of the sphere as he had expected, but upon natural scenes and landscapes. He glimpsed plains and forests, seas and snow-drenched vistas, Ra'Allah and Vensor cities, the clashing rocks and the plaza outside the Eye. One scene in particular drew his gaze: a vast movement of Vensor soldiers with many men hunched like beasts and at their center a caravan of bloated things in huge wagons drawn by teams of lyarts. The gates of Ven were opening before them. His hackles rose. What was happening in Ven during this, his second absence? What powers had been loosed on Maalstrom that could disrupt it so? Other windows disturbed him almost as much. In some he glimpsed alien land-scapes that could exist nowhere on Maalstrom. Bizarre animals; novel machinery; strange cities; stranger people; and selks flying among them in the dead of night in secret. In one, an immense crowd circled an iron rock. In another, they whispered in the ears of priests who wrote franti-cally. He shook his head in confusion–each time he thought he under-stood the gnosis, the code that unlocked the secrets of Maalstrom, something new tore his conception to pieces.

"Do you have your trinket with you, Dweller in cities? Do you not wish to use it?"

Flores thought that if Atasan could smile, he would have done so.

"It is gone."

"Not gone. You have lost it to another. With the consequences you see. But it would do you no good. The bracelets do not work in here. Not in the presence of the greatest bracelet of all. This sphere–the Eye."

Flores lowered his rapier. Raised the bow and notched an arrow. "I need no bauble to bring an end to your life. A single arrow will do." Flores nodded. "Yes, I know that you are mortal, despite your tales and deceit. You can die like me. This is your end, Atasan. You have nowhere else to run."

The voice buzzed. "And why do you wish this?"

Flores blinked. Set firm his shoulders. "I sicken of your exploitation. Your predation on my city and people. We no longer need Atasan–nor malkops–nor Vensor Himself. All lies! Temples, queens, priests, prostitutes, the whole elaborate structure that you and your selks have foisted on Maalstrom since the dawn of time! It must go! Do you hear me, Atasan! We are no longer the children of Vensor, but Men! God is dead! And you must follow!"

Laughter reverberated through the chamber. Flores wondered from what arcane source Atasan's algebra of translation had evoked it.

"Since the dawn of time...and now here you come, a mere thing that breathes, claiming to know the secrets of the Universe. But you cannot know."

"I know you are First among Liars! You may have tricked the priestesses of the temples, but I know that you are nothing more than an insect that lives by depositing its eggs in the bodies of our females, causing them to become huge and bloated, allowing them to produce children for the cities only so long as they also produce your children for you! I know your species feeds off ours! That we men live out our lives in ignorance, never knowing that we exist for your pleasure, serving you and your kind. Even our queens and their priestesses unknowingly serve you!"

The laugh returned. "I, a separate species, feeding off Maalstrom! So the entire world serves Atasan!" In response to his emotion, the windows of the chamber blurred and a rainbow of colors rippled through the glass, the waves and colors creating a kaleidoscope with Atasan at the center. "And you would set it straight, make the converse true to order, by killing me?"

Flores took aim.

"You may attempt it. I will resist. But if you succeed, you will destroy not only me, but yourself, in fact all of Maalstrom." Scorn rendered the glass pink. Its shades flew across Flores like shades on a cuttlefish. He hesitated.

"Dweller!" The ripples turned to scarlet. "Is it possible that you still have not understood any of what you have seen? Look about you! At my subjects that you have slain with such relish! A different species? Nay, Dweller–they are your very flesh and blood! Learn now that I do not plant eggs inside Vensor queens! I do not fertilize Makers-of-Life!" Atasan's emotions heightened and the rainbow waves slipped past so swiftly that Flores grew dizzy from their alternation. "I do the opposite! I *unfertilize* half the eggs the Makers produce, by transforming the females into selks, who are sterile and thus shall never give birth! My act turns potential gilas into images of me."

Flores frowned. "Do you also kidnap gilas then? To live here with you for your lustful purposes?"

"Kidnap? And why should I desire gilas? I have no use for wingless children, and am not inclined to support the vast appetites of my many wives in their temples. Look around you. See the vast hordes of selks that have been summoned and are even now gathering from all corners of Maalstrom. They are your sisters. By creating them, I allow you life. By bringing them here, I civilize you. I save all of you from yourselves. Without me your people would soon return to their ancient barbarous ways, burying female infants in the sand. Before I was, every Vensor female gave birth at will, and the world groaned beneath the weight of their progeny. Now, only a few are allowed to reproduce, and I watch over their health and their happiness, and grant their female offspring a long and glorious life in the Hive, for which all Vensor cities serve as nurseries, while the males live out their lives as they please, feeding their Temples, and by their incessant warfare keep their own numbers in check, on occasion supplying the one male required to father the next millennium. Without my service, every selk you see would be another queen, reproducing as do all animals, giving birth to a million other queens who in turn would spawn millions more with no thought for the consequences, and your numbers would soon overrun not only Maalstrom–but the Universe. As it did long ago, before I was. Before I began my task. I do not create life–I uncreate it! I brake the heedless rush to fecundity that characterizes Womankind everywhere. Do you not see? Woman brings Chaos by creating. I impose Order on that Chaos by uncreating. I do not interrupt Nature. I preserve it. Without me, there is no future. I preserve it for all."

Flores lowered his bow. Slowly he replaced the arrow in its quiver.

Atasan continued. "Now do not anger me. I am not angry yet. If I permit rage to possess me while within the Eye, storms would sweep Maal-strom and cause the world itself to crack. The Eye controls all. Sees all. Bridges all."

"The woman in the cell. The one I spoke with. Did you..."

"I take only queens as my mates. The woman you saw is not yet fertile so doesn't interest me. Weeks ago I had my angels take her to the Land of Gilas–where many gilas live and where she must have come from by mistake. Perhaps you should search there. Now depart. I will not inter-fere with your ships if they remove your warriors. But I tolerate no city dwellers in the Hive. Because they cannot control their emotions the Eye is dangerous in their hands–as your trinkets are dangerous for you. Now go. Your gila is not here. And my servants will soon reclaim every inch of my city and kill all who remain. Not even I could stop them, and I do not wish to."

A minute passed and Flores stood outside the Eye watching it lower into the Abyss. The selks continued to throw themselves at his men with-out pause. The sky, now passing into afternoon, grew black with their numbers, and it became apparent that their attacks would continue until no trespassers remained to oppose them. Flores ordered a retreat back to the caves.

From there they summoned the fleet and embarked. True to Atasan's word, the selks refrained from attacking the ships, and by nightfall the Vens were long at sea, far removed from the Island of the Sun-God.

Flores pondered what he had learned. Can a mortal comprehend the plans of the gods? The structure of the Universe? He nodded. There is no limit, no truth. In fact, one can never arrive at the end, because there is none, but the Universe replicates endlessly as fast as one comprehends it, like a web that spins from itself, with ever more complexity awaiting, the final solution hovering forever just beyond one's grasp. He sighed. His quest had left his life in tatters. It seemed that if you grasp the world, you lose yourself; and if you strive to know yourself, the world must then forever evade your grasp.

CHAPTER 25

KING KOT

Stalkin rubbed his leg. New scars had been added to those caused by hot glass. A falling mast, brought down by selks pulling on the mainsheet, had ripped him with its splinters. He wasn't angry. He had not expected to come through unscathed. It was disappointment he mostly felt. His lip curled with disgust. Despite all their effort, all their planning, the weeks of bribery, cajoling, threats, and the boredom, not to mention nausea, of the days at sea–they had returned with nothing. The crusade had failed.

His companions had also suffered. He looked at the Overseer, whose stubby legs negotiated the esplanade, stumbling over the multitude of wounded they had rescued from the waves. Fish had wanted to leave them. Stalkin was careful to keep well clear of the Overseer's reach– when Numtal met them at the dock, he greeted his assistant with the usual clenched fist to the jaw, then punched several more injured Vawsa too slow to make way. The reception Fish would likely receive upon confronting the King made his mood even worse.

Stalkin lifted each injured man. Whispered in his ear. They each nodded and a growing knot surrounded them as they followed the Overseer to the palace. Mens brought up the rear. The glass-smith did not know what he would say to Kot. Being the King's representative, and the nominal head of the expedition, the vizier's responsibility was greatest. Mens, however, seemed undisturbed by events, and walked steadily, gazing into the distance as was his habit. Stalkin would be glad to leave the talking to him and to Fish. He preferred the rapiers of his companions.

The battered facade of Kot's palace took shape, bright in the morning rays, even more deteriorated than when they had left, if that were possible. The grounds were deserted. The estate had been thrown into confusion by the defeat so that the usual squad of warriors attending the gate was absent, and the returning members of the expedition entered without challenge, a stream of the curious filtering after.

They made their way to the throne room.

The far side came to life.

"What is happening? What? What?" Kot rubbed sleepy eyes. "Would you have me freeze my bottom? Where is my cushion?" He settled onto his rickety chair, and, amid creaking wood, inspected the audience with his one good eye. A horrid cough wracked his body.

"Well, Squawk? Mens?" He squinted. "I see from your faces that the worst has happened. It is as I feared, is it not? Well, what have you to say?" Without waiting for an answer, Kot took a salver from a servant and began cracking sticks.

Fish took a deep breath. "Sire, the number of the selks were as the birds of the sky–"

"Eh?"

"I said the selks–"

"The pelts?"

"–were as the birds–"

"Words? Of course we speak words!"

"–of the sky!"

"Didn't try? Well, if you don't try, you won't gain anything. Anyone can tell you that."

Fish raised his arms. "And our allies, Sire! Abandoned us during the battle! Fled like cowards."

"Who lied?"

"Allies!"

"Oh, realize! Yes, I realize you didn't try. But how can we communicate if you don't use words?" An assistant offered a horn. He stopped him with a palm. "No need. I'm not deaf, you know."

"Sire, I said–"

"Fed?"

"–that–"

"Eh?" Snap!

"Sire, your sticks!"

He shook his finger. "I can listen and crack sticks at the same time. Can't afford to waste time, not like the rest of my spoiled lazy subjects. And especially now that you have returned empty-handed! Now, you were saying?"

Crack!

"I said the cowards abandoned us!"

"Abandoned you? And well they should since you mumble so! Who has the patience to listen, if you won't use words?"

Like a vanquished general vailing his flag for the last time, Fish lowered his arms.

"Oh, enough of this nonsense," said Kot, "I wish to know why you wasted my time and money. I can see you didn't bring anything of value back with you. Well? Whose fault was it?"

Fish looked at Mens.

Mens looked back.

The Overseer's eye roved to Numtal. The rest of the crowd continued to stare at Fish.

The Eye impaled him. "Come here, Squawk."

Fish attempted to swallow, and had he possessed a throat doubtless would have done so. He stepped to the throne.

Producing a fly-swatter, Kot smacked him across the face.

The audience gasped.

A rainbow of colors exploded, imparting to Fish's visage a dark welter of hues as if he had just been hammered with clubs, beauteous as a putrid growth that had never seen the light. For a moment the colors receded and Fish seemed to return to normal. Then the colors returned–the audience held its breath. A terrific struggle ensued, every bit as momentous and hard-fought as that which the fleet had just waged, blotches appearing and disappearing in time with the evanescent dominance of rage and fear as the two emotions vied for control of his blubbery ichthian soul.

He stopped breathing. Like buttons about to pop his eyes bulged. He turned and stared pleadingly at Mens and Stalkin.

"Aaack!"

A puff of smoke blew out his ear. Fish fell on his back and lay motionless, eyes staring like glass.

The audience gasped again. Crowding round, they ringed the body. Newcomers continued to filter in till the throne room was jammed.

"I get his rings! Since he is an employee of the state, all his property belongs to me!" Kot peered at the corpse. "I wonder...what is the price of soap today?" The eye wandered to the other author of the city's disaster. "And you? What have you to say?"

Mens lowered his gaze. "Only this." He motioned to a clot of burly sailors who produced two bales of soiled clothing and a bundle of branches freshly cut from a tree.

The vizier bowed. "With my regards, O King."

The royal jaw dropped. A smile spread across Kot's face. "Yes!" He rocked with glee. "Good Mens! I knew you would not fail me. Squawk did say something about pelts. And here they are!" Mens smiled. "You shall be rewarded generously for this! The expedition was a success after all!"

This was too much for Stalkin. He had been peering into siderooms, searching for armed guards, and now, finding none, he pushed forward. His lip curled in his best sneer. "Good Mens. I knew you would not fail me, he says." His voice reeked sarcasm. "Is that our answer?" He swiveled to face the others. "Is this all our King has to say? Thank you, Mens? We have lost the entire fleet of Vaw and sent much of the city's treasure to the bottom, and you have nothing more to say?"

"Eh? What does yon vagabond say?" Kot motioned for his hearing horn.

Stalkin gestured. "How can we accept this? Our beloved Fish is dead! Our comrades too! And all because this fool of a king–never properly elevated to the ninety-ninth level anyway–refused to equip the expedition as he should but sent us in with too few arrows! Now he blames us, murders our leaders before our eyes, and insults us all by taking twigs as his reward, as if that justifies all his failures!" Stalkin drew his sword. "Vaw-sa! Are we to accept this for our government here in our own sacred city? There is no one to stop us from driving this madman from the throne! His soldiers are gone! We now rule the palace!"

The men roared agreement. Forward they surged and raised the throne into the air with Kot seated in it.

"Eh? You'll have to speak up! There's a draft in here!"

They spun it around.

"Into the cold, the king is too old!" The crowd made for the door with Kot and the throne on their shoulders.

"Sold? No, my throne has not been sold! Give it back at once."

Horrified servants attempted to intervene but under the threat of drawn rapiers soon fell to singing revolutionary songs. The mob passed him once around then pitched the chair, king and all, into a crush in the middle of the room.

Stalkin put one foot on Kot's chest. He laughed. "What shall we do with him? Mens, what do you suggest?"

The vizier–former vizier–looked worried. He seemed about to speak when a strangled cough burst from next the dais.

"Fish!"

The Overseer sat up. "Aaaack!" He spat blood. Shook his head. A second passed and his gaze fell on Kot beneath Stalkin's foot, surrounded by the mob of armed sailors. A wicked grin appeared.

Kot smiled weakly. "Does my Overseer wish...a raise?"

The lips writhed like a plateful of eels. "I am no longer your Overseer. My name is–" The beady eyes loomed. "–*FISH!*" The jaws opened to expose a cavernous interior and double rows of razor-edged teeth.

The crowd roared. Scooping Kot up they paraded him about the room.

"What do we do with him?"

"Out in the cold! Let him wander and beg like the worst of us!"

"A fitting end for a miser who never had a spare coin for the poor!"

"Yes! Let him starve in the street. Let him beg for his daily bread and learn what it is like to do without!"

Kot paled and began to struggle. "No! You can't mean it! Why I'm the King!"

Laughter answered, dimmed as the crowd carried him out the door.

Fish shook himself. Seeing the motley band of hard-eyed men clustered around Stalkin, he opened his arms. "Old friend!" He embraced him. "Can you believe it? No one even came to his aid! A bloodless coup." Their eyes grew crafty together. "We must form a conclave–a cabal–at once."

The visionary suddenly stood by their side. "It is done. It is us." Though a foot shorter, Mens seemed to stare down at them. "First order of business. We must purge all unbelievers."

They returned puzzled stares.

"There can be only one cabal in Vaw," Mens continued.

Fish and Stalkin nodded with sudden comprehension.

"They must swear allegiance to the new god. And to us–His representatives on Maalstrom."

"New god?"

"Yes. Vensed. The rightful god of our world. And join the Order of the Golden Cyclops, which shall henceforth worship Vensed."

They slowly nodded, still not sure they understood.

"Second: we must reward the faithful."

Sudden gleams appeared.

"Of course!"

"Provided they do our bidding. They must assume the places deserted by Kot's former guards in front of the palace." Mens turned to the surrounding ruffians. "Stop all from entering the palace but us and our messengers. The secret password is... 'heretic'. You and you: search all the rooms of the palace and bring all you find to us here in the throne-room. Which is now to be called the 'Hall of Revolutionary Justice.' You three:

visit the docks, the reven-na stables, the customs house. One of you will control and supervise each for the new regime. Numtal: you have been the keeper of the king's keys; you shall be in charge of the buro of taxes."

No one moved.

"And all soldiers of the Revolution will be paid at the end of the day—in cash, at a rate double what they formerly earned."

"Hurrah!" the ruffians cheered and left to do Mens' bidding. Soon the three cabalists stood alone in the chamber. Fish and Stalkin stared in amazement.

Mens breathed deeply. "It is Year One of the New Order." With a look of purest serenity, he resumed staring into the distance. The object of his attention had moved closer.

Fish glanced around. "Good Mens. How are we to pay them? Their allegiance will fall away if we fail to provide them with what we promised."

"Yes. For that, we must return to the Island of Vensor."

Their eyes grew fearful.

"Which means the navy. We must assume personal command over the ships in the harbor and direct the outfitting of a new expedition. This time there shall be no failure. And until we obtain the money—we shall have to use force."

He exited the room. In the lobby were a dozen former members of the palace guard, now under arrest by several of the rabble.

"Release them!"

Mens approached. Handed them back their weapons. "You are now the personal guard of us three—the Committee of Public Safety. You shall follow our orders without question. We hereby place you in command of the new revolutionary army."

"Hurrah!" The soldiers, elated at their sudden reversal of fortune, swaggered, ready to do their bidding.

The following morning Mens, Fish, and Stalkin arrived at the esplanade. The harbor was littered with damaged and half-sunken ships, and floating bodies of reven-na driven to death by the hasty return of the expedition. The populace was sullen.

"It seems, Mens, that the city does not agree with your exactions."

The vizier gazed into the distance. "No matter. They will obey."

The coterie of guardsmen that had accompanied them removed another dozen workers for personal inspection. Every item of wealth and every weapon discovered upon their bodies was confiscated post-haste. The stevedores, seeing that the new regime was not much different from the former one, fell into their former ways, directing resentful glances at their new masters while they beached the ships for repair. The extension of the interrogations to the blocks of tenements adjoining the littoral did not improve their attitude.

"The Revolution must have money. The War must have weapons."

Stalkin shrugged. He counted askance the swords of his own personal guard. As long as they equaled those of Mens and Fish, he was content.

A loud discussion arose from the dock. "What? You would hide a coin from your benefactors, the Commitee of Public Welfare?" Fish roared in the face of an intimidated worker. "We know how to deal with hoarders!" The soldiers seized and commenced to beat him. Fish returned to his companions, leaving Numtal to continue the extortion.

He confronted the new leader of the city. "Mens! We find little. These fools either have no money or they have hidden it all. Someone must have tipped them off to our plans." The Overseer—now Triumvir in charge of Police—stared with confusion and disgust.

The chin shifted. "It is not important."

"Not important, man? How can we run the city? How can we raise a new fleet? Or repair the old one?"

"Ideas, Overseer. Will. That is how we shall attain our goals. Not by mere money."

Fish shrugged. "I fail to see how hot air will help. The kings of Ud and Spelf are in a rage. They expect us to make good their losses."

"They will bear it. And once we complete our repairs they will again join us. The logic of the moment will persuade them. Enthusiasm among the masses can no more be resisted than can the tide. Not even by kings."

A cry went up from the city. Soldiers emerged from the streets leading up to the palace. Several ran to Mens and pointed seaward.

White smudges had appeared. They swelled rapidly.

"Vens!" said Stalkin.

"Yes," added Fish. He tried to put on a brave face, but twitched nervously. "They must come to revenge themselves on us for the death of their leader, whom we flung to the Cyclops."

Stalkin drew his double-pronged sword. Looked to the remaining member of the regime. "What do we do?"

Mens rubbed his chin. Turned to the squad of soldiers that enforced his will in the city. "Flee to the crater! Offer no resistance till the Vens have occupied the City. There we shall make our plans."

His partners were stunned. Before they could intercede, the soldiers were running through the crowd shouting the new instructions at the top of their lungs. Panic swept Vaw.

⪼ ಐ ಚ ⪻

Flores stood beneath the overarching totem of Gethos. Blue paint flecked his fingers. He examined it. All idols tarnish, he reflected. Truth ever disappoints the romantic. Just as facts spell doom for the credulous and the believers in life's illusions. The lines around his eyes–always deep and warped by pain–now betrayed loneliness. He had become an outsider. An unbeliever, a skeptic, an apostate. Although his clansmen and subjects who followed him to the Island had discarded their former deference for the selks, they would never be as he, never possess his knowledge of the whole. Never again could he be carefree in the presence of others. Wear his motives and deeds on his sleeve. Atasan had won. In the end was nought but muscle and sword, and, like Atasan, with those he now prepared to pursue his dreams.

Vaw opened to embrace the violator. His ships, taking advantage of a contrary wind, rode briskly into the harbor and the few boats the natives could muster were quickly boarded, the Ven ships running onto the beach to release their warriors. The attack was swift. Those Vaw-sa who opposed them were surprised and poorly armed, and Flores' men dispersed them into the maze of surrounding flats.

The Turlicum strode among the dead. Oblivious to the occasional arrow that sniped from the tenements, he searched for a certain yellow cap, and a wizened man with a golden medallion. The corpses were few. None were high in rank in the Order.

"One hundred, Sedrech. Half archers, to follow." He set off immediately, knowing his orders would be obeyed.

Thirty minutes passed and Flores stood before the palace ringed by Ven warriors. On the far side of the narrow terrace the Vaw-sa massed, having placed themselves between the invaders and the heart of the city, their Temple. Flores sniffed. It was his enemies he wanted–not Vaw. He had no desire to provoke the city further than necessary by molesting what was most sacred to them. The palace, however, was another matter. He flung his hand and the Vens penetrated the edifice.

After a month at sea, and unparalleled dangers, he stood again in the throne room of Kot, the chamber that had witnessed his former humiliation. Now it was his. Ven soldiers ripped out the walls searching for secret rooms and exits. None were found. Strangely, the throne of the king lay already smashed in the center of the room, the tray on which Kot had habitually stripped his twigs lying bent. What had transpired? Warriors returned with several Vaw-sa in the livery of palace lackeys.

"Do not tremble so." Flores spoke calmly. "Do you remember me?"

One peered. "Yes...but that is impossible! You died the Doom, and none who die the Doom return to the land of the living!"

"I have not only returned from the place of your execution, but from Heaven itself. I have seen the Nether side of the Veil and bring word that the end has come to you and your city." They cringed. "Unless you produce whom I seek."

They exchanged glances. "We surmise that we know whom you mean."

He nodded. "Where are they?"

"Our King was deposed! The mob drove Kot into the street like a dog, with whips and stones." The servants placed their hands over their eyes. "If he is not yet dead in some filthy gutter, he soon will be. Our Master's grief alone will be sufficient to kill him!"

Flores reflected on this. Another strange fate which he felt in the end was undeserved.

"And our new masters..." they continued.

Flores came out of his reverie. "Yes?"

"Fish and Stalkin...entered the corridor behind us, which leads into the interior of the palace. Warriors accompanied them."

"Their goal?"

One shrugged. "I heard something about mir. And the need for dispatch."

꙾ ଞ ଓ ꙾

Ten meters below, a torch fluttered in a tunnel, and faltered. A massive fist drove into the neck of its owner and seized the brand from his grasp. Fish's visage writhed. For an instant the puffy landscape resembled more the face of a worm-ridden corpse than that of a child of Vensor. "Disappoint me once more and I shall extinguish you like this flame."

Numtal whimpered and cast a sidelong glance at Stalkin. The smithy ignored him and inspected his bow.

At a signal from Fish, the band resumed its headlong pace, descending into the earth, where wind from the mysterious depths ahead whipped their hair.

"Why did he tarry?" asked the Overseer. "Does he not wish his share?"

Stalkin shrugged. "Perhaps he has reservations about pilfering his former employer."

The snake-lips smacked. "Empty-headed nonsense. Like his hot air. Gold and gems are worth more than all the talk of all the philosophers on Maalstrom. After a mere day and a half his empire falls. As it should, being the creation of a mere bleater of sounds." Fish wheezed as they mounted a rise in the tunnel.

The party stumbled to a halt.

"Mens! We had thought you fled to Craterside. Neartown is occupied by the Vens–and the palace as well." Fish glanced behind. "Their boots will be sounding behind us soon."

The bleater spoke. "Did you not comprehend what I said upon the esplanade?"

Snorts answered. "We understood! You advised us to abandon the City and the palace, until the barbarians attack the Sacred Spring, then to rally the People behind us and drive them into the sea. What a plan! Surrender all without a struggle, then take it back at a cost of much life! You sophists are all alike. It is no wonder that Kot threw you out. Your brain is addled!"

Fish attempted to push past, and Mens put a hand upon his shoulder. "The problem is the hostility of our subjects. The solution is for them to perceive a threat from foreigners. The result will be perfect loyalty to us. If we take refuge in the crater we may then counterattack."

"Away, tangle-tongue!" Fish flung the hand contemptuously. "I have no more time for your schemes. They are not worth a single gold nugget."

Stalkin smirked, "Or the attentions of a single lovely eunuch."

"Indeed. Not when Kot's treasure room awaits!"

"Treasure room?" queried Mens.

"Kot's secret hoard! Locked in storage!" Fish rubbed his stubby palms together gleefully. "We all know of it! Think! The hoard of the Miser himself–stolen from every city of the southern sea, and including our own recent tribute–guarded by guards and lackeys who themselves are never allowed to glimpse what they protect."

At a sign from Fish, Numtal reached into a pocket.

"The key!"

"Think of the opportunity!" joined Stalkin. "Never before has such a treasure lay for the taking. Do you imagine we will leave it for these foul Vens? Why sail all the way to Vensor's isle when the same lies but a few feet from us here in Vaw?" The smithy drew his double-pronged snake sword. "Now that you have delivered the city to the enemy, we have nought to do but think of ourselves. It is time to make up for the years of our neglect, the time we spent laboring for others instead of enriching our own coffers."

"Indeed!" grunted Fish. "Now—out of our way!"

They thrust Mens aside.

Far from angry, Mens looked puzzled. "But to possess trinkets without power, when you can have both trinkets and power is nonsensical! What is the use of mere trinkets when it is ideas that rule? Did you not understand the ideas behind my strategy?"

"Nonsensical? Ideas?" Stalkin laughed. "Hot air again! With gold we shall have all we need."

"Yes!" called Fish. "Palaces and food!"

"Slaves and eunuchs! And even—" Stalkin peered askance, "—gilas!"

"So you are adamant. You will not desist from your purpose."

"Absolutely!"

"Then I can do nought to help you."

"*You?* Help *us?* That's funny. You and your notions. First your expedition is sunk—then you throw the City into a panic—now you would have us abandon Kot's treasure as well! What else can we expect from you? We have learned. Away, now! You have delayed us long enough."

Fish attempted to push past. Another hand was laid on his arm.

"Overseer. Listen to Mens."

Incredulous, Fish turned a bulging eye on Numtal and drilled his scorned assistant with as hard-eyed a stare as he could muster. "You, scum, dare to contradict your betters?"

The gaunt man shrank back. Fish flung off the offending appendage with such force that Numtal cried out.

"But Overseer, if Mens is right, we throw away what is most important!"

A subtle signal passed from Fish to Stalkin. A signal the latter had seen before.

Numtal continued, overcoming a lifetime of reticence. "Why indeed should we pursue a few trinkets when the means to control the City is at hand? Overseer, I have served you faithfully for a decade. You have made me do many deeds that I did not wish to do. It was I responsible for much that gave you credit; my mind, my work that was largely responsible for your own success before the throne. Now I say that you should listen to me once more. An opportunity such as this may not come again!"

"Keep silent!" The fist raised to repeat its work, but surprisingly its owner calmed and let it fall to his side. "We shall discuss this later. For now, we have no time. We must remove Kot's valuables before the Vens arrive. And you must open the gate to the treasury."

Leaving Mens, the band pushed ahead. The way wound to either side, eventually debouching into an underground grotto whose rough stone had been carved out to create an anteroom of moderate size. Several large iron doors bound with locks bordered the far wall.

"Numtal, is this door the entrance to the treasury?"

"Yes, Overseer." He pointed to the one on the right.

"But you yourself have never seen Kot's treasure?"

"No, chieftain," said Numtal, fingering his newest bruise. "The King never permitted any to see, but guarded his secrets most jealously."

"And of course he never brought any treasure forth, but only added to it." Stalkin and Fish exchanged blissful glances. "The better for us!"

"And the other entrances?"

"They are never opened by anyone but Kot. He never permitted it. These are his most secret chambers, his refuge from the world, and therefore far removed from its influences."

Numtal inserted the key and the lock popped.

The hinges creaked.

Turning to Stalkin, Fish repeated his earlier signal.

Suddenly Numtal lurched up and forward and clawed the air with his fingers. Stalkin stepped back, withdrew the red-tinged blade. Before Numtal fell, the smithy was already contemptuously wiping his weapon clean upon his victim's hair.

The guards shuffled in nervous reaction, but Fish's deep voice resonated through the chamber like a temblor. "Behold! We stand before Kot's treasury. All present shall participate fully in what we find–provided they are deaf, blind, and forgetful."

Vigorously they nodded.

"We must not be disturbed till we have had a chance to examine all of the contents of the treasure room. This will take some moments. But then we must haul it quickly away! The Vens will soon be here, and we must finish and be gone ere they arrive."

The guards moved to the entrance, brandishing bows and rapiers. None would get through while they lived.

Fish and Stalkin dove into the passage. Inside, the tunnel continued down, the raw stone again descending into the bowels of the earth. Abruptly it ceased and Fish and Stalkin stood within a wide chamber shifting in the light of their torches. Along two walls ran the same un-dressed stone as elsewhere, but before them a deep ravine yawned, with steps like an inverted stile carved within, and on the far side a floor of stone slabs adjoining a wall. Set in the wall was a second door behind a small free-standing altar. Toward the left, the floor on which they stood continued without interruption, paralleling the ravine to terminate in a small room that flickered with ghostly light, light that emanated from some source other than their torches. They peered within. Inside the room rested an unadorned table, equipped with two simple chairs of wood, the remnants of a meal, now strewn with dust, and a cup. Sur-rounding the room was a sea of black liquid. Far above glittered its sur-face, and they realized with a start that only a thin wall of glass lay between them and the full weight of the water. Kot's secret refuge.

Clambering through the ravine, they turned their attention to the door. They caught their breath. No lock secured it. It shone like polished gold.

"At last!" said Fish, his lips like rubber. "Open it at once!"

Stalkin's eyes narrowed as might that of a gladiator about to deliver the killing blow. "The treasures we seek must lie beyond–and if they match the door itself, must be valuable indeed!"

They opened it. Another door lay behind the first.

"Is there no end to these portals?" groaned Stalkin. "What was he about, the old goat?"

"No, dear Stalkin," smiled his friend. "Think again! If Kot would guard it so, the treasure must be truly great! Test the strength of this door! Noth-ing can break it. Nothing penetrate. Clearly the fool kept what he valued most within the room that lies just beyond."

"Ah! An enclosure, with a small box!"

They placed it upon the altar.

"It is of plain make." Putting aside his bow, Stalkin opened it.

"The last key to the last door!" Their eyebrows inched up.

Returning to the inner door, they inserted the key. Turned it.

Slowly the door gave way.

"What do you see?" Fish peered over his companion's shoulder while Stalkin thrust his torch into the darkness.

The smithy choked.

"Chests?! Gold?! Jewels?!"

Stalkin frowned. "Look again." Placing his torch into a niche on the wall, Stalkin stepped into the shallow room and dragged one of the chests into the light.

The beauteous growths that had previously rendered Fish unconscious returned. He picked up the chest and smashed it onto the pavement, scattering its contents into the ravine.

"Twigs."

"It cannot be..." The smithy dropped to his knees. Broke open several more. "Sticks. And patched cloth." He threw them into the crevasse. "Nothing more."

The Overseer tossed bundle after bundle after them. Incredulity twisted his features. "What kind of man throws away gold, then locks up twigs and cloth?"

Stalkin laughed, his voice dripping bitterness and sarcasm. "Of course. What else did you expect? He valued this above all else. In the end, the idiot cared for nothing more than a few rotten sticks!"

"Look again! There must be something more! Search!"

"No." Stalkin shook his head. "There will be nothing. Except these–" He let a handful of crushed bark fall to the floor.

"Huuck! Huuck!"

For the first time Fish and Stalkin observed ten feet above their heads a narrow balcony that circumscribed the chamber. Upon this catwalk, above the room of glass, stood an old man whose motley gown was torn, patches falling from his torso with each movement of a limb. A wracking cough seized him.

"No..." Fish gasped.

"Hi-ho! So you've come at last!" Kot leaned forward and cackled. "Well, what took you? I've been waiting for quite some time–yes quite some time. But I knew you wouldn't disappoint me. Yes, I knew it was just a matter of hours before you sought to take from me all that I had left. And that was enough time to prepare. Now you aren't so smart! Oh no! You aren't so smart now, are you? Heeeh-heh-heh!" He placed his hand upon a lever embedded in the wall, and pulled.

❧ ⬧ ⬥ ☙

"Now," whispered Flores.

Two Vens burst from the tunnel. One fell transfixed by a pike. The second parried the blades that sought his flesh, and cut the jugular of an assailant. More Ven-sa plunged into the chamber, and in a few moments the remaining Vaw-sa lay crumpled.

Even before they fell, the Turlicum had entered an open door on the far side and jogged silently but swiftly after his quarry, torch in hand. Flickering light met his gaze. He slowed near the tunnel's terminus, and peered. Nothing he had witnessed on the Island of the Sun-God surprised him more than what next he viewed.

Fish and Stalkin stood on the far side of what appeared to be a grotto, alcoved brands casting eerie shadows about them. At their feet, and separating the two from Flores, swirled a stream of water whose level was slowly rising. Already too deep to cross, the stream seeped from beneath a wall of irsrem on his left, and passed through a room equipped with a table and chairs, only to fall into a steep ravine that separated him from his prey. From somewhere beyond the glass, a deep roar shook the cavern as from the lungs of a huge predator. The glass shook with dull thumps.

"Heh-heh! It is time to come in, my sweet! Time to send these spendthrifts to their Doom! Yes, to their Doom!"

Flores started. On a balcony overlooking the scene was King Kot, his minuscule form suspended from a heavy lever, an arrow preventing it from lowering into its socket. Blocked by the arrow from closing the switch, Kot swung with all his weight, but to no effect.

"Yes, time, I say! Come down! Release the water and let the Cyclops eat its fill!"

The lever lowered a trifle and the wall rose another inch, releasing a second wave. The table and chairs swept into the ditch.

"Kot!"

The old man's feet found the floor again, but his arm remained on the lever. The sleeve was transfixed by the arrow that blocked the device. He peered in Flores' direction.

"Hi-ho! So you've come at last! Yes, I knew you would return as well. And now you arrive! Just in time to assist me—"

"Assist you...?"

"Of course! Why do you think I allowed you to escape, you great fool!"

Flores saw in his mind a sign that read TO VEN.

"The signs—"

"My signs, of course! I hoped you would get back to Ven. I gambled that you were the true king of your city, that you would eventually return with your army to take revenge. So you see, it was I saved your life! I had need of you—need of an ally in my struggle against my thieving subjects, whom I knew would eventually turn on me. So now you have returned, and now you must help me, help an old man, even as I helped you!"

Fish and Stalkin said nothing, but stared open-mouthed. This was too much of a surprise even for them, threatened as they were by the rising tide.

"And why should I bother, King Kot? I care not who rules in Vaw."

"Precisely. So it may as well be me! Besides, you now have the opportunity to revenge yourself for the many insults that have been heaped upon you—you do wish revenge, do you not? You can do so now by aiding me...just...help me...pull this lever." He struggled, his feet rising in the air again. "As you can see," he chuckled, "yon vagabond has impaled me with a shaft which has frozen my device. It doesn't work well—despite the princely sum I paid those who built it. Yes, times are bad. But if you could pull on it as well, we can then release the Cyclops to kill them both! Then all will be as it was, and you can return to your city, having accomplished your goal."

"How—"

"Quickly! Before yon archer draws his bow again! Hurry back up the tunnel, and proceed through the door on the left. It leads to the balcony. Hurry, or his next shaft will end me!"

Flores hesitated.

Fish finally found his voice. He bellowed "Shoot him now, good Stalkin! Before the Ven does his bidding! And then shoot the Ven—before it is too late!"

Stalkin drew the string.

"Quick!" cried Kot.

Ignoring the danger, the Ven leaped upon the roughly hewn wall and climbed toward the balcony.

The rumble of Fish's chuckle reverberated through the chamber. "You are too late, Flores! The first arrow shall end Kot; the second shall take your life. This time you will not escape my vengeance—or the Doom!"

Flores clambered. He slipped. Struggled again. Almost reached the coping.

"Blundering imbecile!" thundered the Overseer. "Meddlesome fool! You cannot make it! Now I will finally take my revenge for all your insults, and meddling in my affairs."

Stalkin drew further. Paused.

Upon the balcony another hand had appeared. It grasped the lever. Numtal emerged, spitting blood. "So you thought to end me...slice me open and leave me dead. After a decade of service, you thought to throw me aside? Behold, Fish! Your life is in my hands!" With that he yanked free the arrow, then slammed the lever into its socket.

"Nooo!"

The glass jerked up and released a torrent of water. In its midst wallowed and roared a huge slug-like thing that slopped through the ravine to the platform. Fish and Stalkin, swept off their feet by the tide, scrambled to recover their balance, but failed.

There was no escape.

It seized Stalkin. "Fish, your sword–before it consumes me!"

The Overseer shook off Stalkin's hand as if it were venomous and backed away. As the Cyclops began its ugly work, Fish watched stricken. In a moment, it dropped the ragged remnants and peered for another victim. The Cyclops sighted Fish. The jaws opened to reveal a row of razored teeth, and, with a sudden lurch forward that belied its vast weight, clamped on Fish's stubby arm. With a wrench it removed it. Fish's own cavernous gullet opened, but from shock or hesitation froze in that position. The Cyclops' jaws closed on a leg and began to work, each gnashing of the jaws matched by a similar movement of Fish's jaws upon air.

The current took them under.

Flores sprang over the coping and inspected Numtal. He no longer breathed.

"Yes, indeed!" gloated Kot, dancing in triumph, "Indeed, yes! My plan worked in the end, as I wished. The City is mine again! Oh," he grew serious, "I have lost my twigs." He gazed disconsolately at the sticks floating in the brine. "Oh well," He shrugged. "My enemies are dead. I will retrieve them and let them dry in the suns."

Flores turned to go.

"Behind you!"

Spinning, Flores blocked a downthrusting blade. He sent it flying.

"Aaiiee!" Kot clutched his wrist. "You have broken my arm!"

"It seems you are no more to be trusted than the rest of your city." Flores gripped both of Kot's wrists in one hand. His arm apparently intact, the former king struggled, then submitted. "Except for Macius..." Flores glanced at the thief who stood on the threshold of the balcony. "My thanks again for a timely warning."

Macius swiveled his head from Kot to Flores and back. "I recalled your unfamiliarity with Vaw and thought to aid you in your task. But this," he glanced over the railing to the now-flooded grotto, "is new to me as well."

Both gazed into the rippling pool. The Queen had exited the grotto, leaving debris and a darker cloud to remind them of her passage. A shape appeared in the depths.

"Look out!"

Bursting from the water, Stalkin's face, shorn of flesh, grinned hideously for an instant, one hand slithering for a hold upon the rock, the other clutching his bow. He took aim, then emitted a harsh cry–the mangled corpus slipped back into the water and sank.

Flores and Macius breathed again. "Kot–he is gone." Flores turned and glimpsed a portion of the tunnel wall slide back into place. He shook his head. "He saves my life, then seeks to take it."

"Perhaps it is time to go." Macius' puppet gaze searched the grotto for new hazards. "Kot has had many years to prepare. I would feel safer in the open." The Turlicum nodded.

Soon they stood again within Kot's throne room surrounded by Ven soldiery.

Isav and Dos entered from the plaza. "Their numbers grow, Flores. We have beat them off twice, but we cannot hold them much longer. They will not rest while we remain within bowshot of the Temple. Our troops are nervous. When the Vaw-sa regain their courage, we will be hard put to regain the boats."

Flores summoned the king's former servants. A wooden chair of solid construction was found in a sideroom hidden by piles of stitched cloth. It bore the Vaw herald of a single golden eye. Ven soldiers entered, escorting several captive Vaw nobles in headgear of various shades of yellow.

"Kot is no more," Flores said. "My purpose in invading your city has been accomplished. I wish no harm to your Temple but seek only assurance that your government in the future will respect the rights of Vensor-sa."

The nobles exchanged wary glances. "We can but assure you that all who declare belief in Vensor shall be killed without mercy. Our city is henceforth dedicated to the cause of Vensed. His mouthpiece has told us that only His devotees should be spared. The throne has been destroyed, and we will accept no leader but the Voice of Vensed."

Flores looked puzzled. He turned to Macius. "I offer the throne to you, Macius. You deserve it more than anyone I know."

The murshid and thief froze in the midst of a sinuous stretching of his back. Never before had Flores seen so much as a muscle on his face move. Now, while Macius stood in the midst of Kot's throne room surrounded by Ven soldiers and a disheveled collection of high-ranking members of the Cult of the Cyclops, one ear twitched. Flores nearly staggered from surprise.

"I want it not. My time is free... I am free..."

Flores pushed out his lips in disappointment. He raised his eyebrows.

"Of course. It would not be in your nature to accept such a duty."

The Vaw's arms wove an imaginary net in the air.

"I shall return to Ven. With you. With your permission."

Flores shrugged. "No matter. You realize that we return to war. Ven is now occupied–by whom and for what reason I cannot tell. I hope to reclaim it, but I have not the bracelets any more. It may be that you will accompany us only to meet death."

"So it may be."

At that moment a wave of sound rose from afar and swiftly grew–the throats of warriors in battle. Exiting the palace, Flores emerged into the plaza where a line of Ven soldiers threatened to break. The Turlicum's appearance inspired the Vens to further effort even as it caused the Vaw-sa to hesitate. Tales of his exploits and inexplicable abilities had spread through the city, and his mysterious return from the Doom increased his reputation. The fighting stopped, and Flores ordered the Vens to fall back to the harbor.

Once on the esplanade, they began to embark. Suddenly, out of the midst of the Vaw-sa emerged a small man in a white robe. Facing the suns, he cast something in the air, and Flores momentarily believed he saw one of the twin suns darken. The Vaws rushed to the attack.

Hundreds perished, but at length Flores and what remained of the army that had departed Ven two months earlier was again at sea. They were reduced to a thin remnant, broken, virtually without arms, and limping back with nothing to show for their efforts except the return of their chieftain and king. Overhead, the watchers of the sky eyed their progress like the stars, as eternal, as vigilant, taking on form only to retrieve the corpses as the surviving crew cast their deceased overboard. Disconsolate, the Vens looked to Flores for guidance. Neither inspired nor afraid, he but stood next to Gethos and awaited the arrival of the Hedronmas. The vision that had drawn him across half a world still rose before him, but like a mirage had at last begun to fade. The pain lines were deeper. Only Macius, astride the rudder at the stern, seemed the same.

♾ ∞ ∞ ♾

CHAPTER 26

VENSA

Before Ven came into view, Flores realized that the usual activity was lacking. In normal times the Hedronmas and Suma would be alive with boats and the banks lined with fishermen, while traders and merchants plied their wares on the docks and hauled their loads into the side streets that led to the central plaza. The ships of the expedition touched the dock.

No boat was visible. No one greeted them.

Flores leaped to the clapboards. A hundred men clambered ashore about him, leaving an equal number of injured behind. Lashing the ships to the dock, they entered the Avenue of Murfenmas.

The city was empty. Each tenement they passed, each street they glimpsed betrayed no evidence of habitation, though Flores was certain he could feel eyes upon them. The disrepair Flores had viewed in the palace of Vaw was here reproduced on a wider scale, and he found himself thinking how quickly civilization falls apart when there is no one to hold it together.

The band reached the central plaza. Ingots and furs lay strewn. He glanced upward. Workers of Atasan glided lazily in the azure sky, having already resumed their ancient task. Rumors of war. Were it not for their efficiency, he supposed, the plaza would be strewn with corpses. Flores and his men proceeded to the Assembly to put Ven's affairs in order.

The gates were open; one was off its hinges, and, from the rust that was visible on the joint, had been for some time. Flores hesitated before entering. From the appearance of the city, he should conclude that the Assembly Hall was deserted—but he knew it was not, that something awaited within, something he had glimpsed in the Eye while confronting Atasan.

He entered the Hall. Despite his precaution, he caught his breath.

He himself sat on Ven's irsrem throne.

But it was not he.

Swathed in a black enveloping cloth, Flores rose from the throne to stand calmly before the intruders. In a flash too quick to see, Flores vanished, and the cloth sprouted gems that glowed and smoked. The blackness vanished, replaced by glittering silver that threw the rays from the sunroof about the chamber in a kaleidoscope. A succession of alien visages followed one upon another like rain. Finally, the images ceased and a man of nondescript features appeared. The real Flores noted the simple robe lined with red thread, the prismed jaw, the bright gleam of the eyes, took in the row of dirty slavers with whips and swords, and half a dozen nude gilas with chained necks.

"From death to death. Poor slow Flores of the vagabond clan. How comical you looked away in the sky without your helmet, your robe, or...your Jewel." Soorkrul smiled. The prisms melted into a caricature of humor, the grin of a thousand jokes shining through.

Flores frowned. He had suspected. Now he knew.

"Yes, dear Flores, that is correct!" Insane laughter rang out as the thing on the throne raised one arm. "Here it is. What you missed when you searched the others in the apartments of Ust–the *second* bracelet on my right wrist. You should have directed the guards to check both my wrists for, you see, before I entered Ust's palace that night," Soorkrul chuckled, unable to restrain his bubbling humor, "I had found another of the baubles. And here are the rest, which I took from your safe after you had gone. Six in all. So simple, it was unworthy of a child."

Flores stood in the proscenium directly before the massive irsrem throne, which had been relocated closer to the floor of the chamber than had the previous throne of Numsenmur. A score of Flores' clansmen collected behind him. Macius appeared at the end, beyond the row of slavers.

"I have never learned where the bracelets came from," Soorkrul continued. "A full year ago I stumbled on one in the forest. I always supposed that it dropped from the saddlepack of the one whose reven I saw disappear over a far ridge–after eluding your unkind soldiers when they ambushed my slavers at the Palmate Stone. But I never learned the rider's identity and I had supposed there were no more. I found the second outside the private quarters of Ust while posing as one of his mute guardsmen." He shook his head in puzzlement. "Only when you and I crossed wits with Sendas and Ust did I finally learn that the 'raper of lox'–Sendas, who was my best source of information on the Assembly– was he whom I had glimpsed in the forest, and he who had supplied the one to Ust, and dropped the second which I found." Soorkrul placed his chin in his hand. "I suspect that still one more exists, for there was another present on that day in Ust's palace whose demeanor was altered." He shrugged. "But whoever held it must be dead–or a coward–else he would have challenged me in my conquest of the Three Valleys. No patriot of Ven would have stood by these months doing nothing while I changed the face of Maalstrom."

Flores exchanged glances with Macius.

"Oh yes, slow Flores, my rule extends across the Three Valleys. My slavers enforce my will further each day. Every city contributes men for the conquest of the next, and youths and gilas for my pleasure. And banquets. Banquets without end!" He laughed to the sky. "What life has in store for the enterprising! How fate rewards those who act!" He looked at Flores with round eyes. "The jewels make one farsighted, you know. I saw your fleet miles before it touched the dock. The visions mix with the revelations–*are* the revelations! I see not only what is, but what may be. And the jewels are indestructible. They are made of the hardest irsrem, a sort unknown to the Guild. They can be used to enforce obedience. But, when used on others, their effect is...unfortunate. They rob the victim of his mind so that he reverts to an animal of the forest, a mere beast of Talen." He tsk-tsked sadly. "And due to the recalcitrance of the rabble of Ven, I have been forced to compel many. The enthusiasm of my followers for my revelations from the Morbius concerning Ven was insufficient to persuade all. But see for yourself." Soorkrul raised one arm and placed his left hand over the wrist of his right. The bracelets had been invisible while he spoke. Now they flashed iridescent.

A low rumble grew from beyond the exits. Within a minute a mob burst upon them.

Flores recoiled. The behavior of the intruders, who now surrounded the band of Turlicum and blocked the exits, was reminiscent of the freaks whom Flores had driven off that distant day in the western glade when he had saved Macius. Advancing on bent legs and extended knuckles, the mob paused to roar like ros-na.

"Yes, Flores." The grin reappeared. "They are Turlicum. Your clansmen. They are now most cooperative–much more so than when I slept in your bed and they answered my request for a banquet in such poor fashion."

"The City–" Flores began.

"The City cowers in its alleys and tenements and will not interfere," interrupted Soorkrul. "They know their turn will come and are none too eager to join the realm of Talen since the beasts of the forest may not fly to Heaven. As all know, the workers of the sky will not touch them. Only men have souls. Only those with souls go to Heaven."

The Turlicum drew his sword. "I have chased such into the hills before."

In reaction, more slavers in bandoleers and baldrics appeared behind the beast-men, and a number of priests occupied the backbenches behind Soorkrul.

Flores shook his head. "If you expect to preserve your life with the likes of these, Soorkrul, you will fail. My men will butcher the lot and seize you in a few moments."

The Guildmaster but smiled. "How little you guess, Flores. How little have you apparently learned of the power of the bracelets." He gestured again and looked at one of the priests beside him. The priest returned his glance with fear-drenched eyes. Suddenly, with a crack, his head thrust forward. The priest gasped. He began to shudder, shaking himself free of his black enveloping cloth till he stood naked.

"You see, Flores," purred Soorkrul, "how easily I command even the strongest." He turned to his companion. "Swart, let our guests see your inner nature. Bow down like the beasts of the field!"

The priest lurched forward till his knuckles touched the ground. The rays inpouring through the sunroof bathed his fat shuddering face in its soft oval of light. He sucked a breath. A howl tore itself from his lungs. The other priests recoiled in horror at seeing one of their own transformed as the Turlicum clan had been.

Soorkrul smiled. "This is but the beginning. All will become as Swart. All will obey. My slavers are already bringing the queens of the Three Valleys. They will all be brought to Ven where they can be properly supervised."

Flores' brows raised. "So that is what I saw."

"My slavers and beast-men have done what the Empire of Ven failed to accomplish in centuries of war, Flores. Nesta, queen of Neset, approaches even now in a caravan on the southern road, in the company of the queens of Asan and Sipan, a thousand of my slaves pulling them in vast iron tubs. Soon we will look upon their fabled secrets with our own eyes—do with them as we please. Power, Flores! That is what the bracelets bring. Power to perform miracles. And youth! Have you not noticed the years they have added to me? In truth I am no longer mortal like you, but an equal with the Urlis, an equal with Vensor Himself. When I have consummated my marriage to each gila I can find, and give each the sting of the leroo hornet, they will each become queens. Each will then join my queens in a new Sacred Spring–a lake my slaves are excavating even now in the Fells of Sish. Under the command of my Brethren, my armies of beast-men will overcome all resistance."

Flores wondered what would be the reaction of Atasan to the moving of several of his Makers of Life. Atasan's anger at the murder of Vensa had been great. Perhaps, he shrugged, Atasan would consider it but a small matter. Vensor cities lay strewn across Maalstrom as numerous as anthills. The shock required to upset the balance of such a vast and time-worn stability as of that of the plant-men, queens, and selks would have to be profound indeed. But should Atasan be roused, Flores had no confidence that Ven, Soorkrul, or even the bracelets could preserve them. After all, Flores had seen the Eye. Even the knowledge that he had now solved the mystery of the leroo-sa, being the means by which normal females–*gilas*–become like Vensa, failed to stir him.

"Your eye wanders, Flores. Are you unimpressed? Or could it be that you require something more personal to capture your attention?" Soorkrul glanced at the gilas at his feet. One more was brought from behind the throne. "Mayhaps you recognize your former companion in the wilderness, my former trainee in the arts of love–the gila Crestal?"

Flores caught his breath. Crestal was not an abstraction, like Amina, but his friend and companion whom, he suddenly realized, he cared for more than he had guessed. Subtlely, gradually, the image of Amina had faded. Crestal's remained.

"Oh, yes, Flores. You are indeed slow if you have failed to see what all others have seen for months. You wish to possess Crestal–have always wanted her. But you are too late. I possessed her long before you or anyone else in Ven laid eyes upon her. It was I brought her to Ven. I trained her between the bedsheets, improving on what the Guildmaster of Tumset had himself taught her when she was brought fresh to him from Klopus. As I trained every gila that the Elders of my Order introduced to Ven. But they were valuable items, essential to my plans to control the Assembly. Even though they had defiled me with their evil energies, I followed the instructions of the Elders and refrained from harming any of their gilas. Now, however, upon my return to Klopus and its fields of wonder, I will instruct the Elders as well. And henceforth my harem will pay for their sins–and mine. Starting with her, whose heart is so deeply tied to yours."

He clapped, and the slavers dragged a thick wooden board into the chamber, barrels of water, caskets, and brands. The board was equipped with manacles. Amid tools of torture they placed a glowing brazier on the floor. Soorkrul pointed. Effortlessly, the dwarf Malag lifted Crestal to one hugely muscled shoulder and approached the torture board. He clamped her upon it. A grimace of terror transformed her visage.

"Malag will now prepare her for my marriage. She will survive the ordeal. Though she may wish she hadn't." Soorkrul turned his face into the sunlight. He sighed. "Her screams–her flesh. Nepenthe for my soul. Enabling peaceful meditation conducive to the best revelations. Yes, Flores, I have seen the Thirteenth Revelation, thus fulfilling the ambitions of generations of my Order." Soorkrul closed his eyes and laid his head upon the back of the throne, a relaxed smile on his face while Malag stoked the coals.

Flores leaped.

Before any could react, he was upon Malag. The idiot grin of the torturer turned to dismay as an irsrem blade flashed with a speed too quick to measure. In surprise, Malag stared down at his mutilated chest. Blood gushed onto the brazier in a torrent poisoning the chamber with the stench of its boil. Flores twirled, slashing two more slavers. A severed arm flew; the other lost his head which rolled then halted, its wide eyes still focused on Flores. Flores picked up the vat of water that Malag had prepared for cooling the irons. Turning toward the diseased thing on the throne, he threw it.

Soorkrul gasped. He stood. Water drenched his cassock and he shook himself and wiped water from his eyes.

"Now, Guildmaster," pronounced Flores, "you are master of nothing more. For I have learned not only the power of the bracelets, but their weaknesses as well. Try your hand now, if you can cease your gloating for a moment. Do your worst! For where water contacts the devices, they become mere baubles once again and powerless to harm anyone." Flores put his fists on his hips and smiled a grand smile. "And now I am going to finish you so it will be as if you had never been." He placed a foot on the first bench.

Soorkrul had been listening, his mouth round with surprise. As Flores advanced, he raised his hand and touched his wrist.

Flores froze. Something had caught his throat. He tried to speak; only hissed. The Assembly Hall seemed to melt and he was aware that his companions now looked as surprised as had Soorkrul. An indescribable feeling stole over him as if his body had become an automaton and he only witnessed its movement from outside, similar to what he had felt on the Isle of Vensor when fatigue had induced hallucination–but this was different, he was flush, charged with emotion. Energies unsuspected rushed upon him, urges whose terrible nature he had never guessed and would have denied to the end of his days. The blood of the slaver upon the floor, a sight that would have repulsed him a few moments earlier now excited him in a vague indefinable way. A knot rose in his stomach. He realized it was hunger and a fear possessed him such as he had never felt before. Menace from others he could handle, he could oppose, because his mind and body were Simet-trained and obedient. But the passions that now enveloped him obeyed no mind, but seized him with a deadly grip of desire. He realized that he did not wish his mind to control them, that he had lost all interest in rationality–he now rooted for the beast. He had become–*was* beast.

"Yes, well, I suppose you were wrong," said Soorkrul matter-of-factly. He rattled his wrist to reassure himself of the bracelets' proper functioning. "Wet or not, they still work. Now get back with the others and wait your turn. I'll have some work for you later." With a chill, Flores realized that not only would he obey, but that he did not regret the outcome. The sense of freedom made him giddy. It was both exhilarating and frightening. He could hardly wait for when his master gave permission for him to run free, to chase, to devour. His eyes wandered to the likely prey and he felt his pulse jump. Plump and slow gilas. Tired and ill-armed Vensors. Easy prey for strong teeth and coiled sinews. He could already taste the rich aroma of blood. He gathered his energy for a leap into their midst, taking no notice of the dark figure that had appeared behind Soorkrul.

"My eyes!" the Guildmaster screamed. In a moment a gush of tears enabled Soorkrul to see again and Flores saw Macius behind him with an empty purse. Salt from the purse covered Soorkrul, including his wrists.

Flores awoke from the dream. He looked around. Every Ven citizen, including those of his clan who had been ruled by the bracelets recovered in the span of a single moment and bolted before the Guildmaster could regain control.

The Turlicum snatched up his rapier. "Clear Ven of these rabble," he said to his men. As the mob clashed, and the Vens and Turlicum burst through the slavers as through senile old men, Flores rushed up the benches and gripped Soorkrul in a handlock that he could never break. Quickly he stripped every bracelet from both wrists of his nemesis. Throwing Soorkrul down and placing a foot on his neck, he handed all six of the devices to Macius.

"Go with Sandol, and take these to the safe on my estate. The energies that gilas unleash on Maalstrom is nothing compared to the evil these have wrought." Flores laughed to himself. "Of course. Salt water. The Sacred Spring of Vaw contains a backwash from the sea. The Doom was imbrued with salt. It was the salt, not the water that affected it."

Macius said nothing, but bowed and left.

Sedrech and Lirsus dragged a snapping and growling Soorkrul down to the prison cells of Vim. Another moment and Flores had freed Crestal. Wrapping her in a blanket, he stared into her eyes. She was embarrassed and humiliated, but not injured or scarred. In seconds, her backbone had returned. But she averted her gaze.

"I'm sorry. I should not have deceived you, Flores. But the years of hiding, the warnings of Soorkrul and Numsenmur that I should always conceal myself, or risk instant death from the mob, made me afraid that you would be repulsed." She shivered. "Or that you would turn me over to...him."

"Sssh. Don't worry now. You are under the protection of the King of Ven, and the new Emperor of the Three Valleys."

Crestal looked suddenly vulnerable again. "And Amina?"

He sighed. The chamber was now empty but for corpses. "She was gone by the time we arrived. The selks took her away to a place called the Land of Gilas."

"The far side of Klopus," Crestal said.

Flores looked puzzled.

"Don't you recall? That is where I am from. Where the Order obtains its gilas."

"The far side of Klopus?" Flores' brows contracted. "Land of the Mok-sa."

"If that is what you call us." Crestal took a breath. "What will you do now, Flores."

"Remember, Amina saved my life. I must save hers no matter how long it takes."

She nodded. Looked up. "But...Amina. I–" She bit her lip. "Go if you must. But before you go, I must tell you of my people."

Flores lifted a finger. "I am tired. We will speak of it in the morning. Now, I must sleep."

Outside the Assembly Hall, Flores summoned a dozen clansmen and charged them with Crestal's care. Flores then ordered that the queens of Neset and the other Vensor cities be returned to their respective Springs. As his clansmen hurried to execute his instructions, Flores sighted a familiar figure. He laid a friendly hand on Macius' shoulder.

"Are they now well-guarded in my safe? Whom did you assign to watch over the devices?"

Macius returned a blank stare. "Safe? What safe? Watch over which devices?"

"Why, the six bracelets which I gave you after you threw salt on Soorkrul and saved Ven! Are you ill that you are so confused?"

The electric current suffused the length of Macius' spine. As it reached the end, he snapped alert. "Flores, my friend. I have been on the docks seeing that the ships are well tended in case we have to make a quick getaway from the city. I have not been in the Assembly Hall since we arrived."

Flores deflated like a ripped jellyfish. He sat heavily by the Assembly gate. One panel drifted noisily on its unrepaired hinge in time to his sighs.

"Yezd," he whispered, "who can finally return to his portal."

Macius sat beside him.

Several minutes passed.

Flores sighed. "Maalstrom will return to normal, Macius, but I am no closer to finding Amina than the day I left." Suddenly he turned to gaze on Macius. "You knew that she was never on Vensor's Isle, did you not, Macius?"

The thief said nought, but squirmed. "You wished her to be there. I could not be certain."

"Ven has a new queen," continued Flores, "*had* a new queen even while I spoke with whom I thought was Amina in the latticework. The calling for sons had resumed even before I left. I wonder why I did not think of that."

The dark man placed one arm above the other and moved them in parallel with the horizon. Flores would once have thought this some enigmatic code. Now he knew it was just Macius' boundless energy expressing itself in dance.

"Soorkrul said that the sting of the leroo makes gilas become like Vensa." Flores stared at the sky. "Was Amina stung?"

"Yes."

Flores turned to face him.

"On the night you entered my castle, after all had gone to sleep and I had paused to watch the night-spiders consume the bodies of the beast-men and enjoy my new freedom, Amina confronted me. She had stolen away from you, and followed me outside, and there she sought to persuade me to accompany her to Ven. She told me that she received the kiss of the leroo on the banks of the Hedronmas and now wished to waste no more time in the wilderness and beseeched me to help her fulfill her destiny... I had not wished to tell you of her insistence, of her attempted seduction. You had already told me of the gills, and where they were buried, so I departed without taking your leave. My apologies. But I did not know how else to proceed. Amina was a lesson that you would have to learn alone."

"Stung. Therefore, Amina must become...must already be..."

Flores leaped to his feet. He felt his wrist, pursed his lips in frustration, then took off at a run. Minutes later he stood beside the secret passageway. He tapped furtively at the opening. Soon came the familiar scraping as the block was drawn into the fortress. The familiar face appeared, perplexed. Before Wijah recognized him, Flores was upon her. Roughly he dragged her through the dark passageway, through the trapdoor and into her chambers.

"You knew all along, didn't you, foul witch!"

Wijah glared hatred.

"Didn't you?!" He shook her hard.

At last she softened. She nodded. "It will do you no good, man. The Queen is far along in her duties. Glory has returned to the Temple. There is a new Vensa, young and beautiful. She is strong and fair and will produce warriors for millennia to come."

"Because Amina...and I..."

Wijah dropped her gaze as if ashamed. "You will be king not only of your city...but of the next generation of malkops."

"I–King of the Selks," Flores pondered.

"A goodly portion will be the offspring of your loins. But there were others... many others."

"And the woman I spoke with across the world, who even now has departed to the land of the Mok-sa. Need I guess her name?"

Wijah shrugged. "Nara wished to have you from the first meeting. She was love-struck and sentimental and therefore unfit to rule. Amina thought of nought but herself and her own needs. That is best for the Temple. With Amina stung by Atasan's offspring in the wilds and already pregnant by you, the Temple had no need of another gila corrupted by contact with men, therefore I made certain the malkops took Nara by clubbing her myself and telling Amina to descend from the tower by another trapdoor. If the malkops had not taken Nara, we Sisters would have killed her, as we will if she ever returns. Once a Queen has been selected, no Sister of the age of vulnerability can be allowed to live after having been corrupted by a man. It would in time destroy the Temple–and all Maalstrom. There can be only one Queen. Only one may ever be pregnant in the Temple."

Flores lost his anger. "Now, Wijah. It is time."

She nodded. Reluctantly, she led the way into the hall. A wave of the hand turned aside the outraged expressions on the faces of the other priestesses, who lowered their pinwheel weapons. Soon they came to the Sacred Spring. Dozens of large reddish gourds in the outer chamber were followed in the next chamber by smaller paler objects, and in the last chamber by a larger number of small white eggs.

"After the failure of the Divine Communion, the Queen demanded we secure men from any source. We succeeded. At least a score were recruited and subsequently banished. The numbers of eggs are still small, but within months there will be thousands. The Temple will again rule the Three Valleys–and further." Wijah pulled aside the imbricated sheaves, newly repaired.

Flores entered.

The Queen's gaze was fixed on the orifice at the top of the dome. She floated in the tank–long cleared of the debris of battle and the corpse of her predecessor and scrubbed sterile. Flores noted her increased size. She was not to be compared to the hulk he had previously encountered, but, if what Wijah had said was true, Amina would one day surpass even Vensa in her service to the state, long after Flores' brief lifespan had ended. Her dark eyes, still gorgeous with subtle beauty, lit in recognition.

"Flores," she smiled.

He stared. This was Amina, but not the Amina he had known, or the ghostly image he had carried with him for the year past, the image that had haunted his days and his dreams. "My Queen, your most loyal servant has returned."

She smiled. "How are your affairs? Your debates with your friends? It was all so...exciting!"

He opened his mouth to answer but she interrupted, motioning to one of the many nursemaids on the concentric stonework that surrounded the bubbling pool. Several rushed to offer sweetmeats, ses, and other choice foods.

"Yes, our time was...sweet. From the moment I found you sleeping peacefully in the cave, water and vok-cheese and shredded lyart by your side, I knew I had to have you. You were so lovely laid out on your little makeshift bed that someone had prepared for you. It was generous of whoever was caring for you to ensure that you would live just so you could serve me. Of course, I had to wait till you were well, since I may not approach any person who is ill." She sighed. A turn of her head brought a new clutch of priestesses running with fresh water and dunmelons. When she had finished, Flores noticed that her gaze had returned to the opening above them.

She had forgotten him.

Slowly he turned away. As he departed, he thought he glimpsed a shadow as from furtive wings descend. He shrugged.

His legs seemed to know where to go and proceeded without direction from his mind. Before him, in his private compartments, he knew another gila awaited, one infinitely more caring, with infinitely more substance, and one who not only deserved more than Amina had deserved, but one who had earned far better than Flores had given her–she who had selflessly cared for him in that long ago cavern until discovered by Amina.

Once outside the Temple, Flores found he could no longer recall any of Amina's features, that he had barely in fact recognized her, and that her image had been replaced by the yellow and auburn hair, amber eyes and indigo lashes that he had first glimpsed in a greenish moonlit tower so very long ago. This time the inner strength and patience of Crestal would be matched by his own.

Flores of the Turlicum

Maalstrom
Tumsenet
Vedeg
Nene
Nasvetin
Tes
Lunsen
Sish
Toor
Ror
VEN
Klopus
Tlat
Lesel
Asan
Sipan
Neset
Lim
Ud
Vaw

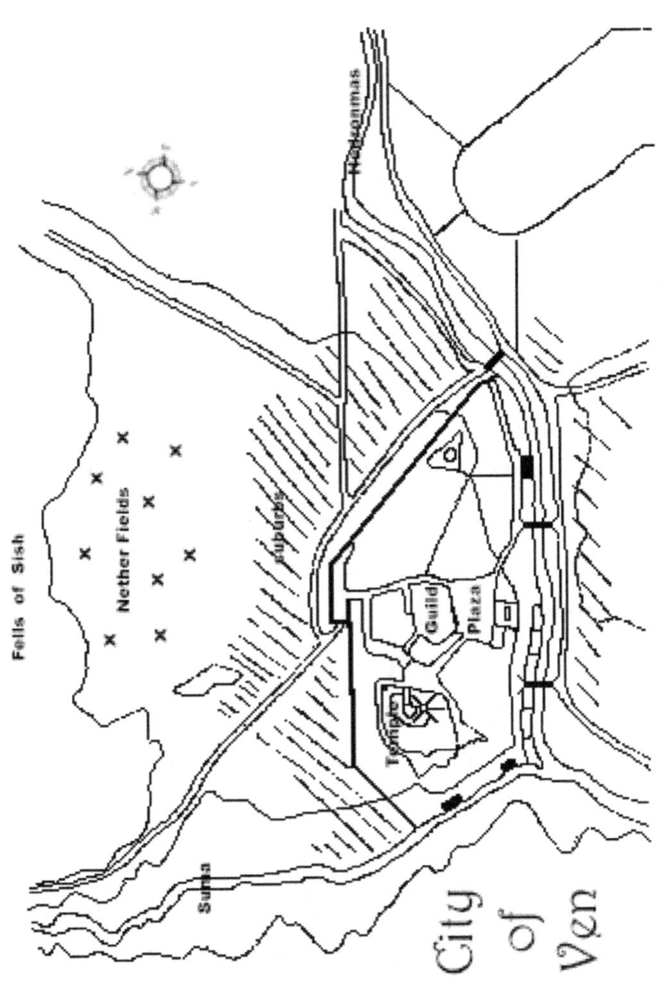

Hadonnas
Fells of Sish
Nether Fields
Suburbs
Guild
Plaza
Temple
Suma
City of Ven

NOTE FROM THE AUTHOR

The Selk King was written over a four year period in the early 1990's, the product of an education in history, philosophy, and anthropology, subsequently immersed in Nietzsche, the origins of mythology, and a degree in Islamic studies. To sum up: the problems of humanity are an eternal part of the human condition, and, whatever planet humans may happen to inhabit, these problems will persist. They can be reduced to The Greek versus The Islamic.

Behind the Veil, Secrets lurk. The Veil is Nature Herself, personified by God, or Allah, and Its dictates, which subject Man to the eternal struggle that philosophers have wrestled with since the beginning of time: Can he master himself and be 'captain of his soul' or is he destined to be an atom in a greater Cause, whether that Cause be religion, the passions, or a Darwinian 'balance' that permits survival only to those species that will reproduce without limit.

The Black Tower is the mystical Mountain that touches the Divine, and also the Tree of Life, which symbolizes the eternal mystery of Death from Life, Life from Death.

The malkops, or selks, are the semi-divine Messengers or angels who guard access to Heaven, and when properly ritually addressed will transmit the Hero's questions to the Divine.

The talismanic bracelets represent the mystical insight that enables penetration of the levels of Heaven by the eponymous Hero, Flores. Yezd is the shaman who transmits the technique.

On his first trip to the Isle of the Sun-God under cover of storm, Macius observed Yezd controlling selks by means of the bracelets (symbolizing the shaman's mystical access to Heaven). Ever the thief, Macius (the Loki archetype) followed Yezd to his castle in the wilds in order to steal the bracelets for himself. After Yezd's malkop flew away with the bracelets attached to its leg, Macius used the gills (a loan from the Sea God archetype Gethos) which Flores took from Numsenmur to travel back to the Island, anticipating that Yezd's malkop would fly the bracelets there. What Macius did not expect was that Flores would find the prize before he did.

Understanding the danger to Universal Order, i.e, that the bracelets can be misused in the wrong hands, Yezd, like any good shaman, seeks to recover all the bracelets in order to restore Heaven's inaccessibility to mortals. While delayed in Ven, Yezd discovers that not all the bracelets have been taken to the Island, but, thanks to Sendas' clumsiness, have been scattered throughout the city, amplifying the danger.

In Flores' struggle to assert himself against millennia of hidebound tradition which bars mortals from Heaven, and the imperative of maximum reproduction that all Vensor-sa (and humans) are forever subject to, he comes to his own conclusions regarding the utility of access to Heaven, i.e., the The Greek versus The Islamic. Though Vensor-sa, including Flores, are not—or more precisely no longer—human, the original human colonists on Maalstrom having long ago fragmented into mutually dependent sub-species and variants of species, his conclusions I think are equally valid for us.

There remain the Mok-sa. A few descendants of the original colonists, whose relics litter Maalstrom in the form of decrepit guns, rusting helicopters (Eternal Whirling Sceptre), etc., still survive on the planet uncontaminated by the sting of the hornet. They are at a severe disadvantage since the Vensor Queens are flooding Maalstrom wtih their limitless reproduction, and on occasion their women are abducted and sold clandestinely to powerful Vensors who are dissatisfied with relations with eunuchs, like Crestal, even the eunuchs themselves participating in this heretical trade.

Both Mok-sa and Vensor priestesses are vulnerable to having their DNA compromised by the sting of the hornets. But whereas Mok-sa like Crestal seek to avoid this by remaining thickly clothed and cloistered, Vensor priestesses like Amina and Nara, eager to become semi-immortal Queens themselves, welcome it and pursue it by covering themselves with althea pollen in order to attract the hornets.

Maalstrom was originally conceived as a trilogy. The story of the Mok-sa and the hornets was to be Book 3, but that book has yet to be written.

Maalstrom and The Selk King, I hope, remain as relevant today as when written to Seekers of Knowledge in their efforts to break free of Society's conventions and penetrate the Veil.

I have spared the reader Arabic phrases where possible, but given that the language of the selks–like the angels of Islamic mythology–is Arabic, the inclusion of some phraseology was unavoidable. The word 'Ra' is Arabic for the imperative 'Look!' The phrase 'Ra'Allah' is therefore 'Look upon God' or 'See-Face-of-God.' Atasan speaks Arabic.

Long after I completed The Selk King, it occurred to me that I had unconsciously followed the example of The Iliad and The Odyssey. Not to compare my feeble scribblings with the giant Homer, or any other master story-teller, but Maalstrom does seem to follow the pattern of The Iliad, while The Selk King parallels The Odyssey, with the Hero going on a mystical quest across the waters of Chaos to slay demons and match wits with various semi-divine opponents, succeeding or failing at the whim of the gods and his own divine-like Will to Power. Flores even encounters the equivalent of a race of Cyclops, here called Dragabonds.

The Selk King also owes much to Robert E. Howard's novella Almuric, which involves a hero mounting a tower at the ends of the Earth populated by winged demons or angels. This also did not occur to me until after The Selk King was finished.

Leaving aside philosophy and myth, The Selk King is an entertaining tale in the tradition of Robert E. Howard's swashbuckling Conan, and Edgar Rice Burroughs' John Carter on Mars. Unique and Just Plain Weird, the story can be read merely for fun.

—Glenn Lazar Roberts

October 1, 2016

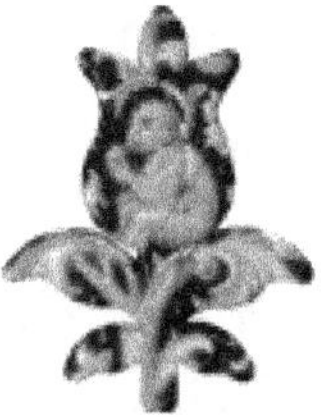

Dreams of the Dark Lotus